Gerald W Grantham

I0615817

Redemption for a Lonely Man

Fiction

Editions Dedicaces

REDEMPTION FOR A LONELY MAN

Published by:
Editions Dedicaces LLC
12759 NE Whitaker Way, Suite D833
Portland, Oregon, 97230
www.dedicaces.us

Library of Congress Cataloging-in-Publication Data
Grantham, Gerald W.
Redemption for a Lonely Man / by Gerald W Grantham.
p. cm.
ISBN-13: 978-1-77076-395-1 (alk. paper)
ISBN-10: 1-77076-395-3 (alk. paper)

Gerald W Grantham

Redemption for a Lonely Man

Chapter One

June, 2010, Sunday:

The late June sun peaked over the mountains, bathing the Valley in crimson and gold. Most of the forest creatures were awake, only the lazy humans were still abed. Local Indians could tell you, that the Sun had risen over this northern California valley for eons. But there had been humans here only for about the last five hundred years. At first, it had been various Indian tribes, mostly peaceful hunter/gatherers. Later on, had been white men, Spanish, Mexican, then Americans. The Valley that was fast becoming sun drenched, now held all colors of mankind. The Indians were still here, of course. The Valley was dominated by two things, a Washo Indian Reservation and the town of Sierra Vista. In Spanish, this meant 'Mountain View'. Indeed, the whole Valley had a breathtaking view of the Cascade Mountains. The high peaks were still capped with snow. Tall evergreens and oaks covered much of the land, but most of the old growth had already been cut. Rugged foothills dominated the eastern end of the Valley, and these held several old gold mines. A few of these still produced low-grade gold ore, but most had cease production decades ago. Many were owned by absentee landlords, not always American. Gold was increasing in price. Soon it may pay to restart the better mines. For now, they sat behind their steel and wooden barricades, Bean Counters deciding their fates. Timber, cattle, and tourism now provided the income for the locals. There were several streams, and a few small lakes. These lakes could hold large native trout, and planted largemouth bass. In August, there was a fishing tournament in the Valley that attracted visitors from around the world. In season, there were deer in the hills. Occasionally, hunting licenses for bear and mountain lions were issued. Theses drew the professionals, and very skilled amateurs to the Valley. There were hiking and photography for those so inclined. Motels, and the odd B&B were scattered around to care for the

5

visitors. These drew many repeat clients to this peaceful place. If it ceased to be peaceful, then there was the Sheriff's Department. It happens, that the current Sheriff lives on one of the small lakes. He was up now, preparing for his morning run. The house is large, a two storied log house built by his Grandfather. It was in this house that he grew up. There once had been his parents, and a younger sister. None were still living. He lived alone in the house, with two pets. He fed them, first thing, then started the coffee. He wore a dark-blue sweat suit, with matching shoes. Navy blue for the Reserve Naval Officer that he was. Bill Andrews warmed up on the front porch, it was deep, and as wide as the house. As he stretched, his mind drifted back. He stretched here getting ready for football. He had been a teen then. After that, he had done most of his stretching at U.S.C., on a football scholarship. Then there was the Navy, through Naval ROTC. He had chosen the SEALs. It had been hard work, but very satisfying. As he rose in rank, it got more political. He chose to leave, after a dozen years. He walked down the steps, and started running now, along the path that circumvented the lake. After the SEALs, it had been the NCIS. He became a Criminal Investigator for the Navy. It was good work, and he had come to realize what his Father saw in law enforcement. Then, the death of his Parents brought him back here. The County Board had been very persuasive about him becoming the Acting Sheriff, until the next election. Who better than the son of the late Sheriff? That had been a month ago. He took a leave from the NCIS, had moved into his childhood home. Bill ran on, at a brisk pace. He still trained hard, perhaps harder than before. He was over forty. As he approached the far end of the lake, the Sanders House came into view. A much larger house than his, much younger, too. Jason Saunder was a also Widower, just like him. He had heard about her bout with Cancer. Just like his Mother. Jason had a grown Daughter, but he had never met her. Joyce, his own twenty-four-year-old, had yet to visit. He wondered when she would make the trip from LA. He saw two of Jason's Security Team. One had the look of an ex-Special Forces. Some senior Green Berets chose private security over manning a desk. The other one waved at him, he waved back. As he rounded the end of the lake, Bill again thought of the coming election. Would he stay and run? That was the big question. It would be a big change. He was on the homeward leg now. He knew that his cousin, Russ, a Captain in the Department, wanted to be Sheriff in the worst way. And that was exactly how Bill saw him doing it, in the worst way. Better him, than Russ. But then, this was not San Diego! That was where he had been living for the past three years. The NCIS crew there was first rate. This Department would need work. More money wouldn't hurt. Would the Supervisors find more money in the budget? He ran on. By July, he was sure that he would not need the top to his sweat suit. A Tee shirt would do, even at this early hour. This area could get plenty hot, and August could see the temperature in the 100's! It felt odd, not seeing smoke rising from the old lumber mill. There was a moratorium on cutting timber, which had closed the mill. He had grown up with the smoking mill always in the background. He and Mary had necked in its shadow. She was lucid then. His Sister had been alive then, and his Grandparents. They were his Mother's folks, his Father came from out of state. He remembered his Grandmother. She was a Washo. Dark skinned, dark haired, wise in the ways of nature, and of man. His Mother had been like her. He missed them both. Bill could see his house now. Soon, he would shower and dress for a rare Sunday in the Sheriffs Department. Harry Truman had said that "the buck stops here," that was true of his job, as well. The County Board was not very understanding of others' short-comings. They never seemed to notice their own. Fortunately, his Father's files held many incidents involving the members of the Board, or their family members. There was a special folder with these accounts. Would he ever use them to get his way? He was sure that his Father had. Bill had grown rather cynical about elected officials. To him, their actions were all about getting reelected. This board seemed to be as short sighted as any he had heard of. Bill walked up the steps to the porch, using his key to let himself in. A check on the water bowls of his 'friends', then upstairs to take a shower. Breakfast would follow.

He was driving a nearly new Jeep Commander. Bill liked the four wheel drive, but hated the big V8. What a gas hog! Still, the power was fun to use on the highway, even if it was not PC. A silver Range Rover passed him, on the two lane road. Since Bill was at the speed limit, he knew the Rover was doing considerably more. He flipped on the red dash light, and sped up. No response from the Rover. Bill hit the siren. The Rover was quickly stopped on the shoulder. He pulled in behind it. When out of the Jeep, he put on his hat. Some of his men preferred a 'Smokey the Bear' Campaign hat, but not their boss. He wore a visored cap, like the cap he wore as a Navy Officer. It was tan, like his uniform. The car window was down when he got to the driver. She was an attractive, thirtyish Blonde, pony tail tied with a white bow. Same color as the tennis outfit she wore. "Good morning, Officer!" Her smile was dazzling. Her blouse was open enough to show a bit of cleavage, and the shorts revealed some very nice legs. "Good morning, Ma'am. May I see your license and registration?" She seemed a little flustered, as she dug in her small purse, "My mind must have been miles away! Did I do something wrong?" "Only speeding and passing in a no passing zone." She handed him her drivers license, "I did two things wrong? I'm on my way to a breakfast appointment. I'm running late." Bill looked at her license, "Mrs. Abbot, I still need to see your car registration." She was stunned, she had been so busy looking at the tall, handsome policeman, that she forgotten! Bill was distracting, at 6' 3" and 235 lbs. His dark hair had only a few flecks of gray. Hellene found the vehicle registration card, and she handed it to him. She made sure to touch his hand as she did. "I will be back in a minute, Mrs. Abbot." He took the documents back to his vehicle, wants and warrants were requested. Bill had to wait for Dispatch to check the computer. Both the car and driver were clean. He wrote out the two citations, then walked back to the Rover, "Here are your license and registration, Mrs. Abbot. I have two citations for you, as I explained. I need you to sign each one. This is not an admission of guilt, just an acknowledgment that you have received a copy of the citations." Hellene smiled and nodded her under-standing, quickly signing both forms. Bill tore off her copies, handing them to her. "The back of the citation has the instructions for payment of the fine. You have the option of a trial. Please drive more carefully, Mrs. Abbot." "I will Officer. My name is Hellene, what is yours?" "Sheriff Bill Andrews, Mrs. Abbot." Her face clouded, "I thought that the Sheriff was an older man!" "That was my Father, Mrs. Abbot. Good day!" He turned and walked back to his vehicle. Hellene Abbot stared after him. She watched him pull back onto the road and pass her. It took her a moment to compose herself. Then she resumed her trip into town. The pool boy was okay, but now she wanted to know a lot more about the Sheriff! She had vision of him in her bed! The Sheriff knew quite a bit

8

about Hellene Abbot. He figured that she was one of the trophy wives that inhabited the Summer homes in the area. Summer Widows was their local tag. Their wealthy husbands generally spent their time at work, in San Francisco or Sacramento. Did he want a tryst with the lovely Hellene? It was something to consider. Wonder if she had kids?

Bill pulled into his marked parking space, near the rear door. Rank definitely had its privileges. He used his key to open the steel door. Bill felt the female stares, as he walked through the patrol area. The female members of the department enjoyed the view, Bill in his short sleeved uniform shirt. His biceps were most impressive! As he approached the Admin area of the Department, he noticed Wanda's desk, his Administrative Assistant, and long time friend. He checked her in-basket for the Saturday Log. He scanned it, as he walked to his office. Ella Jones was arrested, drunk again. Bill gave the news a wry smile, "Must be heredity, I remember when my Dad used to arrest her old man." He knew that Ella's cause was a bad marriage, to an abusive man. He was in jail now, but he would be out soon. So Ella drank. Wanda had been married to a wife beater. He drank and beat her, until his Father had leaned on him. Later, he killed himself in a car wreck. He was drunk at the time. Wanda was still an attractive woman, but she had never remarried. He knew a lot about that, trust was hard. Twenty years, an abusive spouse, and two kids, had not changed her or her view of life. She had put on weight. Wanda was no longer the skinny teenager Sis used to bring home with her. They had been inseparable. He looked over the log sheet. Saturday showed the usual domestic disturbances, teenage pranks, and bar fights. Saturday also showed a rash of speeding by some of the teens. He would talk to Lieutenant Bearpaw about this, it was his domain. Besides, Jim could be counted on to use good judgement. Captain Russ Baker could be counted on to yell a lot and knock heads. Not the best move with juveniles males. Cousin Russ was heavy handed with most things. He left his wife of eighteen years, to shack up with a pretty nineteen year old. Bill wondered what kind of relationship he had with his seventeen-year old Daughter, or his fourteen-year old son. He could drop a fatherly word, for whatever good that did. Russ never seemed to take anyone's advice. Bill grabbed a large ringed binder from the book case behind him. Off the bookcase top, he retrieved a three-hole punch, which he used on the log sheets. Then he inserted it into the binder. As he closed the three rings, Bill thought of his NCIS duty in San Diego. They usually did not deal with misdemeanors. Felonies were usually the order of the day. Law enforcement seemed rather mundane in this part of northern California. Would he be happy here, for the next twenty years? Did he really want to be involved in petty crimes in this Valley? Cleaning up after drunk drivers was as serious as things usually got. There was Joyce's death, it was still open. Bill had an idea how to move his Sister's case forward. Had his Father never thought of it, or was he too proud to seek outside help from the FBI? A pretty twenty year old, found dead in someone's car. Why was she driving? Unanswered questions that defied local ability to solve. He put the binder back in his bookcase. He read another document, which prompted a phone call.

The noisy entrance of Russ Baker ended his thoughts, "You here checking on me, cuz?" Russ had the weekend duty, it was his turn. He was a large man, 6' 2", and maybe two hundred fifty pounds. "Paperwork, Russ. We need things, so I need to apply for another grant. I hope that things are quiet, on Sunday." "I'm glad it's you doing it. I hate all that red tape!" "You wanted this job, Russ. Paperwork is a big part of it." "Jim is better at that, maybe I'd delegate most of it to him." "You were on the phone, when I came in, Russ. What did Lassen County want?" Russ looked surprised, as he sat down. "The usual, they want us to do their job." Bill was grim, "Meaning what, Russ?" Russ wasn't cowed, "Meaning they want us to look for a fugitive Modoc they think is headed our way." "Did they send us a bulletin on him?" "Yeah, Bill. Wanda has a copy. You aren't going to look for this Modoc, are you?" Bill acted like he was talking to a child, "Captain Baker, Lassen County has asked for our assistance to capture a fugitive. A man wanted for assault with a deadly weapon. That is what the bulletin says." He held up the document. "They are entitled to our full cooperation, under the Five Counties Joint Agreement. You do recall that their Deputies have no jurisdiction in our County? How are they supposed to capture this man, without our help?" It was a rhetorical question, Russ did not reply. Bill went on, "I think Jim and his Washo Rangers can handle this one, he hit speed dial, "Jim Bearpaw." "Jim, it's Bill. Lassen County has a Modoc wanted on assault charges. They say he is headed our way. Russ thinks this is their problem. How would you handle this problem?" The Indian Lieutenant was ready for the question, "Six to eight men on horseback. He should be paralleling the highway, through the pass. We capture him, jail him, then Lassen County picks him up from our jail." Bill smiled, "Very good, Jim. Pick your men, the horses are being loaded. Double trailers, I hope we have enough vehicles to pull them. Get going!" "Yes, Sir!" At home, Jim jumped in his Jeep, and took off. Bill turned his attention to his scowling cousin, "Now, where were we?" The other man's anger was apparent, "I don't appreciate being shown up, in front of Jim. That Modoc is not our problem!" "Russ, you are suppose to be liaison with the State and the surrounding four Counties. Yet, you pull this stunt! My inbox is becoming the depository for complaint after complaint about how you cannot get along with this agency, or that County. You are the Operations Officer for this Depart-ment, yet I find no current status reports. Our contingency plans have not been updated for over two years. In short, you are not doing the job!" A defensive Russ interrupted, "Look, Bill. I have been distracted a little. Just give me more time!" "Russ, I know about your domestic problems, but I can't let it damage this Department. If I don't see a big improvement in the next thirty days, I will have to ask for your resignation." "You can't fire me!" Bill looked grim, as he spoke, "What will stop me, Russ? The Board of Supervisors? I see that look! With your Father-in-law now head of the Board, I think that they would enjoy firing you. You left his Daughter, to shack up with a nineteen-year-old! How do you think that makes him feel? I don't think that you have any friends left on the Board." Russ looked grim, "So that's how it is. You're turning on me too!" Bill just shook his head, "This is not about you! It is about this Department! It needs a good Captain. You are not doing the job! Now, either get the job done, or resign. This county can't wait around while you get your domestic problems sorted out!" Obviously angry, Russ got up and stomped out. Bill just shook his head, "Some things never change." He wondered just how far would Russ push, trying to get his own way? Russ was the type that only wanted to do what he liked. To hell with the rest!

It was early afternoon, a young Deputy Sheriff escorted a petit young redhead into a house protected by yellow crime scene tape. He ducked under the tape, then helped the girl do the same,

"I shouldn't be helping you! This is a crime scene, until the Medical Examiner releases it." His name was Brent Carter, a one year veteran of the Department. He was in his tan uniform, minus his hat and gun belt. "I don't know what all the mystery is! Everybody knows what Mama died of! How many times has she been hauled to the Hospital with an OD?" Her name was Mona Barrett, a pretty eighteen year old, recently graduated from High School. She had woken him up this morning, "Help me! I can't wake up Mama!" He had called 911, the Paramedics pronounced her dead, she had been for sometime. Mona had been out the night before. Brent wondered who she had been with? She was now wearing shorts and a blouse. She looked so cute, Brent did not miss her pretty legs. They made their way to her bedroom. Mona got Brent to get her suitcase off the top shelf of the closet. She began filling it from the small dresser. "I suppose you have seen women's underwear before?" She looked a bit embarrassed. He smiled at her, "Sure, lots of times. I grew up with my Mother, and Ellen." "I meant the women you slept with." He looked serious, "Yes, those too. I didn't think you knew." Mona emptied another drawer, "I knew a lot about what you were up to. We have lived next door to each other for ten years." That remark caused Brent to think, "That reminds me. Where are you going to sleep tonight?" Her brow wrinkled, "I start my new job tonight, maybe I can sleep there?" "Where are you working?" She checked the contents of one drawer, "I have the front desk at the Pinecrest Inn, from 4:30 to 1:00 AM." The look on Brent's face showed that he didn't like that at all. "I don't think it's a good idea for you to stay at that place! In the Summer, we have to break up fights there. The damn guys just come up here to drink and party! I think it would be better if you used Ellen's room." She stopped and looked at him, "Where's Ellen? Isn't she using her room?" He shook his head, "No, Ellen has a summer job in LA. She and her room mate are staying down there this summer. I doubt I'll see her until Christmas." This gave Mona pause, you could see her mind at work, "Would Ellen mind my using her room?" Brent shook his head, "You and she always got along. Why would she mind, you need a place?" "I need to get a big paper sack," Mona said, by way of explanation. She headed for the kitchen, pausing at the doorway of her Mother's room. Yellow tape barred the opening, but in her mind, she saw her unconscious Mother. She had been laying on the

12

bed, in her own vomit. Brent saw her shudder. He put his arm around her shoulders, "She's at peace now. It's all over. I'll take you to work tonight, then pick you up after." Her eyes flashed, as she looked up at him, he bent over so they could share a kiss. "Thank you for looking after me," She said, looking up at him. "I like looking after you." He spoke the truth, something he had just come to realize. They held hands as they retrieved a large paper sack. Back in her room, Mona stuffed the contents of the last drawer into the bag. Looking at Brent, she announced, "That's all I need now! I can pick up the rest later!" Brent closed the suitcase, then grabbed it. Mona grabbed the paper bag, and some things on hangers. From the bathroom, she took her toothbrush and hairbrush. "You know, Mona, we have to plan something for Dinner. We both have to work tonight! I'm on the Front Desk at the Department, for the four to midnight." Mona looked at him, skeptically, "Can you cook?" He looked at her, "I might ask you the same thing." She grinned at him, "We will just have to see, won't we!" With that, the pair walked side by side, out the front door.

Bill Andrews stood at his desk, placing a couple of things into his briefcase. Time to go home, it was Sunday. "I didn't know Sheriffs worked weekends!" He looked to his doorway, and there was Hellene Abbot. She wore a blue sleeveless dress. She was lovely. He smiled, "There is always something more to do!" She smiled back, "I thought that only happened to Mothers." She stepped into his office. "I wanted to apologize to you, about this morning. I was rather rude." Bill shook his head, "Not at all. I caught you off guard." She walked over to his desk, "I wanted to invite you to dinner, my way of making it up to you. Have you eaten yet?" He closed the briefcase, "As a matter of fact, I haven't. Did you have a place in mind?" Hellene followed him to the Del Norte Restaurant, she had been here before with her husband. But that had been two years ago. Bill chose a secluded table, toward the rear. They were both mindful of her marital status. "So, you know about the demands of motherhood. How many children do you have?" "I have a Daughter, Bill. My husband is quite a bit older than I, and he spends a great deal of time at his Company. I have had to raise our Daughter pretty much by myself." "That sounds very familiar, Hellene. My wife died when our daughter was only four. I had her to raise, and a full time career. She saw a lot of baby sitters." Hellene was interested, "How old is your Daughter?" "She is a very adventurous twenty-four. She has a degree in Journalism from UCLA. For the past year plus, she has been a reporter for KNBC-TV in LA." "Bill, that's wonderful! You must be so proud. I hope I can meet her, one of these days." "You never can tell about these things." They talked on. Hellene told him about growing up in San Jose, graduating from San Jose State University. She worked as a junior broker at a large firm. She met her husband there, it was right after his first wife had died. Bill saw her great beauty, even in her thirties. Hellene saw his look. She felt the same about him. She paid the check, then she followed him to his place. He gave her a quick tour, then poured them each some white wine. Hellene got to meet his two animals. She was charmed by the small blonde Cocker. The large orange striped cat was rather standoffish, as usual. "He is beautiful, and so large!" Bill stroked the huge head, and he purred loudly. "See, he takes a while to make up to people, but you see how he is with me." They took their wine into the Living Room. The sofa was convenient for their purpose. Hellene was especially eager for this meeting. She thought that Bill was very slow, until he embraced and kissed her. She responded, eagerly. She was fit and toned. Bill ventured to use his hands, she obviously enjoyed it. He was sure that he could have taken her right on the sofa. It was long enough, but Bill escorted her upstairs. In his bedroom, Hellene was undressed. He thought that she was a very beautiful woman. She had proved to be a skilled lover. He assumed that she was experienced, women like her usually are. He wondered, was the husband really neglectful, or was that just her excuse? Hellene was sure she had hit the jackpot! What a physicque! What a lover! He always seemed to be one step ahead of her! She had played a hunch and won! Their lovemaking was quite prolonged. They were both rather competi-tive, each trying to make the other climax. Finally, they came together, in an explosive orgasm! Then they dozed, wrapped in each others arms.

Brent had dropped Mona off on the way to work. She said that she didn't mind going in a little early, there were still things to learn! When he took over the Front Desk, the day Deputy filled him in on the fugitive Modoc. He also heard about the fit that Captain Baker threw. Lately, that man was always throwing a fit. His shift was fairly uneventful, only a few calls. Despatch took the

14

911 calls, so what the Desk caught were locals registering their complaints. If you had the duty for very long, the Deputies quickly found that there was a few perpetual callers. They were mostly of the right wing fringe, Tea Partiests, Birthers, and such. Brent had noticed that they seemed to jump on anything in the news that served their purpose. He figured that they probably watched Fox News. Only Fox News. Brent was devoted to CNN. That made him wonder, did Mona watch the News? Since Mona did not get off until one, he gossiped with his relief. Brent passed on the evening's events. They talked a bit about Mona's Mom. There were not many OD deaths in this County. Both were privately glad of that, it was one of the most undesirable jobs in law enforcement, and that was saying something! Russ Baker was discussed, along with the fugitive Modoc. He had been booked about eight PM. Neither Deputy wanted Lt Bearpaw, or his Washo posse, after them. Brent got over to the Pinecrest Inn a little early. He had to park well out in the Lot, everything close to the office was taken. The Summer tourist season had begun. He noticed two teenage boys hanging around the front door. Brent put on his hat, and marched right up to them. He recognized the shorter one, "Hello, Mike. Are you or your friend guests of the Inn?" "No, Deputy Carter. We're just hanging out." The taller kid was of a different stripe, "Look, Pig! We can stand wherever we want. And there's nothing you can do about it!" Brent smiled at him, "And what is your name, Hotshot?" He leered, "None of your business!" "That makes two errors. First of all our Loitering laws mean you can't stand around a business without using it. Secondly, the name of someone I arrest for loitering is my business!" The Kid was maybe six one, four inches taller than Brent. But neither kid had his width of shoulders, nor his gun belt. They begged his pardon and left. "Thank you for getting rid of those two." Mona stood by the door, in her white, short sleeve blouse and black slacks. Her red hair was up, making her look older. "They have been here for almost three hours. I was afraid they wanted to rob the Inn." "I know the shorter kid, he's just a follower. The other kid could be trouble. I'll have the patrol car cruise by a few times a night." She went on tiptoes to kiss his cheek. Mona was only five three. Back home, Mona insisted on making them some scrambled eggs. Brent told her he could do it, but she insisted. Watching her at the stove, he had a strong urge to kiss her neck. She was very cute. They each talked

15

about their night, as they ate. Mona said that her work at the Front Desk was more interesting than she imagined. Brent was glad of that, he found that he wanted her to be happy. They did the dishes, planned their dinner tomorrow, then it was time for bed. Each went to their own room. Brent had a lot on his mind, as he readied for bed. He knew he had strong feelings for Mona. He had always thought that she was cute, but now she was a young woman. She was a pretty young woman with no one but him to depend on. He felt the respon- sibility. He also felt something else, more primal. He got into bed, but just lay there thinking. Then, there was a knock on his door! "Come in." The door opened, as he turned on his table lamp. There stood Mona, in a short 'nightie'. "I know you find me attractive, and I've always had a thing for you. But I don't want to be alone tonight. Could you just hold me?" Brent threw open the sheet or her, "You just lost your Mother. Come here." He patted the empty side of the King size bed. She came around and climbed in. Brent covered her with the sheet. They cuddled. As they lay there, he wondered if she realized the effect it had on him. Then he thought that tonight, that was not very important. Tonight, she needed to be held. They were soon asleep, tomorrow they would talk about them, and this new found feeling that they had for each other. For now, they would sleep on it.

Chapter Two

Monday:

Bill rose a bit past the usual time, this morning his heart was not in it. Hellene had left about four, she wanted to be home for her Daughter. He knew he would pay for last night, but it had been fun. Bill started the coffee, then fed his animals. Today, he waited for the coffee, poured himself a cup, then drank deeply. Only then, did he begin his warmup on the front porch. Later, he might regret his liaison with the lovely Hellene, but right now, Bill relished every moment. She was a great lover, and her marriage made for safety when the relationship eventually broke down. These affairs always flared, then faded. Such was the way of lust. He began his run, along the usual route. Along the east side of the Lake, around the south end, then return via the west side. He ran on, it hurt more this morning. Bill considered cutting his run short, then shook it off. He had this battle with himself every so often. That urge to slack off, Bill had dealt with for years. It occurred to him, that Russ gave into this urge whenever he could. The trail rose ahead. As his head cleared the rise, he saw a spot of pink! Then he saw the camo pants, with a dark green tee shirt. The glint of a rifle? Reflex took over, Bill ducked behind a large rock. He continued moving to his right, around the rock. Between the rock and a tree, he could observe the trail, unseen. There was a tall, blonde woman being held at gunpoint by a long haired Indian in camo. Who were they? Were there more people? Bill crawled up the back of the rock, he lay on top of it. From there, he could see through the trees. To the east, on the Reservation, he saw many men working. There was a wisp of smoke, probably a campfire. Sheriff Bill Andrews thought he knew what was happening. Quickly climbing down, Bill took his Cell from his fanny pack. He had the number on speed dial. "Sierra Vista Sheriff's Department. Wanda speaking." "Hi, Wanda! This is Bill. Is Russ, I mean Captain Baker in?" "No, he is not, Sheriff. But Lieutenant

Bearpaw is. Should I connect you?" "Please, Wanda. It's important!" A moment later, Jim came on the line, "Jim Bearpaw! What's up?" "I think we have a 'grass' farm on the Reservation, east of Bear Lake. Call the DEA. Tell then that I am on the scene, and that there is a female hostage." "Who is it, Bill?" "Probably a guest of Jason Saunders. I'll try to take out the guard. Tell the DEA to hurry! Then form a posse and meet me on the trail! Move it!" "Yes, Sir!" The line went dead. Bill stashed his Cell, as he began planning his next move, "I need to take out that guard, before the cavalry gets here." The guard had his back to the rock. He seemed totally focused on the big Blonde! Bill slipped across the trail and into the trees. He was able to move quietly, despite the forest debris. "Thank God, this stuff isn't very dry, yet." Bill's mind was busy. He had glimpses of the pair. He saw the Blonde unzip her jacket, she looked very unhappy. He got glimpses of a very full sports bra. No wonder the guard was preoccupied. Bill sincerely hoped that this little scene lasted long enough for him to strike. The closer he got, the slower he moved. Then, he was nearly behind the Indian. Bill wondered how many times an Indian got surprised like this. He had to handle the guard quietly, or the whole camp would be alerted! Bill stopped directly behind the man. He could hear him call for the Blonde to remove her top. Then, he moved! The edge of each hand hit the man's collarbones, the rifle hit the ground! One chop to the back of his neck! The Indian was out, he lay unconscious at Bill's feet. His pulse was checked, Bill was sure he would live. Out came his handcuffs, from his fanny pack. The Indian was quickly cuffed. It was only then that he looked at the Blonde. She had a scared look, and a pistol in her left hand. He smiled at her, "Hi, I'm Sheriff Bill Andrews." She lowered the gun, "My name is Jennifer Saunders. I'm here visiting my Father." He stood up, "Miss Saunders, do you have a carry permit for that gun?" "I do in LA, Sheriff. Will that be okay?" "Sure, but I will need a copy for my files. May I suggest that you zip up, before the troops get here?" The gun went back in her fanny pack, then she zipped her top, "Who is coming?" "Miss Saunders, the DEA should be arriving by helicopter, plus a posse of Deputies will arrive by foot." She was subdued, "He was going to rape me!" Bill saw that as a matter of fact, "Yes, then he would have shot you and buried the body. We have had disappearances in the past." He saw the fear in her face. "Maybe we should get further back. That hill looks good. That was where I spotted you." He took her arm and they started walking. "What is this all about?" She asked. Bill gestured to the east, "Over there is a Marijuana field. That man was a guard. He was probably checking the trail, when you surprised him. I'm sure he thought it was his lucky day." She was grim, "And my worse one!" "Something like that. By the way, who taught you to shoot?" "My Father, first. Then an ex-Navy SEAL, named Adrian Truscott." He looked straight ahead, "Good man." "Do you know him?" She was surprised. Bill smiled, "Did he ever tell you how he got that limp?" "No, he always changed the subject, when I asked." "He was kicked by a camel, I just can't tell you where he was at the time. It was a classified mission." Jennifer was about to ask several questions, when she heard the buzz of a helicopter! It quickly got louder. As the pair climbed the small hill, a small Kiowa scout 'chopper', appeared over the Lake. It flew fast toward the east. The Observer radioed what he saw as they flew over the crop. Bill could hear random shots, probably directed at the Kiowa. Bill was sure none of them hit the fast moving machine. A line of uniformed Deputies appeared on the path. Lt. Jim Bearpaw led several Deputies, pass them and down the trail. Jim smiled as he passed. Captain Russ Baker huffed along at the end of the line. This concerned Bill, "You're out of shape, Russ. Looks like more PT for the Department leadership." Russ flipped him the 'finger' and smiled. All eyes went toward the Lake. Two Blackhawk helicopters came in low. They flared and landed beyond the nearby trees. Random shots were heard, and the Blackhawks' engine grew quiet. Suddenly, two armed Indians burst out of the trees. The Deputies quickly disarmed and handcuffed them. Sporadic shooting continued, accompanied by the shouts of DEA agents for them to surrender. As the pair stood watching from the hill, Bill had a chance to check out Jennifer. Even without makeup, she was beautiful. Nordic good looks. Around thirty, maybe five eleven, and not thin. She had a large bust, narrow waist, and long legs. He did not kid himself, he wanted to see Jennifer nude! He was sure that was the standard response to the lovely Blonde. Jennifer estimated Bill at about six three. She figured that he was older than her thirty-one years. She wondered what he was like in bed? She knew that she was going to find out as much about Bill Andrews as she could. She was sure that her Father could help. Something

19

suddenly occurred to her, "Why aren't you and your Deputies over there with the DEA?" "Jennifer, the Washo Indian Reservation begins about one hundred yards east of the Lake. I have no jurisdiction there. It is Federal Territory, the DEA and FBI are in charge." Jennifer nodded her understanding. Sporadic shouts and shots continued to sound from the trees, then grew infrequent. More Indians reached the trail, driven by the DEA. Each was disarmed and handcuffed. One resisted, Jim quickly put him on the ground. Someone forgot to tell him not to pull a knife on a Ranger. Bill was sure that he would not be so foolish, and he knew how to use a knife. Few lived to praise how well he used the stiletto-like blade that was strapped to his right ankle. It was called a 'Fairbairn', developed before World War II by an ex-Shanghai Policeman of Scottish decent. The British SOE and SBS made use of it, as did the famed Darby's Rangers. He knew members of the Special Forces that never went out without one. A line of fatigue-clad DEA agents emerged from the woods. They piled up the captured weapon, a mixture of lever action .30-30's, and bolt action hunting rifles. Every DEA agent carried an M-16. The lack of AK-47s or other automatic weapons told Bill that this was a local operation. No Cartel involvement, yet. Soon, two wounded Indians arrived on stretchers. They were trailed by three DEA walking wounded. Bill saw one DEA agent talking to a Deputy. His man gestured in the Sheriff's direction. "This must be the Boss." Jennifer saw him gesture at the approaching figure in Camo. Bill recognized the character of the fatigue clad man marching purposefully for him. Type A, aggressive, probably ex-military. "Sheriff Andrew!" Bill noticed that it was not a question, the man assumed he knew who he was addressing. "And you are?" "Special Agent-in-Charge, Charlie Stevens! The DEA thanks you for this timely tip." Bill had his hand forcibly shook. He had the pleasure of seeing the shorter man wince from the strength of his grip. "Glad we could be of service. It was Miss Saunders that actually found the Field. I was second on the scene." "I see! Well, thank you, Miss Saunders!" Charlie quickly found that the big Blonde had a good grip of her own. He wondered what she did for a living, Pro basketball? As he shook some blood back into his right hand, Charlie Stevens revealed the real purpose for his visit, "Sheriff, could you accommodate these would be 'grass farmers' in your jail?" "No problem, Charlie. I suppose you will need us to

20

transport them? How about the wounded?" Charlie was embarrassed now, Bill was getting ahead of him. What he had heard about the man must be true. "Absolutely, Sheriff. We will be tied up here for quite a while. Later, we need to talk." Charlie started to walk away, then turned, "I hear that you were with the Seals!" "You heard right!" "Rangers lead the way!" Charlie turned and walked back into the woods. Jennifer was curious, "What was that about?" Bill had a slight smile, "Apparently, SAC Stevens was with the US Army Rangers. Lieutenant Bearpaw is an Officer in that august group. They do much of the scouting and reconnaissance for the Army. You saw my Cousin, Russ Baker. He was with Marine Recon, they take care of the same things for his branch." That prompted her question, "What do the SEALs do for the Navy?" Bill was straight faced, "Whatever they are assigned to do." He motioned to Jim to join him, then he relayed the needs of the DEA. Jim got on the walkie-talkie that he carried on his belt. Transportation was arranged! Then Bill rejoined Jennifer, "You need to come with me. We need your statement about the Indian, if we want to charge him with attempted rape." She agreed. "Do you mind accompanying me to my house? I need to change." She followed him up the trail. Behind them, the DEA was busy burning much of the crop. The rest would be held as evidence.

As the pair walked along the path, the Lake and trees made Jennifer remember. She had walked this path many times, with her Mother. She had been healthy then. The Cancer had taken all that away. She missed her Mother so much! They walked beside one another. Bill saw the tears start down her cheeks, he was sure it was delayed shock. "When were you going to shoot him?" She dabbed her eyes, "When he demanded that I remove my pants. I was going to pull my gun and shoot the Bastard!" Bill nodded his approval, "Might have surprised him. He didn't know you were armed." Privately, he thought it was a desperate move. The Indian had his gun ready, watching her. Still, the sight of that big bust probably clouded his mind. The Russians were rumored to use busty female Special Ops personnel for exactly that reason. His house loomed ahead, so he started to tell her about it. "My Grandfather built this house. He had married into the tribe, so several Washo carpenters worked with him. It was built of whole logs, the interior is knotty pine paneling." Jennifer noted the many Department vehicles parked in the front yard. Not for the first time, Bill was glad that his Folks had paved the area. No mud or dust would mar the stained fir planking of the stairs or deck. They mounted the steps to the big porch. Jennifer took note, "I wish Dad had put a big front porch on our house. This is a much better idea." Bill considered that, he had not imagined that Jason Saunders's house was deficient in any way. Live and learn. He unlocked the front door, letting Jennifer enter first. As he shut the door, Bill began the tour. "This is the Entry, the Living Room is through that door, to the right." A small blonde Cocker eagerly rushed to Bill, "Hello, Susie!" He knelt to pet his little friend. "I remember Susie, she followed your Mother everywhere!" Bill looked up at the big Blonde, "That's right. She was devoted to Mom. How did you know that?" "Your Mother helped us when my Mother got sick, then when Mom died, she helped my Father get permission to bury her on our land." Bill could see it, special rules for the rich. His family had their own cemetery, but it was nearly one hundred years old. His Grandfather's family had come from Scotland. They were all buried here. Next to the remains of the old house. So were his folks, and his sister. "Jennifer, would you mind waiting here, while I grab a quick shower, and change into my uniform?" "No, Bill. Go ahead. I'll stay here with Susie." He went upstairs, while she knelt to pet the friendly dog. "Hello, Susie! Do you remember me?" Susie's bobbed tail wagged furiously! This continued for a few minutes, Jennifer heard the sound of a shower running. She left the dog, trying to remember the layout of the house. She did recall that the Den was to the left. The room was spacious, it contained two old bookcases filled with California Law Books. These had been his Father's. Against the far wall was an elaborate computer table. A large, flat screen monitor stared at her, a printer rested on a shelf above. She figured that the computer was in the lower left compartment. There was a newer bookcase on either side of the table. Boxes of books sat in front of each. They were open, but not yet unpacked. Jennifer could not resist taking a peak at the books. "What does this man read?" She found books on history, western lore, many books about American Indians. "Maybe we have something in common!" She tired of investigating books, choosing to checkout the rest of the lower floor. The Living Room was right across from the Den. Jennifer found Susie laying on the large sofa, "You are a spoiled little animal!" Susie watched her, betrayed by a rapidly wagging tail. Jennifer looked

22

around, then moved on, into the Dinning Room. There sat a huge dinning table, surrounded by ten ornate chairs. An ornate sideboard graced the opposite wall, topped by a china hutch. This she started to inspect, when her bladder told her of a more pressing need! Fortunately, she soon found the large oak door hiding the old fashioned bathroom. The was a large claw foot bathtub, the overhead tank toilet flushed via a pull chain. It had a polished oak seat, Jennifer put it to good use. After, as she washed her hands, Jennifer caught sight of her image in the mirror, "Help!" No makeup, hair mussed, and a streak of dirt on her left cheek. She straightened her hair, as best she could, washed her face off, then hurriedly applied some lipstick. Opening the door, she was face to face will Bill Andrews! He looked so good, in his uniform! "There you are! We should get moving, Jennifer. The other vehicles have nearly all pulled out." Outside, he was right. Only one Sheriff's vehicle remained, the pair of Deputies were just seating their prisoners in the rear. Bill opened the passenger door of his Jeep for her. Jennifer thought of Bill as 'old school', but she liked it. In no time, the pair was down the driveway, and onto the highway. All of sudden, Jennifer remembered! Dad!" She pulled her cell out of her fanny pack, hitting speed dial. "Yes, Jennifer. Where are you?" "All right, Dad. So you have Caller ID! Did you see the helicopters?" "Yes, my Darling Daughter. A raid on a marijuana field, so the boys tell me." "One of their guards had me at gunpoint. He was going to rape and kill me! But Sheriff Andrews saved me. The DEA should be burning the field now!" "Yes, I can see the smoke. Where are you?" "The Sheriff is driving me to his office, to give my statement. Then I can come home." "Very good, Jennifer. We will hold lunch for you." "Goodbye, Dad." He hung up, then Jennifer did. "Bill, can we stop somewhere? I need something to eat." "We have muffins at the Station." The thought of muffins, made Jennifer very happy. Her stomach was growling! Bill's was too, he could hardly wait. Maybe he should go back to carrying cereal bars.

The Sheriff's office was hectic, the captured Indians were being booked, and fatigue-clad DEA agents lounged on chairs and desks everywhere. Exchanging greetings with some of them, Bill ushered Jennifer into a free interrogation room. He motioned to a free Deputy to join them. Bill introduced Jennifer to the Deputy and asked him to take her statement. Excusing himself, Bill headed for his office. Wanda had several messages for him, when he got there. He glanced at the message slips as he went into his office, and sat as his desk. Wanda quickly brought him a cup of coffee and a muffin. "You read my mind, Wanda. Could you see that Miss Saunders gets a muffin? She was almost raped on the Bear Lake trail." Taking the cup, he added, "Thanks." She smiled and went on a muffin mission. Bill had calls to return, none of them took very long. He then started going through his mail. A moment later, Jim Bearpaw burst into his office. "These guys aren't talking," he exclaimed, exasperated. He was a darkly handsome man in his 30's, six feet tall and about 180 lbs. Leaning on the Sheriff's desk, Jim proceeded to tell him that the prisoners would not tell him who their boss was. "They had a generator, power equipment, and camouflage netting." He told Bill, "Somebody paid for that stuff." "Do any of them have a record?" Bill asked. Jim nodded, "Two of them have priors." "Then work on those two," Bill advised, "A prior felony conviction will make it tough on them in court. Check what Federal Charges could mean for those two. Are you aware of the Attempted rape charges awaiting the guard I captured?" Jim nodded, then slumped into one of the chair that fronted Bill's desk, "Most of these men are out of work loggers or mill hands. They just need jobs. Shutting down the Sawmill has destroyed my people!" It was an old rant, Jim felt it deeply. "It has hurt everyone, white and Indian!" Bill reminded Jim. "I am sorry Bill, I'm just so frustrated. Watching my people turn to crime to support their families! This goes against the traditions and customs of my people." "What about Johnny Eagle and his plans for an Indian Casino?" Bill responded. Johnny was a Harvard educated lawyer working with the Tribal Council. "Johnny Eagle!" Jim parroted. "He is a Modoc, for gods sake! Whatever he knew about our traditions, he has forgotten back East. He talks big, but nothing happens." Jim was interrupted by Russ suddenly appearing in the doorway. He motioned for them to follow him towards the front of the Sheriff's Building, "You need to see this." Looking out on to the front steps, the three officers saw District Attorney Ray Van Cleef and DEA Agent-in-Charge Stevens were holding a Press Conference. Bill saw at least one TV cameraman, the others were Radio and newspaper reporters. "Look at those bastards bullshit the Press," was how Russ summed up the proceedings. "Your Cousin has always had a way with words,

24

Bill." Was Jim's comment. "Our beloved DA also has a way with words," noted Bill, "By now, I am sure, he has told them how he singlehandedly planned and executed this huge drug raid." "Agent Stevens probably doesn't know what hit him," Russ assessed the situation. "You boys are being hard on our DA, I bet he ..." Bill's attention was redirected by Jennifer calling to him, "Sheriff, I have finished giving my statement, can you have someone drive me home?" Bill was surprised to hear his voice tell her that he "would be happy to drive her home himself." "What the hell," he thought, "there is nothing on my desk that needs my immediate attention." Jennifer could not help herself, she was very pleased. They said goodbye to the two officers, and headed out the rear door to the parking lot.

The Saunders home was a large, rustic structure. It evoked a feeling of taste, and of blending with the surrounding forest. A mixture of half and whole timbers, left natural in color, created a house with a warm, inviting feeling. A six stall garage in the same style stood near the house. Next to it, was a large office building. Above the office door was a sign, 'The Nature Coalition'. In front of the house, beyond the driveway, was a Landing Pad. Parked on it was a shining Bell 430 Helicopter, in Green and Silver corporate colors. As Bill and Jennifer exited the SUV, Jason Saunders met them on the front porch. He was a large, blonde man, 6' 5" and 270 lbs. Although he was nearly 60, Jason exuded energy and drive. Attending Stanford on a football scholarship, he had been an All-American Tackle. Passing up a Pro career, he graduated Cum Laude with a degree in Electrical Engineering. He then went on to found five Silicon Valley firms, three of which he still controlled. He was Chairman of the Board for all three of his firms, for which the combined value was currently some hundred and twenty-seven billion dollars. He was the Founder and Executive Director of the Nature Coalition, one of the largest nonprofit conservation organizations in the world. Putting an arm around his Daughter, he offered his hand to Bill. "I don't know how to thank you for saving my Daughter's life," his voice boomed out. Bill protested this verison of the events of this morning. "From what I have seen of your Daughter," Bill pointed out, "She probably would have gotten herself out of that situation." "I think you are too modest," was Jennifer's quick response. Turning to her father, she excitedly described Bill assault on the Indian guard, "He just appeared, and the

Indian was on the ground, out cold. One blow, and the man collapsed" Jason looked knowingly at Bill, "No doubt, something you learned as a SEAL." "Yes it was," Bill admitted, "a basic stalking skill, used very successfully by the Indians." "However, it was usually the Indians doing it to us," Jason observed, "Nice reversal of roles." "But the fact is, I am one quarter Washo myself." Jason smiled at that, "Please come in," he offered, ushering the pair into his entry hall. A young Hispanic woman met them in the hall. "Ah Maria, I think there will be three of us for lunch," Jason said, smiling at Bill. "You will join us, Sheriff?" Bill nodded his consent, "Call me Bill, and I would be happy to stay." "Good," exclaimed Jennifer. "I'm starving," she declared as she grabbed Bill's arm and guided him into the Dinning Room. "As you have observed, my Daughter is a shy, retiring scientist." Jason added dryly as he followed behind them. In the huge Dinning Room, Bill said a hello to Maria, and inquired as to her parent's health. "They are fine, Sheriff Andrews," she answered shyly and slipped into the kitchen. As Jason directed Bill to a chair, he remembered the Sheriff's playing days at U.S.C., "I used to love to watch you play. I remember the big win against UCLA. You were faster than we were when I played. Your team had more weapons than we did." "We were different," Bill responded, "Not really better."

The food was simple, but good. No caviar was served at Jason's table. Bill and Jennifer ate ravenously, washing it down with Sierra Nevada Brewery's Summerfest beer. Bill was still contentedly eating, when Jennifer stood up and excused herself. "I need a shower," was all she said, as she headed out of the room. When he had finished eating, Bill sat back to finish his glass of beer. Looking at Jason, Bill commented, "I would have never connected Jason Saunders the Conservationist with this house." "You should," Jason was quick to reply, "It is all made of natural or recycled material. All biodegradable, I might add." Bill nodded his acknowledgment, and spoke of another matter, "Your group hasn't made many friends in this area. The logging moratorium you won, put a lot of locals out of work." Jason leaned forward in his chair as he explained, "If they had kept cutting the way they were, they would have been out of business within five years. This way, they can sustain moderate logging for the foreseeable future. Next year they can start logging again, but at a sustainable pace.

26

We have to make our resources last." "I'm on your side," offered Bill, "my grandfather said these same things fifty years ago." "Yes he did," agreed Jason. Raising his glass, he offered a toast, "To your grandfather's wisdom." They touched glasses, then drank. Jason sat back in his chair. After a moment, he looked out of the one of the windows that dominated one wall, "We have another fight to win." "You mean AW Fairbanks and her condo development?" Bill inquired. "A condo development doesn't begin to describe what that woman has in mind," Jason snorted, "She plans on building a hotel and shopping mall as well as two hundred fifty Condos. The only thing that stands in their way is the Injunction that we are seeking. In clearing the land, they uncovered Indian artifacts. We think it is a five hundred year old village. AW tried to hide the items they found, but we got a tip." "That land touches the Washo Reservation. Maybe Johnny Eagle wants an Indian Casino next door," Bill speculated. "Do you think that people would come to a Casino this far North?" Jason asked. Bill quickly replied, "They already come here to hunt, fish, and ski. Why not to gamble?" Jason sat silent for a moment, scowling. "This is as bad as clear cutting!" He exclaimed. He rose, pounding the table, "We have to stop this!" Bill looked at him for a moment, "I agree with you. Your Court Injunction better work." Jason decided to confide in Bill, "Our Geologist, Bob Moore, thinks that there are fault lines in that area. That could stop any development plans." Glancing at this watch, Bill stood up, "I've got to get back to my office. Thank you for the your hospitality." Jason accompanied him to the front door, thanking him again for Jennifer's safety. Bill played down his actions of the morning, and bid Jason goodby. Jason waved as the Sheriff pulled away. He then grabbed his Cell phone and quickly dialed a number. The phone rang and rang, no answer, then went to Voice Mail. Dropping that call, he dialed another. "Good Afternoon, Brown and Caldwell." "And a good afternoon to you. This is Jason Saunders, can I speak to the Councilor?" After a moment, "Hello Jason." "Allen, have you heard from Bob Moore?" "Not for two days, Jason." "Really! What is he playing at? We need that report. Well, let me know if you hear from him" "Will do." " Have a good one." Scowling, he put the phone away and headed into the house.

Entering the house, Jason met Jennifer coming down the stairs. "Where's the Sheriff?" She asked, finishing her hair. Jason looked at his Daughter, wearing a tasteful sun dress, "The Sheriff headed back to town." The disappointment on her face was obvious. "Oh," was all she said. Jason thought of the men in his Daughter's past, "This one seems different than your usual choice." Scowling, she started into the living room. "That's not fair, Dad," she said, not looking at him. Following her into the living room, he responded, "Fair or not, this man is something new in your life. A mature, accomplished male, not at all interested in my money." Looking out a window, she denied her interest in Sheriff Bill Andrews, "I don't think that he is interested in me. He's older than I am, maybe too old." Jason said smirking, "Oh, he is interested in you, and his age is a relative thing. Did you know that he has been a widower for many years? His late wife was apparently mentally ill. He has a grown daughter in LA. She is a rookie reporter for KNBC. Bill and his Daughter are close. She is only a few years younger than you." Jennifer turned toward her father, "You are just full of information about Bill Andrews, aren't you." "Not as much as I will be when your Uncle Roy calls me back with the information I requested," he smirking slightly. "On a more serious note," the smirk fading from his face, "Bill Andrews won't lay a hand on you, unless you want him to. I don't think there will be another incident like Mexico." Stiffening, Jennifer started to say something, then turned back to the window. Jason came up behind his Daughter. Placing his hands on her shoulders, he spoke softly to her, "Honey, you have to get on with your life. You can't keep drifting. Working in LA, then Mexico, where next? Drifting from man to man. You are interested in this man. But the ball is in your court. If you want something with Bill, you will have to start it. He won't. He has baggage. He has responsibilities and duties. Everything I know about him says he is a good man." "Thank you, Dad." She said turning to look into her Fathers eyes. She hugged him. "I want you to be happy," he said softly. A moment later, the quiet was broken by the ringing of a phone. Jason grabbed the phone off the table, "Hello." "This Bernadette Saint Clair" "Hello, Doctor Saint Clair." "We have found several Indian graves. Is your Daughter there?" "Really, graves! She's right here, I'll put her on." He handed the phone to Jennifer. "Hello, Bernadette," she spoke tentatively, not knowing exactly what was up with the archaeologist. "How many graves have you found?" "Jennifer, we've found four so far. Can you come over and take a look?" "Good. Yes, I can come over." "When, Jennifer?" "Right away, Bernadette." She handed the phone back to her Father. Jason spoke to Bernadette, "Yes, we will be right over. I'll drive her over myself!" Hanging up, Jason followed Jennifer out of the living room, and through the front door.

Ten minutes later, Jason and Jennifer pulled up to the excavation site in their Land Rover. Dr Bernadette St Clair, a petite woman with wire-rim glasses and short, graying hair, was arguing with another middle aged woman. A W Fairbanks was a short woman, with reading glasses, and bright red, styled hair (obviously dyed). The two were facing each other, about a foot apart. "Anything found on this land is mine, "snarled A W. "I want everything found on my land." Bernadette responded calmly, "All artifacts must be examined first, then the State will decide their deposition." "They are mine." screamed A W. "The State has nothing to do with my land. I want my things now!" Jason moved up to A W. "Madam, I am Jason Saunders. What seems to be the problem? You first, Doctor Saint Clair. "Mr Saunders, she replied patiently, "I am the State appointed Archaeologist for this project. Per state law, I am collecting artifacts and holding them in trust." "She is holding my things," snarled A W, "I have come to collect them. See to it that I receive everything taken from my land." Taken aback by the audacity of her demands, Jason attempted to placate the obviously overwrought land owner. "Ms Fairbanks, State law prohibits artifacts held in trust from being distributed, except by the State." "The State is not going to steal anything that belongs to me," A W screamed, attempting to push past Bernadette, pushing her out of the way. She stopped short when Jason's huge hand landed on her shoulder. "Please don't do anything rash, you will be compensated for the artifacts." He said very firmly. A W looked at him with venom in her eyes. She snarled, "Get your hand off of me!" Jason's hand stayed on her shoulder, "You re not going to bother Doctor Saint Clair or her project," his grip was now hurting A W, "You are going to get in your car and leave." A W Fairbanks' anger changed to fear as she realized what this giant could do to her. She backed up. Jason let go. "Jason Saunders, I am going to have you arrested," she said, rubbing her shoulder. "I don't think you will," Lt. Jim Bearpaw was walking toward them from his parked SUV. "I saw your attempted attack on Doctor Saint Clair. Mr. Saunders may have prevented you from being arrested for Assault." "That is outrageous," screamed A W. "I was the one assaulted." Jim Bearpaw was standing three feet from AW by this time, "Mr. Saunders was defending Doctor Saint Clair from your attack. If she chooses to press charges, you could still be the one going to Jail." "You're on their side," She screamed, "You Indians think you still own this land." Pointing to the far edge of the field, Jim Bearpaw spoke, "Well, from those trees on, we do." This sent A W off in disarray, muttering loudly "about her rights being violated and how they weren't going to get away this!" She got into her car and sped away, a cloud of dust spreading behind her. A rental truck containing two men followed her. "Well done," said Jason, offering his hand to Jim, "Your timing was perfect." Jim motioned toward the excavation, "One of the crew called us when they saw her pull up. She has a hell of a temper." Bernadette St Clair spoke up, "So we noticed," she said, rubbing her shoulder. "Why is she allowed run around threatening people," Jennifer asked, indignantly. "She can until she breaks the law," was Jim's matter of fact reply, "If you win your injunction, there is no telling what she will do." "We will win the Injunction hearing," stated Jason, "So we must be ready for her. I do not think we are dealing simply with an angry woman. There is something seriously wrong with her." Jim volunteered, "I'll speak to the Sheriff about it." "Some of my people will stay here at night," offered Bernadette. Jim seemed concerned about that, "Let me talk to Sheriff Andrews about a night Deputy for the site. That would be better." With that, he said his goodbyes and headed for his car. As they watched him drive away, Jason confided in Dr. St Clair and Jennifer, "I am going to make some phone calls. This woman is not going to get her way with any tricks, even if she has the County Supervisors in her pocket." "What are you going to do, Mr Saunders?" inquired Bernadette, concerned about her 'dig.' "Why Doctor Saint Clair," he replied slyly," I am simply going to call the State Attorney General about our little problem." "Why is it that I believe you know our Attorney General," she said, smiling. Smiling back at her, he admitted, "Perhaps, because he use to be one of my Corporate Attorneys." Still smiling, Jason looked at Bernadette, "Would you like to join my Daughter and I for dinner tonight?" Looking first at Jason, then Jennifer, Bernadette replied, "If I have time to clean up first." "I"ll pick you up at 6:30, if that is alright with you." "Mr Saunders," Bernadette replied, "that would be fine." "Call me Jason," he responded. "I am Bernadette," she said. The two walked off, deeply involved in conversation. Jennifer just stood and watched them. "What are you up to, Dad?" She thought. After a moment, she headed for the 'dig' and the Indian graves.

Sheriff Bill Anderson was back at his desk, immersed in the never ending paperwork that seemed to rule his life now. For this reason, he did not mind when Charlie Stevens of the DEA stood in his doorway, "I see rural Sheriffs fight paperwork too!" "You can say that again! Come on in, Charlie." Instead, Charlie stepped back, ushering a young woman into the room. "Bill, I would like you to meet our PR person. Anita Brubaker, this is Sheriff Bill Andrews." She noticed that he stood to meet them. He noticed an attractive woman perhaps in her late twenties. Tasteful pantsuit, styled light brown hair, and a smile that probably melted most men that she meets. When they shook hands, each noticed the lack of rings for the other. He thought her blue eyes sparkled. Bill invited them to sit down, "Welcome to Sierra Vista, Ms Brubaker." Charlie explained that they were on their way to dinner. Bill asked them if they had somewhere in mind? When they said no, he asked if he could recommend a place? The three of them ended by dinning together. During dinner, Anita found that Bill was a widower, with a grown Daughter in LA. Bill discovered that Anita was from Susanville, and divorced. Charlie was sure that Anita and Bill would be seeing more of each other. They certainly hit it off! Charlie could tell his wife that he had met the famous Sheriff of Sierra Vista, and so had Anita. Charlie found it no surprise when Bill would offer to escort Anita to her car. "Have you lived your entire life in Susanville?" They talked as they walked. "No, Bill. I'm an Army brat. I've lived all over. I went to college at Georgetown, then I worked in Public Relations around the DC area. That was where I met my husband." Bill found that interesting, "We may know some of the same spots. I spent a great deal of time in the area, first with the Navy, then with NCIS." She smiled her wonderful smile, "Yes, we may know some of the same places. We should talk more about DC." He thought that even her blues eyes seemed to smile. They said goodbye at her car, a simple hand shake. As he watched her drive away, Bill wondered when he would see her again?

Anita thought about Bill Andrews on the long drive back to Susanville. It was easy for a bright woman like Anita to see that Bill was the best thing going in these parts. Did he have a girlfriend? Was he looking for a relationship? Anita intended to find out. She had some interest in his area for her to do their PR work. She intended to pursue these opportunities. It could mean more money, for one thing. It could also mean meeting Bill again! Anita did not kid herself. Men of Bill's age usually did not make quick moves where women were concerned. She would have to do the moving. She softly smile, as she continued her drive home.

Chapter Three

Monday:

The men of Fire Station One knew about the Raid. Cal Fire, the California State Forestry Fire Service, was connected to the Law Enforcement Radio Network. The professional firefighters had been monitoring their scanner from the beginning. The DEA helicopters had flown right over them! They occupied an open space cut into the surrounding forest. The paved road to this facility, came off of County Road One, just inside the Washo Reservation. This was Indian land, Cal Fire leased it from the Tribe. In turn, Cal Fire provided protection for the Reservation. Cal Fire liked it because of its central location. This also prompted locating the Battalion Headquarter on the same acreage. There were two other Fire Stations in the County, the Battalion Chief was in charge of all three. The men of Station One were following the Raid with only half a mind. Today, they were getting a new Engineer! This grade of Firefighter was responsible for the Pumper Fire Engine they depended on so heavily. The Engineer drove the Pumper Engine, operating the water pumps and hose connections visible on the stainless steel side panel. Many could drive an Engine, but few were qualified to maintain the water tank, pumps, filters, and gauges necessary to put water on a fire. Captain Grayson hoped that the B. Dawson assigned was an experienced Engineer. He did not have a file for the Firefighter, yet. The veteran Captain did not like that. Usually, he could expect to get the file a week or so ahead, but not now. Budget cuts and layoffs had everything in disarray. He liked that word, the Captain had started doing crossword puzzles, between fires and drills. Increase your word power! There could be boring downtime. There could also be a Forest Fire! Then life got real exciting, and busy! People got injured then, too. Their previous Engineer had helped with a brush fire, along with several Volunteers. This was common practice in rural areas. Volunteers are trained amateurs. One

33

Volunteer made a mistake, the Engineer was badly injured. Captain Grayson was pretty sure that the man would never return, not to this Station. All three men assigned to the Station were in the lounge, off the Station's eat-in kitchen. The Radio blared loudly, but it was getting boring now, just mopping up of the 'farmers'. A light green compact sedan pulled up in front of the station. Everyone watched for who got out. A blue Uniformed person was driving. Blue was the Cal Fire uniform color. The door opened, the driver got out! It was a woman! Long brown hair, down to her shoulders! She walked toward the front door, a folder in her hand. The Cal Fire jacket was warm for this time of year, but Grayson figured that she was being formal. No reason not to impress your new Station. When she entered, the Captain saw her name badge, 'DAWSON'. He knew that this would be interesting. "Hello, Captain. I'm your new Engineer, Brenda Dawson." She handed him the folder. It held her file, Grayson thumbed through it. The other pair were silent. Young Danny Cunningham was twenty, and just off probation. An open, friendly sort. Jake Sawyer was two years older, and of quite a different temperament. He had been driving the Engine, temporarily. The Captain was not happy with his performance. Jake thought that he was doing just great. They didn't need an Engineer, to his simple mind. Captain Grayson looked from the file, Brenda's eyes met his. "Dawson, you have a good record. Five years of Service, the last one as a Fire Apparatus Engineer. Do you mind leaving Bass Lake?" She shook her head, "No Captain. That is not a happy Station. Too many fires, not enough Pros." Grayson nodded. It was a common complaint. "Couldn't cut it, Dawson?" Jake sneered at the tall Brunette. Grayson was quick, "Shut your stupid mouth, Jake. We already had a demonstration of your sorry skills!" Danny giggle, "He kept charging the wrong outlet! Took us forever to get water in our hose!" Jake jabbed him with an elbow. Brenda never acknowledge his remark. She had learned not to. Don't encourage the fools. The Captain studied Brenda. She was 5' 10", 155 lbs. He figured that she would pull her weight. There had been female Cal Fire recruits that really could not do some of the work. Humping rolls of hose is hard labor. After a fire, all used hose must be drained and rolled, then stowed back on the Engine. All hands on an Engine should be able to do their share. He stood up, offering his right hand, "Welcome to Station One, Brenda. You can call me

34

Gary, we will be working together. They shook hands. "Okay, Brenda, this is how it lays out. We have two Engines here, all of our Stations do. One Engine is run by Pros, like this crew. The other belongs to the County, and is manned by Volunteers." Her forehead wrinkled, "What do they do for an Engineer?" "Well, in our case, the Engineer is a retired Air Force firefighter. He is really good." She nodded her understanding. She now knew that their immediate back up were Volunteers. Nothing rare about that in Cal Fire. Volunteers were a vital part of their work. "The local Volunteers are good, mostly ex-military. They train regularly, most are very dedicated. Brenda, you will probably be happy to know that our Volunteer crew contains one woman." She smiled, "Really? That's great! But what I need to know right now is where to I sleep?" Gary's smile turned to a frown, "I was afraid you'd get around to that! Our Sleeping Quarters are off limits. We had a roof leak last year, no one knew that it had dripped into the outside wall. Now, it's all moldy. The boys are bunking in the Engine Bay, with our Pumper." Brenda was obviously upset, "When will it be fixed?" Gary was vague, "The request for repair is in, but money is limited. No contracts will be issued until after the new budget comes out." Gary saw her nose wrinkle, "What do I do in the meantime?" Gary scowled, "My house is full," he gestured toward the house that sat behind the Station, "so I suggest you take your file across to the Chief. Maybe he has an idea." He pointed out the front. The Battalion Headquarters was about fifty yards away. She took the offered file, "Wish me luck!" She set off across the asphalt.

Brenda strode across the warm asphalt. She knew that soon, this same paving would be hot enough to become soft. Moving the multi-ton Engine over it would require care. She had seen paving that carried deep groves from careless summer use. The Battalion Office door was unlocked, so Brenda went right in. Behind the counter, was a short, plump Brunette, maybe twenty. "Hi, is the Chief in?" "Who wants to know?" Brenda was a bit taken aback by the response. She looked down on the much shorter woman, "Tell him that his new Engineer is reporting for duty." Surprised, the chubby gal waddled to a closed door. She knocked twice, then opened it, "Boss, it looks like your new Engineer is reporting." Brenda heard the response, "Send him in." She walked back toward the counter with a big grin, "My name is Janet, go on in and surprise him!" Brenda did just that, coming to the office door, she knocked twice. "Enter!" She threw the door open, and stepped in. "Fire Apparatus Engineer Brenda Dawson reporting for duty!" Chief Stan Jensen looked up from his desk, "Brenda! What the hell are you doing here?" He got up, all 6' 4" of him, and came around the desk. "The usual, Stan. I put in for a transfer, and this is where they sent me!" Stan hugged the big woman. She was almost smothered by the behemoth. "I never imagined you'd end up here!" He held her at arms length, "Still the prettiest firefighter I've ever seen!" "Stan, you could get in a lot of trouble, if the press got a hold of your remark!" "Am I in trouble with you?" She hugged him, "No, Stan! It is so good to see you. I couldn't believe that I'd be working for you!" "Have you checked in with Gary Grayson?" "Yeah, Stan. He seems okay. Now, I need to find somewhere to live." Stan looked uncertain, "I have one suggestion, but you may not like it." "Okay, Stan. What is it?" "You could use the spare room in my place. I have the house out back." She broke into a smile, "Share a place with you and Sue? That would be great!" Stan grew somber, "Brenda, Sue died six months ago. It was Cancer, she was sick for about two years." Brenda got upset, "You should have written me! I could've come to see her. Where is she buried?" "Fresno, she was buried between her Mom and our Daughter. That was what she wanted. She never wanted any fuss over her. I wrote you in Riverside, there was no response." "It was never forwarded to me at Bass Lake." He saw the tears trickle down her cheeks, "Come on, Brenda! Let me show you the place." He put one long arm around her, ushering her out of the office. "Janet, I'll be at the house for a few minutes." Janet stared at the large pair, as they exited the office. Behind the small Battalion Office Building, lay a three bedroom, two bath, seventeen hundred square foot house. Plain and spartan on the outside, Brenda wondered about the interior. "I think you will be surprised, Brenda. Sue did a good job of decorating, but she didn't get to quite finish. Stan unlocked the front door, letting her enter first. She made it two steps into the Living Room, before she stopped to look. She was impressed! There was a nice sectional sofa, two easy chairs, an all wood coffee table, and several lamps. A painting over the flagstone fireplace, set the whole thing off. She turned to Stan, who had entered behind her, "Sue has such a good eye! I mean, she did have a good eye. Oh, Stan! You must miss her so much!" He looked about with a frown, "I suppose that I should have redone the room, but I really didn't want to change a thing." Brenda put her arm around him, kissing him on the cheek. "You two were so happy together, I'm so sorry." "Thanks, Brenda. Let me show you the place." He took her hand, leading her to the small Dining Room, the spacious Kitchen, a Laundry Room, Master Bedroom, the Sewing Room (really, another bedroom), and the Guest Room. This was to be her place. Brenda liked what she saw. There was a Queen size bed, two lamp tables, nice lamps for reading, a good sized dresser, and a small desk. She figured that her computer would go there. She was all smiles, as she turned to Stan. "I love it! But you have to let me pay rent!" He knew better than argue with the tall, young woman, so an amount was quickly agreed on. She checked on the Bathroom, noted some changes she would make, then went to get her car. First order of business would be unloading her stuff! Stan watched her walk away from the front doorway. He wondered what had prompted her transfer, personality clash or an affair gone sour? She was twenty-five years old, did she feel the urge to marry? It would only be natural. But there was still so much unnatural about being a female in Cal Fire. Stan pulled himself back to his work. He sat down at his desk, with Breda's file.

Mona slowly woke up. When she reached out for Brent, she got nothing but empty bed. She had to go into her room to find her robe. Would she ever get use to Air Conditioning? Where was he? She walked down the hall, tying her robe. Then she heard a noise! He was in the Kitchen! She found him at the stove, cooking eggs. Mona hugged him from behind, "Thank you for last night. You've been so good to me." He turned and kissed her. She put her arms around his neck, pulling him down to her. They shared a long kiss. "Sorry, Mona. I have to stir the eggs." She laughed, then let him go, the orange juice needed pouring. She was pouring two cups of coffee, when the eggs were done. They ate a quiet meal, what talk went on was about them. Brent was not sure about a relationship with her. "You're so young, Mona. I bet you haven't dated much." "I have dated. I never felt about them like I do about you. We have known each other for ten year. That means some-thing." They discussed their situation, as they cleaned up the Kitchen. Then they went back to the Master Bedroom. Mona closed the discussion by dropping her robe, and hugging Brent in her skimpy nightgown. As he hugged her back, Mona whispered in his ear, "Make love to me. I want my first time to be with you." Well, Brent was only so strong. He got a condom out of his night stand, removed Mona's nightie, and tenderly took her virginity. For Mona it was a fantasy come true. Of course, the petit eighteen year old was absolutely sure that Brent was all hers. She had bought him with her body. For Brent, it had been something of a solemn occasion. He was taking the virginity of a young woman, who had just lost her Mother. He knew that she was vulnerable. He felt like he was taking advantage of her. Then, he remembered her wearing shorts. How she felt in her nightie. How she felt now, without her nightie. He was very gentle, as he introduced Mona to sex. She didn't feel much pain, and there was not much blood. Brent told her that it was probably her years of gymnastics. She felt glad that those years were of some benefit. To her, those years had been the time of Mom's drug use. After, Brent cradled her in his arms. She felt so soft and warm! Cuddling with her lover was a new one for Mona, she found it so wonderful. Today, her happiness knew no bounds! Laying there, Brent was struck by the oddness of the situation. Mona had given him her virginity, and the use of her fit young body. He had been given a gift. Yet, Mona seemed so thankful, so happy about it happening. Did she see it as ridding herself of a burden? The young Deputy was just beginning to discover the mysteries of sex. Mona saw the loss of her virginity, as gaining her security. She now had Brent, and his house. She sure that she loved him, wasn't that the feeling that she felt? She felt so good, then she thought, "Now we can do this any time we want!" Brent had another condom, so they did it again. They could do it when ever they wanted!

Her hair was up, she was now wearing blue, short sleeve overalls. Management tried to tell them that this was a jumpsuit. The fire crew all knew better. She had her clipboard, she checked off items as she inspected the Pumper. Anything out of spec was noted, it was her job to see that it was fixed. Simple repairs were her responsibility, major repairs required the District Mechanic. It was her practice to require the Mechanic only for major vehicle problems. The plumbing was her domain. Danny was swapping out worn hoses from the Pumper, so the two talked. He confided in Brenda, that Jake was suppose to be helping him. "Does Gary know about this?" She inquired. Danny shook his head, "I don't think so. Jake knows the Captain is busy doing paperwork for the Chief. I hear you know the Chief from before, is that true?" Brenda smiled, "Danny, Stan was my first Captain. I was right out of the Academy, tripping over my own feet. Stan Jensen got me squared away. He and his wife, Sue, took good care of me." Danny looked serious, "You knew his wife? I hear she died of cancer. What a horrible way to die!" "Yes it is, Danny. Would you excuse me for a minute?" Danny nodded that he would. Brenda went into the Living Area. She found Gary in the small office set aside for the Captain. "Gary, I'm going over the log of the Pumper. Jake didn't put his logs into the binder with the rest." Gary looked up from his reports, "Jake should be with Danny. They're swapping hoses." "Gary, Danny is working alone, Jake is nowhere to be seen." Gary rolled his eyes and stood up. "Excuse me, I need to visit my house for a moment" As he went out the back door, he spoke over his shoulder, "My cute seventeen year old niece is visiting for the Summer. I do believe that Jake will appear shortly." Mission accomplished, Brenda went back to her inspection.

Eventually, Mona and Brent surfaced from the Master bedroom. It was agreed, they needed to shop! In the Grocery Store, the young couple got noticed. Or rather, Mona got noticed. She was wearing shorts again. Neither of them was a picky eater, but they each had their own favorites. Mona's style was more open and informal, her Mother's influence. Brent found nothing too objectionable, or was it that Mona was very persuasive? As they loaded their booty in his trunk, the young Deputy started to notice how things had changed. As he drove them home, he thought about how things had happened recently. His parents had retired, early. Both were offered early retirement incentives. It was arranged that he would buy their house, so they bought a Motor Home. Now, they were out traveling, and he was here working. Younger Sister Ellen decided to stay and work in LA. Within two days, he found that he was living with Mona. She was snuggled up against him, on the bench seat. He could feel her presence, her body was soft and warm. She approached most things with enthusiasm and energy. It was interesting to watch her, but stimulating too. He could never forget the naked Mona in his bed this morning. Was this how it was going to be? Mona had surprised him. When they were checking out, she told him that she would pay for groceries with her first paycheck! He had no idea how much she was making, but he liked the idea. He was making house payments to his Parents, then there was the utilities, property tax, and insurance. A young Deputy only made so much. The young couple had to talk.

There had been words between the crew members. Jake was sore about being caught with Gary's niece! He was AWOL from his duty, but that never mattered with a 'citizen' like Jake. It was all about him, someone had betrayed him! He was in Danny's face, but Danny had done nothing, he knew nothing about it. Jake then knew, it must be the bitch, Brenda. He confronted her! Brenda started asking him question about the Engine Logbook. She asked him about the pages he was supposed to have filled out. "Stick that shit! I want to know who turned me in!" "Jake, you have until Friday to bring the Log up to date. Or do you want me to take it to the Chief?" That settled him right down. No way the slim six footer wanted to face huge Stan! He walked away, deep in thought. "I'll get this Bitch! No body is going to get me, without I get them back, double!" His thoughts, such as they were, got sidetracked by a blaring horn. Fire! Jake and Danny ran for their fire gear. Brenda threw her clipboard into the Engine cab, grabbing her gear out of the Driver's seat. Pulling off her cross trainers, she thrust her feet through the pants, and into her boots. The suspenders went over her shoulders, then she fastened the front. Brenda grabbed the coat from the back of her seat, pulled it on, then climbed into the seat. She started the Diesel engine, then bent over to fasten her boots. Her helmet was on the dash, it went onto her head. She fastened the strap under her chin. Danny and Jake climbed into the seats behind her, it was a four man crew cabin. Captain Grayson climbed in, next to Brenda. "Kitchen fire, I'll guide you, Brenda. You haven't had time to learn the Valley!" The big front door was already open, so Brenda pulled out. Lights and siren, that was standard for driving to a fire. The Pumper handled smoothly! Brenda was happy with the handling. Gary was clear with his directions, she was lucky there. She noted that a car in front of the Pumper, pulled over. She had a clear path. She liked the courtesy, discipline was good at stop lights, too. No cars pulled in front of her, no driver failed to hear the siren. Smooth sailing, all the way to the fire. The houses were all built sometime in the nineteen twenties, Brenda noticed that no two seem to be alike.

40

She stopped the Engine before the house with the small crowd in the front yard. They waved frantically at the firefighters, the Captain jumped out. He ran ahead to check the fire, while his crew prepared to pull hoses and charge them with water. They would use their 300 gallon internal tank, if the fire was small. Grayson came running from the house calling to Danny, "Grab a CO2 bottle, it's a grease fire." He told Jake to roll the hose back up, and stow it. "Standby, Brenda. We may need another CO2 bottle!" The extinguishers were kept in a side compartment of the Pumper. They had Oxygen bottles too, sometimes they had to go into a burning building to bring someone out, or to fight a fire. After a few minutes, Danny arrived back at the Pumper, with a big smile, "It was great! A couple of blasts, and the fire was out! Gary stayed to open the doors and windows." Danny stashed his bottle, and shut the compartment. Then he grinned at Jake, struggling to put a roll of hose back on the truck. Jake managed to give him the 'finger'. Danny returned to the crew compartment. Brenda saw the whole thing, she just smiled and shook her head. They had to wait for Gary. He was deep in discussion with the home owner. The pour woman was distraught, she was terrified at what her husband would say, and do, about her carelessness. She had left the skillet on, while she tended to the baby. Now, their Kitchen would need work. All four firefighters knew, it could have been a lot worse. When they got back to the Station, Brenda hauled her gear over to her new home. A Nice shower was in order! This was always risky for a firefighter. An alarm could sound at any time. Breda washed her hair, the ultimate tempting of fate. She won her bet, no fire while she showered and changed. It was a warm afternoon, so Brenda decided on shorts and a blouse. Her fire gear was setup by her bed. She needed fast access to everything. In Winter, long johns would feel good, under her fire gear. This time of year, she liked slacks and a short sleeved shirt. She sat at her desk, trying to bring the Pumper log up to date. "Damn Jake." She figured that setting up her computer would be next. Then a thought struck her, "What about dinner?" She knew a discussion with Stan was in order. Brenda did not mind cooking, but not all of the time. Firefighters took turns, gender was irrelevant!

Afternoon found Brent and Mona fixing their dinner. Dinner in the afternoon, lunch at night. That's how it was with night shifts. Both of the young people were happy, things were working out! There were frequent glances at each other. Mona had a little smile, life was much better than with her Mother. It did not bother her to think that, her Mother had put her through so much. The drugs had made her selfish, so often she was not there for her Daughter. Not that she wasn't home, it was just that the drugs made her forget her obligations. She floated, her mind drifting. Even when she was sober, life was about getting more drugs. Brent had no real idea what living with a druggie was like. He was always on the periphery, he saw the ambulance come for her. No way he could know what it was like, day to day. It was not something Mona wanted to talk to him about. She was ashamed of her past, druggies made their families ashamed. Brent knew enough to leave the topic alone, it was an ugly past. He was willing to let it alone, if that was what his lover wanted. In time, maybe she would bring it up. The ringing phone interrupted their meaningful silence, Brent grabbed it. "Hello!" "Brent, this is Sargent Wolfe. I have a new assignment for you." "What is it, Sarge?" "You know the construction site on Route One?" "Yeah, Sarge." "You are assigned to guard the site, four to midnight. Watch the shed where the Indian artifacts are stored, also the heavy equipment. We don't want any vandalism on that site. Any questions Carter?" "No, Sarge. I have my Cell phone if anything happens." "Until we get our new radios, that will have to do. There is a tent that the archeology crew is using, you might make that your base. Keep you eyes and ears open. People have all kinds of issues with that site. Don't trust anyone, get their ID!" "Yes, Sargent Wolfe. I understand." Wolfe hung up, Brent put the handset away. Mona was watching him, expectantly, so he told her what was up. Her smile faded, to be replaced by a worried look, "You be careful! I want you coming back to me!" Brent put his arm around her shoulders, hugging her. "I promise, Mona! If I hear anything, I will call for backup." Her lower lip slightly protruded, was that a pout? "You better! I want you safe at home tonight. We have plans!" He hugged the little redhead, now reminded of just what he meant to her. "It will be quiet tonight, wait and see! I'll be there to pick you up, at one." She had both arms around him, "You better!"

When Stan entered the house, he was surprised by Brenda's attire. Her long legs were nicely displayed by her shorts. She started discussing dinner with the Battalion Chief. He told her

42

what was available, for which he was soundly chastise, "Didn't Sue teach you anything about a balanced meal?" Stan defended himself, the best he could. He made his point about living alone, it was hard cooking for one. That gave Breda pause, she had never been alone. In Foster care, she had always lived with families, then came Cal Fire. At Cal Fire Stations, the firefighters usually ate together. She insisted, she would run to the market. Stan noticed she had her things in a fanny pack. Brenda was an efficient, modern gal. Stan just wished that she wasn't so damn good looking! He had been without a bed partner for over two years, and he missed it.

Brent dropped off a worried Mona. He had done his best to calm her fears. She kissed him goodbye, then gave him a crushing hug. Mona was a strong little lady! She had a small thermal bag for her lunch. Brent used a good sized thermal lunch box. He didn't know whether he should take a cold or hot drink for tonight, so he took both. Over at the construction site, he found the crew at the Indian Village still working. He was surprised at how attractive some of the young women were. There was this one very tall Blonde. What a build! Brent was sure the Babe was as tall as he, maybe taller! She didn't seem to be in a very good mood. She seemed distracted. He met Dr Bernadette St Clair, who was in charge of the 'Dig'. She seemed friendly, as did some of the students helping her. By the time Brent got there, the crew was tired and dirty. They joked a bit, but most just wanted to put away their tool, and go back to the Motel. It seemed that a hot shower, then dinner was on everyone's agenda. Even Dr St Clair's! One chubby gal gave him the eye. Brent thought that she had a cute face, but he had never been a 'chubby lover'. By five thirty, he was alone. He did a circuit around the site, noting the piece of heavy equip- ment. Everyone had heard about the Court Trial, maybe no one would be using these machines here. There was a substantial building on site. It now held Indian artifacts for the State. His patrol turned up nothing, so he made himself comfort-table under the canopy set up for the 'dig'. They had a small refrigerator, three small tables, and several chairs. He took a position so that he could see the road and the machines. It looked to be a long, slow night. Brent found a few magazines laying around, he glanced at a couple. Soon, it was time to make another circuit.

When Breda got back from shopping, she went right to cooking Dinner. Stan watched her with interest, he was hungry. They ate a rather quiet meal. Both had things on their minds. She broke the silence, by asking about Jake. Stan prodded her, until she spilled out the whole story. He told that he was aware of Jake's attitude. Gary Grayson had given him a poor review six months ago. Instead of steering Jake to a better path, it only sent him into a fit. He saw it as some conspiracy to deny him the credit he felt he deserved. Stan saw him as warped, someone who could not see reality. So far, Jake had done nothing for which he could be fired. Brenda wondered what that meant? Would he improve, or go off the deep end? Stan though he knew the answer about Jake. The kid would keep on, until he screwed up big, then Gary and Stan would fire him. What Stan did not know, was the presence of Brenda going to be a problem in his life? Did she know how attractive she is?

At dusk, Brent decided to have his lunch. Not much was happening. The open air canopy allowed him to keep an eye out. Nothing broke the monotony, except for the odd vehicle on the highway. Brent had found a small radio earlier, it allowed him to get the news. The breeze had picked up, making coffee preferred over something cold. He slipped on his Department jacket, then sat back to sip his coffee. The noise of a small car shattered his peace, it parked near his enclosure. He was not really surprised, when the cubby Brunette got out. She came back for something she forgot. Brent noticed that she had changed, did she shower? She found what she came for, then chatted him up. Her name was Donna, she was from San Diego. Did he have a girlfriend? He told her about Mona. Her disappointment was obvious. Brent was nice to her, but he did not see a future with a visiting 'chubby'. Then, he heard it! From the direction of the shed, tool sounds! Some scraping, or was it prying? He took up his big flashlight in his left hand, his Beretta in his right. He told Donna to stay there, but she did not. Brent made his way toward the back of the building. He heard it again! He quietly moved to a spot where he could see the back. Two figures up against the rear of the building! He knew Donna was near, but there was nothing he could do about that. His light went on, two startled faces turned toward him. "Hold it! This the Sheriff's Department!" The tall figure started to run! Brent fired once, into the air! "Halt, or the next one goes into you!" The

44

runner stopped, then slowly came back. "Now, both of you get face down in the dirt!" They complied. "This aint right!" Brent recognized that voice! It was the kid from the Motel. The other one must be his friend, Mike. He had Donna hold the light on them, while he handcuffed the taller one. For Mike, he had a plastic cuff. It was an oversized tie wrap, handy for multiple suspects. That done, he called it in. The car and two men took about five minutes to arrive. Not bad, except for the mouthy kid's constant bitching. After they were hauled away, Donna gave him a big kiss. She thought he was big hero! He gave a thought to tackling the big girl on one of the tables. But he was never sure that any of them would take her weight! In the end, Donna went back to her Motel. Brent was relieved at Midnight, so he packed up, then went to pick up Mona. She was overjoyed to see him! He had no regrets at all, bedding down with the pretty redhead. She made him feel very important.

Chapter Four

Tuesday:

Sheriff Bill Andrews sat at the small table in his kitchen. He thought about the two women he had met yesterday. The tall, stacked Jennifer, and the shapely Brunette, Anita. He ate his breakfast, drank his coffee, and contemplated his sex life. Jennifer was visiting her Father, no telling how long that would last. Anita lived in Susanville, about an hour's drive away. All he had to do, was pick up the phone. But how could he trust them, after Mary? His relationships had always been of short duration. Sex and lust, with no strings. He did not see either of these woman in that way. But then, there was Hellene Abbot. No question about what she wanted. Hellene already had a rich husband, she wanted fun and games from him. It was no contest, he called Hellene. She was coming over tonight.

It was about nine, Bill was in his office, working at his desk. Suddenly, Russ burst into the office, obviously upset about something. Waving the newspaper at Bill, he loudly asked, "Have you seen this morning's Sentinel?" "No Russ, I haven't," the Sheriff replied. "Our wonderful DA has gone on record that yesterday's raid was his department in a joint operation with the DEA. There is no mention of our department in the whole article," Russ expounded. "Russ, calm down," Bill said patiently, "It was the DEA's show, we just did some cleanup. If the DA needs attention so badly, let him steal some of their thunder." Russ grew more agitated, "How can you take it so calmly? Ray Van Cleef killed your Sister!" "Joyce was alone in his car when she died," Bill said calmly, "there is no proof that he was even there. But I have asked for FBI help to restart the Case." Russ was surprised, "Did you really call in the FBI? Do you think that was a good idea?" "The FBI has the best equipment and the best forensic people around," Bill explained, "Besides, we can't be involved, we're prejudice. She was family. The FBI needs to examine the evidence. If they can prove he was driving the car, he can't yell foul." "I don't like the idea of the FBI taking all the credit," Russ added defiantly, "I want to nail that slimy bastard myself!" "Cousin," Bill said , "you sound just like my Dad. He would never call the FBI. I would like nothing better than nailing Ray myself, but you need to learn which battles to fight and which ones to hand off. That is a problem that you have. You made a lot of waves with the County Supervisors trying to get this Office. It did not help your case that you are separated from the Board President's Daughter, and openly living with a nineteen year old! Hell Russ, you've got a seventeen year old daughter! A wise man would have let it go. A wise man would have laid low for a while." Russ sat down in one of the chairs before the Sheriff's desk, "I wanted this job bad. When you got it instead, I was pissed. It was one more time that you stole the show. First, high school. You were the big Football star. Then at U.S.C., you were the big receiver, All American, while I played linebacker at Cal. Then you married Mary, and joined the Navy. You were accepted for the SEALs. I got shit!" Bill leaned forward, elbows on the desk, "Russ, you partied so much at Cal. You flunked out. I didn't do that. You then joined the Marine Corps. Later, you came home on leave, knocked up Gwen, and had to get married. You did these things, not me. It is about time that you take responsibility for your actions. Every time something goes wrong, you blame someone else." Russ slumped back in his chair and was quiet for a moment, "I'm sorry, Bill. I know you're right. I'm too damn impatient sometimes. I know your life hasn't been a picnic. Life with Mary wasn't easy. I've heard the stories of what she pulled on you. And then to kill herself, with her daughter there!" "She took pills," Bill replied, "she just went to sleep. Joyce didn't know anything was wrong. It wasn't the first time, she did it. But that time no one was home, no one answered her calls for help. She just went to sleep, Joyce couldn't wake her Mommy up. I had gotten help for her, but she could never stick with the program. She stopped taking her meds and just drifted. Maybe she just didn't care anymore." Bill sat there, staring straight ahead. Russ got up and walked around the desk. Putting his hand on Bill's shoulder, he spoke, "Come on Bill. It's been twenty years. Let it go." Bill looked at his cousin, "I know Russ, but sometimes I wonder if I did enough. Maybe I could have done something more." "Cousin," Russ began, "we can always second guess ourselves. What's done is done." "I wish it was that easy," Bill ruefully remarked. Russ wondered how Bill's Daughter liked being named after her dead aunt? Wanda appeared in the doorway. "Captain Baker, there is a call on three for you." "Thanks, Wanda," Russ said, as he headed to his office. Bill looked at Wanda, then spoke, "Could we talk for a moment." "Sure, Sheriff," she said as she walk over to his desk. "Wanda, you were my sister's best friend. I wanted you to know that I have asked the FBI to help jump start her case." "I'm glad you did," Wanda said emotionally, "Ray Van Cleef killed Joyce, he should pay for it!" "Hopefully, the FBI will prove he was driving, not Joyce." Bill responded. Wanda reached for a tissue from Bill's desk and started to dab her eyes, "Thinking about Joyce always makes me cry!" She turned and walk out of his office and on to the Ladies Restroom.

Early afternoon, still the Sheriff's office. Bill was on the phone. "I am glad you called Mike. You didn't have to notify me personally. I thought you would delegate it to one of your army of Special Agents." "You know what they say, Bill. If you want it done right, do it yourself." "Yeah, sometimes it is better to handle things yourself. Thanks Mike." "Bill, I wish you luck with this. Take care." "Same to you." Bill hung up, then made another call, "Wanda, the FBI has decided to help us restart Joyce's case." "Oh, Bill. That is such good news!" "Yes, it is. Please cut the paperwork to have the evidence from her case sent to Quantico. Thank you." Putting the phone down, he looked at the window. Rising, he walked over to the window and stared out. Wanda's appearance at the door broke his mood. "Jason Saunders is here to see you, Sheriff." Turning toward the door, Bill told her, "Please show him in." Jason's large frame filled the doorway as he entered. Bill met him in front of his desk, offering him his hand, "Welcome to the Sheriff's office. What can I do for you?" "Bill, I am concerned about the Geologist we hired, one Bob Moore. No one has talked to him in three days. He has not been back to his Motel, and there is no sign of his car." Motioning him toward the chairs in front of his desk, Bill grabbed a notepad off of the desk and handed it to Jason, "Write everything down, including his car licence, and his description. Does Bob have a cell phone?" Jason replied immediately, "Yes, he does, but it goes right to Voice Mail." As Jason wrote, Bill picked up the phone, "Wanda, please see if Captain Baker and Lieutenant Bearpaw can join us in my office. Thank you." After jotting down several things from a small black book, Jason handed the notepad to Bill. Then, Russ and Jim entered the room. After introducing Jason to the two Officers, Bill explains, "Mr. Saunders and his group have a missing Geologist, Bob Moore by name." Handing the notepad to Russ, he issued his orders, "Captain Baker will setup a search for Mr. Moore. Lieutenant Bearpaw will head the search of Mr Moore's hotel room. Please put out an APB on his vehicle. Mr Saunders will be our contact for information about Mr Moore. Is there anything you would like to add?" Jason stood up, "Bob was working for the Nature Coalition, I don't need to tell you gentlemen that my group has enemies. One of them, might think that removing Bob Moore would hurt our chances at the Injunction Hearing. I suspect A W Fairbanks and her backers." Bill spoke up quickly, cutting Jason off from any more conjecture, "Why don't we see where the evidence takes us. Let's get going on this, time is critical!" Russ and Jim headed out, looking at the notepad. After they were gone, Jason spoke to Bill, "Very efficiently done. I hope we find him alive. He has a wife and three kids." "The APB will reach adjacent counties and the Indian Tribal Council," Bill countered, "it is our best bet for now." Jason nodded, then spoke, "We need his Geological Report for the Hearing." Hesitating for a moment he spoke again, "Can we talk for a bit." Bill gestured toward the chairs before his desk, "Of course. What do you need to discuss?" Jason and Bill moved toward the desk. Jason sat in one of the chairs, "I need to talk to you about what I hear from Sacramento, Johnny Eagle has been spreading around a lot of cash. Apparently, trying to buy friends that can help him with his casino deal." Bill was concerned, "Where would he be getting this money? I'm not aware of him having deep pockets. The Tribe sure doesn't have any money." "Well, my friend, the Attorney General, has started an investigation into the matter. He suspects bribery. If so, they will want to know where the money came from." Bill smirked, "can I count on you keeping me informed about the investigation?" Jason smiled broadly, "I can do more than that. I have certain assets at my disposal. They can reveal amazing things!" Bill bowed to him with a flourish, "I leave it in your capable hands." Jason smiled, then grew more somber, "Bill I need to

50

discuss one other thing with you. I want to talk about my Jennifer." This startled Bill. Jason continued, "You may think of her as a strong, outgoing young woman, but the truth is somewhat different. She has been hurt. She is very insecure and too vulnerable. My Daughter needs to find a relationship with a good man, one who understands her situation." Noticing Bill's puzzled expression, Jason continued, "Jennifer is interested in you. And I think that you are interested in her. I have seen the two of you together. Perhaps it could be a good relationship. You both have baggage, you both have been hurt. I think you both need someone. Most people do." It took Bill a moment to speak. He struggled to find the right words. "How could this man burst in, meddling in his life? Is he pimping his Daughter to me?" Jason watched Bill's struggle, "I am sure it will take some time for you to come around to this way of thinking. We mature men don't make quick decisions where women are concerned, do we? Jennifer wanted me to find out all that I could about you. I talked to my brother Roy about you, he is a Vice Admiral at the Pentagon. He tells me that you are a Commander in the Naval Reserve, that you hold the Navy Cross, the Silver Star, and two Purple Hearts. Not even he can find out what the Navy Cross and one of the Purple Hearts are for. He said that you have a reputation for taking care of your men, on duty and off." Bill was obviously bothered by this information, "I think your Brother has a big mouth. My record is secured, no one is supposed to be making it public." Jason smiled at Bill, "Relax Bill, Roy told me these things in the strictest confidence. I still hold several security clearances. I also checked into your private life. I beg your pardon for that, but as Jennifer's Father, I feel I have a responsibility for her security. Your Sister died in a traffic accident, under suspicious circumstances. That case is still open. Your wife's death was a tragedy, all the more so because you were on a mission at the time. I wonder how much guilt you have suffered for that? I can find nothing that suggests that she was suicidal. No one saw it coming, how could you? You seemed to have raised a fine Daughter, now working for KNBC, I understand. The NCIS speaks very highly of you, in fact, they want you back. You are even highly regarded by the FBI. Now that is a miracle! In short, you seem made to order for my Daughter. Not that you want to hear that. But I am sure you will come around. Jennifer is a special young woman. She is beautiful, isn't she?" With that Jason stood up, smiling, he spoke looking down at Bill, "Well, you have a good day. I am sure that you have a great deal to think about." And with that, he strode out of the office. Bill sat there, stunned. All these feelings came welling up. His Sister, his Wife, his Daughter, and now Jennifer. Did he want to get involved with Jennifer? She had her own problems. Is he an answer for her? Is she an answer for him? Yes, she is beautiful. But was that ever enough? Mary was beautiful too. For now, he had Hellene.

Bill did not have long for his introspection, Wanda's voice came over the intercom. "Sheriff, there is a Captain Davis from the Navy on Line One for Commander Andrews." Reluctantly, Bill answered her, "Thank you, Wanda." He picked up the receiver, and punched the button for Line One. "Commander Andrews." "Commander Andrews, I am Captain Davis from the Bureau of Naval Personnel. I deal with Death Notifications. When you were in San Diego, you volunteered for Death Notification Duty. Are you still available?" "Yes Sir, I did volunteer. What do you have for me?" "Commander, did you know that you are the senior Naval Officer in your area?" "No Sir, I did not realize that I was the senior Naval Officer. What do want, Sir?" "Commander, we have a dead young Marine from your area. We need you to take charge of the Notification of next of Kin, and the funeral arrangement." "Why are the Marines not handling this, Sir?" "There are no Marine Reserve Officers available, They are apparently all on active duty elsewhere. But I have found a senior Marine Reserve noncom. Do you know Master Sargent Russell Baker?" "Yes sir, I do know Master Sargent Baker, he is my Cousin." "Excellent! You will also need a local clergyman." "I understand, Sir, a local minister. Sir, the name of the deceased?" "It is a Private Robert Johnson, did you know him?" Bill's shoulders drooped. "Yes Sir, I did know him. I grew up with his parents. I will handle it, Sir. Goodby, Sir." "I do appreciate this, Commander." Slowly, he hung up the receiver."No Marine Officers are available? They are all in Iraq or Afghanistan." Pushing the Intercom button, he spoke. "Wanda, do you know of a local minister I can talk to right now?" "Yes, Sheriff," She answered quickly. "Reverend Phelps should be available. Let me phone him for you." A moment later, Wanda was back on the Intercom, "Reverend Phelps is on One for you." "Thank you," Bill said as he picked up the receiver. "Reverend

52

Phelps, this is Sheriff Andrews. I need your services for a Military Death Notification call." "Yes, Sheriff. One of our gallant warriors has fallen?" "Yes, a young Marine." "Was this tragic occurrence in Iraq?" "Yes it was Iraq. There will be three of us. We will meet here at my office about five PM.. Can I count on you?" "Of course, Sheriff. I will be honored to help in this matter." "Good, see you at five."

It was about 3:30 pm, Bill was lost in thought. Rob Johnson's death was on his mind. In San Diego, he had served in two death notifications, both for Navy Corpsmen. They had been impersonal. Rob's would not be. His thoughts were interrupted by Wanda on the Intercom, "Sheriff Andrews?" "Yes, Wanda." "Mrs. Abbot and her Daughter are here to see you." The Abbots had purchased the old Van Cleef Estate. They had poured a great deal of money into the old house. So much trouble for a summer home. He wondered if it was it something about the property? "Please send them in, Wanda." She ushered them right in. Bill rose to greet them. He stepped around his desk to greet Mrs Abbot. She was very cool. Was she pretending to be a stranger? Her teenage Daughter was with her. The girl was as tall as her Mother, but not as blonde. Her bronzed arms and shoulders marked her as an outdoor person. Her light brown hair was held in a pony tail and her well developed legs, marked her as a tennis player. The white, short skirt outfit she wore might be suitable for tennis. Bill held out his hand to Hellene, "Mrs Abbot, I am Sheriff Bill Andrews. How can I help you?" Hellene Abbot shook hands with Bill, "Can we speak in private?" He motioned to the two chairs in front of his desk, "Of course, please be seated." Bill walked over and closed his office door, then returned to his chair. "Now, Mrs Abbot, what seems to be the problem?" "Sheriff Andrews, I want you to arrest Don Lee." "What crime has Don committed?" "He had sex with my sixteen year old Daughter, Tiffany." "Mrs Abbot, Don Lee is only about seventeen himself. With what do you wish me to charge him?" "I don't understand, Sheriff. He had sex with my under aged Daughter. Arrest him." "Mrs Abbot. If Don was eighteen, he could be charged with Statutory Rape. If he forced Tiffany, I could charge him with Rape, at any age. Tiffany, did Don force you to have sex?" "Oh no, Sheriff! I love Don!" Tiffany was a slightly slimmer copy of her Mother, very attractive. "Did you use a con- dom, Tiffany?" "Oh yes. Don insisted on it!" "Tiffany, if Don wants to have sex in the future, will you sleep with him?" "Of course, Sheriff. I love Don!" Bill's brow was wrinkled, "Mrs Abbot, there is nothing for me to do in this matter. We have two minors having sex, with a condom. It is a matter for you and your husband to handle." "I do not understand why you will not arrest this person! Do I have to go to the District Attorney to have him arrested?" "Mrs Abbot, the DA can do nothing for you. Don is a minor, just like Tiffany. Minors are not always held responsible for their actions, their parents are. You and your husband should talk to Don and his parents." "Sheriff Andrews, my husband and I are not going to talk to any one. We thought that the law would take care of such people. We thought that we were protected by the law against people like Don and his parents. Obviously, we were mistaken." Bill now knew what the problem was, "Mrs Abbot, am I to understand that the big problem here is who Don and his parents are? Is it that they are Indians, and live on the Reservation in less than grand accommodations?" "Yes, Sheriff Andrews, that is precisely the problem. We do not want our Daughter associating with any degenerate Indian family." "I do not like the word 'degenerate', Mrs Abbot. It does not fit either Don or his parents. The entire Lee family has a good reputation in this area. They are solid citizens, well respected. I should know, I am part of that family. My Grandmother was a Lee. She came from a less than splendid house in the Reservation. Yet, I went to U.S.C. on a football scholarship. Later, I became a Naval Officer. Don has the skills to do the same, if he so chooses." Tiffany Abbot was all smiles when she heard this, her Mother was confused by Bill's statements. Bill spoke quietly, "Mrs. Abbot, this is not a matter for the police, it is a family matter. As a widower with a daughter, I am familiar with this issue. I faced it myself, a few years ago." Hellene Abbot showed interest in this last statement, "What can I do, Sheriff Andrews? I don't want her to ruin her life!" "Mrs Abbot, Tiffany did this out of love. She feels that sex is what males and females do if they love each other. You and your husband may want to help her to know when is the appropriate time for sex. She also needs to understand the risks of sex. Dr. Sarah Davis can help with the physical part. The values have to come from you." She was still somewhat perplexed, and now a bit self conscience, "I am sorry we bothered you, Sheriff Andrews. I

54

will make an appointment for Tiffany with Dr Davis." She stood up, Bill came around the desk to shake her hand, "That is a good start, Mrs Abbot. Please feel free to call on me if I can be of help." "Good Bye, Sheriff Andrews, and thank you." She was not smiling as she turned and walked away. Tiffany, on the other hand, was smiling broadly as she left. Bill had to ask, "Tiffany, when did you first meet Don?" "Last summer, at the Washo Ceremonies. We sent each other emails all Winter." At the doorway, she looked back at Bill with such a look! When she was gone, Bill thought about this family, "There is trouble. Tiffany has no discretion. I wonder about her Mother? What has Tiffany seen in her parents lives? What sex lessons has she had before this? Her Father does not seem to be here. Does she see her Mother 'entertain'?" That reminded Bill of so many rich sorority girls he had met at U.S.C. They could be so jaded and amoral. The Sheriff wondered what would the increase in the number of these wealthy families mean to his Department? More DUIs, more theft, more sexual liaisons? Bill knew one other thing. He would not be seeing Hellene tonight, she was embarrassed. Bill was embarrassed for her.

After 5:00 PM that afternoon, a Sheriff's Dept SUV pulled up before a modest house on a rural road. Three men got out. Bill and Russ in their dress uniforms, Reverend Brian Phelps in a dark suit. Reverend Phelps was quick to speak, "I am glad that I am with two veteran warriors on this sad mission. Such a noble sacrifice, such a brave young man. To give everything for his country! I am sure that his parents are proud of his brave sacrifice!" "Reverend Phelps," Bill spoke firmly, "I think it best that you let Sargent Baker and myself do the talking. We know the parents. We knew their son, he was their only child. Please let us handle it." Reverend Phelps was somewhat disappointed, but he agreed to the request. They made their way to the front door, Bill knocked. A stocky, dark haired woman in her forties answered the door. She opened the screen door, "Hello Bill." She then saw Russ and the uniforms. "No," she sobbed and backed into the house, letting the screen door slam. "Go away!" She wailed. Bill and Russ quickly entered the house. One took position on either side of her They eased the sobbing woman to the sofa and sat down with her. "We know, Abby." Bill spoke softly, "go ahead and let it out." She wept, now with her head on Bill's shoulder. Russ stood as her Husband came into th room. Hank Johnson was a burly man, of average height, in his late forties. He saw Russ and Bill in Uniform, and the Reverend in his dark suit by the door. He realized what this was. "How did it happen, Russ?" Was all he said. "It was a roadside bomb. It took three of them. Rob never knew what happened." Russ calmly replied. Hank's head dropped forward, "Thank God for that." Russ moved forward and wrapped an arm around the shoulders of the now weeping man. "What did he die for?" Hank asked looking Russ right in the eye. "Hank," Russ replied, slowly. "They tell us that our country is safer from attack, and that the Iraqis are building a new nation." "But are they telling us the truth, Russ? So much of what we are told turns out to be shit." Hank spoke bitterly, "They lied to us about what weapons Iraq had. They lied to us about what the Iraqi's would do when we invaded. They lied to us..." "Stop it! " Came the sudden outburst from Abby, "How dare you ask what our son died for! He died to keep our country free." Hank looked at his wife, "What does the death of three Marines in Iraq have to do with keeping our country free? People keep dying in Iraq, everyday, and it doesn't make us one bit freer or safer. It just makes us sad for our dead and wounded sons and daughters. I can't believe the crap we're being fed about Iraq any more." From the sofa, Bill spoke, "Rob was doing what he wanted to do, what he thought he should do. He wrote me about joining the Marines after high school. I tried to tell him what it was like in Iraq. He made up his mind and he went. He wanted to be a combat Marine, just like his Father and Grandfather before him. We raise our children to grow up and to make their own decisions. He made his. We can argue about why we are in Iraq, but your Son make a choice to serve. He chose to risk his life, and he paid the price for it. The three of us took our chances, just like our fathers before us. Hank, I think you should come here and comfort your wife. You need to face this thing together." Hank slowly walked over to his wife and sat down beside her. He put his arm around this woman that he had known most of his life. She put her head on the shoulder of the man she has loved since she was a girl. Their heads touched as they grieved for their Son, their only child. Bill gave them a moment, then leaned down and spoke softly, "We'll take care of the arrangements." Russ moved forward and leaned down to them, "You don't worry about anything. The Valley takes care of its own."As the two cousins headed toward the front door, Bill spoke quietly, "I think you should call Gwen

56

about Hank and Abbey. Someone needs to be with them." "As soon as we get outside," Russ whispered, "I'll call her. She won't be happy to hear my voice, but she will know what to do. After that, let's get rid of Reverend Phelps, and get ourselves a drink." "Or two," Bill whispered back.

Later that evening, Bill Andrews drove into his yard and parked the SUV. It has been a long day. So much had happened, so much to think about. So much he wished he could forget. He unlocked the front door and went in. Flipping the lights on, he instantly noticed a small blonde form sitting before him. "Susie," he smiled, kneeled down and picked up the now wiggling dog. She lick his face and he rubbed the small head. Carrying her into the living room, he sat in an easy chair and petted the overjoyed animal in his lap. "Life does have it's compensations," he thought as he stroked the soft fur. Susie licked his hand and her tail wagged furiously. A large orange stripped cat suddenly appeared on the arm of his chair. "Okay Tiger, we can't leave you out," he smiled as he rubbed the purring cat. "Animal therapy," he thought, as he rubbed the two happy creatures. "It could be worse," he thought, "a lot worse." After several minutes, he read the note he had removed from the door. Jennifer was inviting him to dinner, tomorrow night. He called and made his apologies. She sounded disappointed. He hardly gave it a thought, as he loved his two animals. "You are spoiled creatures. But I wouldn't have it any other way."

Anita Brubaker tried to read, but thought instead. She though about Bill Andrews. She had not counted on him calling, but it did bother her that he did not. A woman likes to feel wanted. Of course, this meant that it was up to her. It was obvious to her that Bill was the best thing going, in this part of the state. On top of that, she felt the attraction. That was important, that electricity she felt around him. It wasn't just sexual, that was part of it, but it was more a matter of comparability between a man and a woman. She simply felt that Bill might be very suitable for her. This, on top of everything else, made Anita to wish with all her heart, for them to get together. Now, she had to plan how that would come about. Recently, she had started talking to the Sierra Vista County Administrator, and the local Hospital. Both organizations were looking for better PR coverage than they had been receiving. They liked Anita's resume. She intended to pursue both possibilities.

This could mean that she would be spending more time in Bill's County. She was interested in what happened after that. It would mean more income, anyway. That was nothing to sneeze at, not in these times. "Look out Bill Andrews, here I come!"

Chapter Five

Wednesday:

Bill was just sitting down at his desk with a cup of coffee, when his phone rang. "Hello." "Bill, I found something in Bob Moore's room that you need to see." "Hi Jim, sounds interesting. Why don't you bring it to my office." "Okay!" The line went dead. Shortly, Jim came in pushing an evidence cart. "Bill, we found that someone had attempted to pick the lock of his room. We think the handyman scared them off. When we searched his room, we found this under the bed," Jim said, holding up a laptop computer bag. Sitting the laptop on Bill's desk, he went on, "I'm afraid it's password protected. I tried to get in, but no luck." "No problem," Bill was not concerned, "I have a program at home that will take care of that. What else did you find?" "We found Johnny Eagles's business card in Mr. Moore's papers. I wonder what their connection is?" "What I am interested in is," Bill said thoughtfully, "who A W has backing her. Do you think you could dig around at the Court House and find out?" Jim looked at him for a moment, "Does this have anything to do with the fact that my Aunt Elizabeth works for the County Records Department and we don't have a Court Order?" "Why Lieutenant Bearpaw," Bill questioned, "Are you suggesting that I would require you to do anything illegal?" "No Sir, Sheriff Andrews," Jim said, standing at attention, "I am sure that you would never ask me to do anything illegal. You might like it if I asked my Aunt to do something illegal, however." "Do you think," Bill said seriously, "that your sainted Aunt Elizabeth would do anything illegal, even if asked to by her favorite nephew." "Now that we have handled that," Jim spoke as he grabbed the cart, "I think I will go visit my Aunt Elizabeth." With that, he headed out of the door. The remaining items on the cart rattled as he moved. As Jim left, Russ came into the office. "Bill, Gwen and Amy are at the Johnson's. Gwen has a schedule set up, she has people lined up to visit the Johnsons night and

59

day." "What about the funeral arrangements? Bill inquired. "I got the American Legion working on it," Russ replied, "When will Rob be here?" Bill seemed frustrated, "The Marine Corp has not gotten back to me. The funeral home will have to stay on hold. Are the Johnsons going to be happy with this?" "Yeah," Russ replied, "Gwen talked to them last night about it. Rob will be buried in the Vets section, the American Legion will provide the Honor Guard, and little Ronny will blow taps." Bill nodded his approval, then inquired of Russ, "How is your nephew?" Russ smiled as he spoke, "Growing like a weed. He'll be twelve soon, looks like he's fourteen." Bill looked at Russ, "I hope he doesn't end up in somewhere like Iraq." Russ frowned, but did not reply. He started to leave. "If I hear from the Marines," Bill said, "I will let you know." Russ left. Bill reluctantly turned his attention to his inbox. He thought about Gwen, estranged wife of Russ. He had always found her to be an attractive, concerned member of her community. She and her Daughter, Amy, were helping the Johnsons. Who is helping Gwen and Amy? Gwen loved Russ, yet he had abandoned her, and their kids. He did not see how Russ rated such love. A short while later, Wanda's voice came over the intercom, "Sheriff?" "Yes, Wanda," he replied. "District Attorney Van Cleef would like to see you." Reluctantly, Bill told Wanda to send the DA in. "To what do I owe the honor of a visit from our esteemed District Attorney," he barely hid his contempt. Undeterred, Van Cleef strode up to Bill's desk. "What is this I hear about you reopening a cold case without notifying the DA's office? " Bill noted his anxiety, it pleased him immensely, "Mr. Van Cleef," Bill spoke with a smirk, "My Sister's Case was not a Cold Case. My Father kept it open all these years." The DA was growing more anxious, "But you have asked the FBI to assist with the case." Bill's smirk grew larger, "That is correct. Their lab in Quantico will be going over the evidence. I received confirmation from the FBI yesterday." This news hit the DA hard. "Well," he managed to say, "It looks like you have it all under control." "Yes I do," was Bill's cool reply. "I even have a 24 hour guard on the Evidence Room, with orders to shoot." With that, Van Cleef's jaw clenched, he turned and hurried toward the door. "Be sure to give my regards to your family," Bill called after him. Leaning back in his chair, he tried not to think of how easily he could snap the asshole's neck. He worked on his inbox again. After handling the first paper, Bill

60

looked at the geologists' laptop. Making a decision, Bill picked up his phone and punched Wanda's number, "This is Bill, I am taking some work home with me. If something comes up, contact me there." He hung up and stuffed some of his inbox into his briefcase. He picked up his briefcase, the laptop, and headed out the door.

A short time later, Bill parked the SUV in his carport. Gathering up the briefcase and laptop, he carried everything to his front door. Inside, he found no animal greetings. He shut the door and set the items down on the hall table. Curious about the absence of animals, he peeked into the Living Room. He noticed a dog asleep on the sofa, and a cat sleeping in an easy chair. "What do we have here?" He said aloud. Both animals were instantly awake. Susie quick came wagging over to Bill. He knelt down to pet the little dog. Tiger the cat, came slowly over, in a dignified walk. Reaching out with one hand to pet the large cat, Bill commented, "Yes, Tiger. I know you are totally indifferent to this. Right." He rubbed Tiger behind the ears. Tiger leaned into it and started to purr loudly. After a few minutes on his knees petting the two animals, Bill got up. "Enough for now. I need to get some work done." He walked back into the Entry Hall. As he moved toward the Hall table, someone rang the front door bell. Bill headed for the front door, trailed by the two animals. Much to his surprise, Jennifer was standing at his door. He greatly admired her tanned form, so nicely displayed by the sun dress she wore. Nice legs, and a bit of exposed cleavage. At 5' 11" and 170 lbs, she was a big woman, but every thing seemed to be in its proper location. "Not a brick out of place," as Russ would say. He smiled as he spoke, "What brings you calling on this fine afternoon?" She smiled back as she replied, "Dad said that you had found Bob Moore's Laptop. I can help with the geographic maps. I called your office and they said that you were here." He quickly asked, "Was it Wanda that you spoke to?" "Yes it was", she replied innocently, "she was very helpful." "Won't you come in?" He said gesturing her in. He shut the door behind her. "Wanda was my Sister's best friend, so I not only have a secretary, but a surrogate mother as well." She smiled at that, "I guess it is one of the fringe benefits of living in a small town. People care about each other." "Fringe benefit or not, he looked serious, "I wish she would stop meddling." He gestured toward the Laptop on the Hall Table, "Shall we take a look at the computer?" Seeing the two pets, she remarked to Bill, "I see your little friend is right with you. But who's cat is this? She knelt down stroked the very happy dog. Bill watched her, intrigued by her natural grace. "The cat is mine", he replied, "his name is Tiger." She reached out and stroked the big head, "Where was he when I was here before?" "Probably out terrorizing the wildlife", he said, knowingly. Stroking the big cat, she was unbelieving, "I can't believe that this cat could hurt anything!" Feeling that he had her hooked, he confidently went on, "Believe it! In San Diego, he use to regularly beat up the neighborhood dogs. He weighs twenty-five pounds!" He looked up at him, not knowing whether to believe his revelation about the cat. Then she saw the gleam in his eye and the beginning of a smile. Standing up, she looked him in the eye, "You are bad! Telling me stories about this lovely cat!" Even as he smiled at her, he thought how much he would like to kiss that very attractive mouth. His defensive move was to mention the Laptop again. "Let's take a look at the Laptop. We will need to get around the password. I have a program for that." "I suppose that was something you picked up in the NCIS?" She inquired as they walked to the Hall Table. He picked up the Laptop, "I did a lot of my own computer work. We never seemed to have enough forensic computer Techs." She sat her purse on the table as they headed into the office. He setup the Laptop on the Computer Desk. Bill grabbed another chair and placed it in front of the Desk, beside his. Susie was sitting next to his chair. Without hesitation, he picked up the dog and sat down with her in front of the Laptop. Tiger jumped up on the Computer desk, sniffed the Laptop, and began to rub the edge of the Laptop lid. "Careful Tiger," he warned, "you are going to knock the computer off. You big ox!" "They cluster around him," she thought, "they like him and he likes them." After booting the computer up, he opened the CD drive and put a CD in it, then closed the drive. When the CD spun up, Bill used the mouse to initiate the program. As the program started, he turned to Jennifer. "This program will find the password to the computer. It may take a while." Jennifer had been looking around the room, "I see that you have finished unpacking your books." She gestured to the adjoining bookcases. I like your choice of topics. You even have some on American Indians." "Jennifer, my Grandmother was a Washo. I grew up with some members of the tribe." Bill replied, "I have tried to learn more

62

about them, but all I can find is about the Nevada Washo tribe." "California Indians are my field," she said, "what do you want to know." He was surprised by this revelation, but was eager to ask, "When did the two Washo bands split?" Her brow furrowed, "You would ask me that! We think that the Washo tribe split up about the time of Columbus, in the late1400's. Possibly the increasing pressure of the Northern Paiutes caused part of the tribe to split off and head west. When the Spanish explorers got to this area in the mid 1500's, the Washo were well established here. A typical hunter/ gatherer society, they seemed to have few horses, even after the Spanish arrived. They traded with the Spanish, and accepted Priests living among them, I have found religious arti- facts in some of the burials I've examined." Bill had other questions about the Washo tribe, "What was their relationship with the Modoc tribe?" "I thought you knew," she quickly responded, "They have been fierce enemies, they still are in many ways. But then, the Modocs were hostile to everyone, White or Indian." He did not look at her as he spoke, "That makes it all the more strange that a Modoc, like Johnny Eagle, would be their Tribal Counsel." At this point, the beeping of the Laptop, and the accompanying flashing screen announced that the program had found the password. The noise startled the two animals, both jumped down and headed out of the room. Bill quickly entered the operating system of the computer. "We need to see what files are here." He scanned the directory, "Here are some Word files. This bunch are graphic files. They are probably the maps he was making." Jennifer seemed perplexed, "How do we know what program he used to make them?" "It doesn't matter," Bill assured her, "When I open one of the files, Windows automatically opens the necessary program. See!" They both examined the map image on the screen. "I wish we could blow this image up," Jennifer exclaimed, frustrated. Bill quickly volunteered, "I can print these maps on my plotter. Would 22 X 17 inches be large enough?" Jennifer looked surprised, "That would be fine." He got up and walked past her to a covered piece of furniture beyond the bookcases. Pulling off the cover, he revealed a large plotter on it's stand. A sheet feeder of wide format paper was mounted on the back of the cabinet. Bill picked up the plotter cable and came back over to the Laptop. "That," Jennifer said, pointing at the plotter, "is not a typical home printer. I could use something like that to plot some of the 'Digs' I

63

work on." Bill smiled at her as he plugged the plotter cable into the Laptop, "It is reconditioned. I got a good deal on it from a friend. I used it to plot crime scenes and some building plans I drew up. Now, I need to download the driver for this plotter." He sat down and set up the download. Jennifer looked around, "What do you use for Internet access?" The download having started, he turned to her, "I have Satellite Internet, that was the only thing available to me, other than slow dial-up." She looked at Bill, then realized that she wanted him to kiss her, badly. He did want to kiss her. She leaned forward, they kissed. "Damn!" He thought, this is just what I did not want to happen." When they pulled apart, Bill said,"We should get these maps printed." With that, he walked over and turned on the plotter, then sat down at the Laptop. "She is very willing," he thought, "Watch yourself!" As he worked to lineup the drawing for the plotter, Jennifer watched him. Finally, she spoke, "You have dealt with lots of women before, in your work, I mean!" Stopping to look at her, Bill responded, "Yes I have. When you work with crimes in the Military, you have to deal with rapes and assaults on women. Too many Servicemen are angry, sick, or hurt. They rape and beat their women. They do drugs or alcohol, then attack a women on the street, or their neighbor's wife. NCIS or Army CID has to deal with it. It can get very messy." He went back to work on the Laptop. The plotter started to make noise, then started to print. Jennifer leaned toward him and put her hand on his arm, "It really got to you, didn't it." He turned and put his hand over her's, "Yes, it did get to me. Beaten wives and raped girlfriends were bad, but abused children were the worst. Helpless kids abused by their own parents, the people that were supposed to protect them! Those are the cases that haunt me." Her other hand came up and touched his cheek. Then they kissed, a gentle, tender kiss. They embraced. He then stood up and offered her his hand, "Shall we take a look at the maps?" She took his hand and stood up. He led her over to the plotter. With his free hand, he scooped up the maps from the plotters basket. "Let's take them into the Dining Room," he said, looking at Jennifer, "We can spread these out on the table." Hand in hand they walked to the Dining Room. Together, they spread the drawings over the large oak table. Bill noticed that Susie was now in one of the chairs. He reached down and stroked her head. Soon, Tiger jumped up on the table and began to sniff the maps. "Okay, you two. How are we supposed to get anything done?" With that, Tiger laid down and rolled on his side. Turning to Jennifer, he exclaimed, "See! I get no cooperation." Jennifer laughed, then started examining one of the maps. She moved on to the next sheet. "This map covers the southern end of the County." Bill joined her examining the map. She became excited by what she read, "See his notations! These are fault lines coming from the south. See how they run due North. Where is the map of the next section to the North?" Bill spotted the missing map. Tiger was laying on it. Carefully he slid the map out from under the protesting cat. Spreading it out, they traced the fault lines. "Look at this!" She yelled, pointing at the map. "Here the fault lines come into the Valley!" "That area is the purposed development," Bill exclaimed, pointing, "The fault lines extend right through the site. There is no way that they can go ahead with their plans. Not if we can get these facts to the Judge." Jennifer looked worried, "How can we convince the Judge with just this map. We need Bob Moore's testimony." "One of those Word documents must be his report," Bill spoke excitedly, "we can give that to the Judge." Jennifer got excited again, "We need that report, we should look for it right now." Bill headed for the Office with Jennifer close behind him. In the Office, he got into the Laptop's files. He opened file after file with no luck, then he got it. "Look at this," he yelled, "Its all here. The suspected Fault, the threat to any development, and the mention of a report to the USGS." Jennifer responded by grabbing him and kissing him. He kissed her back. Things got progressively more intense. Finally Jennifer whispered in his ear, "You got a good look at me on the trail, would you like to see the rest?" Breaking their embrace, Bill gently held her face in his hands, "Are you sure?" "Yes I am," she softly responded and kissed his hand. Bill led her out of the Office and up the stairs, stopping only to remove his gunbelt and hang it in the closet. They went across the Landing and into the Master Bedroom. Stopping at the foot of the huge oak bed, Bill faced her and asked, "Jennifer, what are you using for birth control?" "I have a Diaphragm in my LA apartment, but I haven't been using it lately." "Don't worry, then I will take care of it. Do you still want to do this?" She answered by starting to unbutton his uniform shirt. She thought of him as silly, couldn't he see she wanted him badly. He helped her remove the shirt. He then turned her around and unfastened her dress, she let it fall to the ground. He sat down on the bed and removed his shoes and socks. She kick off her sandals. She help him undo his belt and drop his uniform pants on the floor. He undid her bra and she let it fall. "You are very beautiful, Jennifer," he spoke softly. "So are you," she said, earnestly. Looking at her protruding breasts, he smiled and noted, "Those are quite a bit more than a mouthful." Smiling, she crossed to him, "I'm glad you like them." She presented them for his inspection. He demonstrated how much he liked them, then showed his appreciation for the rest of her wonderful body. In short order, she was naked, spreadeagled on the bed. A naked Bill was licking her various parts. Jennifer softly moaned. This was repeated on her neck and breasts, for several minutes. Then he changed his focus. She moaned more loudly. She grew wet, his tongue found her Clit. She moaned more loudly. Gently, he continued to use his tongue. She moaned and called to him, "Do it to me, now!" He started to take her right there, but hesitated. Then he into the draw of the night stand, he brought out a small packet. "One of my going away presents from the NCIS was a box of condoms." Smiling, Jennifer responded, "Thank your friends for me." He laid beside her on the bed. They kissed and embraced. "I haven't used one of these for a while," he whispered, slipping on the condom. "I bet you say that to all the girls," she whispered back.

Hours later, Jennifer was gently kissing Bill's ear. Bill woke and smiled as he saw her. He reached out to her and drew her on top of him. They kissed. They are soon joined by Susie and Tiger. Resigned to his situation, Bill spoke, "Jennifer, I think we have company." "Isn't it wonderful, we have our little friends," she said, dreamily. Bill hugged her as he said, "I hate to dis-illusion you, but our little friends are hungry. They are here to remind me to feed them." "What time is it?" Jennifer asked. Bill looked at his watch, "Seven twenty." She groaned softly, "I need to call my Dad." "Okay, I will feed the animals," He said reluctantly, "You can call your Father. Arise, Sleeping Beauty." He pushed her into a sitting position. Suddenly concerned, she asked Bill, "What should I tell Dad." Dressing himself, Bill replied, "Why don't you tell him how you ripped off my clothes and ravished me on the sofa." "You are not funny," she said, pouting, "I don't know what to tell him." "Jennifer," Bill said gently, "Your Father is a very bright, very experienced man. He seems to know just about everything that happens around him.

What makes you think that he doesn't already know about you and me?" Jennifer considered this for a minute, You are probably right. I bet he does know." Bill placed his robe around her shoulders, "Wear this, please. Or we won't get anything accomplished." Jennifer looked longingly at him, "I think we got a lot accomplished already." "No argument there, and I enjoyed every minute of it. Right now we have other things to do." "Alright," she said smiling at him, "we do need to get Bob's report for the Hearing." She stood and put the robe on and went to Bill, who was buttoning his shirt. Touching his face, she whispered to him, "Thank you. I needed today." Touching her cheek, Bill spoke softly, "I needed today also. I am not big on trust, too many disappointments." They kissed, then hand in hand, they headed out of the bedroom and down the stairs. Jennifer went to the Hall table and got her Cell phone out of her purse. She headed into the office. Bill headed into the Kitchen, trailed by the two animals. While being watched intently, he filled a food bowel for each pet, and placed them on the floor. Both animals just sat there and watched him. He just said, "Okay," and they both rush to their own bowel and proceeded to eat. He smiled as he watched them. "You are both special little creatures." Still smiling, he headed toward the Office. He could hear Jennifer speaking to someone. "You used my own purse to find me? Global Positioning? Well, I called to tell you that we have found Bob Moore's report and maps. Bill is making us a copy. What? Okay, I will ask for three copies. No Dad, I don't know when I will bring them home, "she said as Bill walked into the room. She looked at him as she told her Father, "We have a lot of work to do here." He gave her a look of disapproval, as he walked over to the Computer table. "I love you too," Jennifer told her Father, then hung up. She watched Bill unplug the cable to his printer from his computer, and plug it into the Laptop. "You were right," she told Bill, "Dad knew where I was. He had my purse tracked, he had a G.P.S. devise planted in it. I bet this isn't the first time he has done this." Bill was placing a CD into the Laptop. He finished, and turned to look at her. "Your Father loves you. He went to a lot of trouble and expense to track you." He turned back to the Laptop and used the mouse to start the download of the printer driver. She sat down beside him, "I know he loves me. He has been very good to me, very understanding. But since Mom died, he seems to concentrate most of his attention on me. I should say the Nature Coalition and me." Bill smiled, "Sounds very normal to me. You are his only child, the closest living thing to him. I'll bet some of his security people are assigned to watch over you." Thoughtfully, Jennifer spoke almost to herself, "Do you really think so? I guess I take so many things for granted. I wonder what else he does that I have missed." Bill was back on the Laptop, "I do believe he has the men in your life investigated. Do you blame him?" She wondered about that comment. Just what did he know about her past? The printer started in printing. Just a test page. Bill picked it up, checked it, then threw it away. He sat back down at the Laptop. "He does the same thing for the executives that he hires," she said matter-of-factly, "it is just his way." As the printer began to print again, Bill stood up. Offering Jennifer his hand, "While the reports are printed, why don't we get something to eat?" As she took his hand, she was enthusiastic, "I am hungry. What are we going to have?" Pulling her toward the Office door, Bill thought for a moment, then said, "Ham and cheese omelet. You can have a choice of Sharp or Mild Cheddar Cheese." "Oh, Sharp Cheddar please," she responded with enthusiasm. They trailed through the Dining room and into the Kitchen. Arriving in the Kitchen, Bill went into the refrigerator, emerging with a carton of eggs, a brick of Sharp Cheddar Cheese, and a container of sliced Ham. He sat the item on the counter next to the stove. He then got a large skillet out of a lower cabinet. Opening the container of Ham, Jennifer inquired, "Where are the knives?" Bill looked at her, then motioned at a drawer near to her, "One drawer over to your right." She opened the drawer and selected a knife. She pulled down a cutting board from its peg on the wall and sat both items on the counter next to the Ham. She rolled up the overly long sleeves of the robe. "Are you sure you know what your are doing?" Was Bill's taunting comment. Jennifer stuck her tongue out at him. He returned to lighting the stove burner. Grabbing a piece of Ham and the knife, Jennifer expertly created a small mound of Ham cubes. Bill brought over a bowl for the Ham, "Beauty, brains, and she can cook." That got him a big kiss. Jennifer took the bowl from Bill and scooped the Ham off of the cutting board and into it. "Got any margarine?" She asked. Bill got it out of the refrigerator and handed it to her. Grabbing it with her free hand, she motioned to a small table and chairs. "Why don't you go sit down, I can handle this." "Okay," he said and sat down in a chair at the table, he turned to face the stove. Jennifer took the items over by the stove and sat them down. She scooped up some of the margarine with the turner and plopped it into the skillet. She brought over the cutting board and knife, and quickly chopped up some of the Sharp Cheddar. She then placed the skillet on the lit burner, and stirred the margarine around until it was melted. She put some of the Cheese in, then some of the Ham. Quickly, Jennifer added three eggs to the skillet, then seasoned them. After a few moments, she expertly flipped the half cooked omelette. Letting it cook for a bit, she commented, "I am glad that you have gas, it is so much better than electric." "We have Propane in this area. It is good for cooking and heating." Without looking away from the stove, Jennifer yelled, "Plate please!" Bill rushed over to an upper cabinet and brought out two plates. He held out one to Jennifer. She flipped the omelet on to the plate in one quick movement. "Well done! You have done this before, obviously." "Now go and eat," she said, "while I fix mine." She turned back to the stove. Bill kissed her on the cheek, then asked, "Beer or white wine?" "White wine, please!" She answered, smiling. He put his omelet on the table, then got out two wine glasses. The bottle of chilled wine came next. He poured two glasses, and carried them to the table. With two forks from the silverware draw, he sat down and watched Jennifer. Noticing this, she commanded, "Go ahead and eat, I will be done soon." Reluctantly, he began to eat. A few minutes later, Jennifer flipped the second omelet on to the plate Bill had left for her. Bill got up and shut off the burner as she sat down the skillet and picked up her plate. They both sat down and ate. Susie was quietly sitting by Jennifer. Jennifer slipped a piece of ham to her. "I saw that," Bill warned. Jennifer giggled and looked down at the little dog, "Busted." The mood was broken by the ringing of the phone on the wall behind Bill. He got up and answered it, "Sheriff Andrews." "Commander Andrews, this Lt. Colonel Jamison at Camp Pendleton. This is your notification, the body of Private Robert Johnson is on post. Where do you wish it to be delivered?" "Deliver him to Sierra Vista, California, Handley's Funeral Home. Thank you for your call." "Commander, this is the least I can do for these fine young people. He will be delivered within 24 hours, with escort. Did you know Private Johnson?" "Yes I did. He was a fine young man." "I am very sorry for your loss. Goodbye, Commander." "Goodbye, Colonel. Thank you for

69

your courtesy." His mood had changed, Bill looked more somber than before. Jennifer noticed the change, "Who was that? What is wrong Bill?" "That was the US Marine Corps notifying me of the arrival time of a shipment." "What sort of shipment?" She asked, growing concerned. Seeing that she was already suspicious, Bill decided not to hide what was happening, "The body of a young Marine will arrive tomorrow. He is a local boy, killed in Iraq. We will be burying him in about 48 hours." Jennifer grew more concerned, "Oh, Bill. I am so sorry. Did you know him?" He returned to his chair, "Yes, I did. I grew up with his parents." He told her about the visit to the Johnsons. He ate the remaining portion of his omelet and finished his wine. Bill then excused himself, "I need to make a couple of calls. Please finish eating, I will be back in a few minutes." Jennifer nodded her acknow-ledgment. Bill left the room. Jennifer wondered about what was happening. "Did he volunteered for this duty?" She thought. "This on top of being Sheriff. He is giving so much of himself. Just like his Mother." She recalled his Mother, "They both put so much into this community. I wish that I had somewhere to give myself to." She finished eating and put her dishes in the sink. "This man is so strong, yet he is so tender to me. So good in bed." That got her thinking, "What are we going to do tonight?" Jennifer decided to go and find out. She left the Kitchen, walked through the Dining Room into the Entry Hall. She heard Bill talking in the Office. She smiled when she saw Susie lying in the Office doorway. "Yes, Russ," Bill said into the phone, "That's it. It is up to the American Legion now. Camp on them.... Same to you. Bye." Jennifer was kneeling in the doorway, petting Susie. Bill noticed that the robe had opened and one of her long, lovely legs was exposed. He spoke to her, "Russ is handling the funeral, with the help of the local American Legion. The Funeral Home will be on time. The victim was their nephew. This is the downside of small towns, everyone is family or a friend." "Or a lover," Jennifer added, crossing to him. Bill raised his eye brows, "That is right. So, Lover, what do you have on your mind." They kissed and embraced. Holding her away from himself, Bill reminded her, "We need to get the reports together for your Father." They went over to the printer, Bill retrieved the pages from the printer and handed part of them to Jennifer. As each copy of the report was com-pleted, Bill stapled it together. Bill then handed all three reports to

Jennifer, "Give these to your Father, I hope that they help at the Hearing." Jennifer put the reports on the Hall Table, next to her purse. Bill joined her. Seeing Susie standing next to Bill, she was curious, "Shouldn't you be taking Susie for a walk about now." "Susie and Tiger take themselves for a walk, Bill explained, "They have a Pet Door in the Laundry, off of the Kitchen. The back yard is fenced." "That is smart," she said, "They can go in and out when they choose." Bill frowned, "But rainy days are a mess, they track mud into the house." "You could put old carpet samples or a piece of outdoor carpet in front of the Pet Door." Jennifer then added, "You could put outdoor carpet down in the Laundry Room and into the Kitchen to catch the mud and water. The carpet could be taken out and washed off afterwards." Bill looked at her for a moment, "As I have said before, you are an appealing mix of beauty and brains." "I am just a practical woman." she said as she took Bill's hand and led him up the stairs. "I did notice the woman part," Bill responded, "But am not sure about the practical part." Jennifer smiled, "Well, Sheriff, there is one way to find out about that." She then led him into the Master Bedroom.

Chapter Six

Thursday:

Bzzzz Bzzzz! Brenda was suddenly awake! She grabbed the Beeper off the night stand, pressing the button showed 'House Fire'! She was up, dressing. Underwear, short sleeve shirt, pants, and socks. What ever you wanted in your pockets at a fire, you put in before bed. She thrust her feet through the fire trousers, into her boots. Pull the pants up, suspenders over each shoulder. Sit on bed, fasten boots. Fire coat on, not buttoned. Grab hat, open door. Time to run! Almost ran into Stan, as he ran for his truck in the garage! "Second alarm, Brenda! Big Victorian went up!" He went into the garage, she went out the front door. Helmet on, strap fastened. Her hands worked as she ran to her Engine. Brenda slid behind the wheel, just as Captain Grayson jumped in. She saw the Chief pull out in his Cal Fire pickup, lights only. No siren at 3:30 AM. Brenda followed suit. Everyone put on a head set, she heard the other three sound off. Everyone aboard, head out! Gary Grayson used the microphone on his headset to bring everyone up to date. "Station Three has one Engine on site! Their backup in on a medical call. Volunteers are on their way!" As she drove toward the visible glow of the fire, Brenda had to ask, "Who contacts the Volunteers?" "You met Janet, the Chief's assistant? She calls from home." "Kind of young, isn't she?" "Don't worry, Brenda. She grew up around Cal Fire. Her Dad is Captain at Station Three, and her Brother is at Station two." The Captain guided her through a maze of streets, Brenda was glad for the headsets. Even without a screaming siren, the Engine's big Diesel made plenty of noise! As they neared the fire, Grayson found the nearest water hydrant was in use, first Engine on site get dibs on the nearby water. The Captain had Brenda drive down a sides street, there was a hydrant! She turned the Engine around, then stopped at the hydrant, as two sections of four inch hose were dropped off on to the pavement. Several feet closer to the fire, she stopped again, more hose dropped off. The Captain was on the radio, soon two big Volunteers joined them. They jumped right on connecting the hose. Brenda would have preferred to use five inch hose, but her inventory of the Engine let her know that there was not enough aboard. When all the four inch was on the ground, Jake and Danny jumped out to hook it up. Brenda hooked up the last section to the Engine Input. She hoped that she guessed right on the distance. It would be embarrassing to have to move the Engine back. Captain Grayson was conferring with the Chief, and Captain Taylor of Station Three. Volunteer Firefighters were arriving in a steady stream. With the last hose connection, the four inch line was charged with water. Brenda saw her gauges react, the pressure rose rapidly. Jake and Danny grabbed a two inch line from its compartment, unfolding it as they walked toward the burning building. Jake had the nozzle cradled in his arms, the big shut off handle on top. Captain Grayson met them part way, he ordered them back. They were going inside! Oxygen tanks and masks were required! They were ordered to drop the hose and grab their equipment. Grayson helped them strap on the bottles, the large masks covered the whole face with a clear shield. Both sets check out, the boys headed back for their hose. Captain Grayson had Brenda charge their line. The two Cal Fire men found two Volunteers waiting with their line. Together, the four men approached the burning house. The Chief told them to go up the staircase, Engine Three had the First floor. The entry hall was smokey, visibility was down to a few feet. They found the stairs, then moved up at a steady pace. Toward the top, the fire on the second floor flared! Flame reached out, but went over their heads. Jake stopped, trying to back up! The other three, pushed him forward, "Turn on your nozzle!" Danny reach around him, and pulled the lever. A circle of water flowed before them. They continued on up. The flames before them were smothered by the strong mist. First, the flames on the landing were put out. Then, the first bedroom was reduced to smoking debris. Captain Grayson brought a Volunteer hose crew to their aid. Doors were opened, fires extinguished, the hose crews leapfrogged each other. Grayson told them that the fire downstairs was out. The Attic remained, they could feel the heat! Back to the stairs, up to the top. Repeat the process. Except, the Attic was one big room. The two crews fought side by side, smothering flames. One hour after Engine One arrived, the fire was out. Now, cleanup began. In the Attic, both crews used long handed hooks to separate burnt material. Two men manned a hose to douse any live embers. One hose went with some of the boys, they started working on the second floor. Engine Three was doing the same thing on floor one. It was slow, dirty work. Everyone was hot, dirty, and tired. The adrenalin of the fire was gone. Back at Engine One, Brenda was watching her gauges, the excitement was gone. A short firefighter approached her, nothing special about that. As the person got close, Brenda caught a glimpse of the face as she drank from her water bottle, female? "Hi, you must be Brenda!" It was an alto voice, from a bronze face. "Yes, my name is Brenda, are you a Volunteer?" She tore her glove off, to shake the offered hand. "Rhonda is the name, you probably couldn't pronounce my last name. I'm Washo!" Brenda could see Rhonda in the spotlight from her truck, round face, flat nose, dark eyes. Maybe 5'6" and stocky. "You are a tall one! Pretty too!" A smile filled the Indian face. The two Ladies talked for a bit, until Rhonda's break was over. She went back to cleanup. Brenda had time to discover that Rhonda was married, she was thirty, and she had two kids. Her husband was a out of work mill hand. He baby sat, while Rhonda fought fires. She had learned her craft in the Navy. When not fighting fires, Rhonda made authentic Indian pottery, with her Mother! Cleanup went on, until every possible spark was extinguished. Then, the great joy of hose retrieval began! All sections of hose were uncoupled from each other, and anything that they were attached to. Every piece must be drained of water, and stored back on the Engine that they came from. Professional and Volunteer alike, everyone did hose! They toiled on, even as the sun turned the mountains crimson. Captain Grayson told his crew, "County Arson found lab equipment in the rear annex. Looked like another Meth lab." The Sheriff would have another crime to solve. As Brenda and crew pulled out, the Sheriff's Forensic team arrived at the badly damaged Victorian.

Back at Station One, cleanup continued. After Brenda had backed the Engine into it's Bay, Captain Grayson got everyone working. Brenda inventoried the Pumper. Danny and Jake had to remove the used oxygen bottles, replacing them with new ones. The only sound they heard was the cracking and groaning of the Pumper, as its hot engine cooled. No one talked, too tired or something. Danny was confused, did Jake try to bolt on the stairs?

Fires often flared, firefighters ducked, then watched the fire to see what it did next. Usually, it just settled back. That's what happened on the stairs of the Victorian. Danny wondered, would Jake break, if the fire was a bad one? Having doubts about your coworkers is never good, not for a firefighter. Unbeknown to the crew, Captain Grayson soon got a phone call from the Volunteer Captain. His men told him about Jake on the Stairs. It was a quiet word of warning, one Captain to another. It gave Gary Grayson much to think on. He already had his doubts about Jake Sawyer. Brenda, on the other hand, was working out. It helped that she would take no shit from Jake. Danny would be okay, when he learned to stand up to Jake. Too often, Danny let him slide. Gary decided on a little talk with Danny, a bit of man to man about Jake. Gary and Stan would also be having a heart to heart about Jake. Gary had decided, this would be Jake's last Summer at Station One.

Sgt Ernie Yeager was studying the layout of the Meth lab. Preliminary tests had been positive for Methamphetamine. Most of the glassware was broken and melted, even Pyrex has its limits. He wondered if the average citizen had any idea how hot a structure fire can get inside? He had already photographed the entire room, now it was time to divine the layout as it had been at the time of the fire. The County Arson Investigator had provided a through analysis of how he thought that the fire had begun. It was Yeager, and his two Technicians, that had to deduce who did this. Who had caused this fire and all the trouble it took to stop it? The property management firm had provided names, but none of the renters had a record. Further checks showed that both names were phony, nothing new for this kind of work. Fingerprints may give more information, there were many unburned surfaces. The Techs already had a dozen samples of good prints, many in the Kitchen. Running them would have to wait until they returned to the Department, this afternoon. This was an Annex, built behind the main house. He had been told, that it was nearly one hundred years old. Meant as a storage room for food stuffs, it was needed when the Rittenhaus Family entertained their many guests. The stories of that time were fabulous. Sumptuous meals, gallons of champaign, the old Timber Barron and his Family really knew how to live! But the Income Tax, and the Depression ruined their business. They finally abandoned the house, it was taken over by the bank. The

76

house passed through many hands, before it was purchased by one Silicon Valley Billionaire. The renovation was massive. New plumbing, wiring, even air conditioning. The young family only had a few Summers here, before the parents were killed in a highway accident. Since then, it had attracted only short term renters. Now, the fire made it uninhabitable, without a great deal of work. Ernie just hoped that it had been insured. He was one of a number of locals that wanted the old house and its surrounding land as a park.

Brent and Mona got the word from the local news. Both knew about the old Mansion, Brent's Dad had been one of those working on the renovation. Both had played on the massive lawn. Mona had interesting information for him, last night. It seems that the owners of the Pinecrest Inn were both retired Highway Patrol officers! She told him that both husband and wife were armed. They had installed a silent alarm switch under the counter, she could trip it with her knee! No one would know she had pushed it! Brent thought about that, it made him nervous. Mona might get brave during a holdup. She didn't realize that a silent alarm would start a series of events. She could be caught in the office with an armed man or two, and deputies outside. A stand off could be deadly! What would the armed owners do? It sounded very dangerous, to Brent! He asked his petite lover to please be careful! They ended up necking in the Kitchen. It didn't take much. Brent did not tell Mona about Donna, nothing had happened. He did give some thought to her big tits.

After leaving Bill's house, Jennifer carried her things to the Land Rover, then drove home. Jason heard her come in, then asked Maria to prepare breakfast for his Daughter. In her room, Jennifer found a note about taking her Meds. She had skipped them last night. She frowned, but did go to her bathroom and take her pills. "Soon, I won't need these," she thought, "Bill will make me happy, and I can throw my pills away!" She then used her phone to make an appointment with Dr Sarah Davis. It was all part of her plan. From now on, it would be Bill and her. She went down, and ate a hearty breakfast. She felt fantastic! Jason noted her joy, it was more than he hoped for, this soon. Her time with Bill Andrews had a wonderful affect on his only child. So far, his plan was working! She had given her Father the Geology Report, he was thankful for that, as well. He was set to deliver it to the Judge.

Now, if they could just find Bob Moore, his testimony was vital to their Court case. Where could the man be?

Jim Bearpaw received a gift this morning, or rather, the Department did. Part of their Justice Department Grant, had been a new sniper rifle. What a weapon! Jim opened the rectangular box first. In it, was a camouflaged case. It looked like an ABS plastic bass guitar case. Jim hoisted it out of the box. The box went on the floor, while the case went on his desk. With trembling hands, the veteran sniper unsnapped the case. Throwing open the lid, revealed a huge rifle! With the manual open on his desk, Jim began to explore this wonder weapon. It was not a .50 BMG rifle, they were like a single shot .50 caliber machine gun. This was slightly smaller, and easier to handle. Still, it's .408 caliber round was large and powerful! From the range table, Jim learned the accurate shot at one and a half miles was entirely possible. With his Army M40 rifle, shots of a mile had not been recommended. The NATO .308 caliber round just lacked the power. Jim had made kills at a thousand yards. The new rifle was capable of kills at two thousand yards! Reading the manual corrected that figure. The M200, was capable of making kills out past two thousand meters! Jim had to think about that, it increased his effective reach by more than one hundred percent! For long range work, the rifle needed a scope. It was in the case, the instructions for mounting were simple enough. Attaching the device, allowed him to consider some information he had received. Maria Sanchez, who works for the Saunders, told her Mother that Jennifer had gone over to Bill's house yesterday. She was not at home this morning. He thought that he might just probe the Sheriff later, just to check out that information. Jim found that he needed to open the other box. This beast could mount a laser rangefinder!

After the Engine was made ready for its next call, the crew ate, washed up, then grabbed some sleep. The Volunteer crew made it back in. The two Engineers got to meet. Brenda, then drug her gear over to the house. Stan wasn't home yet, so she made herself some eggs, took a long shower, then retired. Man, she loved this air conditioning! It was ninety degrees outside, in her room, it was seventy-five. Good sleeping weather! When she woke up that afternoon, Brenda found that Stan was asleep. She operated on 'silent routine', typical for firefighters on different schedules. She put on her Cal Fire shorts and Tee shirt, both dark blue. She had decided to clean out her car. It was still a mess, from her move. A few minutes in the ninety plus heat changed her mind! She ended up talking to Janet, in the air conditioned Battalion Office. Janet told her about growing up in the Valley, and being a Cal Fire brat! She and Janet talk a lot about the Rittenhaus Mansion. Janet had been inside when it had been remodeled. She got a strange look on her face as she described how it was decorate for Christmas! Brenda could not recall experiencing anything like that, not in Foster Care.

Brent and Mona decided to do some cleaning. Brent had noticed how Mona's nose wrinkled when she thought that something was not clean. His concerns about how her Mother had affected the little redhead, had all been a waste. Mona could have become a slob, but she was made of tougher material. Brent noticed how she got this tight jawed look, then tackled a job. She was a tough little character! In no time, the Living Room was cleaned, this on top of the Kitchen having been already done. She was a good partner, on taking care of the house. In the Bedroom, it was still a matter of Brent entertaining Mona. She was young and inexperienced, nocure for that. He would have to educate her in the ways of sex. He was sure that his petite lover would be a willing student. All too soon, it was time for them both to get ready for work. Her Mother had forbidden her to see Don again, but Tiffany's heart would not let her stay away. Her Cell phone had allowed her to make a date. The Acura convertible she had received for her Sixteenth birthday, allowed her to drive to the Lumber Mill. Mother was busy with something, or someone. She wondered if Mother had slept with Sheriff Andrews. There was a Stud! She did not care if he was lots older, what a bod! But she had Don. In the empty Truckers Bunkhouse, Don was waiting. They had their favorite room, where he would undress her. They would make love, all afternoon! It was wonderful, she felt so good. After, she would feel even better! She still wondered about Mother. She slept with several men, here and at home in Atherton. She could not understand that. For Tiffany, one young man was all she wanted! All she could think about was how it would be. She parked her car out of sight, behind the Bunkhouse. The back door was unlocked. She made her way to the second floor, the door to their favorite room was ajar. Tiffany pushed it open. Don was there, waiting! They embraced, there were long kisses. Tiffany willingly shed her clothes. Don's hands and tongue were everywhere! It was wonderful, she could think of nothing but Don. Her body did the thinking for her. In the Fall, both Don and Tiffany would be Seniors. In a year, they would both be going off to college. She was sure that they would attend the same institution! They might be able to live together. What heaven!

Brent called in, before heading out. Sargent Wolfe told him about the Sheriff finding Bob Moore. The young Deputy wondered who could have killed the Geologist? Murder was not the usual thing, not in Sierra Vista. Mona was bothered by the information, murder in the County was unsettling. On the way to work, she clung to Brent. Their kiss goodbye was a bit agitated. Brent observed how easily the teenager was upset. He did think that she looked so cute, with her hair up. Over at the 'Dig', he found everyone there, including Donna. She was wearing shorts, and Tee shirt. Brent thought that she had nice legs. Nice legs, big tits, and a wide middle. He did like her ass. It was interesting what you could take in, while you put your lunch in the little refrigerator. He saw that Jennifer was there, what a body! He thought that the big Blonde looked very happy. Brent figured that they must have found something today. The young Deputy made a tour of the grounds, while the crew finished up for the day. He observed them all take off, quickly only his car remained in sight. He settled down for a long evening. He had the newspaper, and the radio for news and music. It could be a lot worse.

Stan was able to shed more light on the morning fire. Arson said that a Meth lab caused the fire. The exact cause was still under investigation. He said that it was probably carelessness, not intentional. Brenda wondered at renting such a big, expensive place for a drug lab. They figured that it was good camouflage, no one suspected to find a drug lab on such an estate. Stan thought that Brenda looked wonderful, in her shorts. Her just washed hair was down, he liked it that way. He caught himself watching her in the Kitchen. She wasn't stupid, she saw it too. The female in her liked the attention. The firefighter side wondered what it would mean? There was nothing to do about it now, so both of them just tried to ignore it. Brenda's beeper interrupted their thoughts, 'Medical Emergency'. She jumped into her gear, and was gone. Stan thought that it was for the best, he needed a rest.

80

Brent was sure, there was going to be a big investigation about Bob Moore's murder. Fat lot that meant to him. As a still green Deputy, he was sure jobs like this one were all he could hope for. He figured that it would be two to three years, before he could take the exam for Corporal. He figured that he would start studying for it about a year ahead of time. He was not optimistic about his chances for promotion, no one was ready for retirement. There hadn't been a death on duty for five years. He thought about his prospects as he did another tour, in the hot evening. He was on the back side of the property, when he heard the car. By the time he got back to the tent, she was waiting for him. "Hi, Brent! How do you like my outfit!" She had on different shorts, with another Tee shirt. "I like the tits and legs, and the ass is nice." Her smile faded a bit, "Yeah, but you don't like the middle!" She was right, that bulge around her middle was not to his liking. She embraced him, he got a big kiss from her. She was a good kisser. "I know you don't want to cheat on your girlfriend, but I won't be here after the Summer. We could have some good times. No strings!" Those big tits were pressing against him. He started to waver. Then she clinched the deal, "My Folks are rich. I'll give you one hundred dollars for everytime you sleep with me!" That bothered him, "What does that do to her, having to buy sex? Does she need it so badly?" She saw his look, "You're thinking about it, aren't you?" He looked at her cute face, "Yeah, I'm thinking about it. I'm buying my folks house, I could use the money." She looked pleased, "So you don't find me too ugly." "I never found you ugly, just fat." She gave him a wry smile, "I guess I can settle for that. You wait here. I'm going over to the enclosure, to get ready. You know, there's a bed in there." "Yeah, I saw it first time I came here." She embraced him again. Her kiss was warm, with much tongue. He had to admit, she was shaping up to be a good lover. He watched her wide form disappear into the enclosure, the flaps were closed. He looked around, nothing unusual. Just the night creatures of the Valley. The Cicada provided an new, but mono-tonous background noise. Every seven years they appeared. He had grown up with those sounds. He had to think about what he was about to do, and with who. What made Donna fat, then feel that she must pay for sex? It bothered him, not to understand what made her tick. She soon called to him. He entered the enclosure, which was pitch black. "Over here, Brent." He made his way to the bed. He undressed, placing his things on the nearby chair. "I have a condom for you," she said in the darkness. "Good, I think that's a good idea." Now nude, he slipped in beside her. She hugged him, her big boobs felt warm and soft. He kissed her, then gave his attention to her big boobs. Donna turned out to be a good bed partner. She was very skilled with her mouth. From the sounds uttered during their lovemaking, she left no doubt how much she enjoyed the evening. Brent was relieved to find that all normal female parts were there, in about the right location. She felt well serviced, by the time he was done. As he started to get up, Donna held his arm, "Thank you, I had a great time. I want to do this again, soon." That was all right with him, they made a date. Brent got dressed, then went back outside to check around. He picked up his hat from the table, then walked around the outside of the tent. Nothing seemed out of place. When Donna emerged from the enclosure, she made a bee line for him. He was solidly kissed, a one hundred dollar bill was slipped in his shirt pocket. "See you tomorrow, Stud." "I look forward to it, Donna. You're quite a woman!" She was beaming, as she drove away. Brent toured the property, after she left. He could still smell her scent. He knew he should shower, before Mona got a whiff. He wondered why Donna didn't lose the weight. She was a pretty girl, and a good lover. It was one of an increasing number of mysteries life seemed determined to throw at him. He would hide the money, until he could deposit it. Fortunately, Mona was not yet involved in his finances. Once deposited, she would have no way of knowing about his arrangement. He went back to the tent, time for lunch, and to write in his log. Of course, most of what had occurred, would never be written. Mona had insisted on making their sandwiches, she did it with enthusiasm. Just like everything she did. She would make love that way, tonight.

The old man had survived the heart attack. The firefighters had gotten him on oxygen and monitored his pulse, until the Paramedics got there. Brenda knew, they had been lucky. She had experienced times when there was only bad luck. Gary had called the Hospital, he was resting quietly. Normal heart sounds. Her mind drifted to the other issue. As a woman, she rather liked Stan staring at her in shorts. Brenda had always liked him, and he was a big blond stud. He was a lot older than she, but she did not mind that, either. What she wondered was, did Cal Fire have something in the Regulations that would interfere with a relationship between a Battalion Chief and an Engineer? She did not report to Stan, she worked for Gary. Would that be a problem? She knew that some would find it unethical, a conflict of interest. She thought of the storm it could unleash. But she had no family to object, what about Stan? He had no living kids, what about siblings? Brenda could not dismiss the possible impact it might have on her career. Her career was all she had, how could she risk that? Stan could keep looking, there was no harm there. But she would do nothing to encourage him. Both of them would keep their careers intact. What kind of relationship could it have been any way? That brought forth a few unexpected images of Stan in the buff, doing wonderful things to her. She shut those images down in a hurry. She was rattled! Those thoughts had been beneath the surface. Had they been there from before? Brenda lay in bed, wondering. Where had those thoughts come from?

Mona had much to relay, on the way home. They had to call for Deputies! There had been a fight in the parking lot, about ten thirty. Four people were arrested, drunk in public. At home, things were normal. Their lunch things needed to be handled, plans made for tomorrow. Brent took his shower. Mona was waiting for him in bed. She was eager to make love, he enjoyed her enthusiasm. She was a sweet person, with a very nice body. He enjoyed both sides of his petite lover. She was rather quiet, unlike Donna. He wondered about that, but decided that it just must be her style. Sometime in the future, Brent meant to talk to her about it. There were several things that lovers need to talk about. For now, Mona slept with her head on his chest. She was obviously very fond of him. Brent felt very fond of her. She was a sweet, foxy young woman. He wondered how much did her Mother's death do to her? Only time would tell.

Chapter Seven

Thursday:

It was after 9 AM, Bill Andrews was at his desk. His mind was not on the papers in his inbox. Jennifer was on his mind. Jennifer in his bed was filling his mind, "She is beautiful. She is very bright. She is special. But why would her Father plant a G.P.S. unit in her purse? Why not a G.P.S. phone? It occurred to him, she could turn that off. Is Jason overly protective of his thirty-one year old daughter, or does he have reason? What am I doing with this woman?" And then he graphically recalled exactly what he was doing with that woman last night. He made another effort to tackle his inbox. A note from Jim, "Sargent Yeager would handle the Drug lab and Fire Investgation." The fire at the Rittenhaus Mansion left a pall over the Valley. "Sheriff," Wanda called over the intercom. Bill pushed the 'Talk' button, "Yes, Wanda." She replied, "Sheriff Andrews, a Special Agent Gorski of the FBI is here to see you." "Please send him in." A stocky man, in his late twenties, and about 5' 10", walked in and moved toward the desk. Bill got up to greet him. They shook hands and exchanged greetings. Bill addressed the Agent, "What do you know about your assignment?" He replied very businesslike, "The Deputy Director himself briefed me. I am to escort the Refer truck load of evidence back to Quantico. He told me about the case. I hope this move turns up something." "Thank you," Bill replied, "If District Attorney Van Cleef interferes in any way, shoot him. He is a suspect in my Sister's death." Agent Gorski was surprised, "No one told me that, Sheriff!" "Well, now you know," Bill said, "Gorski, is that Polish?" The Agent smiled, "You bet your Dupa! My great-grandparents came here in 1907, from Poznan. They ended up in Iowa. The meat packing industry employed a lot of Poles. I was raised in Waterloo, and graduated from the University of Iowa. I could either work in meat packing, farm, or join the FBI. So here I am." Bill looked at the agent warily, "I hope that you made the right choice." Agent Gorski smiled, "So far, I have no big complaints. But I do wish they gave me better assignments. This is the fourth evidence escort that I have done this year. Hey, I need to thank your Secretary for the Bed and Breakfast she recommended. Great breakfast!" Bill smiled, "Yes, they are famous for it. That B and B belongs to my Secretary's parents, by the way. I think she got one up on the FBI." Agent Gorski laughed, "I guess she did. There was this really cute waitress." "That is her seventeen year old daughter, and my god daughter." The Agents face paled, "Well, I'll be shoving off now." Bill offered him his hand, "Give my regards to the Deputy Director. Have a safe trip." They shook hands and the Agent left the office. Bill followed him to the door. After he was gone, Bill spoke to Wanda, "The evidence in Joyce's case is leaving for Virginia. That agent will accompany it all the way. I am glad that you got him into your folk's place. He loved the breakfast, and he thought Pat was cute." As he turned and headed for his desk, he thought about the FBI agent, "And the Bureau wonders why it has a lousy reputation with local law enforcement." Bill went back to his chair and his inbox.

It is early afternoon. Bill leaned back in his chair. The idea of Jennifer in his life was still hard for him to deal with." Where will this relationship go? Where do I want it to go?" Jim Bearpaw burst into the room wearing camouflage fatigues, carrying a large camouflaged ABS case, "It's here," he announced as he laid the case on Bill's conference table. Bill snapped out of his day-dreaming, "You mean the big one?" "Yes sir, the M200." He held the large, beige and brown camouflaged rifle up. It took both hands. Bill walked over to Jim, "The scope is already mounted, so we just have to mount the Laser Rangefinder." "What do you mean 'we' white man?" Jim said with a smile. "Okay, the Desi-gnated Sniper needs to mount the Laser Rangefinder," Bill responded, smiling back at him. "Very well, the Designated Sniper proposes that we take this beast out to the Old Mine Road and check it out," Jim announced. Bill was puzzled, "Why the Old Mine Road?" "Well, it is good country for testing the 'long reach' of this weapon," explained Jim, "Besides, Old Puma Lee told me there was some truck activity around there. He saw tracks." Bill seemed surprised, "Is he still alive? How old is he?" "Around ninety, we figure," Jim looked at Bill, "You know, he's your Grandmother's cousin. You're part of his family, he is the Elder.

We should go see him. Maybe you could take the Saunders woman." Bill was very surprised at this comment, "Why would you mention Jennifer Saunders?" Jim smiled, sheepishly, "Sheriff, Sir, my sources tell me that she went to see you yesterday afternoon, and no one saw her again 'til this morning. Is there something you want to tell me?" Bill looked serious, "What I want to tell you is that it is none of your or your sources business." "Come on, Bill, I was only joking," Jim explained, "we just want you to be happy." We want you to stay here and be our Sheriff. You need to be happy for that to work. If Jennifer Saunders makes you happy, that's great." "Look Jim," a somewhat embarrassed Bill began, "I don't know what is happening with Jennifer and myself. We have to see where this relationship goes." "Well, Bill, that is all I wanted to know, Jim smirked, "See how easy it was." Bill drew himself up to his full height, "Okay, you clown, grab your toy and let's get on the road before I get hung up by a phone call."

"Why do people try to marry off their friends?" Bill thought as Jim drove them out of Sierra Vista, "Did Mary and I do that to our friends?" His memories of Mary answered that question, "We were too busy with her problems. We didn't have many friends. Mary's outbursts saw to that." They drove on. Jim was silent. Jim was usually silent. He had been raised to appreciate silence. So had Bill. Silence had always been a friend, allowing him to concentrate on the matter at hand. In law enforcement, or in the Military, silence was good for business. Jim chose to break the silence, "I wonder what a truck would be doing around the old mines? Drug transport?" Bill joined the speculation, "Maybe they are storing drugs in one of the mines. I should talk to the DEA." "It could be stolen car parts," Jim offered, " There's big money in that racket" "If we mention stolen car parts, the DEA won't loan us their Helicopter," Bill pointed out. That prompted Jim to respond, "We may need that Infrared capability for night work." The silence resumed. Bill thought of the sniper rifle and felt the need to speak, "Jim, what do you feel when you are looking at a target." Jim took his time answering, "In Bosnia, we targeted their snipers. They were trying to kill us. I felt a sense of power, of control. I was glad I was getting them before they could get any one else." "For me," Bill began, "it was usually up close and personal, sometimes with a knife. Often it was sudden, they surprised us or we surprised them. You could often smell them."Jim thought about that for a bit, then spoke, "The closest I ever was to a target was about 100 meters. We were far enough away to pretend that our targets were anything but men. You didn't kill a man, you 'zapped a target'." Bill nodded, knowingly, "In my After Action Reports it was always 'neutralized one sentry' instead of 'slit throat of one cold and wet 18 year old kid'." "I heard about the Johnson kid," Jim said, changing the subject, "that is sad. He wasn't a bad kid." Bill looked at Jim, "You knew Rob?" "Yeah, I had to arrest him and his friends when he was 15. They papered AW Fairbanks' house," Jim recalled, "Did a good job of it." Bill responded glumly, "He should be going to college now, not his own funeral. How many locals have we lost in Iraq and Afghanistan?" Jim replied after a moment, "Three dead, so far. Five wounded. Greg Forrester probably won't walk again." "Viet Nam, the Middle East, the Balkans, Afghanistan, Granada, Panama, we keep finding places to send our young men and women. Always, some of them don't come back like they left." "It has been the same for my tribe, Jim observed, "We fought the Northern Paiute, the Mono, the Modoc, and the White Man. Since World War I, we have fought for the USA. We have two boys and a girl in Iraq right now." "You know," Bill began, my Grandmother used to tell me about her people that fought in both World Wars, and Korea, some were in Viet Nam at the time. She was proud of their service for our country. I would look at the tribes poverty, and wonder what they were fighting for." "Bill," Jim said slowly, "You do not know us. We may be poor, but we are warrior, and patriots. You are 1/4 Washo. You should know more about us. Why don't you join the Tribe? If you apply to the Tribal Council, you would be approved. Johnny Eagle got in, and they like you a lot better than him." Bill was curious, "Johnny Eagle is a member of the Tribe?" "Any one of at least half Indian blood, who marries into the Tribe, can apply for membership," Jim responded. "Who did Johnny marry?" Bill was very interested. Jim went on with his wealth of local knowledge, "He married Linda Littlewolf, she works for A W Fairbanks." "Johnny seems to be positioning himself for something. He is Legal Counsel to the Tribe, a member of the Tribe, and he has his wife inside A W Fairbanks' office. What is there for a sharp, Harvard trained lawyer? Why is he here, and not helping his tribe, the Modocs?" "What about the Indian Casino we keep hearing about?" Jim reminded him. Bill considered that for only a moment, "What did you find about backers for A W's project?" "Sorry Bill," Jim said, apologetically, "I forgot to tell you. She is partners with the Sierra Development Corporation, a Delaware company, and Charlie O'Brien. It will be hard for us to get anything out of the State of Delaware about that outfit." "We are not going to try," responded Bill, "But I know someone who might." With that he grabbed his Cell phone and hit dial for a number he selected from a list. The call went through, and it was answered, "Hello, Jason Saunders." "Jason, this is Bill Andrews." "Bill, how are you?" "Fine. How are you?" "Just fine!" "I am glad to hear it. Jason, the reason I called is that we need some information about a Delaware Corporation." "Which company, Bill?" "The Sierra Development Corporation, it is partners with AW in her development." "Now you're talking! I would love to know that myself. I will look into it." "You will? Jason, I do appreciate this." "Think nothing of it. When I have something to share, I will be in touch. You take care." "Same to you. Please say hello to Jennifer for me. Goodbye." Jim glanced at Bill, "Do you know what he thinks about you and his daughter?" Bill laughed, "He practically welcomed me into the family the day after I met her. I think he believes me to be perfect for his daughter." "Thank God for that," Jim exclaimed, "That is one man I don't want mad at me." That reminded Bill of what Jennifer said about her Father and a death in a Mexican Prison, "I think you are right. He is dangerous on many levels. I would hate to have him after me." They drove on in silence.

When they reached the Old Mine Road, Jim turned off on to it and parked next to the gully. Jim and Bill got out, and Jim examined the gravel roadway. After covering the area back to the first mine, then the roadway back to the County road, Jim turn toward Bill, and walked back toward the SUV, "There has been at least one truck through here recently, probably a dump truck pulling a trailer. It looks like it left heavier than it came." This information had Bill's attention, "What would a dump truck be hauling around here. Drugs?" Jim thought for a moment, "Drugs make sense. This area's remote. If it hadn't been for Old Man Lee coming out here to gather paint pigments, we wouldn't know anything. They could haul a lot of drugs out in a tandem dump rig." "Are they hauling the drugs in the same way?" Bill asked. "I can't tell much from this gravel road," Jim admitted, "But it looks like they are coming from the south. Susanville maybe. They left heavier, than they arrived. Drugs in, Rock out?" Bill looked pleased, "I think that we have enough to interest the DEA. It could be more than just storing a few keys of 'grass'. Jim was moving toward the rear of the SUV, "Okay, you contact the DEA, and I'll set up our new toy. Bill reached for his cell phone and looked at the screen, "No Cell service. Maybe I can get a signal up there." He pointed at the ridge above them, beyond the gully. Jim nodded, "That looks like a good spot to test our toy. Grab the ammo box and follow me up." Jim used the gun case strap to sling it onto his back. "Like hell I'll follow you," Bill yelled as he grabbed the ammo box and rushed past Jim, leaping over the small gully. The two men scrambled up the side of the ridge. Bill was first, but barely. Jim laughed, "You old guys are always trying to reclaim your youth." "And you kids never show respect for your betters," was Bill quick retort. Jim laughed and slung the gun case off his back and onto the ground. He opened the case and took out the rifle. Bill found that he had Cell phone reception, so he placed his call. "DEA Office." "SAC Stevens, please." "Who may I say is calling?" "Sheriff Andrews." "One moment please." "Hello Sheriff. How are you doing?" "Hello Agent Stevens. Fine, how about you?" "I can't complain." "Good. The reason I called concerns suspected drug transportation in my county." "Sheriff, I thought we cleaned out the area by the lake." "This time it's in the Old Mine area. Please call me Bill." "That area is isolated. They could be hiding drugs in the mines. You can call me Charlie." "I agree, the mines could be used for storage." "If they are, they're probably doing it at night." "You're right, Charlie, that is why we need one of your helicopter for some night work." The one with Infrared, I expect." "Yes, we need FLIR capability." "Bill, I could give you two Surveillance Vehicles." "No, ground units might spook them. This is lonely country at night. You can see a car or a light a long ways off. I'm thinking of infiltrating a ground team into the area at night. There is an old logging road nearby, my guys will sneak in from there after dark." "Probably some of your boys were Rangers." "Right, Charlie. Despite that handicap, I think we can get the job done." "Very funny. Is that a Squid joke? All kidding aside. I will put the FLIR unit on call for you. The crew won't like the night standby, but that's life. Let me know if I can do any other little favors for you, Bill." "Okay, Charlie. Nice talking to you, too." Jim looked up from the rifle, "What's the word on the Helicopter?" Bill put up his Cell phone, "One ship and crew will be standing by for us. Now all we need is some eyes around here, starting tonight." "Leave that to me, Bill," Jim looked up from the Rifle, "Two of us should be able to cover it." "You think that two of you can infiltrate this ridge after dark," Bill asked. "Bill, we have been infiltrating this ridge for five hundred years, I think we can handle a few more nights." "Okay Jim, you and your 'Native American Scouts have got it." Jim stood and bowed at the waist, "On behalf of my 'Native American Scouts', we thank you." Bill looked Jim in the eye, "Take the new radios and night vision sets." Jim nodded, "It's about time we got some use out of that grant money." "Speaking of grant money," Bill said, looking at the now assembled Rifle, "When do we get to try out the toy." Jim held up the Sniper rifle, flipping open the bipod under the forestock, "It's ready. Pick out a target for me." Bill took the lens caps off of the binoculars that hung from his neck and studied the area. He studied the range chart for the rifle. Jim took a prone position with the bipod on the ridge top, his body resting on the backside. Only his head and the rifle were visible on the ridge line. "See the small rock left of the Red Dog Mine? At ten o'clock." Bill coached. Jim swivelled the rifle slightly, "Laser Range, three hundred fifty-seven meters." He chambered a round. His finger slowly squeezed the trigger. The sound of the shot was milder than expected for such a powerful round. "One click high and two to the right," Bill called out, still watching through the binoculars. Jim made his adjustments to the sights quickly, and chambered another round. The shooting routine was repeated. The second shot struck the rock dead center. Bill glanced at Jim, "Bulls eye!" "Find one further out," was Jim's emotionless response. Bill scanned to his right, "Mesquite tree near the Molly Bee Mine. Bottom branch on right." Jim chambered another round, as he acquired the target, "six hundred fifty-four meters." He fired. Bill observed the shot, "One click low." Jim made the adjustment, and chambered a round. Another shot echoed off of the rocky wall in front of them. "Bulls eye!" Bill announced, "How about one over by the Midas Mine?" "Past it," Jim requested. "How about the Keep Out sign?" Bill asked. Jim responded by shifting the rifle and acquiring the new target, "Twelve Hundred seventy-six meters. Top bolt holding the sign." He chambered a round and focused on the target. Slowly, he squeezed the trigger. Another sharp crack, and the sign moved. "You hit the lower bolt," Bill reported, "Low one click." "Too bad this isn't Horse Shoes," Jim muttered as he dropped the empty magazine. Bill heard the magazine hit the ground and grabbed a fresh one from the Ammo box, "These .408 rounds are heavy." He handed it to Jim who was adjusting the Scope. Jim took the new Magazine and carefully inserted it, without disturbing the alignment of the rifle. He chambered a round. His eye never left the Scope. "You don't expect it to still be aligned?" Bill asked, skeptically. Jim did not answer. The rifle spoke again as Bill watched the target. "Damn," was all Bill said. He took the binoculars from his eyes and turned to Jim, "Another Bull's eye." Jim chambered another round, "Challenge me this time." Bill put the binoculars to his eyes, and looked further down the Old Mine Road. The road turned right past the Midas Mine, then turned back to the left. At this turn to the left, there was a rock about the size of a man's head. Bill had Jim shifted the rifle to the new target, "Seventeen hundred nineteen meters," Jim announced without emotion. A slight adjustment to the scope focus, then the slow squeeze of the trigger. Another sharp crack and echo. "Damn, Bull's eye!" Bill was surprised, "This is why I went for such a long range weapon. Let's try one with the Silencer." He got the camouflaged cylinder out the Rifle case and installed it on the end of the barrel. Jim chambered another round and repeated the shooting process. When the bullet hit, Bill called out, "One click low." "Not bad," exclaimed Jim, "This is one hell of a sniper package! This makes an M40 seem like a .22!" He stood up and motioned to Bill, "Look at this Ballistics Computer." Bill stepped over to the unit and knelt down to examine the Computer, "Looks like a PDA. Are those sensors attached? " "Yeah, wind and temp," Jim said, "And there is a Night Vision Module with IR laser." Looking back to the last target, Bill was impressed, "That is one flat shooting Bastard.... Jim, I just saw a reflection off of something." Still on his knees, Bill shifted his body back and forth until he found the reflection again. "There is something in the gully near the Midas Mine," Bill estimated, "I have a glass reflection at that point." Jim started to break down the Rifle, "Let's go check it out." "Let me give you a hand, "Bill said as he picked up the PDA, unplugged it's sensor cable, and placed it in the Rifle case. He then rolled up the Sensor cable and stored it. Jim returned

92

the Rifle to the case, and snapped the lid shut. Bill picked up the empty ammo magazine and put it in the ammo box. Jim slung the rifle case onto his back and Bill grabbed the ammo box. Together, they rushed down the slope to their SUV. Bill unlocked it, and got in the Drivers seat. Jim put the rifle case in the back, then got into the Passenger seat. They drove up Old Mine Road, watching the gully. There lay a late model SUV on it's roof. Jim grabbed the clipboard with the Hot Sheet, as he exit the vehicle before it quite stopped. "I got the license," Jim yelled as he scanned the Hot Sheet, "It belongs to the Geologist, Bob Moore." "Secure a rope while I call it in," Bill called to Jim. While Bill used the radio, Jim took a rope from the rear of the SUV. He secured one end to a ring on the rear bumper and threw the coil of rope into the gully. He removed a Repel Rig from the SUV and started to put it on. Bill joined him at the rear of the SUV, "The Crime Scene Unit is on its way. We need to find the driver, head down when you're ready. I'll join you in a few minutes." Bill grabbed a Repel Rig for himself and put it on. Jim checked his rig and then grabbed the rope. He attached the rope to his belt, gripped the rope with both gloved hands, and backed over the edge of the gully. He repelled down the gully wall, trailing the rope out behind him with one hand. He quickly reached the gully bottom and detached himself from the rope. As he approached the Driver side of the inverted SUV, the stench of death was strong. The Driver's side window was shattered, the center of it was missing. Kneeling beside the window, Jim saw a man in his forties was strapped in his seat, upside down. There was an obvious bullet hole in the side of the man's head, possibly the cause of death. Jim turned and shouted, "Gunshot to the head, possibly through the side window." Bill was repelling into the gully, he soon joined Jim at the wreck. He pulled a digital camera out of his pocket and activated it. Jim stood aside while Bill shot pictures of the victim and his vehicle. "What do you think he was doing out here and who was he with?" Jim asked the rectorial questions. Bill spoke as he took photos, "There is nothing out here but these old mines, and most of them have been closed since the 1960's. Might be a good place to meet if you have something to hide." "Any connection to the truck activity I found?" Jim wondered. Bill wrinkled his brow and replied, "That's what we need to find out. When I get home, I intend to look at his computer again. There might be some clue to his murder in his files." That caused Jim to think of other possible clues, "I think I should go back up and check the area for tracks. Maybe I can find some clue about what happened. Bill nodded his agreement. Jim attached himself to the rope, and used it to pull himself out of the gully. He examined the ground where the SUV had gone over the edge. Then he worked his way out, towards the Midas Mine. Both men heard the approaching Helicopter about the same time. Jim walked back to the gully and yelled down to Bill, "Are you expecting guests?" "Not by 'Chopper, the DEA knows nothing about this," Bill responded. Shortly, their curiosity was satisfied when a green and silver Bell 430 came into view. "That's Jason Saunders machine," Bill yelled up to Jim. "How did he know we were here?" Jim yelled back. Bill yelled to Jim, "Send him down. He can ID the victim." The area in front of the Midas Mine was wide enough for the Helicopter to land. Jason Saunders jumped out, instinctively ducking to avoid the still spinning Blades. He rushed over to the Sheriff's SUV, where Jim waited for him. The Helicopter grew quiet as it's engine was shut off, it's blades slowed down and stopped. Jim reached out to shake Jason's extended hand, "Mr. Saunders, Sheriff Andrews wants you to come down to the wreck and identify the body." Jim showed him the rope and helped him put on a repelling rig. Jim was surprised that Jason knew about repelling, he was even more surprised that the older man did it so well. On the floor of the gully, Jason detached himself from the rope and strode over to the wreck. "Bill, I understand you want me to identify Bob. I assume it is Bob." Bill motioned him to the Driver's window, "I hope the smell doesn't bother you." Jason move forward and got down on his knees, in order to see in the window. After a moment studying the swollen form, he shook his head and stood up. Turning to Bill, he spoke softly, "That is Bob Moore. Poor Man, I feel for his wife and children." Bill had questions to ask, "Do you know why he was out here?" "No Bill, he was not here for me or my group," Jason was genuinely puzzled. "He was essentially done with our project, perhaps he took on a new client." Bill considered this information, "That could be one reason for coming out here. But, why meet here? Not to be seen? I think I need to take another look at Bob's computer. He may have left some clue to what he was doing, and who he was working for. Jason, you and I need to talk about your people monitoring my radio communications." Jason simply

94

smiled. About twenty minutes later, two vehicles came to the wreck site. One was the Crime Unit SUV, the other was an ambulance commandeered by the County Coroner. The Crime Unit, a Sergeant and two men, started to unload their equipment. Dr. Barbara Davis, County Coroner and local physician got out of the ambulance cab, and walked over to the Jim standing by his SUV. Dr. Davis was a tall, attractive brunette in her early 30's. Divorced, she moved to Sierra Vista to start over. The air, the trees, and the people were a big change for her. Men like Jim Bearpaw were not part of her New York experience. "Lieutenant Bearpaw, I take it that the deceased is in the ravine." Jim noticed how the jeans and blouse complemented her well endowed figure, there was just a hint of cleavage, "That is correct, Dr. Davis, you may need assistance getting down there." She looked into the gully and at the rope attached to the vehicle's bumper, "I assume that this is the only way down." "Yes it is," Jim replied, "I take it that you have never repelled." He obtained the proper size climbing belt from the Crime Unit, and helped her put it on. He attached both of their belts to the rope, Barbara Davis in front of him. He guided her to the edge of the gully, and they backed over the edge. Barbara bumped into Jim several times on the way down, at the bottom she seemed embarrassed. Jim noticed that she seemed a bit upset by their descent, incorrectly concluding that the trip frightened her. Backing into Jim Bearpaw did many things to Dr Barbara Davis, fear was not one them. Barbara's mind was racing, "God, get hold of yourself. You have had a man's arms around you before. What is wrong with you?" Her interest in Jim had begun six weeks before, when they had been introduced at a Board of Supervisor's Award banquet. With great effort, she regained her composure. She went over to the wreck and started her exam. Her bag was quickly brought to her, allowing her to probe the head wound. The ambulance driver joined her in time to remove the body from the vehicle and lay it in a body bag. The Crime Unit had rigged a SKED Rescue Stretcher to raise and lower their equipment. The loaded Stretcher had come down and was being unloaded by Jim and one of the Crime Unit Deputies. Seeing that the deceased was in a body bag, Jim came over to Barbara. "We can take the body up on the Rescue Stretcher, whenever you are ready." "Thank you, Lieutenant," She said and smiled, "I appreciate your help." The Crime Unit was beginning to go over the wreck, as she zipped the body bag closed. Jim and the Driver lifted it and placed it on the Rescue Stretcher. They strapped it to the Stretcher, as Barbara Davis tied her bag to the Stretcher foot. At Jim's signal, the Stretcher was hauled up to the road. Jim watched as Barbara hooked the rope to her rig and pulled herself up by it. Barbara's mother was Italian, as a result she had a 36DD bust that, like now, usually drew a lot of attention. Jim noticed, so did every other male within a mile. But Jim wondered why she needed help going down, but not going up? He thought he knew. One of the Deputies helped Barbara and the Driver put the body bag on a Gurney and get it into the Ambulance. Jim repelled out of the gully in time to see the Ambulance pull out. He was soon joined by Bill, "Bill, I found bits of auto glass over by the Molly Bee Mine, the Crime Unit is on it." "Good. Jim, I want you to take charge here. I am hitching a ride back with Jason Saunders. I want to take another look at Bob Moore's computer." "I hope you find something about what he was doing here, "Jim looked glum, "This murder doesn't make sense. What does a geologist have to do with drugs?" "Maybe drugs are the problem, Jim," Bill looked very serious, "a geologist up here could be dealing with tunneling or excavation. Maybe they are enlarging one of the Mines." "I could look around, Bill." "Leave it alone for now, Jim. Start your surveillance tomorrow night. If the truck comes back, we will have it followed. When we know what they are doing, then we will come back here in force." "Okay Bill, you got it." "See you later," Bill gestured to Jim. Bill saw Jason standing by the Helicopter, talking to his pilot. He strode over to the pair, "Jason, are you heading back now?" "Yes Bill, I am." "Can I beg a ride back with you?" Bill asked the big man. "Sure. Get on. We can leave right now," Jason said as he scrambled into the machine with surprising agility. Bill got in, and the doors were shut as the rotors start to spin.

　　As the Ambulance drove back to town, Dr. Barbara Davis wondered about Lt. Jim Bearpaw. "What goes on behind that stoic face? She thought, "What does he think about me? Would he be interested in a white woman? How do I go about getting to know him?" Barbara was sure that he noticed her. Men had noticed her since she was fifteen. "I wonder if he will attend the autopsy? I could invite him to the autopsy." She smile at that.

Jason and Bill climbed out of the Helicopter and walked over to the house. Jennifer met them on the Front Porch. She was still dressed in dirty jeans from the 'Dig'. "At least you could have given me a chance to shower," spoke a smiling Jennifer, as she grabbed Bill and gave him a very energetic kiss. She slipped her arm around his waist and turned to her Father, "You could have told me you were bringing Bill back with you!" Jason smiled at the two of them, "It was a surprise for both of us. I am glad you liked the surprise!" Bill seemed embarrassed by their display, but Jennifer was obviously happy about the whole thing. Jason spoke to Bill, "I need to find someone to drive you home." "No you don't," Jennifer exclaimed happily, "I'll drive him. Dad, you entertain him will I change." With that, she rushed inside. "It looks like we have our orders," Jason spoke ruefully to Bill, "Seriously, thank you for giving me back my Daughter. She is back to her old self, passionate about life." Bill looked a bit shaken, "I think I have been hit by a blond hurricane. I was also concerned about what 'Dad' would think about my keeping his little girl out all night." "Relax Bill," Jason said, still smiling, "It seems to be the cure for her problem. The important thing is what comes next." Bill looked serious, "Yes sir, that is important." Jason was philosophical, "Time will tell, Bill. In the mean time we have a very happy young woman on our hands." "Jason, I can't help being concerned about what it will take to keep her happy." Jason did not reply to this comment, but had something else on his mind. "Bill, tomorrow is our Injunction Hearing. The Judge has had time to consider the facts. You know what this injunction means to the whole area. If we get it, I am worried about A W Fairbanks and her crew. You heard about how she carried on at the 'Dig'. What will she do if she loses her case? She is one sick puppy." "Don't worry about A W, I will have her watched," Bill reassured, "If she steps out of line, we will arrest her." Further discussion of A W was interrupted by the reappearance of Jennifer. Bill noticed that she was still wearing the same outfit, but an overnight shoulder bag was over her right shoulder. A thin wardrobe bag was in her left hand. Bill looked at Jason, surprised and perplexed. Jason simply shrugged. "Okay, let's go," said an unabashed Jennifer. And so they did.

Dr. Barbara Davis entered the Kitchen of the large old house she shared with her Aunt Sarah, who was washing vegetables at the sink. Dr. Sarah Davis was an almost petit woman in her 60's. Her niece Barbara towered over her by a good four inches. Sarah had been a doctor in this area for almost thirty years, ever since she had purchased the practice of Old Doc Petersen. "So how was it," Sarah asked her niece, "Was he badly decomposed?" "Dead about a week, "Barbara told her Aunt, "It was not pleasant." "Well why don't you take a bath while I fix dinner," Sarah suggested. "Aunt Sarah, sometimes I think you are a mind reader, "Barbara started to leave, then stopped, "What do you know about Lieutenant Jim Bearpaw ?" Sarah stopped washing and looked at her niece, "So that is what's been bothering you! Jim Bearpaw is thirty-five years old, single, and a dedicated police officer. He is active in Washo tribal affairs, his Uncle sits on their Tribal Council. He is active in the Army Reserve. He built himself a nice house on the Reservation. Barbara, many of the local young women have gone after the handsome Lieutenant, with limited success. He dates them a time or two, maybe a few times, then he moves on." "You mean he dumps them?" Barbara asked, unbeliefving. "No," replied her Aunt, "He seems to part with them gently, no one seems angry with him." "I am not surprised," remarked a relieved Barbara, "He seems so nice." "My dear niece, you have it bad," she resumed washing, "I suggest that you do something about it." "Aunt Sarah, I am working on it," Barbara said as she left for her bath. "Barbara," her Aunt thought to herself, "you have achieved everything that you have gone after. It has not always made you happy."

Bill walked with Jennifer from the car to the Front Porch, "We need to talk more about this, Jennifer." "Of course we do," She said, "I want to talk about us." Bill jumped on that comment, "Whether or not there is an us, depends on what happens in our relationship." "Don't you think a lot has happened already," Jennifer spoke emphatically. "Yes I do," Bill spoke as he unlocked the Front Door, "Maybe too much, too soon." Jennifer seemed skeptical, "I don't think things are happening too fast. I think things are going just fine." As she stepped into the house, she took the overnight bag from Bill. Shouldering the bag Jennifer headed for the Stairs, "We can talk about it after I take a shower." An exasperated Bill, watched her head upstairs, then headed to the Kitchen. He was joined by two hungry animals. He kneeled down and stroked the two eager pets, "Okay you two, chow time." The three moved to the refrigerator. Bill grabbed the two open cans and put them on the counter. He got out a bowl for each pet, and used a fork to clean each can into a bowl. "Chow down you two," Bill place a bowl before each one. He stood up and watch his two animals for a moment, then looked up, anticipating the conversation that he knew he had to have with Jennifer. First, however he needed to check his messages. He checked the answer machine, and found nothing new. Reluctantly, he headed out into the Entry Hall, took off his gun belt and hat, as he climbed the stairs, putting them in the closet. As he reached the Master Bedroom, he found Jennifer's blouse on the floor. Between the door and the bed lay her bra. At the foot of the bed lay her shoes, socks, and jeans. By the door to the Master Bath lay her high cut briefs. Standing before the closed door, Bill could hear the water running. "Jennifer!" he called. The water stopped, "I'll be out in a minute," she called out. In a moment, she came out wrapped in a towel. Considering her height, it did not cover very much. She hugged Bill, her short blonde hair was damp. "Jennifer," he spoke softly into her ear, "What happened here last night was an explosion of emotions. I am not sorry it happened, but we shouldn't read too much into it. But, if we sleep together tonight, it will be an intentional act. This is an important decision for us. I want you to think about it carefully." Jennifer stepped back, loosened the towel and let it fall to the ground. She stepped forward and pulled his head into her large breasts, then whispered in his ear, "Dr. Davis fitted me with a diaphragm today." Bill knew that they would be dining late tonight. A man could only do so much. He did have one thought, "Man, thou are weak!"

Chapter Eight

Friday, 8:30am:

Quietly, Bill emerged from the Master Bathroom. He was dressed in his Navy Dress White Uniform, the jacket was still unbuttoned. "It is going to be too warm for this monkey suit today," he thought, regretfully. Looking at the still sleeping Jennifer, he also had regrets there. She was bright, beautiful, and full of life. But why did her Father keep close tabs on her. It sure was not to guard her chastity. She was going to the Hearing this morning. He was going to a funeral. "How I wish I was spending the day with you," he thought as he watched her sleep. Duty called, so he headed downstairs. He went into the kitchen and fixed the coffee. While it brewed, he fixed some toast, with butter and Jam. The two sleepy animals had joined him by this time. He got a can of food for each of them out of the Pantry, and used a fork to place ½ of a can in each bowl. They waited for his okay, then eagerly dove into their bowls. Bill watched them eat for a moment, then poured himself a cup of the now brewed coffee. Grabbing the paper towel holding the toast, he carried it and the coffee into the office. He sipped from the coffee before he sat it down. He then turned on the laptop computer. He ate on a piece of toast as he waited for the computer to boot. Bill typed in Bob Moore's password when prompted. He was quickly searching through Bob's files. One file was a geological report on the Old Mine Road area. Bill scanned its pages very carefully. He heard a sound behind him. Turning, he saw a sleepy Jennifer standing in the doorway, wearing his too large bathrobe. "Good morning, Sleeping Beauty." He started printing the report, then walked over to her. He gently embraced her and kissed her on the cheek. She took his head in her hands and kissed him strongly on the mouth. "I like the way you say hello," he spoke to her softly. There is coffee in the Kitchen. I found a report on Bob Moore's computer, it is printing now." She shook her head, "I'll look at it after I have some coffee." Hand in hand, they walked into the Kitchen. Bill showed her where the cups were kept. She got one and poured herself a cup of coffee. "You make good coffee," she said appreciatively. "I bet you say that to all the sailors," he kidded her. Jennifer smiled back, then sipped her coffee. Bill reluctantly announced his departure, "I've got to go now. I have to pick up Russ on the way." She put down her cup and grabbed Bill. They kissed for a long time. Afterwards, he touched her cheek,"Good luck today. Call me if the Judge renders a verdict. My Cell number is on the pad by the phone." Reluctantly, he pulled himself away and headed for the Front Door. Jim had dropped off his SUV last night. Bill was glad he already knew about Jennifer. With the morning, some of the doubts returned about the big Blonde.

Dr. Barbara Davis stood in the Kitchen, finishing her coffee. The local phonebook lay open on the counter next to the phone. She seemed to be making a decision about something. Then she put down her coffee cup and picked up the receiver. Reading from the phone book, she punched in a number. "Sierra Vista Sheriff's Department, Wanda speaking." "Hello Wanda, this is Barbara Davis." "Hello, Barbara. How are you?" "I am fine. How are you?" "Feeling old. My son will be a sophomore in college in September." "Sorry, I have no cure for age, Wanda. Is Lieutenant Bearpaw in his office?" "Yes, he is." "May I speak to him?" "Hang on a minute." "Thank you." A moment later, "This is Jim Bearpaw." "Hello Jim, this is Barbara Davis.""Hello Barbara, how are you?" "Fine, thank you. The reason that I called is to let you know that I will be doing the Bob Moore autopsy at nine this morning, if you would care to attend." "I have no other commitment. I'll be glad to attend." "You will? That will be fine. See you then." She was noticeably relieved as she hung up the phone. Barbara smiled to herself as she put her coffee cup in the sink and headed for the garage. Aunt Sarah was watching her, she just shook her head. "I hope you know what your doing," she thought as she prepared to leave for her office. "First, the Saunders woman, then Barbara. Is there something in the water?"

It was 9 am, Barbara and her assistant were just entering the Autopsy Room of the Sierra Vista Memorial Hospital. Today they wore masks as well as gowns, not for fear of infection, but to help counteract the smell. The body of Bob Moore was on the table, under a sheet. The room was filled with it's aroma. Jim

102

Bearpaw was already there, the expression on his face showed the smell was bothering him. Barbara noticed his discomfort, and spoke to the short, heavy woman next to her, "Rachel, will you get a mask for Lieutenant Bearpaw?" Rachel grabbed one from a box near the door they had just used, and gave it to Jim. "It is chemically treated," Barbara said, noticing his hesitance to use the mask, "go ahead and put it on. It will help kill the smell." "He is cautious and suspicious," Barbara noted to herself, "Is he also that way with people?" Barbara proceeded to remove the sheet from the body and hand it to Rachel. Rachel stuffed it into a large laundry hamper in one corner of the room. Barbara began an examination of the naked body. Starting with the head, and working her way down. Barbara spoke as she worked, Rachel took notes as she did. "There is a hole in the left side of the head, two centimeters forward of, and at the same level as the Auditory opening." Barbara's shoulder length brown hair was up, she wore a white coat that fastened in the back. She had surgical booties on her feet. "She looks good even in that costume," Jim thought, taking it all in. Barbara was working her way down the corpse, "Lieutenant Bearpaw, we bagged his clothes and sealed it. I hope that we will be able to turn them over to you." "Please call me Jim," he reminded her, "and I will be glad to take custody of the evidence." "Thank you, Jim," she replied without looking up. "There are injuries to the shoulders, arms, chest, and abdomen consistent with an auto overturning while wearing a lap belt and chest belt," she continued. The autopsy went on in the same mode for several more minutes, with the same findings. Barbara then examined the head. She started by separating the skin of the face from that of the skull. She separated the face from the scalp, then peeled the scalp back off of the top of the skull. Using an electric saw, Barbara then removed the top of the skull. She moved the overhead light to better illuminate the interior of the skull. Some of the damage to the brain was now visible. Using a stainless steel probe, she explored the suspected bullet path, "Damage is worst than it appears from outside. Perhaps more than one bullet was used." She continued to probe, "I found it. " Barbara put down the probe and took up a type of long tweezers. With these, she was able to extract a bullet, dropping it into the steel bowl that Rachel held. She picked up the bullet in her gloved hand and examined it, "Jim, perhaps you should look at this. Bullet ID is not my strong suite." Jim walked over to her and she held up the bullet to him. "It looks like a .38 slug, in good condition," Jim quietly announced. He produced a small evidence pouch and held it open. Barbara dropped in the slug. Jim sealed the pouch. He stepped over to a nearby counter and identified the contents with the permanent ink marker he carried. He walked back over to Barbara, "Could you please initial this, Dr. Davis." As she complied, she quietly asked him to, "Please call me Barbara." Their eyes met for a moment, then Barbara went back to the skull. "His eyes are so kind," went through her mind. Probing carefully, she searched for another bullet."I've got another one," she exclaimed. Soon she dropped it into the bowl. Jim came over to take a look. It was badly smashed. Jim was still pleased, "It's not a problem, the first one will give us what we need. I need an evidence bag for this one." Barbara turned to her assistant, "Rachel, can you find an envelope for Lieutenant Bearpaw?" Rachel left the room, heading for her office. Barbara and Jim were facing each other over the bowl. Jim looked her in the eye, "Barbara, would you like to have dinner with me tonight?" Surprised, Barbara quickly recovered, "Why, yes, I would." "Could I pick you up at seven o'clock?" Jim asked, very pleased. Barbara thought for a moment, "Yes, seven would be good. Barbara smiled behind her mask. "Do you have my address?" "Barbara, I know were you live. Do you like your Aunt's house?" "I like that old house, Aunt Sarah has made it very homey." Jim did not need to see her smile, he saw it in her eyes. Rachel came noisily back into the room and handed the small plastic bag to Barbara. She placed the victim's clothes on the counter, near the exit. Barbara popped the bullet into the bag and handed it to Jim. The permanent ink pen came out again and the bag was identified. Barbara initialed it, and it went into Jim's pocket with the first bullet. "Dr. Davis, I need to run these bullets through Ballistics. If you find anything else in your autopsy, please contact me." "Yes, I will, Lieutenant Bearpaw," She answered in her official voice. Jim said goodbye to both women, and left, remembering to pickup the victims's clothes off the counter. He left his mask on the counter by the door. Rachel walked over and picked up the mask. She moved with that side to side waddle the very overweight use. She walked back with the mask and put it in the hamper. The remainder of the autopsy was routine, except that Barbara continued to smile behind her mask. Rachel noted that twice, Dr. Davis started softly humming.

Commander William Andrews, USNR stood in the shade of an old oak tree, looking splendid in his dress white uniform. As the senior military officer present, Bill was in charge. He watched as Master Sargent Russell Baker, USMCR directed the unloading of the Hearst. Russ did look impressive in his Marine Dress Blue "B" Uniform. He wore all of his ribbons, as did Bill. It was a gathering of old military men, Bill knew most of those present. All most every man here had served in one branch of the military or another. So had some of the women. Patriotism ran deep in this valley, so did the desire to 'get the Hell out'. "But most of them came back. Even me," Bill thought reflectively, "not a bad record for so remote a part of California." He looked at the assembled pall bearers: the buck Sargent Marine escort, two Marine reservists, one Army, one Navy, and one Air Force. Most of them knew the deceased, two were his good friends. That is how it was in a small community. Everyone knew everyone else, we are all related in some way. The parents of the deceased sat opposite the open grave, flanked by their parents. One frail white haired lady also sat in the first row, great-grandmother of the dead Marine. She had lost her Father in World War I, a brother in World War II, a son in Viet Nam, and now Rob was gone. What was going through her mind? Did she see it all as some great and noble sacrifice, or as some terrible curse? It was almost enough to make Bill weep. Then, the appearance of Jason Saunders' pale green Land Rover caught his attention. The vehicle stopped and the driver rushed to open the rear passenger door. A Marine Major General in Dress Blue "B" Uniform got out. He looked around at the Funeral Party, spotting Bill in his White Dress Uniform. Two stars gleamed on each shoulder as the General strode over to the oak tree. There were six rows of ribbons on his Jacket. Bill could not help but think, "This guy is a warrior." Bill snapped a sharp salute as the Marine stopped before him. "Commander Andrews," he said, reading Bill's name tag, "I am Major General Bernard Wycliff. My son was killed with the Marine you honor here today. I would be honored if I could be allowed to attend this service." "Sir," Bill quickly responded, "His family is at grave side, why don't we ask them?" The two walked over to Henry and Abby Johnson. Hank stood up for the introduction. Bill did the honors, "Hank, this is

General Wycliff. His son was killed with Rob. General Wycliff, this is Gunnery Sergeant Henry Johnson, USMCR, Retired." One old warrior to another, the General spoke, "Mr. Johnson, I would be honored if you would allow me to observe your son's service." Hank looked at his wife, she nodded yes. He then turned to the Marine Officer, "General Wycliff, we would be honored by your presence. He motioned towards an empty seat. Please sit with the family." He sat down next to the great-grandmother, and nodded his thanks to Bill. Bill moved to the Burial Detail, who was ready to lift the casket. The old woman turned and spoke to the General,"Did you know my great-grandson?" "No Ma'am," He replied, "My son, John, died with him." "How old was he?" the old woman asked. The General looked her in the eye, "He was twenty years old, Mam." "Rob was nineteen," she replied, returning his gaze, "Did they die in vain, General?" Staring straight ahead, at the Grave, he said softly,"Ma'am, I wish I knew." She reached out to his gloved hand and held it, in her small wrinkled one. Tears slowly ran down the General's cheeks. The six pall bearers hoisted the casket to their shoulders with something approaching military precision. They had managed a rehearsal earlier. Bill nodded to the American Legion drummer, and he began to tap out the beat. They did a good job of marching in step, carrying the deceased, Russ softly calling the cadence. When they held the casket over the grave, Russ called a halt. In unison, they lowered the casket onto the webbing over the open pit. Russ softly called the moves as they lower the casket, then released their grips and stood up. The command to "Second section, About Face" was given, the three facing the guests all turned in unison. "Left face" was spoken and all six men complied. "Forward March," Russ softly commanded, and they filed past the casket. As the pall bearers left, Rev Phelps took his place behind the casket, facing the guests. Mercifully, his talk was brief. His enthusiastic rant on sacrifice and patriotism was unneeded for the group before him. Most of the men in attendance had served some time in the military. Many had seen combat and suffered wounds. Most came back changed. This section of the cemetery was the resting place of those that had died for their country in a dozen foreign lands. Two were represented only by markers, their bodies were never recovered. Now some of the young women were joining up. Two had been wounded in Iraq. "It may make me a

106

chauvinist, but I would spare the women from experiencing this trauma," Bill thought, "Hell, I would protect everyone from the pain and trauma of war." Rev. Phelps finished his prayer and moved away from the casket. Bill signaled the young Bugler. Soon the mournful notes of 'Taps' filled the cemetery. The seven members of the Honor Guard filed into line along side the open grave. These seven veterans of wars past raised their 1903 bolt action Springfield rifles. Three times they loaded a blank cartridge into the chamber of their rifle, and three times they fired over the grave and over the heads of those attending. As Taps ended, Bill and Russ marched in from opposite sides and met in the center of the casket. Each grabbed one end of the flag laying on the casket and held it up, as the Honor Guard filed out of view. They proceeded to fold it according to protocol, ending with a triangular bundle, the stars showing. Bill took the folded flag, and each man took a small case from a pocket and placed it on the flag. One case held a Bronze Star Medal with V for Valor device. The other box held a Purple Heart. Bill turned around to face the guests. He moved to Abby Johnson, leaned down to her and held the flag and medals out to her, "On behalf of a grateful nation, please accept these tokens of your loved one." Weeping without shame, Abby took the bundle from Bill, placing it in her lap. Her hands ran over the two cases as if that might bring back her only child. Her husband put his arm around her, she hardly seemed to notice. Russ and Bill resumed their positions on either end of the assembled guests. The motorized devise started lowering the casket according to plan. As the casket lowered beyond ground level, Russ appeared with a chrome shovel. When the casket was fully lowered, four of the pall bearers removed the mechanism. Russ offered the shovel to Hank, then accompanied him to the earthen mound near the grave. Hank scooped up a shovelful of earth and poured it on his son's casket. Hank handed the shovel back to Russ. One by one, the other men lined up for their turn with the shovel. None of the women joined in this ritual, until Rob's cousin, Linda Johnson, stood up. Sgt Johnson, USAF, was determined to join this all male activity. Rob had been like a little brother to her, she was going to say her goodbye. Resplendent in her dark blue dress uniform, she quickly moved from her seat in the third row, and joined the line. Russ frowned when he saw it, but Bill found it hard not to admire her, "Good for you, Linda." Then April Tanner stood, tears streaming down her face. April was Rob's long time girlfriend. Assisted by her best friend, Asumpta, April made her ways over to the line. Little Asumpta was barely five feet tall, but determination showed on her face as she propelled her taller friend forward. The visage of these two young women was too much for the people in the line. One by one, they waved the pair forward until they were at the head of the line. Rob's grandfather, Ralph Johnson, handed the shovel to April. Almost blind from tears, Asumpta had to help her get a little dirt in the shovel and drop it into the grave. This scene was too much for the assembled group, the men just stood there, awed by the site of such profound grief. Most of the women broke into tears, but not Rob's great-grand-mother. She called to the pair, "Please come here. Bring April to me." Little Asumpta handed off the shovel and propelled her friend around the grave to the first row. She eased the grief-stricken girl into the chair next to the old lady, then sat down on April's other side. The distraught nine- teen year old was surrounded, age and experience in these matters on one side, youthful compassion on the other. Bill watched this small drama play out, and simply shook his head. His brain screamed out, "Why do we cause these people such pain? Why can't they live their life in peace?" Suddenly, General Wycliff spoke, "Well Commander, I need to get going." Bill snapped him a salute. He continued, "I need to get to Green Bay, Wisconsin for another funeral." Bill had to ask, "Funeral for the third Marine, Sir?" "Yes," The General replied, "then home." "Sir," Bill began, "I am sure your wife will appreciate that. Can I help you arrange transportation?" "Commander Andrews, my wife was taken five years ago by cancer. I do have another son, he is a Marine Captain. I also have two daughters, both married to Marines, and three grandchildren. I will not be alone. May I ask you a question?" "Sir, of course you may." "That insignia above your ribbons," The General indicated, "SEALS isn't it?" Bill smiled, "Yes, Sir. That is correct." The General was curious, "I notice that you have the Navy Cross, the Silver Star, and two awards of the Purple Heart. I also noticed that Master Sargent Baker, over there, holds the Silver Star, the Bronze Star, and the Purple Heart." "Sir, he was Marine Recon. Desert Storm, Grenada, and Iraq. Now, he is the Captain in the local Sheriff's Department." "Interesting, Commander. What is it that you do now?" "Sir, I am the Sheriff here," Bill replied, "after several years with

NCIS." The General looked at Bill with greater appreciation, "Commander, this is an interesting place. I will have to keep it in mind for my retirement." Bill was interested in that, "Sir, are you thinking of retiring?" The General's brow furrowed, "I am due for reassignment in six months, but if I say what I think about Iraq there may not be one." "Sir, one question." Bill inquired, noticing the SUV he was about to get into, "How long have you known Jason Saunders?" "But Commander, I never met Jason Saunders, until today. I know his brother Roy. We were roommates at Annapolis." With that he was gone. Bill returned to his duties. It was time to get the pall bearers and guests over to the American Legion Hall for the reception. But his heart was not in the reception right now. Bill needed to hold Jennifer in the worst way. He needed a dose of life after this morning with death. But that would have to wait. Duty called. At the American Legion Hall, the somber reception drug on. The bereaved couple were surrounded by friends and family. A couple of the older gentlemen took pity on the obviously uncomfortable Bill Andrews. One of them asked about his Navy Cross. When no details were forthcoming, he asked Bill if he had read yesterday's issue of the Sentinel? "No, I didn't get a chance. Why?" He was told of an article about the DEA raid, seems that the PR gal for the DEA had given an interview. She told about how Sheriff Andrews had spotted the illegal activity, then called the DEA. In the Hall office, he was able to obtain a copy of the paper. Anita had done a masterful job of telling the story, while undercutting everything the DA said. She mentioned the hostage rescue, but not who. Away from the mourners, Bill called Anita's cell, "This is Anita!" This is Bill Andrews. I just got a chance to read your article in the Sentinel." "How did you like it?" "Anita, you did a beautiful job of telling the truth about the Raid. Of course, that totally undercut our beloved DA. Well done!" "I am glad that you liked it, Bill. I'm on my way over to Sierra Vista. After my business with the County, maybe we can get together for coffee?" The idea of seeing Anita again, pleased him greatly, "How about dinner? I Just presided over the funeral of a local Marine. I could sure use the company" "Oh, Bill! I am so sorry to hear that. Did you know him?" "That is what made it so hard. I knew him, and his parents, I had to do the notification. Swing by the Office when you are free." "Will do, Bill!" She now had a concerned look, how quickly her smile faded.

In Court Room 1 of the Sierra Vista County Court House, (there were only two court rooms), the matter of The Nature Coalition vs A W Fairbanks et al was about to convene. One end of the Court Room was dominated by the raised Judge's bench. Facing it were two tables, one for the Plaintiff, one for the Defense. At the Plaintiff's Table were Jason Saunders, his attorney, Allen Brown, and Jennifer. Jason and Allen were deep in conversation. Jennifer wore a pale green Armani suit. Her short blonde hair looked beautiful, as usual. Her mind was drifting. Bill was all she thought about. She had two nights with him, she wanted more. More nights, more days, more time. She did not know it yet, but she was feeling the first urging of her 'biological clock'. For a healthy woman of 31, it was only natural.

The other table belonged to the defense. A W Fairbanks was in heated conversation with her attorney, Marvin Schiller. A W's voice was easily audible to everyone around her. "Nothing this old Fart says means a thing," she snarled. Marvin tried to quiet her, "Don't talk garbage. He is the Judge of the case against you. Whatever he says goes." "No one can tell me what to do with my own land," insisted A W, her voice rising. "It does not belong to just you," Marvin snarled in a loud whisper, "You have partners, remember?" "I'm in charge of this project," she shrieked, "I control everything!" "A W, lower you voice," Marvin warned, "the Bailiff is looking at you." Woodrow Graham was a large, black man and retired MP MSGT. He was Senior Bailiff and he ran a tight ship. He stared at the Defense Table, hoping that A W would cause a scene. When he first came here, to take a Bailiff job, he rented a house from A W. After a career in the Army, he thought he had run into sleazy landlords, but A W was the worst crook he had ever experienced. Now he hoped she would give him one more outburst, and he could eject the bitch from the Court. But wait! Better that she screwed up when Judge O'Reilly was here. "I'd love to get her on a Contempt charge," Woodrow thought with glee. The door behind the Bench opened and the Judge entered the Court Room. The movement caught Woodrow's attention, "All rise. The Superior Court of Sierra Vista County is now in session. The honorable Charles O'Reilly presiding." Everyone rose as the Judge took his seat at the Bench. Judge O'Reilly was a slight man in his early 60's. Most people mistook his affable manner for weakness. That was a large mistake. His concept of the

110

Law was solid and absolute. This Court was his and Justice would be dispensed here. He opened a folder and laid it on the Bench in front of him. He reached for the gavel, and twice rapped for order, "Please be seated. Court is in session." As the Court Room settled itself, the Judge studied the folder before him. As the noise died down, he spoke, "The matter before this Court is 'The Nature Coalition vs A W Fairbanks et al'. "Before we hear from our final witnesses, is there anything new that would be germane to this matter?" Allen Brown spoke, "Your Honor, the Plaintiff wishes to inform the Court of the death of one of our expert witnesses, Robert Moore. I have the Police Report, if it please your Honor, I would like to enter it into evidence." Judge O'Reilly was concerned, "Mr. Brown, do you have a Death Certificate?" "No, your Honor," Allen Brown answered, "The autopsy is being done today." "Please give the Police Report to the Court Clerk," said His Honor, but this matter concerned him. Allen walked over to the Clerk and handed the document to her. The Clerk stamped the page with an evidence number and initialed the stamp. The Clerk noticed that the Judge held out his hand for the document. She quickly stepped over to the Bench and handed it to him, then returned to her chair. Judge O'Reilly examined the Police Report for a few moments, then spoke, "Sheriff's Department found suspected gunshot wound to the head. You will keep me informed on this matter, Mr. Brown." "Of course, your Honor. I would like to remind your Honor that Mr Moore's report was unsigned at the time of his death. Will you rule on it's admissibility?" The Judge looked at Allen Brown, "I rule Mr. Moore's report is admissible as evidence in this matter." He rapped once, with the gavel. Allen, Jason, and Jennifer were very relieved and pleased by this judgement. On the other hand, A W was obviously outraged, "But the report is not signed. The man is dead! How can this moron accept the report?" Marvin Schiller leaned toward her and hissed, "Shut up! Do you want to be jailed for contempt?" Judge O'Reilly's voice seemed to fill the room, "Ms Fairbanks, one more moronic comment from you and you will find yourself jailed for contempt. Now shut up." A W glared at the Judge, but held her tongue. Marvin was relieved, but knew they were on thin ice. Judge O'Reilly had a widely know reputation for a ruthless insistence on respect of the Law and of the Court. Above all else, you did not disrespect the American flag or Judge Charles

O'Reilly. After a career in Military Justice, he had been appoint to this position. Retirement was approaching, but he would stay on the Bench and give 100% until that time came. Two witness for the Plaintiff were allowed to speak. When the last one was again seated behind Jason, the Judge picked up a page from the folder before him and read from it, "All testimony having been given, I am set to render a verdict in this case. In the matter of The Nature Coalition vs A W Fairbanks et al, having given the matter due consideration, I find for the Plaintiff. I hereby grant a Temporary Restraining Order against the group represented by A W Fairbanks. She is enjoined from making any changes to the property described in the Suit. This Temporary Order will last for 180 days, at which time it can be replaced by a Permanent Injunction against said proposed changes." "You senile old man," A W stood and screamed at the Judge, "you wouldn't know Justice if it pissed on your shoe." Marvin Schiller attempted to put his hand across her mouth. "Nobody's going to stop my project! I am in charge!" She ranted on. Her water glass shattered against the back wall, just missing the Judge. Chief Bailiff Graham headed toward the berserk woman. Judge O'Reilly pounded his gavel and called for order. Bailiff Graham grabbed A W from behind, his right hand went over her mouth, his left arm put a choke hold around her neck. A W grew limp and sank back into her chair. Wilson Graham instantly released his grip and let her go. He was an expert at this, having learned on drunk, often belligerent young soldiers. He checked to see that she was breathing okay. Her eye lids fluttered, then slowly opened. Seeing that she was awake, Judge O'Reilly banged his gavel and spoke, "A W Fairbanks, I find you in Contempt of Court. I sentence you to 30 days in jail." A W was fully awake now. "I have nothing but contempt for you and this Mickey Mouse Court," she howled. "Sixty days in Jail," said the Judge, with a bang of his gavel. "This is outrageous!" She yelled. The Judge cut her off, "Would you like to try for 120 days?" AW glared at him and sat down. "We plan on appealing this decision," yelled Marvin. Judge O'Reilly pointed the gavel at Bailiff Graham, "Take Ms Fairbanks into custody, then transport her to the County Jail to begin her 60 day sentence for Contempt. This court is adjourned." He banged the gavel twice. Chief Bailiff Graham leaned down and softy spoke to AW, "Please stand up." "Bullshit," was all she said and she grabbed the chair seat with both hands.

112

The other Bailiff on duty joined Woodrow, and they each grabbed one side of the chair. Still sitting, AW found herself being carried out of the Court Room, "Put me down, you Assholes! This is outrageous!" No one heard Woodrow Graham say to his fellow Bailiff, "Let's use the back door. There's a dumpster back there." AW yelled at them, but without much conviction, "You wouldn't dare!" At that point, the double doors of the exit closed behind them. Shortly afterwards, two Deputies that had been summoned by the Court Clerk, had to assist two Court Bailiffs extradite A W Fairbanks from the dumpster for the Jail Kitchen. It was a terrible 'accident'. "I'm going to sue everybody!" A W whaled. "I'm going to own you all! I'm going to own this whole county!" Woodrow Graham just sniffed, and said, "You stink, Ms Fairbanks, you really stink." Her screaming could be heard for blocks.

Sheriff Bill Andrews parked his SUV in front of the Del Norte Restaurant. He got out of the vehicle and ran around to the passenger side. He wore light gray slacks and a charcoal pinstripe sports coat. Anita was helped out, and they walked toward the Entrance. Anita took his arm, "The lamb better be as good as you described. I have never had Basque style cooking before." "You'll love it," Bill replied, confidently. Anita looked suspicious, "Gourmet tips from a man who eats goat entrails." "Only once," he said very matter of fact, they were quite good. Of course, we were drinking a lot of date wine." Anita hit him on his shoulder. As they entered the restaurant, Bill noticed the hostess tonight was Asumpta. Suddenly somber, he recalled April and Asumpta this morning, "How are you doing," "Hello, Sheriff Andrews," she replied with a weak smile, "I am all right." Her speech was flavored with the soft accent of her native Spain. "April is with the Johnson family. It is all so sad." Bill put his hand on the girl's shoulder, "You were a great help to your friend, today. I am glad you were there." She seemed to shrink a little, "Thank you, you are so kind." "Asumpta," Bill changed the subject, "This is Anita Brubaker, PR person for the DEA. Anita, Asumpta is the daughter of the owners of this restaurant and the Bed & Breakfast next door. She just finished her first year at UC Berkeley." Anita stepped forward and offered her hand, "I am so glad to meet you. You were very brave today." She smiled and shook hands with the petit Brunette. "April has been my friend since my family came here," Asumpta replied, modestly, "My friend needed my help." "And you did a good job. Now Rob's family will help her, and her own parents," Bill said. Asumpta looked better, she gestured toward the seating area, "Let me show you to your table." Bill chose a table in a dark corner of the room. There were only a few other couples in the room. After they had sat down, Anita looked suspiciously at Bill, "And just what do you have in mind with this table, Mr. Andrews." Bill was bemused by her question, "I always sit where I can see the whole room." "Oh,"Anita responded, confused, "I thought you might want to kiss me." He took her hand in his and brought it to his lips, "That too. She leaned toward him and they kissed. A young redheaded waitress came and filled their water glasses. As Bill drank from his glass, he noticed Jim Bearpaw and Dr. Barbara Davis being shown to their table. He squeezed Anita's hand and nodded toward the new arrivals. "How long have they been dating?" Anita whispered. Bill whispered back, "I think that this is their first." The two held hands and watched Jim and Barbara. Barbara was admiring the room, "The decor is so authentic, it is as if you were eating in Spain. Do you come here often." Jim shook his head, "Bill Andrews brought me here once." "Did you order the Lamb?" Barbara asked. "No, I ordered beef. I grew up on Government surplus mutton. But don't let that stop you, Bill loved his Lamb." And so she did, Barbara ordered the Lamb and Jim a steak. They took Asumpta's recommen- dation and had a Spanish Rioja wine with their meal. The food was good, and conversation flowed naturally. Over coffee, Barbara told Jim about growing up in upstate New York, near a Mohawk commu- nity. She went to Cornell for her education, undergraduate through Med school. She had met her husband as a Resident at John Hopkins, "I was very flattered by his attention. He was Chief Resident, I was two years behind. When I finished my residency, I joined him in his New York City practice. The Practice was busy and I thought that everything was going well. Then the State Medical Board started investigating him, charges of negligence, kickbacks, fraud. I believed his claims of innocence. Then I caught him cheating with our Receptionist. What a fool I was. I was lucky to escape criminal charges. After the divorce, I hardly had a bean to my name. My Aunt Sarah asked me to come here and help her with her practice. My Ex is serving time in prison for his crimes. I get to spend my time in this beautiful area." Jim told her of growing up on the Reservation. He went to High School here in

114

town. "I discovered sports," he explained, "Football, Basketball, and Track." Then he joined the Army. "I tried out for the Rangers after Airborne School," Jim went on, "It was like sports, we were very competitive." He made it through Ranger School, shortly afterwards came Desert Storm. "We raced across the desert until we ran into Iraqi units," Jim paused, "I don't think you are interested in the battles we fought. They were all one sided. We lived and they died." Barbara tilted her head slightly to one side, "I don't think that you liked the war. There was no challenge for you." "I never felt threatened," Jim replied, "We had better equipment and training. Our moral was so superior to the Iraqis." He told her how an assignment to Bosnia came after Iraq, "That was different than Desert Storm. There were threats there, artillery, booby traps, and snipers. I trained as a Sniper there." Barbara was interested in this, "Did you do any sniping in Bosnia?" "In Sarajevo, we fought their snipers. They were killing civilians, so we killed them. Then they tried to kill us, so we tried harder to kill them. Finally, the UN worked out a truce." "How long were you there?" Barbara asked. "One year," he replied, "but things improved after the first 6 months. Air strikes made them stop shelling us, and we killed most of their snipers. I finished my enlistment the following year and transferred to the Reserves. I decided to get an education with my Army benefits, so I was admitted to San Jose State University." Barbara wanted to know, "Why San Jose State?" Jim smiled, "I was in the Army with a soldier from San Jose, he told me all about the School and the area. San Jose State was cheap and had a good reputation. We enrolled together, and rented an apartment near the campus. I chose a dual major, Sociology and Criminology, plus Army ROTC. That got me a Lieutenant's commission in the Reserves. It took me four and a half years to graduate, but I got through it. Then I came back here and joined the Sheriff's Department." Barbara smiled at Jim, "You have made rapid progress, you are now the Lieutenant of the Sheriff's Department, the number three man in the Department." Now Jim smiled wryly, "You seem to know a lot about this Department, are you a Groupie?" Barbara was a bit embarrassed about having been caught out, "My Father was Police Chief of Ithaca, New York. I am naturally curious about Law Enforcement wherever I live." Jim chose to pretend to believe this tale, "On behalf of our Department, I thank you for your interest. Perhaps you would like to ride on patrol with me sometime?" Her dignity somewhat restored, Barbara rose to the challenge, "I would like that. Perhaps some weekend?" "I think that can be arranged, as it hap- pens, I am on duty this weekend," Jim replied warmly. "It would mean starting out at 8 am tomorrow." "Not a problem, Doctors are used to rising early," She replied easily. A smiling Jim suggested that they leave, "We both have to work tomorrow." And so he settled the bill and they left the Restaurant. As they walked along toward Barbara's residence, Barbara took Jim's arm. The night was cool, as nights usually were in the Cascades. As they neared her home, they stopped. Jim kissed Barbara. She let him, but she was tentative, somewhat cool in her response. "What is it, Barbara," he softly asked, "Is it what I did in Bosnia? Because I was a Sniper?" She was reticent to reply, it was hard for her to put in words, "I don't know, perhaps. I have dedicated my life to saving life, now you tell me you took lives. It is something I have to think about." They walked on. They soon reached her home, and Jim said his goodbyes, "This is not the first time that the past has come up. It has cost me relationships before." As he turned to leave, Barbara spoke, "I had a nice time tonight, and I would like to see you tomorrow." Jim was pleased, "8 am it is."

Bill let Anita into the Entry Hall. When he switched on the lights, she was amazed, "This is something out of a magazine!" "My Grandfather had this house built to his own design. Here, let me show you to your room. The bedrooms are upstairs." Anita noticed Susie, she sat with one paw out. "What a cute little dog!" She leaned down and shook the paw. Susie's tail wagged furious-ly. "Anita, I think you just made a friend. Her name is Susie, a very spoiled little creature." Anita knelt down, so she and Susie could get to know each other. She looked up at Bill, "Are you sure you don't mind putting me up?" He shook his head, "I think it's better than you driving home, alone. And I don't recommend your plan to stay at the Pinecrest Inn. The Off Road Club is staying there. We have had several incidences, drink and noise, mainly. It is not the place for a young woman alone to stay. I'll put you up in the Guest Room." He took her bag upstairs. Anita nosed around, looking at the Den. She found the Bathroom, and used it. When she emerged, Bill was waiting for her. He took her by the hand, guiding her on a tour of the house. He was showing her the Kitchen, describing how his Mother and Sister worked in here.

116

There was a quiet moment, they were face to face. Then, they embraced and kissed. They held each other. "I've so glad that you called me. Bill. I've been thing about you." "Anita, I hated to see you leave, the other evening." They kissed again, and again. Later, it was agreed that Bill would secure the house, Anita would prepare for bed. When he arrived upstairs, her door was shut. Bill put on his pajamas and brushed his teeth. He heard Anita in the guest Bath. When he checked, her door was closed, "Goodnight!" "Goodnight!" Her voice echoed, from behind the door. He crawled into bed, switching off the light. He lay there, going over his day. Naturally, he concentrated more on the portion with Anita in it. Then, his door quietly opened, he heard bare feet on his carpet. He knew that someone was by his bed. "If you think that we are just going to leave it like this, you are very wrong!" Bill threw back the covers for her, "Anita, get in here!" She removed her nightgown, and complied. Bill found her a good lover. She was fit and toned. She found him everything she hoped for. Whatever their day had been, their night was wonderful! Jennifer never called Bill, on the one day he really need it. He had found out about the Court events from one of the Bailiffs. He guessed Jennifer was busy celebrating.

Jennifer had told herself, "Just a few minutes at the Party, then I call Bill." The Nature Coalition office did look nice, all streamers and banners. The entire Staff was euphoric! Jennifer drank several toasts, the champaign flowed. She did forget that alcohol did not mix well with her Meds. Then there was the tall, blond Swen Hyerdahl, their Environmental Expert. He paid a great deal of attention to her. She took Swen on a tour of the house, ending in her room. He had her out of her Armani in short order. She did, however, remember to install her diaphragm. Swen had to help her with it. Swen never did make it to his room that night. Swen knew she was drunk, he had no idea about her medication. Only her Father knew about her problem.

Chapter Nine

Saturday:

Barbara was ready when Jim knock on the door. She wore jeans and a nice short sleeve blouse, over it she wore a jeans jacket. Her shoulder length brown hair was down. It was a good look for her. "Right on time," she smiled when she greeted him. "So are you," he smiled back. He helped her into the light green Jeep Commander. He put her medical bag behind her, on the floor. "This smells new," Barbara said. Jim looked proudly around the interior as he fastened his safety harness, "It is. We just got it in from Redding. The Dealer did some mods on it for us." Barbara nodded and looked around the vehicle. Jim grabbed the radio Mic. from the dash, "Dispatch, this is Unit Three. Beginning Patrol." "Unit Three, this is Dispatch. Understand starting Patrol." Off they went, Jim explained that they would be taking a tour of most of the County, "Our Patrol will be a large rectangle." As he drove, Jim told her about the history of the area. "Various Native American tribes wandered through this valley. They were all nomadic hunters. Then my people came here from Nevada, and sat up permanent villages. They're excavating one of the main villages right now," Jim gestured to the site. "Are they using that construction equipment for the village excavation?" Barbara asked. "No, that was intended for a Condo development and a Mall," Jim smiled slightly, "but a Court Injunction to stop it was granted yesterday." Barbara stared at the site, "I hate to think of this land paved over for condos and parking lots." "There is a temporary order now," he spoke with great feeling, "in six months it could be permanent. We can uncover the ancient village. Maybe we will be able to build a museum on the Reservation." Barbara turned toward Jim, "I hope that works out. Where is the Reservation?" Jim smiled, "We just entered it." She nodded and looked around at the forest, with the Cascades looming ahead. She saw small houses scattered off the road, interspersed with mobile homes. Some where well kept, others were not. Suddenly, she saw a larger house across a small lake. It was larger and grander than anything she had seen so far, "Who lives there?" Jim glanced at her, "I do. It is not completed inside. I've only finished four room." Barbara was envious, "I'll bet it has a gorgeous view." "It does, and it keeps changing, season by season," Jim explained, "In winter, it is so beautiful when it snows." They drove on about a mile, then Jim signaled and turned off the road. They were on a long gravel driveway. "I have to stop off here for a minute. This is the home of my Sister." A modest frame house came into view. As they drove into the yard of the house, Barbara saw three children playing. One was about five, one about seven or eight, and the eldest about eleven. All of the kids yelled "Uncle Jim!" as the couple got out of the SUV. The five year old little girl ran toward Jim with arms extended, "Uncle Jimmy!" she yelled with glee. He scooped her up and held her above his head, she giggled with joy and excitement. He lowered her to his chest and hugged her, "How is my little skunk?" "I am not a skunk!" She indignantly exclaimed. "A racoon?" he asked. "No, I am Christina!" She replied with great dignity. Jim turned to a smiling Barbara, "This noisy little creature is my niece, Christina. Christina, this lovely lady is Dr. Barbara Davis." Barbara saw the little smiling face, the jet black hair, the big brown eye, the high cheek bones, "I am very happy to meet you Christina. How old are you?" The little girl held up her hand, with the five fingers spread out, "I'm gonna be five years old next Tuesday!" "This big guy over here is my nephew George," he said, nodding to the eleven year old. "Hello George," Barbara said looking at the wary boy, "How are you?" George kept his distance, "Are you really a Doctor?" She nodded, "Yes, George, I really am a Doctor." "This shy guy over here," Jim pointed to the eight year old, "Is my nephew, Michael." "Hi Michael," she said, "How are you." "I'm okay. I don't like Doctors," He spoke, barely making eye contact with her. Barbara's smile got bigger, "Neither did I, when I was your age." He looked at her, "Really?" "You bet," she replied. The front door opened, and a pretty young woman of about thirty came out. She was dressed like Barbara, a blouse and jeans. Her long black hair was in pigtails. Barbara thought, "If she lost about twenty pounds, she'd be gorgeous. The woman did not say anything, just walked rapidly over to Jim, who had put down Christina. She hugged Jim, and let him kiss her on the cheek. With

120

one arm around each other, Jim turned to Barbara, "This is my sister, Anna Redhawk. Ann, this is Dr. Barbara Davis." Anna looked at her with great interest, "I'm glad to meet you. Are you working with Dr. Sarah Davis?" "Yes I am. She is my Aunt. I am glad to meet you." Jim then spoke to Barbara, "Could you excuse us for a minute, Barbara?" Barbara nodded okay, and Jim walked his Sister back toward the front door. "When did you hook up with her?" Anna inquired of her Brother. Jim looked a bit awkward as he grabbed for his wallet, "We just started dating. She is the County Coroner. I work with her." Barbara saw Jim get out his wallet and get a piece of paper out of it. He handed it to Anna, and she unfolded it and read it. She then gave him a kiss on the cheek and happily started to go in the house. She stopped and called to Barbara, "I'm happy to meet you. Goodbye." Barbara waved, and Anna was gone. Jim was walking back toward her, "We better get going." Barbara waved to the three children, "Goodbye, kids. I'm glad to have met you." The three waved back at her, the two boys tentatively, little Christina, with great enthusiasm. Jim started to explain as they drove down the driveway, "Anna follows the tradition of our family. All of the women are maker of traditional beaded baskets. I needed to drop off the latest check for the sale of her baskets. There is a crafts store in town that handles most of our native products. It was meant for the Tourists, but we found that there are also Collectors who come to shop. Anna needed that check, her husband found work in Susanville, but there isn't much left to send home." They turned back onto County Route one. Thinking of the long driveway to Anna's, Barbara wondered about how big was her lot, "How much land does your Sister and her husband own?" Jim got a very patient look on his face, "Barbara, no one owns a lot here. All of us in the Tribe own the whole Reservation, communally. The Federal Government won't let us sell any of our land. Even this County Road One is leased to the County, they can't buy the right of way. We apply to use a certain size area for ninety-nine years. I have ten acres around my house." "I noticed the small lake in front of your house," Barbara recalled, "Is that part of your lease." "Yes, it is part of my Use Permit," Jim answered, "not a lease." Barbara looked out of the window, "It seems so peaceful here. Is there really a need to patrol this area?" "A few years ago," Bill responded," I would have agreed with you. But after they shut down the Lumber Mill, unemployment went up to 35%. Crime shot up. Most of it is small time, but there is an increase in robbery, domestic violence, and theft. My people are hurting. More of our young people are joining the Military, and some are getting injured in Iraq. I wish we could patrol on the Reservation, but this is Federal Land. The FBI, the DEA, and the ATF have jurisdiction here. The Sheriff's Department has the right to pursue a suspect into the Reservation, or to serve warrants here for crimes in the County, but we can't patrol in the Reservation. We are simply driving on this County Road to another part of the County." Barbara was confused by this revelation, "How are crimes in the Reservation handled?" Jim sympathized with her, it was confusing if you had not grown up with the system, "Minor crimes are handled by the Tribal Council, serious crime get investigated by the FBI." "You mean, the FBI comes hundreds of miles to handle cases that your department could handle?" Barbara was incensed by the waste. "That is correct," Jim admitted, "But Sheriff Andrews and I are trying to change all that. We are negotiating a Joint Powers Agreement between The Tribal Council, the FBI, and the County." Barbara snorted, "If the Federal Government has to approve it, you'll have a long wait." Jim knew she was probably right. "Over to our left," Jim pointed, "Is the Tribal Council House. The Council Chamber is on the ground floor, the offices are upstairs." She saw a gas station, a small grocery, and a tiny video shop, clustered around the Tribal Building. "I bet this is all there is for this Tribe," Barbara thought. Jim seemed to read her mind, "There is a gas station and 7-11 at the northern end of the Reservation. Most of us shop in town. You have to travel to Susanville, or Redding to find a Wal-Mart or department store." Barbara suddenly felt very isolated. In New York City, she had so many choices for her shopping. "Well," she thought, "there is always the Internet." "Dispatch to Unit Three," the radio blared, "Dispatch to Unit Three." Jim grabbed the Mic, "Unit Three to Dispatch, over." "Dispatch to Unit Three, proceed to Old Mine Road. Wrecker crew found buried corpse. Over." "Unit Three to Dispatch, ETA to Old Mine Road, ten minutes. Out." Barbara was all business, "I wonder who got buried out there? Anyone missing in the area?" Their speed picked up, Jim flipped on the lights and siren. Down the two lane road they tore, there were only a few other cars on the road, all got out of the way. Barbara felt such a rush, the trees were flying by. "They look like a

122

picket fence," she thought. Nine minutes after getting the call, their SUV turned onto Old Mine Road. They could see the heavy duty Kenworth wrecker of Tiny Pearson & Son backed up to the gully where Bob Moore's SUV lay. Tiny stood toward the rear of the truck with his arms folded, all 300 lbs of him. His son Paul was in the truck cab with the radio on. "This is going to be fun," Jim said, half to himself. Barbara wondered what he meant. "Okay Tiny, where is the corpse?" He asked as he got out of the SUV. Barbara got out and retrieved her bag from the back seat. A big smile spread across Tiny's face, "Well, if it ain't Tonto! I thought I was gonna meet this famous Sheriff that was with the SEALs." Jim stood about three feet from the 6' 4" behemoth, "Sheriff Andrews isn't on duty today, I am. So where is the body?" Tiny's attention was taken by the form of Barbara Davis, "Hey Tonto, who's the babe?" Barbara snapped out an answer, "I'm Dr. Davis, the County Coroner, you fat slob." Tiny smiled real big, "You're not from around here, are ya?" "No, I'm not. I'm from New York, where we don't tolerate people obstructing police. Your red face says that your blood pressure is probably too high. You are pushing hard for a stroke." Tiny looked at Jim, a puzzled expression on this face. Jim smiled at Tiny, "She's not like the locals, is she? Why don't you show us the body, so we can do our work." Paul caught a glimpse of Barbara and decided to kill the radio and join his Dad. Tiny walked over to the gully edge and pointed beyond the now upright SUV, "Down there, where the vehicle was. I saw some bones sticking out of the soil when we rolled it over." Jim went back to the Jeep and got out a coil of rope and two repelling rigs. He tossed the rope to Tiny, "Tie that off on your truck." Tiny complied, as Jim put one belt around Barbara's waist. Paul viewed that with great envy. He was a thinner version of his father. Tiny saw his son's expression, "Boy, that is a woman!" "She sure is," Jim whispered into Barbara's ear. Try as she might to frown at this chauvinistic display, she smiled slightly as she put on a pair of gloves. Jim put on his belt and escorted Barbara over to the truck. "She's going down there?" Tiny seemed skeptical. "You're damn right I am!" She said, looking Tiny in the eye. Jim grabbed the rope and headed down. When he reached the bottom, he signaled Barbara to toss down her bag. She shook her head and hooked the bag to her climbing belt. Then down she came on the rope. Jim lead her around the front of the mangled

SUV, now sitting on its wheels. On the other side, they found that the earth had been disturbed by the impact and removal of the vehicle. Reddish-brown arm and hand bones stuck out of the soil. Barbara undid the clips holding her bag and knelt beside the grave. She examined the exposed bones, "Jim, we will need to uncover the rest of the skeleton. A shovel would be useful." "Tiny should have one on the truck," Jim replied. "Hey Tiny, can we use your shovel?" He yelled up to the watching pair. "Sure thing, Tonto," Tiny yelled back, as he directed Paul to the truck's stowage compartment. Paul got the shovel out and started to throw it down to Jim. Jim had to stop him and directed him to slide the shovel down the slope. Shovel in hand, Jim walked back over to Barbara. She looked up at him, "That kid is not the sharpest tack in the pack, is he?" Jim looked down at her and shook his head, "You mean the pride of Alturas? He's just a chip off the old block." She smiled at the comment, then asked Jim to, "uncover the head, if you can." Without speaking, Jim started gently digging where the head should be. Reddish-brown bone peeked out of the soil, so he dropped the shovel and dug by hand. Soon a skull lay exposed. Jim went on to uncover the shoulders and Barbara worked on the ribs with a small trowel. She spoke to Jim with real interest in this skeleton, "Why don't you work on the legs, I can finish here." Jim used the shovel to scrape away the soil over the leg bones. A few minutes of work by the pair exposed a complete skeleton. Barbara put down her trowel and got out a small tape measure. Unreeling two feet of the tape, Barbara handed the tip to Jim, "Hook this on one of it's feet. Let's get a length measurement." When the tape was drawn tight, she called out, "Five foot three." Jim released the tape and Barbara rolled it back up. She held the tape in one hand and looked at Jim, "This appears to be a small male, possibly Indian or Asian. There are remnants of black cloth on the skeleton. This appears to be an old burial, it is hard to tell how old." Jim thought for a moment, "They used Chinese labor in these old mines in the 1870s and 1880's. They often wore black cotton clothes. There were some labor disputes between the mine owners and the Chinese." Barbara looked disturbed, "Do you think a mine owner killed his Chinese miners?" "Maybe some of them," was his response. "Sometimes they would kill the ring leaders in a dispute." "Jim, this is outside of my expertise. We need a forensic anthropologist to examine this site. There may be more remains

124

here." "Barbara, I know who could do this. Jason Saunders' Daughter is the anthropologist at the Indian Village excavation. She's working on the old graveyard currently." Barbara took that in, then she asked, "How can we reach her? I don't know how she can be paid. I will have to ask the County Board for funding." Her brow furrowed with concern. Jim smiled and said, "Don't worry about payment right now, Jennifer Saunders has a trust fund, she is sole heir to her father's Billion dollar fortune. And as for contacting her, I believe that Sheriff Andrews can help us." "Does he know where she is?" Barbara inquired. Jim tried to think of how to delicately put it, then remembered Barbara's New York back ground, "Bill Andrews and Jennifer Saunders have started sleeping together recently. She is probably at Bill's place." Barbara smiled at Jim's blurting it out, "I am not shocked by that little revelation." Looking at Jim, she thought how good that activity sounded. She tried to stifle that thought, but certain images popped into her mind. Recovering, Barbara thought that Jennifer Saunders sounded like a good idea, "Why don't you call the Sheriff. See if he can reach Jennifer." Jim looked somewhat stricken, "No Cell service here, I need to get to my radio."

Jim was wrong about Sheriff Bill Andrews, he did not know where Jennifer was. He was sitting at the table in his Kitchen, drinking coffee and holding hands with Anita. "I grew up on several Army Bases. We were living at Fort Meade, when I got a scholarship to Georgetown," She continued, "That was where I met my husband." Bill squeezed her hand, "You don't have to talk about him." She smiled, slightly, "No, I don't mind. Wayne was a jock, I suppose I was flattered that he was interested in me." "That tells me that he had good taste," he said, smiling. She smiled back, "But he was unfaithful to me, and every other woman he slept with. I don't think he really wanted to be married, he was after the conquest." Bill frowned, "There are a lot of men like that. None of them seem to be very happy. Always juggling women, lying and sneaking around." "I was working for a Lobbying outfit, when Mom got sick. She and Dad had retired to Susanville, they were both raised there. Her Cancer was bad, Dad had a small heart attack, so my visit turned into my living there and taking care of them. Mom died last year, but Dad is fit again. Now, I work part time for the DEA, and, as of yesterday, I am the PR person for this County." Bill was pleased, "Then you will be spending more time in this area?" She smiled back at him, "Looks that way!" He leaned over and kissed her. Susie, who had been sleeping by Bill's chair, suddenly became alert and sat up. She listened for a moment, then tore off towards the Entry Hall. Noticing Susie, Bill remarked, "Someone must be coming. We may have a visitor." About that time, the Front Door chimes rang. Reluctantly, Bill released Anita's hand and went to the Front Door. He was wearing slippers with his slacks and shirt. Looking through the Security Peephole, he was surprised to see Jason Saunders standing there. As he opened the door, he had sudden visions of Jason angry over the betrayal of his daughter. "Good Morning," Bill said. Jason broke into a big smile, "And a good morning to you, Bill." Jason strode into the Hallway, at Bill's invitation. "To what do I owe this visit," Bill inquired. "I wanted to let you know about the information I have been receiving," Jason gushed. "We're in the Kitchen," Bill gestured, "Would you like some coffee?" "No thanks," he answered as he followed Bill out of the Entry. Anita stood when she saw the visitor. Fortunately, she was dressed, in jeans and a blouse. Bill introduced her as the Public Relations person both the DEA, and the County. Jason smiled at the young woman, "Attractive and accomplished, I recognize your name from a recent article." She smiled, "That seems to be my current claim to fame. I have read may articles about you. I don't recall ever hearing of an interview you have given." Now he smiled, "That is true, until now, I never have." Bill picked up on that, "Does that mean that you have granted an interview?" "Yes, I have granted one to NBC. Winning the Injunction is a big deal for the Nature Coalition. I want to talk about out victory, and our plans." "I look forward to watching it," Bill was genuine in his interest, "do you know when it will be aired?" "Not yet. I will keep you informed. The reason that I stopped by this morning, Bill, is to tell you of my discoveries from the State of Delaware. Is it appropriate for both of you to hear about what I have discovered?" Bill nodded. Jason continued, "Delaware tells me that the Sierra Development Corporation is a wholly owned subsidiary of The Washo Mining Corporation, a Nevada Corporation. Nevada tells me that company is a wholly owned subsidiary of The Lassen Land Corporation, a California Corporation." "Don't keep us in suspense, who is the Lassen Land Corporation?" Bill urged. Jason smiled, "You will love this! The President of The Lassen Land

126

Corporation is Linda Littlewolf of the Washo tribe." Now Bill smiled, "She's Johnny Eagle's wife, and she works for A W Fairbank. Both Jason and Anita looked concerned by this news. "I have more information," Jason injected, "as I mentioned, Johnny has apparently been spreading money around Sacramento, trying to get an Indian Casino for the Washo Tribe." "Jason, how much money has he put out in bribes?" Bill inquired. Jason was quick to respond, "About $50K each to our local State Assemblyman and State Senator. Perhaps another $150K to other State officials who could be of help to him." "Where is he getting all this money?" Anita wanted to know. "Where indeed?," Bill remarked, "He spent $250K in Sacramento, I believe he financed the Pot field we found the other day, and he spent tens of thousands to support AW's project through the Sierra Development Corp. Setting up these dummy corporations can't be cheap. Where is all the money coming from?" Jason obviously relished this hunt for facts, "I won't be able to do much until Monday, but leave it to me. I will uncover his finances." Bill touched Jason on the shoulder, "I do appreciate what you're doing. It would be so difficult for me to do this through official channels, and very slow. Jason beamed, "I'm doing this for my Group as well. We need to stop all this development in the area. It's all uncontrolled, so illadvised ." Bill's Cell phone rang, interrupting the conversation, "Hello, Sheriff Andrews." "Sheriff, this is Dispatch. Lieutenant Bearpaw is out at Old Mine Rd. They found a skeleton under Bob Moore's SUV." "I understand. How many?" "Just one, but they think there may be more. It might be an oriental male. They think Ms Saunders needs to look at it." "I see. Yes, tell him I will be in contact with him shortly. I will see that someone contacts Ms. Saunders to see if she wishes to assist." "I'll tell Lieutenant Bearpaw, Sheriff. 'Bye." Jason was all ears, "What about Jennifer? What have they found?" Bill looked at him a moment, making his plans, then spoke, "Jim found a skeleton buried under Bob Moore's SUV. Barbara Davis thinks its an old burial of an oriental male. She is requesting your Daughter's presence at the site, if she's willing." Jason smiled hugely, "I am sure she will go. This sounds interesting." "Will you inform her?" Bill asked. Jason nodded, "Of course, I will drive her there, it will probably be safer. I will also notify Professor Saint Clair about the finding." Jason bade them goodbye, then headed out the front door. On his way home, he wondered about Bill and

Anita. "Just the meeting of two professionals?" He was concerned, did Bill know about Jennifer's bed partner last night?

Bill excused himself, and went upstairs. He picked up his radio set, switching it on. "Dispatch, this is Sheriff Andrews." "Yes, Sheriff, go ahead." "Dispatch, have Unit Three switch to Channel Two. I will be waiting." "Yes, Sir! Will do!" It was only two minutes later, that his radio crackled, "Hello, Bill!" He was quick to reply, "Hello, Jim! Jason Saunders is on his way home to tell Jennifer. He plans on driving her out to you." "I thought you might bring her out." "No, Jim. I will be out tomorrow, so you can cover Road Patrols. Okay for you?" "Fine, Bill. Sounds like a plan. Out!" Bill switched off his radio. "Why would he think that you would bring Jennifer Saunders out?" Anita was standing in the doorway. Bill turned to her, "Because we were seeing each other. I met her the same day I met you. She injected herself into my investigation, and my life. She's just visiting here, but seems to be trying for a relationship with me." She seemed cool, "And you don't share her interest?" "Anita, I'm with the woman I am interested in. Jennifer is a typical rich girl, it is all about what she wants. I gather from her Father, that she has problems with men. I have a good idea why." "Then, I take it that you that you will not be seeing her any more, socially." "No, Anita. My relations with her will be purely professional. On the other hand, I wish to see a great deal of you, both literally and figuratively." She got a wry smile, at that, "It just so happens, Sheriff Andrews, that I feel the same way about you. By the way, I recently broke up with a DEA Agent. I guess we're even." Bill smiled as he crossed to her, they embraced and kissed. "So much for our recent pasts," Bill said, then they shook hands on it.

Jason tried to keep within the speed limits as he drove them to Old Mine Road. For that reason, along with Jennifer urging him to go faster, they arrived about forty minutes after getting the call. They saw Jim's SUV parked near the gully, Jim was standing next to it. The front passenger door was open, someone was sitting there. Tiny was securing Bob Moore's SUV to a dolly as they pulled up. Jason saw that, "At least the vehicle is out of the way." Jennifer noticed Barbara, "I see Barbara Davis is sitting in Jim's car. Looks like they came out here together. That is interesting." The pair got out of the SUV and walked over to Jim."What are you trying to do, Jim?" Jason said, straight faced. "Drum up more

128

business for your Department?" Jim played along, "Right, I figured two killings would be better than one." He saw Barbara walking up beside Jim, "Dr. Davis, I assume that you have already examined the remains." "That is correct, Mr Saunders," she answered. Jason did the honors, "Dr. Davis, this is Jennifer, my Daughter, and a physical anthropologist from the Getty Museum. Jennifer, this is Dr. Barbara Davis, County Coroner." The five foot eight Brunette shook hands with the five foot eleven Blonde, each was curious about the other. Their attention was soon drawn to a gray State of California van that had just turned onto Old Mine Road. Dr. Bernadette St Clair waved from the front passenger seat. The van stopped next to Jim's SUV, Bernadette jumped out and came around to Jennifer. "What do you have? How many skeletons? How old are they? She eagerly asked. Jennifer looked exasperated, "Calm down! I just got here myself. Barbara, this is Doctor Bernadette Saint Clair, State Archeologist. Bernadette, this is Doctor Barbara Davis, County Coroner." Bernadette step over to Barbara and shook hands, "I am so glad to meet you Doctor Davis." Jennifer thought she saw Bernadette grow visibly taller as she pulled herself up to her full five foot three. Barbara shook her hand, "I have heard so much about you, Doctor Saint Clair." A blast from Tiny's truck horn startled everyone. Tiny waved as he pulled out, towing Bob Moore's SUV, the rear end on the dolly. That made Jennifer's head hurt. She was a bit hung over. Bernadette asked Barbara, "Where is the grave?" Barbara responded, "There is one skeleton down in the gully." Barbara gestured to the rope now tied to the front bumper of the SUV. "Do you have a climbing belt? Bernadette asked. Barbara started toward Jim's vehicle, "Just a minute, I'll get one for you." She took Jennifer with her, "Are you sure Bernadette is up to this?" "Relax," Jennifer said, "she can outwork a twenty-two year old grad student. She has done several projects in the Sierras." Barbara got the belt from the car and handed it to Bernadette. She quickly put it on. Jennifer was still searching in the back of the SUV for a belt to use. She was joined by Jason, "Have you ever repelled before?" She started to put on the belt that she found, "No, but you are going to show me, aren't you?" He smile at her brazen move, "I wonder what you would have done if I said no?" As she walked past him she kiss his cheek, "When have you ever said no to me?" Jason followed her to the rope. Bernadette was already at the bottom, unhooking the rope from her belt. When she was free and stepped away from the rope, Jason hooked up and backed over the gully edge. Jennifer then hooked up, under his watchful eye, and backed over the edge until she rested against him, "Here we go, Little One!" They started backing down the slope. She saw that Jim and Barbara were watching them. So were Jeff and the other students that came in the van. They repelled down the slope and both unhooked. Jennifer walked over to Bernadette, "That's okay, Jennifer, I wish my Dad had shown me." Somewhat embarrassed, Jennifer led the way to the skeleton. Seeing the bones, Jennifer was immediately on her knees, examining them. Shortly, they were joined by Barbara. "I don't know if this is a Chinese male or not," Jennifer announced, "but he is Mongoloid. Could be Native American, even Eskimo." Barbara was not perturbed by this news, "The black clothing he was wearing seemed to say Chinese, according to Lieutenant Bearpaw." "Jim is good amateur archeologist, and he does know the history of this area," Bernadette injected. Jennifer was not pleased by this, "That is good as far as it goes, but I prefer more facts. We need to take a sample of the cloth and have it examined. Same for the bones. Bernadette, what can you do about it?" Bernadette thought for a moment, "I could get the State Crime Lab in Redding to look at them, but UC Berkeley will take weeks, if not months, for a more detailed analysis." "As Coroner, I could help push that," added Barbara. "Okay," Jennifer said, "I think I could get the Getty to examine the item before that. We need to know about the age of the cloth quickly." "We could take it to my Autopsy Room for Examination," Barbara offered, "Then we could package it for shipment. I have all of the evidence bags and labels we should need." Jennifer smiled, "I think I can talk my Father into flying the items to LA. They could be on them by Monday." The three women were satisfied with their arrangement, they were all smiles. Then Jennifer noticed something about the skull. She took a new pencil out of her shirt pocket and stuck it into the skull's Nasal opening, full length. She then pulled it back out. There was now dirt on the tip. Jennifer looked at the other women, "I think I know what killed this man. There appears to be a hole in the back of the skull." She gentle lift the skull and peered underneath. As she did, there was the sound of something rolling. There was a hole in the rear of the skull. She laid the skull back down. Barbara handed her a pair of long handled tweezers,

130

and a small evidence bag. Jennifer probed in the skull with the tweezers until she found something. Lifting the tweezers out of the Nasal cavity, she saw a lead ball being gripped by the tips. She dropped it into the evidence bag, then examined it. Bernadette stepped over to take a look, "I think it is a .44 caliber pistol ball." Barbara produced digital calipers from her bag, and Jennifer handed the bag to her. "I think you're right," Barbara said after examining it, "but I don't know much about bullets." "Barbara, why don't you show it to Jim Bearpaw," Bernadette suggested, "He is our resident ballistics expert." Barbara swiftly took off with the pistol ball, and repelled up the slope to Jim. Bernadette smiled, "They will make a nice couple." Jennifer smiled at this comment. She then looked around the skeleton, "Bernadette, don't you think we need to know what else is buried here?" Bernadette looked at her for a moment, then yelled, "Jeff, bring the crew down. We need shovels, trowels, and screens." The gully soon became a very busy place.

It was early evening. Barbara and Jennifer were working in the Autopsy Room at the Hospital. They had given the skeleton a through examination, and were now readying it for shipment. Several small items lay on the side counter, near the front door. Jim was going over these items that had been found around the body. Barbara was distracted, watching Jim working disturbed her. She wanted more intimacy, but was it with him? Try as she might to concentrate on the remains, she kept coming back to the problem, what should she do about Jim? She remembered him with his niece, the joy on her face, and his. She could not reconcile the Jim she knew, with the Sniper in Bosnia that he had been. "Dad says the helicopter will fly it to Sacramento tonight with our shipment," Jennifer talked as she buttoned up a box. "Every-thing will be flown to LAX in the morning, The Getty will pick it up from there." Barbara snapped back into focus, "Everything is tagged and logged as evidence. Only the small items need to be boxed." Jim spoke up, "I'm on that. I have photos of everything." "He is very bright," Barbara thought, "He instinctively does the right thing. People like him. It would be so easy just to let myself fall into a relationship with him. Just like last time, with Brian. That Bastard didn't get enough prison time, not nearly enough! He seemed so nice, and turned out so deceitful." Jim's Cell phone rang, "Lieutenant Bearpaw." "Lieutenant, this is Dispatch." "Yes,

Dispatch" "Lieutenant, Corporal Elkhorn reports that Doctor Saint Clair and crew have found a total of four skeletons. They are now packing up to leave." "Okay, Dispatch." "Corporal Elkhorn says they will stay out of sight until dark." "Thank you, Dispatch. Bearpaw out." He turned to the two women, "The report from the grave site is interesting. Bernadette and her crew are packing up for the night, but they have found four more skeletons." Jennifer was excited, "Four more! I wonder how many there will be? It was so good of you to arrange for a guard for tonight. And on such short notice." Jim was dismissive, "It's no big deal. This is standard procedure for a crime scene." Barbara wondered about that. "Why a two man team to watch the site? If it is okay with Bernadette, I suppose it should be okay with me." "I'll go tell the van crew to start loading," Jennifer announced. She proceeded out of the room. Barbara moved over to help Jim. "A 1874 dime," said Jim, holding up the plastic bag, "This should help date the site." "Jim," Barbara began, "why are there two armed deputies at the site tonight." Jim continued placing evidence bags into the shipping box, then spoke, "We suspect drug activity around those mines. Their trucks tracks have been seen by members of the Tribe." Barbara frowned, "Did you ever regret having your question answered." "Frequently," Jim laughed. She helped him seal the box. Jennifer came back in with the two men from the Van. "We want this box first," she said, pointing to the boxed skeleton, the men complied. "How are you doing with that box? She asked the pair. Barbara applied the label to the top of the box, "That does it. The last box is ready." Jennifer took charge, "Everyone, grab a box. Let's finish up and get out of here!" It occurred to Barbara, that Jennifer had someone waiting for her. "I don't blame her," she thought, "In her situation, I'd be in a rush." Five minutes later, all boxes were in the van, Barbara and Jim said their goodbyes to Jennifer. Barbara turned to Jim, "I'll lock up and you can take me home." Jim turned to looked at her, I thought you might like to have dinner first." "Why don't I fix something for us at Aunt Sarah's?" She quickly responded. As they closed up the Autopsy Room, Barbara wondered, "Why did I suggest that? But Aunt Sarah will be there, it will be all right." When they arrived at the house, Barbara went into the Kitchen. Jim joined her as she was reading Sarah's note on the Refrigerator. To her consternation, Sarah was out delivering twins. "No problem," she thought,

132

"I'll just fix something quick, and then it will be over." "How about pasta?" She asked Jim. "Sounds fine," he responded, "but isn't that a lot of trouble?" She smiled, "I always keep some pasta around." She said as she opened the Freezer Compartment, "The benefit of having an Italian mother." She took out a container of pasta and one of sauce. Off came the top of each container. She placed both containers into the large Microwave that sat on the counter. "Defrost." She announced to Jim. He then looked in the Refrigerator, "Salad?" He asked. She joined him in looking for salad fixing. They sat their finds on the counter, Barbara got out a bowl and started putting lettuce into it. Jim found a knife for the just washed tomato. The Microwave beeped and Barbara left the lettuce to tend the pasta. Jim moved in to cut the tomato and add it to the lettuce. Barbara mixed the pasta and sauce together, then back it went into the Microwave. While Jim worked on the salad, Barbara found a bottle of Pinot Noir. "I guess this will be okay with the pasta," she said, holding up the bottle. He nodded his approval, and she started to hunt for a corkscrew. What she found was a cork remover, which she did not know about. She held it up to Jim, "Do you know how to work this?" He smiled, "Yes Ma'am, I'll do that if you find some salad dressing." They swapped tasks, Barbara got out two kinds of dressing. Jim removed the cork, then poured some of it into one of the glasses and sampled it, "Nice," he said, "Would you like a taste?" She smiled at him, "Yes, please." He pour some in her glass and handed to her, she sipped it approvingly. The Microwave beeped and she put down her glass and reentered the Kitchen. Jim poured each of them a full glass of the excellent wine. Barbara came from the Kitchen bearing the pasta. She sat it down and went back for the salad. Jim remained standing until she returned. She sat down the salad and bowls, then motioned for Jim to sit. She placed a bowel by each plate, and sat the salad between them. Jim waited for Barbara to serve herself. She thought about that, "Seems like a gentleman. Certainly an improvement over Brian. He shares tasks in the Kitchen. He knows something about food and wine." As they ate, Jim thought about their day," Tiny called her a 'Babe'. That does not seem like enough. She is very attractive, but also very intelligent. She seems to care. She seemed to enjoy meeting my niece and nephews. At the grave site, and later, in the Morgue, she took charge. She did not force the issue, just worked with

Jennifer and Bernadette to solve the mystery. She is confident, but not as much as she appears. Her patients seem to like her." "Aunt Sarah is out delivering twins tonight," Barbara announced. Jim had been curious, "I wondered where she was. I thought it probably was a medical emergency." Barbara looked serious, "What do you suspect is happening at the Mines? How big an operation is it?" Jim finished chewing and swallowed, "This is speculation, so far. We think Bob Moore helped them to open one of the mines. They are probably using the chosen mine to store large quantities of drugs. Everything is going in and out by truck, at night." "It seems so wrong for drugs to come to this area," Barbara responded, "It seems so untouched here." Jim warmed to the subject, "Drugs are not a problem here, yet. It is probably only a matter of time. Once we have drug distribution here, local drug use will follow." Barbara grimaced, "I hope not. I saw enough drug abuse in New York. So many ruined lives. So much waste." Jim finished his wine, "I hate to eat and run, but I'm back on patrol at 8 am." Barbara felt a pang of regret, she had hoped to talk more with him. "Yes, It has been a long day," she heard herself respond. When he rose, she followed him to the Front Door. She spoke first, "Thank you for a very interesting day." "I enjoyed the company," he responded. After a moment, he reached and touched her cheek, then he kissed her, gently. She responded warmly, they held the kiss. The kiss ended, and she laid her head on his chest. Quietly, she said, "I'll be ready at eight, if you want me to go with you." He kissed her hair, "I want that very much. Good night, Barbara." As she watched him walk away, Barbara wanted to kick herself. "My bedroom is just down the hall," she thought, "We could be there right now." She shut the door and headed back to the kitchen, "What will I do when he brings me home tomorrow? What will Aunt Sarah think?" Her mind was full as she cleaned up the Kitchen.

Bill Andrews was in the Living Room of his home, sitting in a big leather easy chair. In one hand he had a Ballistics Report on the .38 slug taken from Bob Moore. His other hand stroked the blond dog curled up in his lap. The Ballistics Report had been handed to him by Sgt. Yeager, when he stopped by the Office earlier. Jim had the bullet run through IBIS (the FBI bullet data-base), the results were in the report he held. The .38 bullet came from a Smith & Wesson Military and Police .38 Special with a five

134

inch barrel. The weapon was used to kill one John Wentworth, 38, on April 16, 1977, in Lanham, Maryland. Wounded, was one Sadie Matson, 19, secretary to Mr. Wentworth. Bill wondered, "What is this gun doing here? Is it still being used by the same killer as in Maryland?" The gun was traced to a James Ferranti of Baltimore, Maryland. Mr. Ferranti reportedly gave the gun to his Daughter, Alice Ferranti Wentworth. Mrs. Wentworth, 32, has been missing since the murder of her husband. "That," Bill thought, "was very interesting. We may have a middle age woman in our area who kills." Bill's thoughts were interrupted by the ringing of the phone on the nearby Lamp table. "Hello." "Hello yourself," said the Deputy Director of the FBI. Bill smiled, "How are you, Mike? To what do I owe the pleasure of hearing from so exalted a person? "Bill, I got an alert that your Department made an IBIS inquiry about a .38 Special slug." "That's right, Mike. IBIS says that it was used in a 1977 shooting in Maryland" "Bill, that was one of my Dad's cases. He spent the last years of his career chasing this woman. Do you have the gun?" "Tell your Dad that we are looking for it, Mike." "Bill, Dad died five years ago. So, I guess it's my case now." "Well, it is not often that a humble Sheriff gets to aid The Deputy Director of the FBI." "Bill, I am about to become a grandfather. That would not be happening if you had not rescued my son. He would have died where he was hit or in a Libyan prison, if you had not carried him back to the boat." "Mike, this line is not secure. You should not be talking about this. I did nothing more than my duty to my men. He was my responsibility." "You received the Navy Cross for what you did. You rescued my son while wounded yourself. The Navy obviously thought you did a little more than just your duty." "Mike, you can pay back whatever you think you owe me by nailing my Sister's killer. Has Quantico received the evidence from her case?" "Yes, Jeff and his boys are on it. As soon as I hear anything, you will know. And Bill, it is not just what I owe you, but what my boy feels he does." "How is he doing? What is he up to, beside impregnating women?" "He's doing fine, based in Chicago now. He just made section head in Antiterrorism. How is your Daughter doing." "She is now a feature reporter for KNBC in Los Angeles. Calls herself Sheila Andrews. She looks a lot like her Mother." "Bill, I hope that doesn't bother you. This raises another question. How is your love life?" At that point, he looked at Anita, who was on the sofa, reading. "Mike, you asked me about my love life. Well, right now, I am looking at a beautiful, blue-eyed young woman, who has honored my home with her presence. She is currently spoiling my cat!" "Come on, Bill. You don't have to fantasize on my account!" Bill held up the phone, "Could you please show him that you're real?" Anita got up and grabbed the phone, "Mike, my name is Anita. I am a 5' 6" Brunette. I measure 36-23-36. As soon as we get rid of you, I plan on taking Bill upstairs and have my way with him." She handed the phone back to Bill with a smug look. "See Mike, I told you." "Wow! Bill, all I can say is have fun. You already have the Good Luck. Talk to you later." "Take care, Mike." He hung up the phone. "Was that really the Deputy Director of the FBI?" "Yes, Anita. He was concerned about my welfare." She slid into his lap, "For that sexist incident, you owe me, big time!" They kissed. "Now, while I take a shower, you can think of how you're going to make this up to me," she cooed in his ear. She gave him another big kiss, then got up and left the room. Susie was sitting patiently next to his chair. He patted his lap, and Susie hopped into it. Bill rubbed the happy little dog, and thought about his situation. "Mike says I am lucky to have Anita. If she were the passive type, we might not even be dating. But she is pro-active and very positive. Maybe it's her age, or being an Army brat, or both. Whatever it is, it worries me. How is she going to fit into the life of a back country sheriff? She needs to think things through more. Will there be enough for her to do? When we get beyond the physical, what will we have? But then, isn't that always the question." Sitting quietly for several minutes, Bill recalled something. He put Susie down, got out of the chair, and headed for the Den. In the Den, he checked the printer and removed the documents from the output tray. With Susie follo-wing, Bill walked back into the Living Room and sat in the same chair. Glancing at the document, he remembered to pat his lap. Susie jumped into his lap and curled up. He looked at what appeared to be a geology report, but he had trouble determining what property it covered. It occurred to him that he had the Geographic Maps of the area in the next room. He picked up little Susie and headed into the Dinning Room. Bill sat down at the table, settled Susie in his lap, and started searching for the maps of the Old Mine Road area. He shuffled maps until he came to two maps of the mine area. Bill was studying these maps when Susie

136

suddenly sat up. A slender hand appeared over each shoulder and wrapped themselves around his neck. Anita put her head next to his and hugged him. He kissed her on the cheek. "What are you doing with the maps?" She spoke softly, in his ear. "I am trying to match Bob's report with the maps of the mine area. His report talks about an excavation project." She pulled up a chair beside him. She was wearing a short, summer robe, when she sat down, her legs were exposed from mid-thigh down. "I wonder if she does this on purpose?" Bill pondered. Looking at the map reminded her of the day's discoveries, "Bernadette and her crew found four more skeletons at the site. I'm going over there tomorrow. There should be a Press Release about the discoveries." "We could go together," Anita offered, with a smile. Bill smiled, "I like that." "We could pack a lunch," She offered, "but I should drive my own car. I need to go home from there." She saw his expression sour. "Can I see Bob's report?" He handed the report to her. She studied it intently for several minutes. Bill noticed her intense look, how she really concentrated on this project. He was developing a new appreciation for the woman who was suddenly in his life. She finished studying the report and grabbed a map of the area. A few minutes of study, then she seemed to see something. "I think he worked on the Midas Mine," she announced, but he mentions earlier work in another mine. It could be the Molly Bee. In both, he planned an enlargement of the mine, a widening of the shaft into a sort of room." Bill frowned, "Are you sure abut this?" Anita replied confidently, "The description of one mine matches the map of the Midas, see the curve of the shaft." Bill studied the map before her, then the report. Finally, he put the paperwork down and looked at her, "You're very good at this! You have done this kind of work before." Anita smiled at him, "I spent several weeks exploring drug caves. There were rooms carved into the walls of the caves that had to be mapped. I was part of the crew that did it." Bill put his hand over hers, "Thank you for helping me. It would have taken me a lot longer." They kissed. "What are you going to do about the Midas Mine?" She inquired. Bill looked puzzled, "I'm not sure. I should poke around tomorrow, while you play with the old bones." She pulled her hand away, "I do not play around with old bones! I will be disclosing the discovery of ancient remains." "I think Bernadette and her crew deserve some recognition for their hard work," Bill pointed out. Anita promised to highlight their efforts. Bill noticed Susie tense, then heard the vehicle in the driveway. "I think we have a visitor." He got up and headed toward the front door. He arrived, about the time that someone rang the bell. He opened the door, to find Jennifer standing there with a small suitcase. She quickly entered, setting down her case. Bill was embraced and kissed. "Hello, Bill!" She bubbled. "Jennifer, what are you doing here?" Her smile was huge, "I came to see you!" Bill was serious, "It is normal for people to call, before going to visit someone. Tonight is not a good time." He held open the door for her, "Please call before you come over, next time." Her look was angry and hurt. She said nothing, just picked up her bag and left. Bill shut the door and locked it. He rejoined Anita, I think that ends the Jennifer problem." She was unsure, "That was harsh! Did she deserve that?" "Yes, Anita. Last night, she was too busy celebrating the Court victory to remember to call me. What I had on my plate was completely forgotten. Now, she come calling, unannounced." "What happens next?" Bill smiled at her, "Since you are leaving tomorrow, my intention is to escort you upstairs, where I am gong to remove all of your clothing. Then I plan on doing many wonderful things to your magnificent body!" "Oh, goody!" Was all she said. Hand in hand, the pair shut off the lights and ascended the stairs. Bill had made his choice. It wasn't hard, given Jennifer's behavior. Whatever doubts Anita may have had, about Bill and his relationship with Jennifer, seemed to dissolve in the heat of their lovemaking. She decided to trust him. She was richly rewarded for it.

Before Anita fell asleep, she thought of Bill and Jennifer. "Why was this rich young woman throwing herself at him?" The answer was obvious, he is a big Stud! "If she slept with him, she must want more. Bill says she went after him, then neglected him. He rejected her, harshly. He thinks that is an end to it. But is it? Will Jennifer be after Bill again? I would, in her shoes."

Chapter Ten

Sunday morning found Barbara in her bathroom. "Should I wear my hair up or down?" She pondered as she stood before the mirror. She thought about Jim, "I don't know what he likes. How does he like me to wear my hair?" Finally she decided the wear it down, "It was easier that way. But Jim hasn't seen me with my hair up. Wait, I had my hair up at the Autopsy." Her hair remained down as she finished dressing. Barbara was mad with herself for wanting to cater to a man, "I should dress to please myself. Jim will just have to take me as I am." Then she noticed her snug fitting blouse and jeans, "Who am I fooling! I have been dressing to please men all of my adult life. When you're built like me, how can I not dress to please men. Wear a Moo-Moo?" Resigned to her situation, Barbara ploughed forward to start another day. She put on a sweater, and walked into the Kitchen. She got a large wicker basket out of the cupboard and started putting items into it. Paper plates and napkins, plastic utensils and cups went into the basket. Then she started loading things from the refrigerator. Barbara muttered to herself, "How good an idea is this picnic? But, we have to eat. We might as well enjoy it." She finished packing, and carried the basket to the Front Door. Setting it on the Hall table required moving a small brass statue, "What does Aunt Sarah see in this thing?" She then peeked through the Security eye hole in the Front Door. Right at eight, Jim came marching up the walk. She opened the door, "I'm trying to be quiet, Aunt Sarah was out late. I want her to sleep." "Not a problem," Jim said, "Shall we go?" "Wait a minute," Barbara said, as she went back into the house. She came back out carrying the basket with both hands. "You come loaded for bear," he said as he took the basket from her. She smiled at him, "I believe in being prepared. Why don't you put that in the car while I get my bag." Jim bowed slightly to her, "Yes Ma'am." He put the basket in the rear of the Jeep Commander, and stood by the passenger door. Barbara came shortly, with her purse and medical bag. Barbara went into the front seat, while Jim put her medical bag into the rear seat. Soon they were on patrol. Barbara was anxious about last night. But neither spoke of it. About the time they reached the Reservation, Jim decided to tell her what Sgt. Yeager had reported to him, "I got the ballistics report back on the slug you removed from Bob Moore. The FBI say that it came from a gun used in a killing thirty years ago in Maryland. A thirty-two year old woman used it to kill her cheating husband. Then she disappeared." This information worried Barbara, "Does that mean the killer from Maryland is here?" Jim was matter of fact, "If she is, she would be in her early 60's. We should be getting more information on the killer. That will help to identify her, if she is still here." "Do you know anyone that age who came here thirty years ago?" She asked. Jim hesitated, then spoke, "Your Aunt Sarah comes to mind." "My Aunt Sarah came here from Syracuse, New York, twenty-eight years ago. She was in a medical partnership there. She hates guns! She won't allow them in the house." Jim was quick to reassure her, "Barbara, I never thought that your Aunt was the Killer. The Killer probably came here after spending time somewhere else." That caused Jim to think of something he had heard. He grabbed the Mic, "Dispatch, this is Unit Three." "Unit Three, go ahead." "Dispatch, tell Sargent Yeager to fingerprint A W Fairbanks and run her prints. Unit Three out." "Roger, Unit Three. Will inform Sargent Yeager. Dispatch out." Barbara jumped on this, "When did A W come here, and from where?" Jim was quick to reply, "She came here about eight years ago, from LA. So she said." "Are you going to investigate her?" Barbara asked. Jim got that 'patient' look on his face, "Yes Barbara, we will check her out. Checking out her fingerprints is just the start. Starting tomorrow, we will do a complete background check on her." Feeling a bit patronized, she just stared down the road. Then it caught her eye, "What is that on the right?" "I think someone is trying to flag us down," said Jim. By now they could see that it was a middle-aged Indian woman, she was obviously distraught. "It is Maria, my Mother's cousin," Jim told her. He pulled off the road and jumped out, "What is it Aunt Maria? What's wrong?" "Oh Jim," she wailed, "My granddaughter is hurt, little Patty fell!" Jim turned back to Barbara, who was standing behind her open door, "Bring your bag, there is a hurt little girl." Barbara gabbed her bag and followed Jim and Maria into the woods. About a quarter of a mile

140

in, they came to a dirt path running along a ravine. The child lay at the bottom, next to her bike, which was partially in the creek. There was a path down to the creek nearby, soon the three were down to the girl. Her Grandmother held her hand and touched her face, "My poor little one! Are you hurt?" The girl looked at her Grandmother and moaned, "My leg hurts, my right leg hurts!" Barbara noticed that the angle of her right foot was wrong. She knelt down and palpitated the lower leg. Maria looked at her with fear and mistrust, "Who are you? What are you doing?" Jim intervened, "Aunt Maria, this is Dr Barbara Davis, the niece of Dr Sarah. Please let her help Patty." Relief filled Maria's eyes, "Oh, Dr Davis! Please help my Granddaughter!" "Jim, her leg is broken," Barbara was all business, "Find something to use as a splint." Jim went off looking for splint material. Barbara started checking for other injuries. Her left leg seemed okay, but her right arm was swollen, possibly broken. Barbara was concerned about her ribs, "Patty, I'm Dr Davis. Do your ribs hurt?" She felt the girls chest, Patty shook her head no. She looked at the little girl's eyes. Good color and reflexes. No obvious sign of internal bleeding or shock. Jim came back with pieces of a shipping crate, "Barbara, I think these will work." He sat the boards down, next to the girl. Barbara stood up and joined Jim, "The boards will work. But I need to set her leg, the broken ends are displaced. It will hurt her. Please try to comfort her while I do it." "Of Course," was all he said, and he knelt down next to Patty. "Hello Patty, I'm your cousin Jim, Do you remember me?" The little girl smiled weakly, "I remember you. You gave out the presents at the Christmas Party." "That's right Patty. Now, I want you to hold on to my hand with your left hand. Dr Davis says it may hurt a little." "Okay Jim," said the stoic little girl and she held on tight. Barbara pulled gently on her right foot, Patty grit her teeth. She felt the broken ends of the Tibia align, and carefully secured a splint on either side of the lower leg, over her jeans. "The worst is over, Patty." Jim still held her hand. Barbara moved her bag and two splints up by Patty's right arm. "Her Ulna may be broken," Barbara said to Jim and Maria, "It shouldn't hurt her. Several minutes later, the arm was securely splinted. "Now," Barbara announced, "we need to get her to the Hospital. Jim, she needs to be checked for internal injuries. Can you take us to the ER?" Jim looked at Patty, then looked at Barbara, "If you think it's okay to move her I can." "It is

141

okay for you to carry her to the car," She said, "if you are very careful." She turned and put her supplies back in her bag. Jim spoke to the anxious girl, "We need to take you to the Hospital, Patty. Tell us if it hurts." With that, he slipped his arms underneath her and picked her up. Slowly he carried her out of the gully and through the woods to the road. Barbara ran ahead and opened the rear passenger door of the Jeep. Jim gently laid little Patty on the rear seat. Barbara got into the rear seat with her bag. She cradled Patty's head in her lap. Jim helped Maria into the front passenger seat. He jumped into the driver's seat and they were off, siren and lights on. "Dispatch, this is Unit three." "Roger, Unit Three. Go ahead." "Dispatch, I am in route to the Hospital with an injured child. Please notify ER. I have a Doctor on board. Unit three, out." "Dispatch. Roger injured child. Acknowledge en route to Hospital with Doctor, Dispatch out." Five minutes later they pulled up to the ER entrance, with lights and siren. Two attendants met them with a Gurney. Patty was quickly placed on the Gurney and wheeled into the ER. Barbara went in with the victim, Jim and Maria close behind. There were problems over who was Patty's legal guardian and who would pay. It turned out that her parents were at Fort Benning, Georgia, where her father was a Drill Instructor. She was visiting her Grandmother for the summer. Jim was able to fix things with a call to her Mother. Soon, a fax arrived giving permission for treatment and information for billing. Barbara reluctantly turned over Patty's care to the ER staff. Maria accompanied her Granddaughter into a treatment room. As they walked back to the Jeep, Jim could tell that Barbara was reluctant to surrender her patient to the Hospital staff. He stopped her with a hand on her shoulder. "Barbara, I know you hate turning Patty over to the staff here. But you should know about them. The ER doctor is ex-army. He served in Bosnia and Kosovo. I met him at a Field Hospital in Bosnia. He is good, and he cares. He came here because he married a local gal. Did you see the little redheaded nurse? That's his wife, Connie, one of the Johnson family, she served in Kosovo with him. They could be working in a big hospital, but they chose to come here. You took good care of Patty, Maria and I thank you for it. Patty is in good hands. We can return to patrol. They will contact me if anything happens." Barbara was somewhat pacified by his words, but her concern was not greatly diminished. "Don't patronize me," Barbara snapped. Jim put a

142

hand on each of her shoulders and looked her in the eye, "Barbara, there are several things I would like to do to you, patronizing isn't one of them." She had to smile at this admission, and they kissed there in the parking lot. In front of God and everybody. Aunt Sarah saw them as she drove into the parking lot. "That could be good." Sarah thought, "If they don't waste too much time, I could deliver their children before I retire." She had a subtle smile on her face and she watched them get in the Jeep and drive off. Although marriage had never interested Sarah, she thought it was just what her niece needed. "Dispatch, this is Unit Three." "Unit Three, this is Dispatch, go ahead." "Dispatch, Unit Three is resuming patrol from the Hospital. Unit Three out." "Unit Three, understand resuming patrol from Hospital. Dispatch out." Jim and Barbara were headed back out on County Route One.

Meanwhile, Bill Andrews was dealing with a problem of his own. Sunday morning found he and Anita in the big four poster that had been his parents and grandparents. Bill was responding to her, "I am sure orgasms early in a relationship are very natural. I have know several women who had the experience." "But I never had that experience before," Anita happily exclaimed. "I didn't know I could experience that." Bill rolled on to his side and looked at her, "Conditions must have been just right, and so were you." She rolled onto her side and looked him in the eye, "Why don't we try for the right conditions right now." He gently took her head in his hands and kissed her passionately. Then he spoke firmly to her, "Madam Publicist, your skeletons await." "You're no fun," she said and rolled out of bed. Jim smiled as he watched her naked form move toward the bathroom, "That is not what you said last night." She stuck her tongue out at him. "Oh, that's mature," he responded. "That's not what you said last night," came her muffled voice from beyond the bathroom door. He smiled and shook his head, his life had grown rather full, rather quickly. "So far, so good," he thought. Reluctantly, he got out of bed. He walked over to the bathroom door and knocked, "Hurry up in there, I need to take a shower." Anita was quick to respond, "If you took a shower at night, like I do, you wouldn't have this problem." She stuck her head out of the room, "I guarantee that if you take a shower at night, I will make it very interesting." He grabbed her by the shoulders, "I am very good at water sports." They kissed. Bill used her distraction to slip into the bathroom and shut the door. "That was a dirty trick," Anita yelled, and opened the door. Bill had started the shower water and stepped into it. He started to soap his rag, when she hugged him from behind, "That was sneaky. Now you need to show me a water trick." Bill turned around, and she noticed his erection. "You must be glad to see me," Anita giggled. Breakfast was delayed for 'water sports'. Later, a very relaxed Bill and Anita, now dressed, headed downstairs to the Kitchen. Of course they were greeted by two hungry animals. Bill fed the animals, while Anita gathered the ingredients for breakfast. They agreed on omelets. There was cheese and meat to cut, she tackled that first. Bill finished feeding the animals, and Bill moved on to fixing coffee. Anita got out a skillet, placed it on a burner, and put the meat and cheese pieces into the skillet. She turned on the burner and went to get the eggs. Bill smelled the unmistakable aroma of gas. He turned and saw the unlit burner, "Anita, please turn off the burner, it is not lit." Horrified, she ran over and flip the burner off, "Is the pilot light out." Bill got a patient tone to his voice, "Dear, there is no pilot light. You have to light it with a match. See the container of matches on the wall? I thought you saw me light the burner for you last night." "I thought you were just adjusting the burner," she exclaimed, "I had no idea that there was no pilot light." Bill crossed over to her and put an arm around her, "This stove is over a hundred years old. It was built long before pilot lights." He went over to the stove, grabbed a match, and lit the burner. "This stove was salvaged from the fire that destroyed the original house on his land." Bill went to Anita and touched her face, "Okay Beautiful, it's all yours." She took the eggs over to the stove, and resumed fixing the omelet. Bill got the coffee brewing and moved on to the toast. She was impressed by the old cast iron skillet, "You were right about the skillet. It is doing this double omelet. I hope the spray stops any sticking." Soon, breakfast was served. They found a fringe benefit to Anita being left handed. They were seated next to each other at the kitchen table, holding hands. Both could still eat, Anita using her left hand, Bill his right. "I think I will be over here on Wednesday, if everything goes according to plan." Bill swallowed, "What about your Press Release?" Don't you have to stay here for that?" She looked at him, "Don't tempt me! I have several things to do in Susanville. I will have to send it out from there." Bill frowned, "Suddenly I hate modern communications." She saw his look.

144

"How like a little boy," she thought, "My little boy." She leaned over to Bill and kissed him gently. They finished breakfast, and got ready to leave. There was a short pause to pet the two pets, then they were off, the skeletons awaited. Bill helped Anita load her things. Neither enjoyed the chore. As they drove away, in separate vehicles, Bill thought, "I almost blew it. Why so possessive? She is not my first Lover. Why did I over react?" He was confused. "We hardly know each other," his mind cried out, "but I over reacted when I heard that she was leaving. She has her plans, I knew that. Maybe it didn't mean as much to me then." "Why did he react that way?" Anita wondered, "He does have a lot on his mind, Bob Moore's murder, for one. Suspected drug trafficking for another. Did that make him say more than he meant to? He really cares if I leave," she thought, "Maybe he does love me. The way he lost his wife and his parents couldn't make him like sudden change. He had confided in her, that his Sheriff Father had injected his terminally ill Mother with an overdose of Morphine. When she was dead, he went out onto the dock and ate his pistol. Mentally, she shuttered at anyone having to deal with that. It was a quiet ride over to Old Mine Road. When they arrived at the grave site, Bernadette and her crew were hard at work. As pair approached the gully, they could see five skeletons exposed in the rocky soil. Bernadette called out to them, "Sleeping in this morning?" Bill headed down the rope ladder they had rigged, and hurried over to the dark colored bones. He dropped to his knees to examine the first skeleton. Anita was soon right behind him. Bill could not miss Jennifer's eagerness, as she did her work on the skeletons. Jennifer was joined by Bernadette, "What do you think?" The Archeologist asked. "Looks like the first one," Jennifer lifted the skull, "Including the hole in the rear of the skull." "It looks like there are at least three more. I think they were buried here and mine tailings were dumped over them. It has taken a hundred plus years of erosion, and a car wreck to expose them," Bernadette speculated. "You may be right," Bill added, "this entire area is covered with mine tailings. The road is paved with it. And this gully is a major drain for the area." Bernadette smiled broadly, "Ah, Sheriff Andrews. Who's you friend?" Bill smiled back, "Bernadette, this is Anita Brubaker, Public Relation Officer for the County. Anita, this is Professor Bernadette Saint Clair, State Archeologist for this area." The ladies shook hands. Anita started to speak, but Jennifer

145

interrupted, "Aren't you going to introduce me?" She stood there, smiling. Bill did the honors. The pair shook hands, during which, each looked the other over. Jennifer didn't know what to think about Anita. The opposite was not true. The Blonde reached into her pocket, and handed something to Bill, "Hang on to this, it is evidence." He watched her walk back to the skeleton. "God," she thought, "I want to jump him right here and tear his clothes off. I have never felt like this before. Is this love or lust?" She went back to her examinations. Bill spoke to Anita, "I'm going to look around while you get your information. I need to go to the SUV for more evidence bags." Back at the vehicle, he picked up the bags. He stared at the Midas Mine, "Did they excavate that mine? Is there any thing in there?" He had about made up his mind to check the mine out, when he heard another vehicle coming. Soon a new Jeep Grand Cherokee 4X4 pulled up next to him. A Washo Tribal Council logo was on the door. Johnny Eagle got out of the drivers side and came around the front of his vehicle. He looked very prosperous in his tailored jacket, slacks and Gucci shoes. "Ah, Sheriff Andrews. What a lucky coincidence, just the man I needed to see. How fortunate that I chose to visit these skeletons." "Nice car," Bill noted, "I didn't realize The Tribal Council could afford such a vehicle." Johnny's smile got a little strained, "It was a donation to the Tribe, a corporate donation." Bill jumped on that, "Would that be the Sierra Development Corporation? Or the Washo Mining Corporation, or the Lassen Land Corporation?" Johnny lost his smile for a moment, then it returned, more strained than before, "Why it was the Sierra Development Corporation, of course. I don't know these other companies." Bill bored in, "How nice for you, and your wife. Linda isn't it?" "Why yes, Sheriff. Linda is my wife's name. But what does this have to do with her?" "Mr. Eagle," Bill began formally, "As the President of The Lassen Land Corporation, which owns the Washo Mining Corporation, which owns the Sierra Development Corporation, your wife gave that vehicle to the Tribe. Her Tribe. Where did the money come from to purchase it? Who decided that you should drive it? How much does the Tribe know about this gift? How much does the Tribe know about the company's involvement with A W Fairbanks. How much does the Tribe know about your bribes in Sacramento?" He tried to hide his nervousness, but Bill was very experienced in this game, "Sheriff Andrews, I resent your accusa-

146

tions. I hope that you can prove that my efforts on behalf of my Tribe involved bribery." "Counselor, it isn't important what I can prove," Bill pounced, "It's important what the Attorney General can prove." Johnny thought a change of topic was the best plan, "I wanted to talk to you about the members of my Tribe that are still being held. Why has no bail been set?" "No bail has been set, Counselor, because all but one have gone to Redding to be arraygned on Federal Charges. Felons in possession of firearms, Assault on Federal law enforcement officers, and use of firearms in commission of a crime. All on Federal Land." Johnny's discomfort was now complete. He had no idea what this would mean. "How much will they tell when faced with Federal time?" He wondered. He smiled at Bill, "That is too bad. I had hoped to help with their rehabilitation. Well, there doesn't appear to be any thing else I can do for them here. I think I will forgo the skeletons today, Perhaps some other time." "Have a nice day, Counselor." Bill smiled, "Please say hello to your wife for me." Johnny went up the road to turn around. When he came back by, Bill could see his grim face. "I didn't tell you what I suspect about the Midas Mine," Bill thought, "What would that have done for your state of mind?" He headed back down into the gully with the evidence bags.

Jim was driving the usual patrol route: east out of Sierra Vista on County Route One, through the southern end of the Reservation to County Route Five, north on Route Five along the eastern edge of the County to County Route Seven, west on Route Seven across the Northern end of the Reservation to Route Nine, and south on Route Nine along the western side of the County until you hit Route One, east on Route One brought you back to Sierra Vista. They were on Route Seven now, in the northern part of the Reservation. Barbara was enthralled by the endless forest of Pines, Firs, and Cedar Trees. Occasionally, there had been a small lake. The lakes had Brown Trout and Bass, Jim had explained. Jim slowed the Jeep at one point, and turned left onto a gravel and dirt road. Down this road they had gone for about two miles, when the road ended at a river and a grassy meadow. Along the edge of the meadow were two picnic tables. It was at one of these tables that Jim stopped and parked the Jeep. "I thought that this might be a good spot for a picnic." Jim gestured to Barbara. She saw the rocky river, the meadow, and the forest all around them. It occurred to her that this maybe a special spot for Jim, "It's lovely here, Jim. Do you come here often?" "No, Barbara. I haven't been here for a while. It is rather special." He got out and came around to help Barbara out. Then he got the picnic basket and a blanket out of the back. Together, they walked over to the table. He put the basket down and turned toward the meadow, "Barbara, this meadow is sacred to my people. For nearly five hundred years we held our ceremonies here. Now we hold them in the field behind the Council House. It is better for the Tourists. There use to be three dozen tables around this meadow, now there are just these two." He felt her hand on his arm, she spoke softly, "Everything changes Jim, look at my life. I know it must be terribly sad to see a way of life altered so much, but I bet it was changing for a long time before you noticed." He smiled and then looked at Barbara, his hand went over hers. He leaned toward her and they kissed. Then he spoke, "You are a very wise woman." "No," she replied, "I am a very wise person." He laughed, "I stand corrected." They started unpacking the basket. Jim spread out the blanket on the wooden bench. Barbara got out a rough old table cloth, and Jim helped her to unfold it and spread it on the table. They spread the contents of the basket onto the table. Jim chuckled, "You packed enough food for a Ranger battalion." She smiled back at him, "I take that as a complement. I always believe in being prepared." They talked as they ate, the topic of change brought out many examples in the world around them. Afterward, they put everything back in the basket. Barbara looked a bit disturbed, so Jim asked her, "What's the matter? You look upset." "What I need," Barbara confessed, "is somewhere private." Jim offered her his hand, "Come with me." He led her over to the Jeep and to the front passenger side, where he produced a paper bag from under the seat. He handed the bag to Barbara. In it she found a roll of toilet paper, a packet of antiseptic towelets, and an empty plastic bag. "Thank you for the 'Mercy Kit'," Barbara said to Jim. Jim offered her his hand, she took it, and they headed into the woods on an old trail. As they approached an old building, Jim spoke," I don't recommend the 'Ladies'." Barbara looked at the derelict building and agreed. He pointed to a clump of bushes beyond the 'Ladies', "I suggest the bushes behind the building. Are you all right with this?" Barbara was quick to respond, "My family used to go camping in the Adirondacks, this won't be the first bush I've used." She headed off with her paper bag. Jim went the opposite

148

way looking for a 'male' bush. Several minutes later, Barbara rejoined Jim on the trail. She held the paper bag and a plastic bag with her "paper waste". Jim was quick to notice, "You look like a proper woodsman." "I prefer 'environmentalist'," she replied with a smile. They walked back to the table and picked up their things. Everything went back into the Jeep. Jim helped Barbara into the front seat, then went around and got in himself. Barbara was putting on her seatbelt, when Jim spoke, "Barbara, I know your still on the fence about me, about what I did in the Army. But I want to continue to see you. I want our relationship to succeed." Barbara let go of her seatbelt, and spoke, "Jim I have a hard time dealing with what you did in Bosnia. I think that I know you well enough now to be sure that you thought you were doing the right thing. Your motives were good. Your intentions are always good. I'm willing to try a relationship with you." Jim put his arm around her and kissed her. She held Jim with both arms and kissed him back. Very quickly, their emotions rose. Barbara responded by unbuttoning the top buttons of her blouse. Jim wasted no time in kissing her neck and cleavage, when the radio blared, "Calling Unit Three! Unit Three, this is Dispatch!" Jim had to grab the Mic. "Dispatch, this is Unit Three." "Unit Three, Sgt. Yeager says he got a hit on AFIS. Please contact him." "Roger Dispatch, I understand hit on AFIS. Unit Three out. When he put down the Mic., Jim noticed that Barbara was buttoning her blouse. "Sorry," Jim said. "Not your fault," she replied. "You owe me, Jim," she thought, "Then she wonder what would happen, later." Jim was thinking too, "I blew it. Now she is having second thoughts about this. One step forward, two steps back." Jim started the Jeep, and away they went. Back on to Route Seven, headed west. When they hit Route Nine, they headed south. When they hit Route One, they headed east. Soon Sierra Vista came into view. Jim headed for the Sheriff's Department and the adjoining jail. Jim jumped out of the Jeep, Barbara jumped out of the other side, and they rushed into the lobby. Sgt Yeager was behind the Duty Desk. Seeing Jim, the Sgt reached for a document he had printed out earlier, "I thought you would want to see this." Jim grabbed the report and started reading. "Oh, Man!" He exclaimed. Barbara moved in to read over his shoulder. "Lieutenant, that was a good call," the Sgt called out. "What were you two up to on this fine summer day?" He thought to himself. Jim looked at Barbara, "A W Fairbanks is the suspected killer Alice Wentworth. They think she shot her husband to death in Maryland, thirty years ago. Apparently, there was a witness that survived the attack. "Sargent, have you told anyone else about this? "No, Lieutenant, I thought you would want that honor." "Thank you, Sargent." "Barbara, I'd like to go to my office and call Bill Andrews." They walked side by side down the hall to his office. Jim turned on the lights, and motioned her into it. Barbara noticed the simply furnished office. "I bet we could do it on that sofa," she thought. Jim sat at his desk and grabbed the phone. The number was dialed from memory, "Damn, it went right to voice mail. Maybe they're at the mines with the skeletons." Barbara was looking at the Commendations on the office walls. There were ones for Deputy Bearpaw, Cpl. Bearpaw, Sgt. Bearpaw, and the latest one for Lt Bearpaw. There was his diplomas from San Jose State University. Various Indian artifacts filled a glass front cabinet. There was also the picture of a middle-aged Indian woman that she assumed was his Mother. "No picture of his Father," she thought. "Barbara, I need to use the Department Radio to reach the Sheriff." "All right, where is it, Jim?" He stood up and offered her his hand, "Come with me." Hand in hand they continued up the hallway to the Dispatch Room. Jim opened the door and ushered Barbara into the room. Dispatcher Margaret "Maggie" Peters was on duty. Maggie was a short, full figured Brunette, about thirty. Jim did the honors, "Maggie, this is Dr. Barbara Davis, our County Coroner. Barbara, Maggie is the mother of two young children, and the widow of one of our finest officers. Barbara was distressed by this and asked, "How did your husband die?" "He was chasing a speeder one night, when a drunk hit him head on. They were both killed," Maggie answered, evenly. Jim noticed Barbara's distress. "She really cares," he thought. "Maggie, I need to reach the Sheriff. His Cell phone must be out of range." "Okay, Lieutenant. I'll see if I can reach him." With that, she grab the Mic. and spoke, "Dispatch to Unit One! Dispatch to Unit one!" She told Jim, "We'll wait a minute for him to answer. I've noticed it takes the Sheriff longer to answer lately." Barbara and Jim looked at each other and smiled. They could think of at least one reason for this delay in answering. The phone on Maggie's desk rang, Maggie answered, "Emergency Operator! Yes Madam, I can dispatch someone to assist you. You are very welcome." She hung up then looked at a list of emergency numbers on the wall. She

150

picked the phone up and dialed one of them, "Hi Jerry, got a stranded tourist for you over on Route Three, at the Mile thirteen marker. Probably out of gas. Take care." She hung up. Jim explained, "This Center takes care of our 911 calls, as well as Sheriff's Department Dispatch. This Section is growing. Next week, our new personal radio units will be operational. Each officer will wear their own radio unit with a shoulder microphone." "That will be a big improvement, like right now, for instance." Maggie chimed in. "Unit One to Dispatch." Maggie grabbed the Mic, "Dispatch To Unit One. Hold on for Lieutenant Bearpaw." She handed the Mic to Jim. "Bill, this is Jim. I had our latest prisoner fingerprinted. AFIS says she is the Maryland killer. Over." "Jim, have you notified Maryland about your little discovery? Over." "Negative, Bill. I thought the Sheriff should know first. Over." "Jim, you notify Maryland. I owe the FBI a courtesy call. Over." "I understand. I will notify Maryland. Over." "Unit One out." Jim handed the Mic back, "Thanks Maggie." "Barbara, I need to fax Maryland about our "guest". We need to go back to my office." Maggie noticed that Barbara took his offered hand. She watched them hold hands as they left the room. Back in Jim's office, Barbara sat on the sofa, while Jim went to his desk. A few minutes on the computer, and Jim had composed a Fax for the State of Maryland. He picked up the form from the printer, and started to the door, "I'm going to go fax this." "Jim, where is the Ladies Room?" He gestured, "Down the hall on the right." Both of them headed for their respective destinations. After Jim had transmitted the Fax, he decided to visit the Men's Room while waiting for confirmation. When he came back by his office, he noticed that Barbara was sitting on the sofa, looking out the window. "She is beautiful. A mixture of self reliance and vulnerability," He thought, "What would have happened in the car if the radio had not interfered?" Barbara turned toward him and smiled. "Barbara, I'll just be another minute, and then I can take you home. I have to check the Fax machine." Barbara joined him, and they walked down the hall together. Maryland's Fax was confirmed, so Jim led them back to his Jeep. As he helped her into it, Barbara looked him in the eye, "I'd like to go to your house. We started something in the car this afternoon." They kissed and held each other. Then she got into the car, Jim got behind the wheel. A moment later, they passed the Hospital. Barbara stared at it as they passed. Jim watched her and smiled, "We can stopped off here when I do take you home." She turned to him and smiled, "You know me pretty well already." "It isn't hard Barbara, you are a caring person. You are also a very attractive woman, very desirable." She slid on the bench seat until she was up against him, he noticed that her top blouse buttons were unbuttoned. A great deal of cleavage was now exposed. Jim drove home with divided attention, but great enthusiasm.

Bill and Anita had been sitting in the shade of a lone tree. They had finished their lunch, when they heard his car radio. When he returned from the car, he helped Anita clean up. They were both uneasy. The time approached for her to leave. Anita found it tougher than she thought. "I might be able to drive over after the Tuesday afternoon DEA meeting." He stopped and looked at her, "I don't want you to cut corners for me!" She smiled at him, "If I cut any corners, it will be for me!" He bowed to her, "I hope you will forgive my assumption." "Forgiveness will require you to come over here." With a smile, he crossed to her. He leaned down, she embraced him. They shared a long kiss. "I will miss you, Anita," he whispered in her ear. She held the hug, "I didn't know it would be so hard." He looked at her face, there were tears in her eyes. He hugged her again. "On Tuesday night, we will be together again. We will live for then." He applied a tissue to her eyes. Then, kissed her. Later, the lovers parted. Bill watched Anita drive away. He had done easier things in his life.

They were soon driving up his driveway, past the lake. He pushed the remote's button, and the Garage Door opened. They parked next to a well worn Jeep CJ7. He got out as the Garage Door closed. He helped Barbara out of the SUV. As they walked past the CJ7, Barbara had to comment, "That looks like an old veteran." "About 250,000 miles worth," was Jim's response. Barbara could only say, "Wow." They entered the house through the Laundry and the Kitchen, Barbara thought that it was a beautiful kitchen. Granite counter tops, and a center island to match. There was an elaborate gas cook top and dual wall mounted ovens. "Did you design this kitchen," Barbara asked in amazement. Jim looked embarrassed for a moment, "I wish I could take credit, but Gwen Baker, Captain Baker's wife did it. She did it for Jason Saunders' house also." "Who built this?" She asked. Jim answered simply, "I did. Let me show you the Living Room."

They stopped at a closet, Jim put his hat and gun belt in it. Then he led her by the hand past an unpainted formal dining room and into a large, but cozy living room. The opposite wall was dominated by a huge granite fireplace. "Did you build that," Barbara exclaimed. Jim answered, "No, but it was built to my design. Members of the Tribe run a small granite quarry. They quarried the granite and built the fireplace, they did the counter tops too. I built the oak mantle." Barbara looked around the room with surprise. The furniture was massive, but attractive. There was lots of exposed wood, oak she thought. The material on the sofa and chairs was in Autumn tones, oranges and browns. She liked this room, "This is beautiful. So warm and friendly. Did you design or build this?" "Both, actually." Jim answered. She looked at Jim with a new appreciation. She put her arms around him. They embraced and kissed. Passion had been building up all afternoon and now it bubbled to the surface. They sat on the nearby sofa. Jim finished unbuttoning her blouse. He kissed her and tried to unfasten her bra with one hand. "Let me do it," she whispered. Then, she clasped her bra with both hands and undid the fastener in the front. Her magnificent breasts pour out of the open bra. Jim did not have to be invited to partake of the bonanza. "Your only the second man I have ever slept with," she confided to him, as he undressed her. He didn't reply, but started kissing her neck. Then he worked his way to her breast. Barbara had intended to use his bedroom. He took her on the sofa first. They coupled again on his custom made bed. Great sex! Then they slept in each others arms.

Chapter Eleven

Monday:

Bill was late getting to his office this morning. He was thinking about Anita. He had trouble sleeping last night, Anita was on his mind. The tears in her eyes when she left, made him realize what this relationship meant to her. That caused him to consider what it meant to him. She was bright and beautiful. Mary had been bright and beautiful. He recalled how it had been with Mary, everything took so much time. So often, the results were disappointing. But this time was different, very different. He smiled at the thought of Anita. Tuesday night seemed so far away. He would call her tonight, that would help! His "In" basket held two things: the AFIS report on Alice Wentworth, and a Fax from someone in the Maryland Attorney General's office. He looked at the AFIS report. It was a 100% match, no doubt there. The fingerprints involved were all sharp and clear. AW fit the profile for Alice Wentworth, it looked open and shut. "Mike was very happy when I phoned him about this. I suppose that the FBI will be involved." The second item was a response to the Fax Jim had sent to Maryland. There was a phone number to call in Annapolis about Alice. So he decided to call it. A moment later, "Attorney General's Office." "Mr. Warner, please." "Who may I say is calling?" "Sheriff Andrews from California." "One moment, please." Their background music was tinny and slurred. He was sure his was better. "Hello, Sheriff Andrews. My name is Darrell Warner. I am on the Attorney General's Staff here in Maryland. I received your Fax about Alice Wentworth. How sure is the identification." "Mr. Wagner, we have a 100% AFIS match. And she does match the profile of Alice. I believe that the FBI will be involved in the identification process, this is an open Fugitive case for them." "I see. Sheriff Andrews, I am going to start extradition proceedings, pending the FBI report. I will be in touch." "Hold on, Mr. Wagner! Alice is the principle suspect in a recent local murder. Our investigation has just started." "I see. Sheriff Andrew, I'm going to take my time with this paperwork. We will try to keep the State of California out of this matter for as long as possible." "I do appreciate your courtesy, Mr Warner. I have a "heads up" for you. The Deputy Director of the FBI has a personal interest in this case. It was his late Father's Fugitive Case." "Thank you very much for that heads up. Sheriff Andrews, we will be in touch. Good day to you." "Good day," Bill put down the phone, "That was easy." He thought for a moment, then reached for the Intercom switch, "Wanda." "Yes, Sheriff Andrews." "Will you ask Captain Baker and Lieutenant Bearpaw to join me." "I'll get them, Sheriff." Bill looked again at the AFIS report. Russ and Jim soon entered the room and sat down in front of his desk. "Gentlemen," Bill began, holding the AFIS report, "We need to deal with this situation. Russ and I will interview AW, Jim will get a search warrant for her home, her car, place of business, and phone records. We need to find that gun! Russ, I want you to start a background search on AW. She said she came from LA, start there. Let me know if either of you find anything. We'll talk to the woman when we have something on her. Right now, she is our number one suspect for Bob Moore's murder." Russ and Jim left. Bill went back to his paper work.

A bit later, Jason Saunders appears in Bill's doorway. "It seems your attractive secretary is away from her desk." "She is a widow, Jason, why don't you ask her out?" He walked over to the Sheriff's desk and sat down, "I might just do that. I'd say she's about forty." Bill corrected him, "Forty-two, actually. I understand that she loves the Del Norte Restaurant. She was my Sister's best friend, I'd like to see her happy. She hasn't had an easy life." "We will talk more about this later. Bill, why I came over, has to do with a phone call I just received. It seems that they want to interview me tomorrow afternoon for TV. This Injunction and the previous Logging Moratorium have made me something of a celebrity. The network is sending a reporter up from LA. On Thursday evening, I have decided on throwing a dinner to celebrate the Injunction and the Interview. You are invited. I figure this is the only way I can clean out my wine cellar." He was smiling at this last statement. "I hope that you are not giving us your rejects," was Bill amused response. "Jason, I ran into Johnny Eagle yesterday, out at the Mines. We had a little talk about his

156

dealings in Sacramento and his wife's involvement with certain corporations." This interested Jason, "How did he take this little talk?" "He seemed very nervous. I'd say our boy was scared. Maybe he'll make a mistake. Right now, I need to know who is involved with him. I need another favor from you." "Bill, anything I do to help you in this matter, helps my cause as well. What do you want done?" "Tell me who he deals with. We need his banking records. How many accounts does he have? Under what names and corporations? Who is he paying off? If I get a court order, he will know what we are up to. Besides, that would be just a fishing expedition." Jason beamed, "My boy, consider it done. He won't know a thing." "Jason, someday you should tell me what all of this illegal activity costs you." "Bill, I would never tell any sheriff about my involvement in any illegal activity. I consider it a normal cost of doing business." "I would not want to be the one trying to compete with you, Jason." "No Bill, that would not be wise," Jason said, smiling. He rose and leaned on Bill's desk, "Now about the lovely Wanda." Bill leaned back in his chair, "She is a lady, Jason. She was married to an abusive drunk. My Father had to put the fear of God into him or he would have continued to beat her. He killed himself in a head on collision with a tree, about five years ago. She has a son and a daughter, the son is away at college. He's on a football scholarship at Oregon. They're good people, Jason. Just what are your intentions?" Jason looked somewhat somber, "Spoken like a good friend. I am glad she has your loyalty. To speak plainly, I am lonely. After my wife died, I tried to bury myself in work. But I already have good men running my companies. Fortunately, I found a place in Conservation. For a while, it fulfilled me. Now, after our victories, that too offers me less comfort. I tried an intellectual relationship, but it was not fulfilling. My wife was not a great intellectual, but she had a great lust for life and had a good deal of common sense. I miss a physical, vibrant relationship. Your Wanda interests me. We have talked on occasion. She is a wise woman. I now understand something of why." Bill was thoughtful, "Go slowly. Both of you need to take it slowly. I do thank you for your efforts on this other matter." "My pleasure, Bill. How much would it take to repay you for helping my Daughter? And Bill, I know you and she are having some difficulties. I know that she is overwhelming. Hopefully, you will learn to love it." With that, he turned and walked out of the office. Bill followed him to the doorway. He saw Jason stopped at Wanda's desk, Wanda laughed. Bill smiled, thoughtfully, "Good for you, Wanda. Good for both of you." As for Jennifer and her problems, he intended to have as little contact as possible.

It was nearing noon in the Autopsy Room. Barbara was taking bones out of an evidence box and placing them on the Autopsy Table. There was a subtle smile on her face and she hummed softly to herself. Jennifer was watching her, from the other side of the table. "Barbara," she said, suddenly, "What are you doing for lunch?" "I'll probably go home for lunch," she answered, still smiling. Jennifer decided, "I think I'll go the to Coffee Shop." "Why don't you come home with me. We could have Pasta Salad." "You're on, Barbara," Jennifer quickly replied, then decided to probe a bit, "Is there something you want to tell me?" Barbara stopped and looked at Jennifer, "What do you mean?" "I mean, you are smiling all the time. You hum to yourself. You are slightly preoccupied. Are you in love?" Barbara looked slightly puzzled for a moment, then answered , "I don't know if it is love. I just know it makes me very happy." "Is it Jim Bearpaw?" Barbara looked at Jennifer, "Yes." "Barbara, tell me. You were with him last night, weren't you?" "Yes I was," Barbara admitted with a smile. "Are you going to see him tonight?" "I'm going over to Jim's for dinner." Jennifer could hardly contain herself, "I think I know what will be for desert." They both burst out laughing. Finally, Barbara started peeling off her gloves, "That's it! Let's go to lunch. I'll open a bottle of wine." They both headed into the office to dump their lab coats. Barbara could not stop thinking about tonight.

It was after two in the afternoon. AW Fairbanks was sitting at one end of the small table in Interview Room one. She wore the bright orange, short sleeved jumpsuit worn by prisoners in the County Jail. She also wore a heavy belt with steel loops on it. Her wrist bracelets were attached to the loops by short chains. There was a chain on each side of her, locked to the belt loops at one end, and locked to eye bolts anchored into the floor at the other. She was not a happy camper. "One of you assholes better unlock me now!" She yelled as Bill and Russ entered the room, Bill carried a manila folder. One of them sat on either side of the table. Russ carried a small tape recorder. He sat it on the table between he and

158

Bill. He pressed a button on the recorder and spoke, "This interview was started at 2:18 pm. Present are Sheriff William Andrews, Captain Russell Baker, and AW Fairbanks." "One of you unlock me right now!" "I'm Sheriff Andrews. I'm afraid that we can't unlock you." "Why not!" "Because it is against the rules. You wouldn't want us to break the rules, would you?" "Fuck your rules! I need a smoke!" Bill looked concerned, "If you talk like that, how can we be friends, AW? What does AW stand for?" This seemed to take AW by surprise, "Friends? AW stands for me, I'm AW." Bill assumed his 'patient mode', "Now, we know that AW stands for Alice Wentworth. Alice Ferranti Wentworth of Lanham, Maryland. Your fingerprints tells us that." "There must be some mistake. I'm AW Fairbanks from Los Angeles," she said in a very affirmative tone, "I've never been to Lanham, Maryland." Russ took over at this point, "We could not find an AW Fairbanks in LA before 1977. We did find an Alicia Fairbanks born in 1945, died in 1962. In 1977, suddenly an AW Fairbanks appeared and took out a Social Security Card. The IRS shows that Social Security number was used by you to obtain employment at various Real Estate and Escrow offices in the LA area. The records show that you also bought and sold several properties in the greater LA area.. Then you sold out in LA and came here in 1999 and started buying rental properties. In 2001, you formed a partnership with one Charles O'Brien, a local realtor." AW was becoming agitated, "I did not die in 1962! I didn't have a Social Security Card before 1977 because I was married! I have done nothing wrong! Why are you doing this to me?" "According to the records," Russ spoke, looking at the reports from the folder, "AW Fairbanks was never married. You never had a Drivers License until 1977." Bill entered the interrogation at that point, "AW, what did you do with the gun?" "What gun?" she snapped back with noticeable anxiety. "The gun you used to kill your husband, John Wentworth." "I didn't kill anyone! I've never been married! You said so your self!" Bill continued, "You were married to John for nine years. There was a witness to your murder of John. The State of Maryland wants you back to stand trial. Not much chance you will walk away from that one. You well might get the Death Penalty." "The Death Penalty? But I didn't do anything! I didn't kill anyone! I've never been to Maryland!" "But AW, your fingerprints are on file in Maryland. You were an Escrow Officer. Your fingerprints say that you're a killer," Bill pushed on, "You followed your husband to a motel and shot him, then you shot Sadie. Sadie lived, you know. She says you shot her and John." "It's a mistake! It wasn't me! Let me go!" Bill heard her increasing anxiety, "A witness saw you. You can't escape your crime. Thirty years ago, you killed John Wentworth, then last week, you killed Bob Moore, with the same gun. You can't escape that murder either." "What? I didn't kill any one! I don't have a gun! I want a lawyer!" "Okay, Alice. Captain Baker will get a phone for you. But you have to use your real name, Alice Ferranti Wentworth. Your fingerprints prove that is who you are." Russ slid the phone down the table to her. She could just reach the receiver, she had to lean toward the phone to hear the dial tone. From memory, she dialed the number for Marvin Schiller in Chico. Bill noted this, "Nothing appears to be wrong with her memory." "Hello, Marvin Schiller's office," his long time secretary answered. "This is AW Fairbanks, put Marvin on." "Please wait, Ms Fairbanks." A minute later, she came back on, "Ms Fairbanks, Mr Schiller asked me to tell you that your case has been appealed. He will contact you when there is any development." "I want to speak to Marvin, right now." "Mr Schiller is with another client right now." "Tell that asshole to get on the phone right now. I'm in the Sierra Vista Jail." The response was colder now, "Ms Fairbanks, we are aware of your contempt charge. There is nothing that Mr Schiller can do about that." "No, you don't understand." AW wailed, "They think I killed someone." "Ms Fairbanks, Mr. Schiller does not do Criminal Law," then she hung up. "No, wait! You don't understand. It's all a mistake! Get me out of here! Tell them I'm innocent!" She let the phone slip from her hand. Russ reached over and hung it up. The wild look in AW's eyes was slowly replaced with the dull look of shock, like she now understood that there was no escape for her. "Marvin Schiller is not a criminal attorney," Bill told her, "You will have to get someone else. We will contact the Public Defenders Office for you." AW did not respond. Bill motioned for Russ to follow him out. Russ announced, "This interview is terminated at 2:33 pm." He switched off the recorder, picked it up, and followed Bill into the hallway. Both Bill and Russ had seen young men 'lose it' in battle. They had seen the hysteria of the wounded. But there was something unnerving about Alice Wentworth. Bill mentioned it to Russ, "I don't think she's lying. I think she really believes she is

160

someone else." "Sargent Yeager told me that she didn't fight his taking her fingerprints," Russ added. Bill acknowledged this information, "That matches what we've seen just now. The fingerprints mean nothing to her, she just wants her freedom. I don't think we'll get anything from her, because I think she is delusional." That upset Russ, "If she's crazy, we wouldn't get her to trial. It makes me pissed off to see justice cheated by an insanity plea." "Maybe she is 'faking', Russ. The Court can get her examined by a 'Shrink', it is up to the court to determine her mental state. Right now, we need to find that gun. Please give Jim a hand with the search. Ask Charlie O'Brien to come see me, before you go." "You got it, Bill" Russ took off to his office. Bill spoke to the Officer on guard outside the Interview Room, "Return her to her cell. Place a female Officer with her. I want a 24 hour suicide watch." Bill then headed down the hall to Wanda's desk. "Wanda, will you contact the Public Defender's Office, and tell them AW Fairbanks needs defending against one possible count of murder, and one extradition for murder." Wanda looked shocked by what she heard, but quickly recovered, "Of course I will, Sheriff Andrews." Bill disappeared into his office. He sat at his desk, and checked his phone list. Satisfied, he dialed the number, "Superior Court Office." "Judge O'Reilly, please." "Who may I say is calling?" asked his clerk. "Sheriff Andrews." "Just a moment, I'll get the Judge." A minute later, the Judge came on the line. "Hello, Sheriff Andrews. What can I do for you?" "Good afternoon, Your honor. I have information for you about AW Fairbanks." "She wishes to beg my forgiveness?" "Sorry, Your Honor, but no. I called to inform you that she has been identified as a fugitive killer from Maryland. Also, she is our prime suspect for Bob Moore's murder. The same gun was used for both." "I can't say I'm surprised. Sheriff Andrews, I have felt for sometime that something was wrong with that woman." "Your Honor, that is what I called to talk about. In questioning her, Captain Baker and I discovered that she may be delusional. She could also be faking it. We need a psychiatric exam for her." "Sheriff, is this request not the responsibility of the District Attorney?" "Yes Sir, it normally is. But I and my staff need to further question her and the State of Maryland will soon file to extradite her. We need to move forward on this. She needs to be evaluated for competency quickly." "You are quite right. We don't have any budget for it, of course. But that is not our problem, is it?" "No Sir, that one belongs to the Board of Supervisor. I believe we are bound by State Law and Court precedent." "State and Federal Courts, my boy, don't forget the Feds. Yes, we are required to give our charges a fair trial. It is not our problem how to pay for it. I believe that they can get funding from the State Department of Justice. Sheriff, I will start the wheels rolling." "Thank you, Your Honor." The Judge hung up. Bill decided to write up his report on AW.

It was about thirty minutes later, that a very curious Charles O'Brien was ushered into Bill's office by Wanda, "Sheriff, Mr. O'Brien says you sent for him." "Yes, Wanda, I did. Thank you." "Mr O'Brien, I am Sheriff Andrews. Please be seated," he gestured to a chair at the small table off to one side in his office. Charlie took a seat on one side of the table. He was a small man about sixty, somewhat overweight, with thinning hair. Bill crossed over to the table and set a small cassette tape recorder and a manilla folder on the table between them. He sat down across the table from Charlie. "Do you mind if I record this meeting?" "Sheriff, what is this meeting about?" "Mr O'Brien, I need to ask you some questions about AW Fairbanks. May I record?" "I don't know what you want to know about AW, but ask away." "This interview is beginning at 3:20 pm. Present are Sheriff William Andrews and Charles O'Brien." "Mr O'Brien, when did you first meet AW Fairbanks?" "Please call me Charlie. AW first contacted me in September, 1999. She bought a house from me." "Did she purchase other properties from you?" "Yes, Sheriff, she has purchased several properties, and sold some through me." "Charlie, what form of payment did she use usually?" "She always paid cash for them. Sometimes using the money from the sale of another property." "Do you know where she got the money for these purchases?" "She has an account with the Chemical Bank of Los Angeles. How money gets into that, I don't know." Bill opened the folder and took out a sheet of paper, "Charlie, I have here a print out from The California Department of Real Estate. It shows that you have had your Brokers Licence temporarily suspended once and restricted twice. You seem to have trouble handing your Trust Account. I'll bet an infusion of capital was very welcomed. Is that why you agreed to a partnership with AW?" "Sheriff Andrews, I admit that our partnership was a real

162

shot in the arm for my business. But I never did anything illegal. Many times, she wanted me to do illegal or unethical things. She got mad when I said no. I found properties for us to buy, and she supplied the capital." "Charlie, didn't you ever wonder where the money was coming from?" "Yeah, I wondered. But if I got curious, AW got really pissed. It occurred to me that I was playing with fire, so I stopped." "What about her gun?" Charlie seemed startled for a moment, then replied, "Yeah, I knew she had one. I found out when she couldn't find it. She kept it in her desk. She claimed someone took it. I told her she should report it stolen. She told me to mind my own business." "When was this?" "Oh, about six months ago. About the time we were working on the condo proposal for the County Supervisors." "Are you aware of the gun's location right now?" "No, Sheriff, I don't know if she got it back. She never said another word about it." "I need to inform you that AW Fairbanks is being held for the murder of her husband thirty years ago in Maryland. Also, she is our prime suspect for the murder of Bob Moore." The effect on Charlie was dramatic, "I had no idea she was a fugitive! I thought she was part of a wealthy family! You have to believe me, I didn't have a clue!" "We need to track her whereabouts for last week. Do you know when she made a trip out of town?" "Sheriff Andrews, I don't think AW has been out of town for over two weeks. She was working on the court case and the plans for a casino, I think. She and Johnny Eagle met a lot. One time she met with our attorney, Marvin Schiller. She was in our office every day last week. Ask our secretary, Linda." "Charlie, I want to thank you for your assistance in this matter. I must inform you that your place of business will be searched by my officers." "They were there when I left. Sheriff Andrews, when will they be out of my office?" "When they are finished. You may go now. Do you know the way out?" Charlie rose to go, "Yes, thank you. I just hope I don't have to find my way back. Goodbye to you." He left the office. Bill spoke to the tape recorder, "This Interview is terminated at 3:40 pm." He switched off the recorder, picked it up, crossed over to his desk, and sat down. He took the tape out of the machine, put it in a manilla envelope, and wrote on the envelope, then sealed it. The sealed envelope when into a desk drawer, which he then locked with a key from his key ring.

Barbara had visited Patty today. She was still in the Hospital, X-rays had found three crack ribs. The Staff preferred to treat the little girl in the Hospital, children of that age tend to be rather careless. The down side was she was very restless now. Her Grandmother was with her, but she seemed unused to 'entertaining' Patty. Was she just allowed to run wild? With the need to limit her movements, Patty could not go to the other children in the Ward. So Barbara had to arranged for some of the kids to visit Patty. It broke up her day quite nicely. Barbara wonder if anyone knew that she was sleeping with a member of Patty's family! That thought trigger a host of carnal images. She hoped no one saw her blush! So far, Aunt Sarah had said little about her 'nights out'. Barbara had her beeper with her. Her bag was in her car, ready for use. She liked to think that she would be ready, if needed. Sarah had not chided her about her duties. Was this her way of approving? Not for the first time, Barbara was having trouble divining her Aunt's mind. It did occur to her, that Sarah had no problem letting one know of her disapproval. Why no outburst now? She saw a glimmer of the truth. Sarah wanted this to happen! She had two more patients to see in the Office, then home to get ready for her Dinner at Jim's. She knew very well, what he had in mind for desert!

Bill was deep into the manual for their new portable radios. Each Officer would soon carry a radio, just like the major police agencies. Wanda stood in the door way and cleared her throat. Bill addressed her, "Yes, Wanda?" She came into the office, and up to his desk, "Bill, Jason Saunders has asked me out. What should I do?" Bill was surprised, first off she never called him Bill any more. Secondly, she rarely mentioned her personal life to anyone. "Wanda, when is the last time you went on a date?" "Bill, I haven't been out on a date for over twenty years. What should I do?" "What has Jason suggested that you do on this date?" "He wants me to go to his house for dinner, he'll send a car for me." "Okay, Wanda, in that house you will be chaperoned by Maria Sanchez and several security men. Maybe even his Daughter will be there. His wife died several years ago, Jason is a lonely man. He is also a formidable man, very bright, very energetic, but very compassionate. Jason is a good man. I think he can be very gentle. I"ve seen him with his Daughter." Wanda

164

looked relieved, "I've talked to him several times. He seems to care about people. He seems to care about me." "Wanda. I am sure he does. He asked me about you. I feel like I need to warn you, Jason wants a physical relationship." Wanda's ample chest swelled, "Bill Andrew, I sure hope he does. There is nothing new about a man wanting that, from me." She smiled as she went back to her desk. He thought of how she had changed from the skinny fourteen year old that use to flirt with him. Bill could not help himself, an image of a naked Wanda pop into his head for a moment. It was quickly replaced by an image of a naked Anita, which lingered much longer. This pleasant diversion was disrupted by Wanda's voice blaring out of the Intercom speaker, "Sheriff Andrews, ADA Metcalfe is here to see you." "Send her in, Wanda." Assistant District Attorney Marion Metcalfe was a plain woman of about the same age of Bill. You might have noticed that she knew how to do her hair, clothes, and makeup to make the most of her rather average attributes. There was nothing average about her mind, however. She strode over to Bill's desk with a serious expression, "What is going on with this AW Fairbanks thing?" "Hello to you too, Marion. This "thing" is that her real name is Alice Ferranti Wentworth and she killed her husband in Maryland, thirty years ago." "How did you find this out?" "We got an IBIS hit on the bullet that killed Bob Moore. The gun used to kill Bob Moore was also used to kill Mr. Wentworth. Jim Bearpaw got the bright idea that AW might be the cause of both, so he had her fingerprinted. We got a hit on AFIS. The State of Maryland will want to extradite her. The FBI wants her on an old Fugitive charge. And she is our number one suspect for Bob Moore's murder." Marion sat down in one of the chairs, somewhat surprised, "You have been busy! How is the Bob Moore Investigation going?" "Russ and I interviewed AW this afternoon. We got nothing out of her about either killing. I really think that she is delusional. I don't think she knows who she really is." "We need to get her examined. I'll contact Judge O'Reilly." "I already did that. Sorry if I stepped on your prerogative, but we need to get her judged competent to stand questioning. I don't know if she's faking or not. Also, she asked for a lawyer." "All right Bill, you're forgiven. What other information do you have on her." Bill reached into his Out basket to retrieve a report. "Here is what we have so far," he handed the document to Marion. She quickly skimmed the pages. "Can I keep this?" "It's yours, Marion." "Thanks. You will keep me informed about this case." "Marion, shortly after I learn something, so will you." "Thanks Bill." She hesitated for a moment, then spoke, "Bill, did you ever think either of us would end up back here?" "No Marion, I never did. I figured when I went off to U.S.C., and you went off to Cal, that was it. I went into the Navy and you went on to Law School. I heard you were working for the San Francisco DA. What did bring you back?" She smiled, "I met a Park Ranger. I was working as a volunteer at the Golden Gate Rec area one weekend and I met this very nice career Ranger. We got married about a year later. We lived on Diamond Heights. You could see the entire city, when there was no fog. Even the fog was beautiful. Three years ago, he got a chance to come here as Chief Ranger for the National Forest. So we moved here, then this job opened up." "How do you like working for our beloved DA?" "He's a jerk, but he knows enough to keep out of my cases. Is it true that you've got the FBI trying to nail him for your Sister's murder?" "The evidence is at Quantico as we speak. They have the best Forensic Lab. If anyone can nail him, they can. Marion, tell me, after San Francisco, how do you like our old home town?" She laughed, "Oh Bill, I like it just fine. I have my husband and my work, and some old friends, like you. Of course, Satellite TV helps." They both laughed. Marion stood to leave, "Please send me a copy of whatever you discover." "You got it, Madam Prosecutor." They both were smiling as Marion left.

Evening at Bill Andrews', found Bill, Jennifer, and Bernadette clustered around the Dinning Room table. Bernadette was unrolling some maps onto the table, "I got these from the USGS in Sacramento. I've found them very co-operative in the past." "If they didn't co-operate, you would probably tell the Governor on them," Bill sneered. She never missed a beat, "I doubt that I'd find the Governor in. I'd have to settle for the Lt. Governor." Bill and Jennifer smiled at this jab at their much traveled Governor. Bill was helping spread out the maps, "Here's one of the southern county line. See if you can find the next one south of that." Bernadette sorted through several before she found the one, "Here it is," she aligned it with the map Bill had laid out. Three heads converged over the maps. "There are the fault lines running North toward the County," Bernadette pointed to the map she had found. Jennifer was seriously examining the map of the southern County, "Where are the fault lines in the County?" Bernadette had been watching her search, "There aren't any. The USGS has not surveyed up here for that, yet." Jennifer was somewhat frustrated, "But that is what Bob Moore was doing, wasn't it?" "Dear, Bob was doing a basic surface survey. He had no equipment or manpower to do anything in depth. His report gives us places to look, but is not proof in its self." "But didn't the Judge give us an injunction based upon Bob's report?" Jennifer demanded. Bernadette was somewhat surprised by this, "Jennifer, Judge O'Reilly gave us an injunction based upon the impact on the environment and infrastructure of the Valley. The Geology Report came late, only two days before the Hearing. Bob's report was only a flag indicating that more study is needed. No one can say at this point that there is a fault in the Valley, only that there may be one." Jennifer was suddenly silent, and looked rather pensive. Bill saw her look and became concerned, "What's the matter, Jennifer?" She screwed up her lips for a moment, then responded, "I think I made a mistake. I told a reporter I know in LA about the fault up here, and about the casino plot." Bill was upset, "Jennifer, you had no right to say anything about these things. You had no facts, just hearsay. I hope this LA reporter bothers to check the stories." Jennifer was stung by this, "We needed to get these things out. What they're trying to do needs to be exposed." "We need facts if we are going to catch Bob's killer," Bill reminded her." We need facts to stop Johnny Eagle and his Casino plan. What we don't need is someone blabbing a bunch of heresay to a reporter. That was very irresponsible of you. You could destroy our credibility. I'm the Sheriff here and Bernadette is a State Archaeologist, our reputations could be damage by your actions. You need to think before you act. I don't want you talking to the press about any of this without my permission." During this, Jennifer's irritation had turned to anger, "I was not irresponsible! I don't need your permission to talk to the press on these issues!" "I'm afraid you do," Bernadette spoke sternly," I represent the State on these issues, and the Sheriff represents the County. There is a murder investigation underway, and another one concerning bribery. We need to get the USGS to survey the county. All these thing could be damaged by careless talk." Shocked by this attack by her friend, Jennifer defended her actions, "We need to get this information out! What are you two trying to hide!" "We aren't trying to hide anything," Bill showed his frustration with Jennifer, "We are trying to conduct scientific investigations here, not produce PR for the Nature Coalition." That was the last straw, Jennifer ran crying from the room and out the front door. The sound of her car starting and driving away could be heard. Bernadette was contrite, "We were hard on her, maybe too hard." Bill was resolved, "We were right. She was irresponsible. She often is, this time it really mattered. She has got to learn that even being Jason Saunders Daughter has its limitations." "Bill, what is this going to do to your relationship?" "We don't have a relationship Bernadette. Our seeing each other was her idea. I'm now seeing someone else" "Is it Anita Brubaker?" "Yes it is." "You could still help her, Bill. Don't let this go on to long. See her soon." "We'll see." Bernadette looks at her watch, "Well, I should be getting back to my motel. The skeletons at the Mines put us behind on our Indian Village. We are starting earlier these mornings. I need my rest. Is it alright for me to leave these maps with you?" "That will be fine, Bernadette. I'll see you out." They both exited the room, and Bill escorted her out to her car.

An hour or so later, Bill was in his easy chair. Susie was in his lap and Tiger was laying on the arm of the chair. Bill was rereading Bob Moore's report. He heard a car come up the driveway and stop. Then there was a car door slam shut. Next, he heard footsteps on the front stairs. He was not surprised when his doorbell rang. He gently placed the sleepy dog on the other chair, and headed for the front door. He flipped on the porch light. Opening the front door, he expected to see Jennifer. Instead, he saw a pretty girl in her 20's, about 5' 7", with auburn hair and a full bust. Immediately, she rushed in and embraced Bill, Bill embraced her back. He slung the door shut with one arm.

Chapter Twelve

Monday:

Sierra Vista Station One stood down. Brenda had been called to the Rittenhaus Mansion. The Fire Marshal had a large cow, when he found out that neither the arson investigator or the Sheriff's CSI team had seen fit to call in someone with a Haz-Mat certificate. As Battalion Chief for Cal Fire, Stan was asked if he could recommend someone. Could he! Brenda Dawson had her State Certificate in Hazardous Materials, she was duly dispatched. That left the Station without and Engineer. Time off was due for this Station anyway, so the rest of the crew made plans for their day off. Danny seemed particularly pleased, after making a phone call. Jake saw his co-worker change into civilian clothes, nice civilian clothes. But he said nothing, just turned on the big floor fan and laid in his bunk. Danny saw this, but paid no attention. Jake had always been moody, always talking about how he had been cheated, or betrayed! "Some people just like to be unhappy," His Mother used to say. Danny was not like that, especially not today! He was taking his girlfriend out. Captain Grayson was taking his family out for the day, including his niece. Too bad Jake! Danny took his old Chevy over to an older, but pretty neighborhood in town. He parked in the driveway, walking quickly up to the door. A cute Blonde of about eighteen answered. He was quickly admitted, her arms went around his neck. They shared a nice kiss. Her Mom and Aunt were in the Living Room, but both ladies smiled at the young couple. Her name was Sally Mae Crabtree, and she thought that Danny was a hero. He had gone into her Parent's burning home to rescue her cat. All three ladies thought the young firefighter was handsome and brave. When Sally had first expressed interest in the twenty year old, no one in her extended family objected. She was pleased that he returned her interest. Sally had him pickup the picnic basket, she took a blanket. Everything went into the backseat, except Sally and

Danny. The bench seat allowed Sally to plant herself solidly against the firefighter. Air conditioning made it comfortable, on this ninety plus degree day. She knew just the place for their outing, but it was a little drive away, beyond the Washo Reservation. Danny had never been there, it was like an adventure!

Over at the Mansion, Brenda was not having an adventure. She was sure it was a nightmare! In the basement, she had found several five gallon containers of solvents. There was Toluene, Acetone, and worst of all, Methylene Chloride! These were tonic, flammable, and cancer causing. She immediately informed the Sargent on site, that these containers had to be removed to a safe place. Redding had a certified facility for handling these chemicals. When asked what would happen to them, Brenda casually mentioned that the usual method was to destroy them, by burning in a closed furnace. She thought that Sargent Yeager was going to faint! He quickly said no! They were all evidence in a drug case! They were to stay right here, under guard, until the case was tried. She asked him if his people had Haz-Mat suits, or even masks? Yeager was at a loss, he was not sure what the his Department had. She told him that her hands were tied, hazardous materials must be handled. She had to notify the State. He said that he could not release evidence in a case. Things seemed to be at a stalemate! The two Deputies pulled their Sargent aside. Neither of them wanted to breathe toxic fumes! What if they burn, or explode! A compromise was quickly reached! Forensic samples would be taken of each one. These would be analyzed, the analysis could be entered into evidence. The chemicals would be photographed from every angle, the serial numbers would be recorded, and a signed receipt would be left by the State, when the containers were picked up. Brenda and Yeager shook on it. As she got ready to leave, one of the Deputies asked her out. He looked okay, and he was a bit taller than her, so she accepted. They exchanged phone numbers. A smiling Brenda drove back to the Fire Station, to make her phone calls, and do her report. She hoped the State cooperated in this little compromise. Yeager told her that two men had been identified from fingerprints found on site. Warrants and APBs had been issued for both. Several sets of unidentified prints had been found.

Sally guided Danny through the Reservation on Route One, out to Route Five, then North to the old fire road. Turn right, then follow the dirt road to Spanish Creek. Sally explained to him that the Creek ran year long, due to an Artesian spring. Danny had never seen anything like that. She showed him a good picnic spot. He had asked her about her Folk's home. How was the work coming? Sally was glad to tell him that the roof was on, they were working on the siding. From that, Danny knew that she would be living at her relatives house for about two more months. He told her he was happy that she would be getting her room back. Sally thanked him, but she knew that her room had become less important to her. It did not include a young firefighter! Danny found that his Lady knew how to pack a picnic lunch. In truth, she had the use of others' experience, her Mother and Aunt. There was an old tradition there, Danny reaped the benefit of their experience. The young couple sat on the blanket, in the shade, eating and talking. The creek bubbled and splashed, as it ran over the rocks. It was warm and so pleasant at the Creek. There was no Jake, no hoses, just Sally's pretty smile. Having eaten their fill, the pair lay side by side on the old blanket. After a few minutes, Danny rolled over, and kissed Sally. To be wanted by her young man, thrilled the young Blonde. They kissed for some time. He ventured to kiss her neck, then the spot above her bra. He ventured to unbutton her blouse, she did not mind. His hand slipped under her bra, he began to message her small breast. Her eyes were closed, enjoying the feeling. Danny enjoyed these sessions, but he could not help wondering, "How much will Sally fill out?" Both her Mother and Aunt had nice sized breasts. He pushed her bra up, then fondled both breasts. Sally was smiling, it felt good, and she liked him exploring her. She was so glad that he was interested! She knew she was skinny. Her shorts showed legs that were long and spindly. She had grown so fast, her body needed time to catch up. She was 5' 8", and only weighted 115 pounds. Danny started licking her breasts. She loved this part! A little of this, and Sally knew to call a halt. She was getting wet, and she wanted more! That was not part of her plan, not yet! Sally was a virgin, so much about sex and her body scared her. But Danny always seemed to understand. He was so gentle. Danny immediately obeyed, pulling her bra down, and redoing her buttons. "Thank you, Danny. That felt so good! Now I want to take you to the Spring." Danny was easy, he did not mind walking with his arm around her waist. He could feel her move! Then the bank narrowed. They walked along

171

the creek, now holding hands. They stopped for a kiss, then Danny heard something! Quietly, the pair moved forward. They heard men, speaking Spanish! They used the bushes for cover, it allowed them to peer around a bend. Danny took it all in. Several men were moving in and out of tents, or placing fresh foliage on them. Was this camouflage? He saw one of the men with a gun, he was on a higher level. He saw the curved ammo magazine, it was an AK-47 assault rifle! He had no doubt, drug smugglers! Mexican drug dealers were camping here! He hustled Sally back to their basket, then the basket and Sally were rushed into his car. Starting the car, nearly gave him a heart attack! He expected to be riddled with bullets at any minute! Slowly, quietly they drove down the fire road, and back onto Route Five. Only then, did Danny feel confident enough to get out his Cell phone. He called 911. They took his information, asking several questions. He had to give them his contact information, before they let him go. Sally was plastered to his side all the way to Station One. They could have been killed!

Lieutenant Jim Bearpaw had been given Danny's information. It was just the conformation that was needed. Several armed Hispanics hiding out in camouflaged tents was a much more substantial proof of drug activity at the Mines. Spanish Creek began very near the end of Old Mine Road. Now, Jim considered when he should pass this tidbit on. Both Bill and the DEA should know, but timing was important. Better to reveal it as part of something bigger. But when could it be done? As usual, Jim felt he would know when the time was right. It was the Washo way.

Brenda went back to Station One. With the Captain out for the day, she felt no qualm about using his desk. First, she made her phone call to the State. Due notification of the solvents was given, and their status as evidence in a Drug Case. Old hat, to the clerk who handled the call. Brenda was told that this happened all the time. The containers of solvents would be picked up, but would remain the property of the Sheriff's Department. The State facility at Redding would hold them in a safe room, until the Court released them for destruction. Brenda was pleased, it was more organized than she expected, a very pleasant surprise. Arrangements having been made, Brenda started working on her report of the Haz-Mat Incident. She was deep into the form, when she heard a noise. Looking up, there was Jake in the doorway. "Oh, hi Jake.

Enjoying your time off?" Her eyes went back to the form. "Don't look away, Bitch!" Brenda heard a click. When she looked up, Jake was at the desk, with a buck knife. "You betrayed me to the Captain! You insulted me! I know you talk about me, behind my back!" Leaning across the desk, he stuck the knife in her face. "Now, its my turn! First, I'm going to have a good look at you!" His free hand reached for her shirt, he grasped the top button. "I'm gonna take your clothes off, then I'm gonna rape you! Brenda's hand went to her belt, the cylinder was in her hand! Jake screamed, as the Pepper Spray hit his eyes and mouth, "You Bitch! I can't see! My eyes!" His knife dropped on the table, Brenda brushed into the top drawer. She grabbed the phone, calling 911, as Jake screamed in pain. Jake started grabbing for her, but she hit him with the handset, then finished her call. A car with two Deputies was there in three minutes. They handcuffed the unconscious Jake, took Brenda's statement, and took custody of the buck knife. Stan and Janet were there, attracted by the Patrol Car. They waited patiently, as she was questioned in great detail. Just what was said? Finally, Jake woke up, had his face scrubbed, then was placed in the back of the Patrol Car. Brenda was told that he would be charged with Assault, and Attempted Rape. Would she come in tomorrow, and sign the Complaint? She certainly would! As Jake was driven away, Stan and Janet ushered a shaken Brenda home. She was fed, hugged, and kissed, before she was urged to take a nap. "Nonsense!" She said, "I have a report to finish." Janet helped her change her torn clothes, while Stan went to get her paperwork. Danny and Sally appeared as he was leaving the Station. They were informed about Jake's behavior, and subsequent arrest. Danny told Stan that he was just going to show Sally the Station and Engine. Stan wished them an enjoyable day off. Danny showed Sally the Kitchen and Lounge. The Captain's office was off limits, it was block off with yellow Crime Tape. Danny told her about the mold problem with their sleeping area. He showed her where they slept now. The big floor fan blew across the two beds, making it almost cool in the area masked off from the Engine Bays. Sally was shown the two Engines, she was able to climb all over Engine One. She sat in the driver's seat, dreaming that she was Brenda, driving to a fire. When her tour was done, she kissed Danny. The pair drifted over to the sleeping area. They pushed the two beds together, then made sure that all the doors were locked.

Danny pulled the plastic curtains together, the beds were entirely masked. He knew, Sally was a shy person. She needed complete privacy to disrobe for him. He showed her the box of condoms, then undressed the slim Blonde. He knew enough to take it slow and easy, although he want to rush things. Sally saw his eagerness, to her it said, "He wants me!" What more could she ask for? She let him go all the way. She always knew she would, some day. After hearing about Brenda's attack, Sally knew it could happen to her. She decided that today was the day. She wanted her first time to be with Danny. She felt a little pain, there was a little bleeding. He had provided paper towels to catch the blood. Afterwards, Sally cuddled with her lover. They talked about the future. Not the distant future, but the near future. Like when could the meet like this again, and where? They had plans to make. It did occur to Sally, how odd this was. She did understand the irony, one woman saved herself from rape, while another young woman decided to lose her virginity. All in the same Fire Station, on the same day. Sally and Danny had no regrets, only plans. And as for Brenda, time would tell.

She tried to write, but the shakes came back. Brenda sat at her desk, trying to finish her report. Her hand shook, she felt queasy, what was wrong? It was no use, she had to do what Stan had suggested, she laid down. She closed her eyes, trying to forget about Jake. She relaxed and thought of pleasant things. She drifted, finally, she slept. Stan knew about shock, he knew what it could do. He peeked in on Brenda periodically. He intended to just let her sleep. He watched her regular breathing, so peaceful. Yet he knew, she could have been raped and killed. What made Jake snap? Did he know what was in store for him? Stan hoped he got sent for a psych evaluation. Both he and Gary Grayson were sure that would finish him with Cal Fire. He was almost finished now. Stan had started the paperwork. His conviction in the local Court would close the chapter on Jake Sawyer. Today had shaken Stan. He had experienced just how much he felt for Brenda. If Jake had not been in police custody, he might have killed the arrogant pervert! The strength of his feelings surprised him. Now Stan knew, he cared very much for the tall, young firefighter. She might be young enough to be his daughter, it did not matter. To Stan, what mattered was how Brenda would greet this revelation. Would he ever tell her?

174

Brent had spent part of his Friday, helping Mona retrieve the remainder of her stuff from her Mama's house. They had talked about what to do with the furniture? Mona planned on getting some boxes for her Mother's stuff. It was all going to the Salvation Army. Much of it had come from their thrift store, originally. Aid to Dependant Children had seen to Mona's wardrobe, until she reached eighteen. Now, she earned her own money. Brent watched his little partner work. She had such a determined look! As they finished in her Mother's room, he gave in to the urge. Brent came up behind her, slipped his arms around her waist, then whispered in her ear, "I can't keep my hands off you! Do you mind?" He was severely kissed, for his efforts. She did like these little surprises. All of Mona's things were soon integrated into Brent's house. The Master Bedroom became thoroughly coed, not that Brent minded. All of this benefitted their time in bed. Little Mona was blossoming, as her confidence grew, so did her sexual appetite. Their time off was a good time for both of them. On Monday, Mona was told the her Mother's body was ready for release. She arranged for if to be cremated. She could not afford a burial. All of the furniture could now be picked up. Brent had arranged for it to be sold by a Consignment Broker. It was the same one that handled his Grandmother's things. Brent watch with pleasure, as his Lover took on more of the chores around the house. Mona was certainly not afraid of work! As for Mona, she cleaned and arranged with great joy. For the first time, she felt like this was her house, too. Brent gave her lots of room to do things, which the little redhead took as trust. He trusted her to make decisions! Mona had grown quite content, very quickly. She liked her job, the owners of the Motel were nice to her. Having no children of their own, they sort of adopted the orphan teen. They knew a Deputy took her to and from work, but not about their sleeping together. They thought that she rented a room from him, an old friend. Well, it was true. The room just happened to be his bedroom. She had no intention of telling. Both of her Bosses were ex-cops, they were both suspicious of the cute young redhead, and her handsome Deputy. They had seen them kiss, in Brent's car. They both smiled at the little deception.

One more whiny loser, that was the impression Sargent Sumner had of Jake. The kid never shut up. He was innocent! He was set up! What a pile of crap! Sumner had the word, the knife he used had his prints all over it. He wore the scabbard for it on his belt. He was going to jail for a long time! Sumner had three inmates in his jail right now. AW might be going to Maryland, rumor had it. Good riddance! What a Bitch that old woman was! Always yell for her rights! AW wouldn't know her rights if they pissed in her ear! Then there was the Indian, Attempted Rape of the Saunders woman. He used a gun in the crime, that would mean more time. "I've seen that Jennifer Saunders, what a body! I'll bet she has all the action she can handle!" Only three inmates right now. But the twenty-five year vet was not optimistic, he saw the signs. There were less arrests for drunkenness, more for serious crime. Times had charged in the Valley. People seemed to be more desperate now. It was the Mill closing, then the loss of the hotel/condo development. Some people just had no more hope. Some just want what they don't have. It saddened him to see it. He knew that it meant more violence, more crime. More work for him and his Deputies. The Sargent went back to his computer, he was entering Jake. Not a pretty picture, but better than AW. That one had fooled him. She came in for Contempt, now being held for Extradition. Wanted for murder in Maryland. A small, old murderer, justice finally caught up with her. On the run for thirty years, not much of a life. The kid, Jake, twenty-two years old. He will be middle-aged, before he gets out. Then he considered the situation. Jake had a mouth, and a bad attitude. Either one could get a rapist killed, in prison. He smiled as he typed.

He sat at his desk, the office was smaller than he liked. The Tribal offices were cramped, Johnny disliked cramped things. Poor and cramped describe his childhood, then he was chosen to attend a private prep school. That scholarship was the first of many, culminating with one to Harvard Law. He had excelled there, showing those Ivy League whites who was the brightest. He was as smart as any of them. Why was he not rich, like them? He had tried working for others, but got tired of making them wealthy. So he looked about for something he could make his own. This was a good spot for an Indian Casino. Soon, he found partners to help with his dream. Now he found that AW was a crazed killer! Maybe they will blame her for the Geologist. Why did that man have to get nosey? Take the money and run, that was the way. Mind your own business and get paid! Linda, his wife, worked for AW, and her partner. Johnny did not like AW in Jail, or the Court Injunc-

176

tion. These things slowed down his plans, made him improvise. He was now on Plan B, the Casino would go through, without the Hotel/condo development. Perhaps he would do it all on the Reservation. There were Traditionalists that opposed him, but the poverty of the Tribe was in his favor. So many of the young members were unemployed, state unemployment all but exhausted. They were restless, even the best of them seemed ready to grow Pot, or brew Meth. The good ones were smart enough not to get caught, or if they did, they did not talk. Johnny made sure that they were taken care of. At least he tried. This new Sheriff was too clever by half. All this information about the Corporations, was nothing by itself. The Sheriff had no probable cause to get into the finances of these groups, his groups. Without that, he knew nothing. If things went right, the Sheriff would have nothing but suspicions, until it was too late. Until then, the Sheriff needed watching. Captain Baker could do that, if he joined our little group. A little bird told Johnny that Russ Baker was in money trouble. Left his wife for a well built teenager, he liked to buy her things. So much the better, a man in need of money, is a man you could deal with. Plan B could work out, it would just take longer. The Sheriff was up for election in the Fall, what if Russ ran against him? The Sheriff could be guilty of something. An affair with a married woman? Too many bed partners? Very unseemly for a Sheriff, even if they were fabricated. Could he ever prove the charges were false? Yes, a smear campaign would keep the Sheriff on the ropes. Money was the key, and money would be plentiful, if the Mines worked out. Johnny Eagle knew there was a problem, Linda. His wife was anxious, would she talk? Linda would have to be reassured, the problem with AW was unimportant. If she kept her mouth shut, it would all work out! If she could not keep silent, she might just have an 'accident'.

When Stan came home, he was surprised to find his Living Room filled with Volunteers, some brought their family. Rhonda was there, close to Brenda. She seemed most affected by the attack. She had been shocked, when she heard. The Dinning table was covered with bowls, casseroles, and plates of food. Everybody sent something! Stan rounded up the plates and silverware, they served themselves, cafeteria style. Some had brought things to drink, Stan noticed the absence of alcohol. He whole heartedly approved, Stan had seen too much foolishness connected to booze.

177

There was air of disbelief that such a thing had occurred! An attack on a firefighter was bad enough, but to come from another firefighter was hard to swallow. As the evening wore on, more people asked Stan about a replacement for Jake. He told them that a fax had gone out, they just had to wait for a reply. Privately, he was not optimistic. Cal Fire was short of manpower, they would probably wait a while, then get a recruit. Someone right out of the Academy! It would take them weeks to pull their weight. Such was life, in tough times. Still, anything would be better than Jake! Those with children were the first to leave. Rhonda insisted on helping Stan clean up. Brenda soon joined them, she was not the kind to sit around. Stan was not surprised, he knew something about the young firefighter. They had crewed a Pumper together for two years. He thought that she was doing okay. No shakes, no drifting, she seemed focused. He figure that a good night's sleep would aid the cause. It could have been much worse.

Late in the day, Charlie received a call from a local Hispanic grocer. It seems that a well educated Mexican was in his store this morning. The man brought a lot of food, sacks of rice and beans, dozens of tortillas, cases of Mexican soft drinks. He paid in cash. The informant said that he spoke like someone born and raised in Mexico City, and very well educated. Most questions were met by silence, or a monosyllable answer. He drove north from Susanville, in a fancy model Jeep, with some logo on the doors. There were two other Hispanic males in the vehicle. Charlie was pissed, why had the man had not called sooner? He might have been able to arrange a tail. Where were they going? Was this connect to the Mines, or a whole different operation? It was the same old story, you got bits and pieces, never the whole story. Well, it was still early. This story had a while to run. Sheriff Andrews had eyes on the Mines, maybe something would come from that. That would be more substantial, than a Hispanic male purchasing supplies in Susanville. "I need more information!" His mind screamed. He was sure it would come, but when? This waiting was the hard part. Better he could corner them, then there would be a shoot out. Better violence, than this waiting. Always waiting for the facts to emerge.

Desert was on the mind of Donna, tonight. She breezed into the Tent, gave Brent a big kiss. Then started making plans. "Long

178

time, no see." Chided the young Deputy. She was quick to explain, "Had my monthly curse, but it's okay now." Brent considered that. He had heard of how bad it was for some women, she must be one. Cramps, bleeding, headaches, the stories were ugly. "Sorry it was bad for you. I know some gals have problems." She frowned, "But you don't know any women like that, do you?" He shook his head, "No, I don't. My Mother and Sister, treated it like nothing special. One gal I dated had some bloating." "Well, I have bloating, cramps, headaches, and bleeding. It really sucks!" He put his hand on hers, as it rested on the tabletop, "I am sorry. How are you, now?" Donna smiled, gripping his hand. "If you care to join me, in the enclosure, I could show you." Donna chose to accompanied him on his circuit around the field. She talked about the Indian artifacts they found, every day. She told him how difficult it was working with Jennifer, the tall Blonde, "What an egotist! Everything has to be her way! Yet because she almost has her PhD, she treats the rest of us like we were High Schoolers!" Brent told her how, in his experience, people like that usually got theirs. "Cheer up!" Later, in the enclosure, Brent gave her much to be happy about. She was very vocal, and very affectionate. Brent noted how well it went, in the dark. He forgot her size, in the throes of sex. The big girl made him forget all else. He was sure that it was the power of those big tits! After, when she had dressed, she kissed him goodbye. When she slipped him the money, he wondered if she wished him to refuse if? Brent had never paid a 'hooker' for sex, so he was uneasy with this arrangement. He had trouble understanding Donna, and her 'situation'. He was more at ease, taking Mona home, undressing her, and 'entertaining' the little redhead. She made him feel so good! He was sure that he was the center of her life. He had no idea what constituted the center of life for someone like Donna. She liked sex, but what else? He cuddled with Mona, falling asleep with his teenage lover. He had dealt with enough mysteries today.

At seven o'clock that evening, Jim's doorbell rang (actually it chimed). Jim dried his hands and went to the door. Opening the door revealed Dr Barbara Davis, wearing a dark colored coat and heels. "Hello Barbara, please come in." "Thank you." She stepped in and Jim closed the door. "Can I take your coat?" Barbara unbuttoned it and turned her back to him. Jim took her coat by the lapels and slipped it off, revealing Barbara's 'simple black dress'. It had thin straps, was low cut enough to show an interesting amount of cleavage, and ended high enough above the knee to display Barbara's shapely legs. Jim was able to hang her coat in the closet and still get an eye full of Barbara. His hands now free, he embraced her and they kiss. Embracing again, he whispered in her ear, "You look beautiful, Barbara. You do great things for that dress." She flushed a bit, it had been a while since she had heard such words from someone she cared for. Jim stepped back from her and extended his hand, "Dinner is just about ready." She took his hand and asked, "What are we having?" "Poached trout," was the answer, as he led her into the unpainted Dinning Room. He pulled out the chair at the head of the table for her. She sat in it and became aware the table seemed to glow, a deep, rich reddish-brown glow. There were two place settings, then this large expanse of glowing wood. She looked up at him and asked, "What kind of wood is this? Did you make this table?" "It is Brazilian Rosewood, and no Barbara, I did not build it. It was built in a shop run by members of my tribe. My cousin, Clint, designed it. He also designed the table at Jason Saunders house." "The light of the chandelier is reflected by the table. I've never seen anything with that luster." "It is a time consuming process, involving many layers of finish," Jim said, patiently." Each layer must be lightly sanded before the next is added. After all layers have been added, the finish must be buffed and polished, mostly by hand." "This must have cost a fortune, Bill." "Not really. A picture of this table is in their catalog. They sometimes bring clients here to see it. Please excuse me, I need to check on our dinner." Smiling, he left the room. Barbara watched him go, "Could I help with any thing?" "Thanks, but no," he called out from the Kitchen, "If you came in here, dinner would be delayed." She smiled, and thought, "He is probably right. This dress still works, with a little help from me." In her heart of hearts, she wanted to go into the Kitchen. "No, I'm going to be a good girl and wait right here. There will be time for that after dinner. Besides, I'm hungry!" Shortly, dinner was served. The trout was delicious, served with Asparagus and a chilled Chardonnay. Barbara noted that he never touched her during dinner. Not once. This intrigued her, "Is he mad at me, for canceling last night? He was told that it was a medical emergency." What ever it is, she was going to find out. She had

180

been surprised by the intensity of their love making. Barbara hated losing control like that. Jim cleared their plates. Then they went into the Living Room to enjoy their wine. She sat on the sofa and then he sat a respectable distance from her. She slid over, next to him. He raised his eyebrow for a moment, but said nothing about it. She continued to ask questions about the room and the house, and he continued to answer them. Suddenly, she put her hand on his knee and looked him in the eye. Jim put down his wine, put an arm around her waist, and pulled her to him. She put down her wine glass, put her arm around his neck and kissed him. He kissed her back. They were locked together like that when a sound from the bedroom hallway caught Jim's attention, "Dispatch to Unit Three! Dispatch to Unit Three!" Jim released Barbara and stood up, "Excuse me. I have to get this." He rushed out of the Living Room into the hallway, Barbara trailing after him. "Dispatch to Unit Three!, Dispatch to Unit Three!" Jim entered his bedroom and grabbed the radio Mic. on his dresser. Pushing the button, he responded, "Unit Three to Dispatch. Over." "Unit Three, Unit Twelve reports one tandem dump truck at Midas Mine being loaded by a Bobcat. Over" "Thank you, Dispatch, Unit Three over and out." Barbara spoke from behind him, "Looks like your suspicions were right." He sat down the radio and turned to her, "Yes, now I need to alert the DEA about this." He turned back to his dresser and grabbed the Cell phone out of its charger. He hit speed dial, and a moment later, "DEA, Special Ops." "This is Lieutenant Bearpaw of the Sierra Vista Sheriff's office" "Good Evening Lieutenant, what can I do for you." "Do you have a bird on standby for us?" "Yes Sir, I do." "Then wind it up. There is a truck parked at The Midas Mine. We need to see where it goes. This is surveillance only, I repeat, surveillance only." "I got you, sneak and peak." "Rangers, right." "You got it, Sir" "Me too. Have a good one." He hung up and put the phone back in its charger. Barbara had to ask, "Do you have to leave?" He turned to her and smiled, "No, the DEA and my guys can handle it tonight." "Good," she said, and slipped her arms around him. Now face to face, she softly said, "Now, would you like to tell me why you are reluctant to touch me?" He took her face in his hands, "Barbara, I want to do nothing but touch you. I know how I feel about you, but I'm not sure how you feel about me. I don't want to always be the aggressor." "That I can understand," she said as she unbuttoned his shirt, "You need a small demonstration." She turned her back to him, "Please undo my Zipper." Very seriously, he unzipped her dress. She quickly stepped out of it and draped it over the chair by the dresser. She sat on the chair's edge and took off her heels. "I avoided wearing panty hose, aren't you glad," She then stood up and opened her bra, then it dropped to the floor. He could see that her nipples were erect. Her bikini briefs then dropped to the floor, and she walked over to an enthralled Jim. She rubbed against him, her nipples rubbing against his bare chest. This excited both of them. Her hand groped his obvious erection, "It would be a shame not to use that thing." He picked her up and carried her to the bed. He laid her on it, then sat on the edge and took off his shoes and socks. His shirt and pants went flying. Then his underwear. He was on her in an instant. He cover her with kisses. Their first coupling was monumental. And so it went, mutual pleasure til they fell asleep in each others arms. Now each knew how the other felt. Barbara would come to understand just how much she had wanted this sex. That would bother her to a great degree.

Chapter Thirteen

Tuesday:

The early June morning was still and warm. The few whiffs of clouds overhead warned of the heat that this day would bring. A familiar Cadillac came rapidly down the driveway toward the house. It stopped before the Andrews house, and a tired and worried Jennifer got out. There had not been much sleep for her last night. She feared going to the front door, but she feared not going more, "What should I say to Bill? What will he say to me? Why do I hurt so much?" Determinedly, she marched up to the front door and pushed the bell button. There was no answer, so after a minute or two she pushed the button again. The door suddenly flew open, revealing the auburn haired lovely from last night. She was wearing a light, short robe that left a lot of leg exposed. They were nice legs. Jennifer managed to recover from her shock enough to ask, "Is Sheriff Andrews here?" "I guess not," came the relaxed reply, "if it was left for me to open the door. He's probably out on his run. Who should I say called?" "Just tell him Jennifer came by. I'll talk to him later." She turned and fled back to her car. The young lovely just watched as Jennifer jumped in the car and sped away. "That was a tall, beautiful woman," she thought, "She looked anxious, I can guess about who." She shrugged and headed back to bed.

Jennifer was sobbing as she drove the short distance back to her Father's house. "How could he! Where did she come from? I bet that car was her's! I bet she came from San Diego, that's where he met her! Probably on a case, I bet she was a victim!" She sobbed again, remembering her own rape and assault. "How could you do this to me? Was it all a con?" She sobbed her way home. Arriving at the house, she stopped the car in front. One of her Father's men took the car and parked it. She rushed into the house. Her Father was in the Entry hall talking to Maria about the evening's dinner. "Oh Dad, how could he?" Jennifer wailed, "He has another woman in his house!" Jason looked at his approaching Daughter, then spoke to Maria, "Would you excuse us?" "Of course, Mr. Saunders," she said as she returned to the Kitchen. He grabbed Jennifer by the shoulders. "Now, what is this all about? You found another woman at Bill's house. Who is she?" "I don't know who she is. How could he do this?" "Jennifer, if you don't know who she is, how do you know she is involved with Bill?" "She slept there last night. We had a fight, and then this." "Jennifer, calm down! You had a fight with Bill last night, then you think he went out and found himself a woman?" "Yes, Bill went out and found himself a twenty-something redhead." Jason started to doubt this whole event, "Do you recognize her? Are you sure she is from this area?" "No, Dad, I don't recognize her. I don't know many people around here." "I know someone who does, Maria, will you come out here!" Maria came into the Hall drying her hands, "Yes, Mr. Saunders?" "Maria, my Daughter is going to describe a young woman to you. Tell us if you know her. Go ahead, Jennifer." "She's in her twenties, about 5' 6", reddish brown hair, and she is very attractive." "That sounds like Ellen Johnson. But she joined the Navy several years ago. I think she lives in San Diego now." Jennifer jumped on that, "See, I knew it! She met him in San Diego, now she came here to be with him!" "Thank you, Maria. You may return to your duties." "Yes, Mr Saunders." She exited to the Kitchen. "Jennifer, you and Bill had an argument last night, then this young woman suddenly appears at Bill's. I don't believe that the two things are connected. She arrived too quickly. She had to be on her way before you had your fight with Bill. You need to find out who she is, and what Bill did last night." "Dad, how am I suppose to find out?" "Why don't you ask him or you could ask her. I thought you liked Bill." "Dad, I love him!" "Then why don't you trust him?" She had no answer for this, and seemed to sag under the weight of what was happening. "Why don't you have some breakfast. Jennifer, this is the time for you to decide: either you trust Bill or you don't. It is not the time to assume anything." With that, he headed into his Den, there was work waiting for him on his desk. Plus there was an inter- view for which he needed to prepare. Jennifer dragged herself off toward the Kitchen. Jennifer thought of Anita, but this woman was not her. Who is she?

Morning found Barbara awakened by Jim sitting on the edge of the bed. She reached out and grabbed his arm, "Don't go. Stay with me awhile." He turned and laid across the bed and kissed her, "Barbara, I was just coming back to bed." "Oh," she giggled. Her breasts jiggled when she did. That caught Jim's attention, and he began to kiss and lick each breast in turn. Before long, Barbara was facing Jim while enthusiastically riding his most significant digit. She moaned, and thought, "Brian was never spontaneous like this!" Her back arched with the shear pleasure of it. It passed over her in waves. Each wave was a bit higher, until she finally climaxed. Her back arched and her body grew ridged. Jim grunted as his most tender member was squeezed by her orgasm, then he came too. Both bodies stayed ridged for a moment, then slowly relaxed. Barbara slid off of Jim, and lay panting beside him, her head on his arm. Jim pulled her to him and held her. "God, I love this!" Filled both minds as they lay there. "Thank you," she whispered to Jim. "My pleasure," he whispered back. "Not all of it," she replied. Jim smiled and squeezed her. But, Jim could not shake off a little voice that whispered, "This is too early to be sure of her! What will happen when you have to kill someone on duty?"

By 8:30 am, Bill was in his office. Checking his voice mails, he found Jim's report about the truck at the Midas Mine, and Danny's report of men and tents. "What did the DEA find?" He wondered. "Wanda, is Lieutenant. Bearpaw in yet?" "No, Sheriff Andrews." "Please have him see me when he does." "I will, Sheriff Andrews." "I wonder why Jim is late?" He thought, then he remembered Barbara Davis. He smiled at the thought Jim and Barbara, together. Then he thought of Jennifer, and his smile faded. Once again, he ran over their argument of last night, "How could she talk to a reporter on her own? How could she represent speculation as fact? Why did I react so strongly?" The argument played over and over in his mind. He regretted that it happened, but with Jennifer, it was almost inevitable. His thoughts were interrupted by the noisy entrance of Russ, carrying a large cardboard box. "This is the files from AW's office," Russ explainned, "Where should I put it?" "Russ, why don't you put them on the table." He nodded toward the table in his office. Bill joined Russ at the table. Russ was taking folders out of the box when he got there. "This," he said, holding up a folder, "is her dealings with the Sierra Development Corporation." Bill took the folder and sat down, Russ sat next to him. Together they paged through the many papers in the folder. Bill spread several of the documents on the table, "Notice that these are all signed by Linda Littlewolf. Who got her to sign them, her Husband or AW?" Russ was sure he knew, "AW is crazy. She forced Linda to do it. She was crazy to get the condo development built." "Maybe, but where did the money for it come from?" Bill asked. Russ had the folder open and started sorting out email printouts. Bill's phone rang. As he walked over to the desk, he saw that it was his direct line. "Sheriff Andrews." "Hi, it's me!" "Good Morning, sleepy head." "Yeah, I slept right through breakfast and your leaving." "Well you can have breakfast now. Mrs. Garcia will be in shortly, she'll clean up the Kitchen." "What I called you about was that a tall blonde called Jennifer came by while you were running." "What did she say?" "Only that she would talk to you later. Care to tell me about her?" "Her name is Jennifer Saunders." "As in Jason Saunders?" "That is correct." "Have you been seeing her?" "Yes, I have." "Is it serious?" "It is probably over. We have not been getting along. We had a fight last night, before you came." "She probably came over this morning to make up. I bet I was a surprise for her." "I bet you were. Did you introduce yourself to her?" "No, she rushed away before I could. I was pretty sleepy." "I am sure she'll meet you later." "You're probably right. See you later. Love you!" "Love you too!" With that he hung up. Jim Bearpaw was in the doorway. "Oh, Jim. Please come in. Russ, could you leave us alone?" "Oh sure, Bill," Russ started gathering the folder contents. Bill noticed this,"Just leave that on the table, Russ, I'll get back to it later." Russ hesitated, then shrugged and left. Jim came over to the desk. "Why shut Russ out of our conversation?" Bill did not reply, but walked over to the table. With his right hand he lifted the box of files, his left hand pulled several forms out from under. He walked over to the door and shut it, then started back to the desk, examining the stack of forms, "This is why. These are copies of bank transactions for A W. Each one shows a deposit in her account from the Sierra Development Corp." "Bill, why would he want to hide those?" "I don't know, Jim. Maybe he wants to hoard the evidence for himself. Make himself look better in this investigation." "I think he needs it, Bill. Leaving Gwen and moving in

186

with a nineteen year old killed his reputation with most folks around here." "Yes, and he shot his mouth off when I was appointed interim Sheriff." "You two are very competitive, aren't you?" "Take a seat, it's a long story. Jim, it goes back to his Mother and her Father, our Grandfather. Apparently he did not approve of her choice in men. Russ's Father was a wild one, heavy drinking, gambling, and womanizing. When his Mom got pregnant, with him, she and Jack ran off and got married. They probably thought that her Dad would eventually forgive them. He never did. Her Dad disowned her, Grandfather was very straitlaced. They came back here to live, and Jack got a job as a lumberjack. My Grandmother tried to help them. Russ and his Mom needed help, Jack blew their money, and there was a string of other women. When Russ was thirteen, his Dad was killed in a logging accident. Some say he was drinking, but no one is sure. Russ and his Mom got some insurance money, but not much. Jack didn't think he needed much insurance coverage. Money got really tight. Grandmother tried to help as she could, but she had to work around Grandfather. Russ and I got very competitive in High School. He is younger, so he felt like he was always following in my wake. I got the headlines catching the passes, he got bruises blocking for the quarterback. After he flunked out of Cal, he acted like I had caused it. Then I made second team All-American at U.S.C. He had left to join the Marine Corp, he was gone for three years. When he got back here on leave, he and Gwen rekindled their relationship. Then, he shipped out again. When Gwen found out she was pregnant, her Dad, you know what he's like, demanded that the Corp send him back here. So Russ returned and married Gwen. It was all so badly handled, so public. Our Grandparents died later, and left everything to my Mother. Russ really resented that. The House, 3,000 acres of timber, and the Lake all went to my Mother, and now to me. I found that there were investments, my Father was pretty good at investing, or maybe he got good advise. I came back here to handle my folks' funeral, and tie up some things. Then the Board of Supervisors asked me to be their Interim Sheriff. You heard about Russ cussing out the Board, starting with his Father-in-Law. He could not see that leaving his wife and shacking up with a nineteen year old might hurt his chances of being Sheriff. Perhaps he is trying to upstage me with these bank statements." "Bill, I don't envy you this situation. He could be dangerous. What if he uses what he learns here?" "What do you mean use? Do you think he might sell the information?" "He could make money out of it. He's going to need money, Bill. Marlene is pregnant, Barbara told me. She's Sarah's patient, Barbara overheard them talking." "Jim, I hope you told Barbara it was unethical for her to divulge that information. I haven't heard about Russ having any money problems. I think he might have said something to one of us if he was." "I hope you're right, but I would watch him from now on. Have you told him about the Midas Mine?" "No, I have not. Jim, I would appreciate if you didn't mention it either." Jim looked surprised at that, but didn't say anything. Bill chose to change the topic, "Can you give me a report on your search of A W's property?" "Not much to tell. They're not done with her car yet. You have the files from her office. There is no sign of a gun." "Well then, we should go through those files," Bill gestured toward the table, "There may be other evidence besides these bank statements." Jim yawned and tried to hide it with his hand. "Feeling tired, Jim? Perhaps you should go see a doctor," Bill said with a smirk. Jim gave a weak smile. They both left the desk and went over to the table. They had not been working for long, when Wanda interrupted on the Intercom, "Sheriff Andrews!" Bill walked over to his desk,"Yes, Wanda." "DEA Special Agent-in-Charge Stevens is on Line One." "Thank you," Bill called out as he sat down. He picked up the handset and pushed the flashing button on the phone, "Sheriff Andrews." "Bill, this is Charlie Stevens. I need to report our observations from last night." "Go ahead, Charlie." "Okay, Bill. You requested covert observation of a truck at the Midas Mine, so my guys picked it up on FLIR at about 10 miles out. They followed the truck to Susanville, where it stopped at the Sierra Metals Smelter. Ground units observed the truck pull into the Smelter, where it dumped its load of what appeared to be rock and dirt. After unloading, the truck pulled out and moved to the yard of Tucker Trucking, and parked. The driver got out, turned in the keys, and left the yard. He was followed to the Starlight Motel, where he is registered as Bob White. We sent his picture and fingerprints to Washington. The truck is a 2001 Kenworth, registered to Tucker Trucking." "Good report, Charlie, as long as no one saw you. Now we need to know who owns Sierra Metals and Tucker Trucking." "I will see what we can do. So far, this looks like a case of rustled rock. Bill, I don't see any sign of drugs." "Charlie, bear with me. We have a local spending hundreds of thousands on bribes in Sacramento and on buying land here, and I can't tell where his money is coming from. What does that sound like to you?" "It sounds like he's laundering drug money. We'll keep on it. Keep me informed of any developments on your side. I'll do the same for you." "You got it, Charlie. Thanks for your help." "No problem. You take care." Charlie hung up, so did Bill. Jim was anxious to know, "What did the DEA have to say?" Bill walked back to the table, "Charlie Stevens says the truck dumped its load at the smelter in Susanville. He says it belongs to Tucker Trucking and is now parked in their lot. They are checking out the driver, one Bob White." "I heard you ask about the Smelter and Tucker Trucking. Is he going to check them out? The reason I ask is that my brother-in-law is working as a mechanic at Tucker Trucking." "Jim if this is drugs, it could be dangerous for anyone poking around that outfit." "I'll tell him to be careful. If anything happened to him, my Sister would kill me." "Jim, I don't like amateurs getting involved with investigations. It can get really messy." "Wayne was with me in the Rangers. He's no dummy." "Jim, I'm going to leave it up to you and Wayne. Just keep me updated." "Yes sir, " Jim said with a salute. "Knock it off, Jim" "Okay, Bill. We will be very careful." With that, they went back to the files.

Noon found the Saunders household a busy place. The planned celebration had everyone involved with preparation for Thursday evening. It was for this reason, that Jason had to answer the front door himself. Opening the door revealed the Auburn-Haired Lovely from this morning. She was soberly dressed in a white, long sleeved blouse and tight, black skirt. She immediately spoke, "Mr. Saunders, I'm Sheila Andrews from NBC. I believe you were advised that someone was coming." "Yes, Ms Andrews, I was informed that someone would be coming for my interview today. Would you please come in?" "Of course, Mr Saunders. I have my crew with me, one cameraman, and a sound person. They will need to set up." "Please come in, all of you. Let me show you to my Den." A tall, thin cameraman and a short, wide sound woman followed them to the room, pushing cases on a dolly. He spoke to Sheila as the walked, "Andrews? Any relation to Sheriff Bill Andrews?" "Yes, Mr Saunders. He is my Father." Jason got the crew started on setting the lights and microphones. "Miss Andrews," he address Sheila. "Yes, Mr Saunders?" "Please call me Jason. While we wait for the setup, I would like to have you meet someone." "First, you must call me Sheila. I would be pleased to meet whoever you have in mind." Jason grabbed his Cell phone and hit speed dial, "Could you please come to the Den? I have someone I would like you to meet." He hung up and clipped the phone to his belt. "It will just be a minute, Sheila." "Not a problem, my time is your time." Jason smiled at her, "I find it interesting that the network chose you for this interview." "Well, I am young for this, but someone in New York must have known of my connection with this place. When Dad was appointed Sheriff, it did get a lot of coverage. My name was mentioned." "Of course you never did any campaigning for this job. Did you Sheila?" "Okay, I'm busted. Yes Jason, I did a lot of campaigning for this interview. This is the kind of break that can make a career." It was at this point that Jennifer joined them. When she saw Sheila, her mouth dropped. "Jennifer, I would like you to meet Sheila Andrews from NBC, she is going be interviewing me this afternoon." Sheila offered her hand to Jennifer, "Hello again. My Father said I might run into you." Jennifer took her hand, "Bill Andrews is your Father?" Sheila's smile broadened, "He was, last time I checked. He doesn't look old enough to have a Daughter my age, does he." "No, he doesn't. I mean, I was told about you, but I didn't think I would be meeting you any time soon." Sheila saw her cameraman signal to her, "I have to go right now. When the interview is over, we should talk." She rushed into the Den, followed by Jason. The door was shut, and Jennifer was left in the Hall feeling very strange. First of all, she felt a profound sense of relief, Bill was not cheating on her. Secondly, she felt ashamed for believing such a thing about him, very ashamed. "Dad was right," she thought, "Why did I think that he was unfaithful? Was it because we had a fight? Why did we fight? Because, I did something I shouldn't have done. I made a mistake and caused Bill and Bernadette possible problems. Before that, I got drunk and was unfaithful to Bill. Perhaps I thought he should be mad at me, mad enough to find another woman. Bill was right, I acted impulsively. I could hurt our cause if I tell reporters something false, or even half false. What was I trying to prove? And who was I trying to prove it to? Why do I care so much about Bill's opinion

190

of me? Only my parents opinions mattered so much before. I guess that I admire Bill. Dad said that he is an accomplished man. Is that what intimidates me? I love Bill, but am I intimidated by him? Why did I ignore him? There is nothing more important to me." "Damn," she said aloud, "I need to help Maria." She hurried off to the Kitchen.

Jason's interview lasted for over an hour. When he exited the Den, Jennifer was decorating the Front Hall table. "She does a very sharp interview." "But not sharp enough to ruffle your feather, right Dad." "No, Little One. She ruffled no feathers." Jennifer smiled at her Father, "You are the only one who thinks of me as 'little'. "Jennifer, you will always be my little girl." Jennifer smiled as she watched Jason walk toward the Dinning Room. "You like your Father, don't you?" Jennifer turned to see Sheila standing in the Den doorway. "Yes, I do. He is a very special man." Sheila walked toward her, "I think you're right. He is a dynamic man, full of surprises. He surprised me by inviting me to this Dinner you're throwing. I don't have anything to wear to it." Jennifer looked at Sheila, "Neither did I, until Dad flew something in for me. But we don't have that option, in your case. Fortunately, I have another idea." Jennifer grabbed her Cell phone from her fanny pack and dialed a number from memory. "Hello, Dr. Davis' office." "Hi, this is Jennifer Saunders. Is Dr Barbara Davis in?" "Yes Miss Saunders, she is. Please hang on." One minute later, "Hello Jennifer, what's up?" "Barbara, I have Bill's Daughter with me at the House. She needs something to wear for the Party. Dad just gave her a surprise invitation." "I don't know if I have anything for her. My things are all so big." "Trust me Barbara, I don't think Sheila will have too much trouble filling things out, if you read me." "Really! Well then, meet me at Aunt Sarah's and we'll see what we can do." Jennifer put away her phone, "Follow me, we're going to see a very well dressed Doctor." She took off out the Front Door, with a curious Sheila following close behind. They piled into the white Cadillac Escalade. "Barbara Davis came here from New York City. I've been dying to have a look at her wardrobe. She and Lieutenant Jim Bearpaw have been seeing each other." "By 'seeing each other' you mean they're sleeping toge-ther," Sheila said, matter-of-factly. "As a matter of fact, they are." Sheila hesitated for a moment, then plunged ahead, "What about you, Jennifer? Are you and my Father 'seeing each other'?"

Jennifer glanced at Sheila, then back at the road, "Not that it is any of your business, but yes. Your Father is helping me get over a traumatic incident that happened to me a few years ago." "Jennifer, were you raped?" "Yes, I was. Your Father is helping me put it behind me." "Who made the first move, you or my Father?" "I guess I did, but it was sort of a mutual explosion." "Jennifer, I am going to tell you a few things about my Father. One thing is, he has dealt with lots of rape victims. I don't believe that he ever slept with one before. Secondly, you and your Dad are very wealthy. As a rule, my Father does not like rich people. He seems to like both of you. Thirdly, most men my Father's age do not like surprises. Whatever you surprised him with last night, fix it. This is the most involved I seen my Father in a long time. And Jennifer, to answer your unasked question , I look a lot like my Mother. Her hair was redder, and her eyes were green, not hazel like mine, but everything else is very close." "Sheila, how do you know so much? You just got here." "I talk to Aunt Wanda, Dad's Assistant. She was my Aunt's best friend and she knew my Mother. She gives me all the gossip. Wanda doesn't miss much." "She will be at the Dinner, Dad invited her." You don't mean Aunt Wanda and your Dad! Jason Saunders and Aunt Wanda, who would have thought!" She turned to Jennifer suddenly, "Your Father better not hurt Wanda! She deserves some happiness in her life!" "I think your Father already had this conversation with my Father." "Well, good for Dad!" "Sheila, my Father isn't like that. If it does not work out between Wanda and my Dad, he will be gracious and generous." "That is not the Jason Andrews that I've heard about. Jennifer, your Father has a reputation for ruthlessness in the business world." "Sheila, that's what his enemies say about him, check what his friends say. Check on the activities of his Ellen Saunders Foundation, or the Nature Coalition. These two institutions are what my Father is really about." "Ellen Saunders was your Mother, wasn't she." "Yes she was." "We have that in common, Jennifer, we both lost our Mothers." "We have one other thing in common, Sheila. We both love your Father." Sheila looked at Jennifer, but said nothing. She turned to the road and stared at the scenery, with a subtle smile.

Five minutes later, the Escalade pulled up in front of the restored Victorian of Sarah Davis. Barbara's vehicle was parked in the driveway. Jennifer and Sheila jumped out and ran up to the

192

Front Door. Barbara answered the door a moment after Jennifer rang the bell. "Come on in." Barbara took a long look at Sheila, "You are lovely, my dear. I see what you mean," she said to Jennifer, "I should be able to help. You two come to my room." She led them down the Hall and into her bedroom. On her queen size bed, four cocktail dresses were laid out. "Sheila, I'm wearing the pale blue. Do you like any of the others?" Sheila didn't hesitate, she quickly picked up a red one. She held it up in front of herself, "I think this one suits me." Barbara looked at her critically, "I think your right. It goes with your coloring." Jennifer couldn't resist a comment, "It matches her personality too." Jennifer and Sheila smiled at each other. Barbara was a bit impatient, "Go ahead and try it on. If it needs alteration, we're short of time." Sheila gave Jennifer the red dress to hold, then stepped out of her skirt and laid it on the bed. She quickly unbuttoned her blouse, slipped out of it, and laid it on the bed. "Wait," Barbara commanded and stepped over to her dresser. Reaching into the second drawer, she came out with two strapless bras. "In New York, we attended a lot of charity Black Tie events." She handed one of the bras to Sheila. Sheila quickly discarded her own bra, and put on the strapless one. It was silk. Jennifer helped her put on the red dress. When Jennifer finished zipping up the dress, she stood back. The two older women looked Sheila over. "It feels a little large around the waist, and around here, she gestured around her bust. "I'll overlook the crack about the waist," Barbara smiled ruefully, "We need to take you and this dress over to Mrs. Valdez, Aunt Sarah says she is great with alterations. She was told we were coming." "What about shoes?" Jennifer suddenly called out. Barbara rushed to her closet and swung open the door. On the inside of the door was a wire rack containing row after row of shoes. Barbara chose a pair of red heels and handed them to Sheila, who kicked off her black pair and slipped on the red ones. Walking around for a moment caused her to note, "They seem a little large." "So now I have big feet!" Barbara exclaimed, "Never mind, we can stuff tissue into the toes! Lets go!" Barbara and Jennifer gathered up Sheila's clothes, and the three women rushed down the Hall and out the Front Door. After a visit to the Valdez residence, the trio went to Jennifer's quarters, and drank champagne!

Long after lunch time, Russ made it back to his office. Wanda greeted him, he did grunt a response to her greeting. He lurched into his office, closing the door. She thought about it for a bit, then alerted Lt Bearpaw. Jim sneaked a peak into his office, only to find him asleep, his head on his desk. Jim considered for a moment, then told Bill. Bill had a hunch about his cousin, he wasted no time checking it out. His nose told the story, booze! Bill lifted his Cousin's head, "Wake up, Russ! Time to go home and sleep it off!" The Captain struggled to arouse himself, "What's up? Who's pullin' my head?" Bill and Jim together struggle to get the big man up. "That's it, Cousin. Up we go!" Russ was standing, "Okay, Bill! Where we goin'?" "Home, Russ. Time to go home!" Jim was talking right in his ear. "Home? Is it time already? Where are my keys? Time to go home!" As the keys came out of the pocket, Bill grabbed them, "I got the keys, Russ. My turn to drive!" A bleary eyed Russ looked at him, "You gonna drive? Okay, Bill you drive the old piece a shit! My car's a piece a shit!" They walked him out the back door, he went peacefully into the back seat. Very soon, he fell over and went to sleep. Jim took the keys from Bill, "I'll drive him. Have Sargent Yeager follow me to Marlene's." Bill considered that, then agreed. He felt strange just walking away from Russ. But it was for the best. Bill really did not want to see Russ disgrace himself, again. Drunk on duty! Poor Marlene, nineteen and saddled to a loser! That was the first time he used that word in connection with Russ.

Anita rolled in about four thirty, Mrs Garcia let her in. She hung her gown in the Spare bedroom, she had found Sheila's things in the Guest Room. Mrs Garcia told her about Joyce, A.K.A. Sheila's visit. Anita asked her about the availably of an iron and board. Mrs Garcia insisted on doing it. Bill had asked her to be especially nice to Anita. That told her all she needed to know. Anita talked to her as she worked. Questions about Bill, and his Daughter were answered. Mrs Garcia found out more about Anita. She was profusely thanked for the beautiful job on the Cocktail dress. As Anita ran it upstair for safe keeping, Mrs Garcia decided that she liked Anita. Jennifer was not in her good graces, she had been cold to the older woman. Anita showered and changed, just in time for Bill's homecoming. They made no attempt to keep their hands off of each other. It had been two day!

Before she left, Mrs Garcia had turned over a nice meal. As she served it, Anita was very thankful. The couple cleaned up the Kitchen, loved on the animals, they went right to bed. Two whole days!

Chapter Fourteen

Wednesday:

Sheila opened one eye, then she heard it again. Someone was knocking on her door. "Hello?" She called out. "Hello yourself," it was her Father's voice, "Rise and shine, Sleepy Head. Time to get up if we're going to get in our run." "Give me a minute, Dad." "I'll go put the coffee on." "Sounds good to me." She threw off the covers, and pulled her nightgown over her head. She felt the coolness of the early morning, "Much different than LA," she thought. Suddenly she was almost knocked over by a large orange-striped cat who was rubbing her leg, "Tiger! You big moose!" She was down on her knees, petting the cat with both hands. "You snuck into my room last night, didn't you," she cooed to the purring cat. She got back up and grabbed her Sports bra. Putting it on, she watched Tiger rubbing the chair leg near the bed, "He remembers me, I haven't seen him for months, but he remembers." She then thought of the past, "I remember too. I remember all of the phone calls to Grandma, to this house. Those wonderful visits, usually for Christmas. And those long talks with Wanda. She slipped on her 'sweats', then sat on the bed to put her shoes and socks on. She also remembered last night! Her head ached a bit. She left her room and slipped into the Master bedroom. There, she saw that the bed had been used on both sides! Meanwhile, Bill had the coffee on and was laying out some 'goodies'. Sheila made a noisy entrance, Susie heard her coming down the stairs and went into the Hall to greet her. On seeing the little dog, she smiled and went down on one knee, briskly rubbing the happy animal. Then she was up and walked into the Kitchen. "Oh good, you got some of those great little pastries! Did Jennifer get them for you?" Bill looked at his Daughter, "No, she did not. Maria, who runs their Kitchen did." She noticed Anita, who was seated at the small table, nibbling on something. "Oh," she said, accepting the cup of coffee from her Father. "What happened to

Jennifer?" He was pouring coffee for himself and Anita. Bill acknowledged her question with raised eyebrows, and a mouth full of pastry, which he swallowed. "She offered to help me with the murdered Geologist's files. In the middle of that, she kissed me. Later, she wanted to make love. She then wanted to play house. I wasn't asked what I thought. When she got busy, she forgot all about me. Anita and I then got together. We had met a few days earlier. We started a relationship. I asked her to come over from Susanville, for a few days. I invited her to accompany me to the Party. Jennifer seems to have problems with men, her Father as much as told me so. My personal experience showed me several problems with her behavior." Sheila knew that statement was the death knell for her Father's interest in any woman. Her Mother had made him very wary. "I think that I should confess. Yesterday, I spent a lot of time talking to Jennifer, about you. Dad, I thought I was doing you a favor!" "Some favor." Was his sour response. Sheila looked embarrassed. "I should have beaten you more as a child," He said, smiling at her. She smiled back at him, "You didn't beat me at all as a child!" "That was my mistake," he informed her. She drank her coffee. Bill introduced the two ladies to each other. Anita was all smiles, "Your Father told me about Jennifer. Saturday evening, she barged in here, without even calling him. I had been with him all day. He had to attend a funeral on Friday, for a young Marine that he knew. She knew about it, but never even called to check on him! He called me, about an article I had written. I was already on my way over here on business. We had dinner together, then he invited me to stay here." She broke into a wry smile, "I went into your Father's room, hoping to sleep with him. He invited me into his bed. I hope he continues to do so. He's a great lover!" "Too much information, Anita! But I wish you both every happiness." She walked over and kissed Anita on the cheek. The three finished in the in the Kitchen, then it was out onto the front Porch, for warmups. After which, they began their run. The two women had to curb Bill's need for speed, he was in better shape than either of them! After the run, it was showers for everyone. Anita and Bill shared one. Saving hot water? Bill had taken the morning off, to be with his two Ladies. They were most appreciative. The two women talked, while Bill called his office. He found that Wanda was not yet in. That brought forth an image of naked Wanda cavorting with a naked

198

Jason in a palatial bedroom. It was too early for that picture! While Sheila checked with LA about her interview, Bill and Anita walked along the Lake. The day was warm, and they were alone. The kisses were many and long. Too soon, they headed back to the house. Sheila informed them that the A P had picked up on Anita's Press Release about AW. Her Boss at KNBC, wanted the story covered. Bill climbed into his Tan Uniform, becoming Sheriff Andrews again. Mrs Garcia made sure he had a good lunch before he left. His women were in the Den, working on the AW story.

Bill was just arriving for the day. As he approached Wanda's desk, he saw a bald, middle aged man sitting in the waiting area. Wanda saw him coming, "Sheriff Andrews, this gentleman is here to see you." She seemed to be smiling a bit more broadly than usual, Bill noticed. At the mention of Bill's name, the man stood up. Bill could see that he was about 5'8", and slight of build. He had the look of an academician. As the Sheriff stopped in front of Wanda, he was addressed, "Sheriff Andrews, I am Doctor Simon Cohen. ADA Marion Metcalfe arranged for me to interview A W Fairbanks. I am a Forensic Psychiatrist with the San Francisco Police." "Doctor Cohen, I am glad you could come and help us with ths case." They shook hands, Bill was sur- prised that his handshake was so firm. "Doctor Cohen, why don't we go into my office?" "Very good, Sheriff. Why don't you call me Simon." Bill led the way, "Simon it is. Please call me Bill." He gestured for Simon to sit in one of the chairs before his desk. He walked around the desk and sat. "Simon, how much to you know about AW?" "Bill, Marion filled me in on the case." "That brings us to the heart of the matter How do you want to handle her? Do you want her to be first into the room, be their waiting for you?" "Bill, since your people will bring her in and secure her, I assume, I want that done first. After your people leave the room, I will wait a bit, then enter. I think it will aid our cause if she is forced to wait a bit. It seemed to work for you." Bill smiled at Simon, "You caught that, did you. I will ask for her to be brought to Interview One. I think you will find it suitable. We only have two rooms suitable for interrogations." "Bill, that sounds fine. I am ready whenever you are." "Let me make a call," Bill then picked up his phone and dialed. "Jail, Sargent Sumner speaking" "Sargent Sumner, this is the Sheriff. Please have A W brought to Interview One and secured. No guard will be needed." "Yes Sheriff, I'll have it done immediately." "Thank you, Sargent." He spoke to Simon, as he hung up, "All right Simon, she will be taken to the room in a few minutes. We have some time to kill." "Marion also sent a copy of your interview tape to me, Bill. May I say, you do a very fine interview. FBI training?" "Thank you Simon. No, I worked with the NCIS before I came here." "Then you must have run into Doctor Ed Kotke during your time with them." "My first NCIS assignment was Norfolk, VA. I was able to observe Ed interrogate several suspects over the next three years. He played those bastards like a fish. I learned a lot." "Yes, Ed is very good, very good indeed." "Simon, you're not so bad yourself. I believe it was you that got the Tenderloin Killer to confess." "Well we did get lucky with that one. Now we need to concentrate on A W Fairbanks, I take it you are not sure about her mental state." "Simon, I know about her irrational behavior around here. I know what she is accused of in Maryland. I think she has some real mental problems, but I do not think she is insane. I think she is aware of right and wrong. And she has managed to escape discovery for thirty years. That is not the product of insanity." "Very logical, Bill, but I have seen some amazing feats of self preservation by persons unfit to stand trial. I am going to reserve my judge- ment until after I have examined her." Simon looked at Bill with interest, "You mentioned irrational local behavior, Marion didn't cover that." "AW is involved in a land development out- side of town. An old Indian Village was found on the site, and a State Archeologist was appointed. A W showed up with a rental truck and two men to take the items excavated by the State. My Lieutenant had to stop her from assaulting the State Archeologist when she refused to turn over the material. Then there is the reason she was in jail to be fingerprinted in the first place." "Which is what?" "She was being held for contempt. A W insulted the Judge after losing an important case. She showed no awareness of the time or place, just vented her anger at the Judge over losing control over her building project. He gave her sixty days, because she would not stop her abuse. Then she resisted arrest. Next day, however, she showed no resistance to being fingerprinted. That is the one act that I can not reconcile with her character, as I know it. Perhaps she gave up, after losing her project." "Thank you Bill, for sharing those events with me. I consider them very pertinent. I agree that allowing herself to be fingerprinted does seem to be a

200

'surrender' of sorts, but consider her age and size. How long could she resist your men? This could be a matter of practicality. If we look at the transcript of your interview with her, she simply ignored the fingerprint evidence, then denied she is who the fingerprints say she is. She calls on you to let her go, then seeks the same thing from her lawyer. She seems to have avoided being fingerprinted over the last thirty years. There is no record of her marrying under any name. There is no apparent contact with anyone from her past life. She has a younger sister in Maryland who claims to have had no contact with her since the murder. She seems to have no close friends here. She seems to be a good business woman, but has a host of legal problems resulting from her treatment of tenants. Her attempt to seize the Indian Artifacts taken from her land, and her performance in Court all show a certain mind set. She intends to do whatever she sees fit. There is marked aggression, often attempting to get her way through sheer force of will." "I can attest to the accuracy of that statement," Jason Saunders was standing in the doorway, "I hope you will forgive my intrusion." Bill was quick to respond, "No problem, come in, Jason," Jason moved toward the desk, I would like you to meet Doctor Simon Cohen, Forensic Psychiatrist for the San Francisco P.D. Simon, this is Jason Saunders owner of several companies and holder of many patents." "I know Jason Saunders by reputation, of course. I am very glad to meet you." Simon and Jason shook hands. "Doctor Cohen, I was present at the 'dig' when A W attacked the State Archeologist, I was also in the Court to witness her outburst at the Judge. Both incidence were chilling to observe, she seemed oblivious to the world around her. It was all about what she wanted." "Mr Saunders, how would you describe your relationship with A W Fairbanks?" "I am probably her greatest aggravation, currently. I stopped her from assaulting the State Architect, and she lost an important lawsuit to me and my organization." "Then you would say that your name would probably upset her?" "Doctor Cohen, I believe that my name would probably enrage her." "That knowledge may come in very handy, Mister Saunders. I may use your name in my interview, if it proves necessary." "Be my guest. If it settles A W's situation, it will would be worth a great deal more than that. On another note, Doctor Cohen, I need to transact a bit of business with the Sheriff." He took a sheet of paper out of the folder that he carried and placed it, face up, on the desk in front of Bill. "Please read this. You will find it very interesting." Bill glanced at the paper, then showed it to Simon, "If Jason will excuse us, we should go see A W now." "I will not stand in the way of such a meaningful endeavor. I bid you gentlemen adieu," With that, Jason headed out the door. He made it only as far as Wanda's desk, however. Bill saw him hovering over Wanda, as he and Simon walked toward Interview One. Bill had never seen Jason touch Wanda, he wondered how was it when they were alone. When the pair reached the room, Bill opened the door with his key and stepped in. A W was seated as before, chained to the floor, wearing a short sleeve orange jumpsuit. Her eyes were two narrow slits. "Get me the hell out of these chains!" She yelled, "You have no right to do this. I want out now!" "A W, I have brought you a visitor," Bill said with little emotion. He motioned for Simon to enter. "Who the hell is this creep!" She roared. "I could be a lawyer come to free you, but then you know that is impossible. My name is Doctor Simon Cohen, I am a psychiatrist." "Oh hell," A W roared, "Screw you. I have nothing to say to you!" Bill and Simon sat down at the table, Simon next to A W, Bill opposite her. "I want my lawyer!" She yelled. Bill looked A W in the eye, "Your lawyer has been watching you through that mirror since shortly after you came in here," he nodded toward the mirror opposite the door. Bill saw Simon's look, "Standard procedure, the defense attorney is always called when the client is to be moved to an interview room." Simon did not acknowledge, but returned his gaze to A W. "A W Fairbanks," he spoke to her, "Do you know why you are in jail?" "Some senile old fart who thinks he's a judge didn't like hearing the truth from me." "He charged you with Contempt. You received sixty days in jail." Simon casually watched her. "I have nothing but contempt for him," A W snarled. Simon looked at his notes and then at her, "You insulted a Judge in his own Court. Was that smart?" "He was a moron! I told him what I thought of him." "Because he did not rule in your favor?" "Yes. He accepted all the bullshit from the tree hugging assholes. He tried to tell me what I could do with my own land!" "It is not your land, A W. You have partners, they own a larger share than you do. The Sierra Development Corp owns 51%, your partner, Charlie, owns another 20%. That means you only own 29%. You only own that much because of the payments you have received. I guess this means

202

Linda Littlewolf and her Husband control the land." "I control that land! I am in charge! No one is going to tell me what to do with my land!" "A W, you seem obsessed with controlling things. Indian Artifacts, land, court hearings, your tenants, you try to control them all. Even to the point of violating the law. Getting your way seems to be very important to you. Why is that?" "I know my rights! No one can tell me what to do with my property!" "But you exceed your rights all the time. Then you get in trouble. It would have been smarter not to violate the law. People noticed you. You got jailed. You got fingerprinted. Not smart, A W." "I defended my property! I control it! I decided what to do! What do I care about fingerprints!" "But you did care. You cared enough to stop being an Escrow Officer in California, when fingerprints became a requirement. Then you managed various offices. All the time, your Father sent you money every month. Until 1999, when he died. You then sold your property in LA, and moved here. Your partner Charlie handled all of the official stuff. You kept a low profile, no fingerprints. No photos either. But then the problems with tenants began, usually male tenants. Your involvement with the current Condo Project seems to have run into problems. First, the discovery of Indian Artifacts stopped work. Was it Jason Saunders and his group that called in the State?" "Yeah, that bastard Jason Saunders and his tree huggers, and that Hank Bearpaw and the Tribal Council all lied to the State. Then the State sent that Bitch to try and steal my artifacts." "You were almost arrested for assaulting the State Archeologist. Jason Saunders stopped you then, did he not? Then Jason and his group asked for the Injunction that stopped the Condo Project. You seem to have a lot of problems involving men." "These assholes are all against me! They hate me because I'm a successful woman! They're always plotting to stop me!" "AW, was that how it was with your husband?" "My husband?" "You told the Sheriff in your last interview that you were married up until 1977. How long were you married?" "I got married when I was twenty-three." "So you were married for nine years. Was your husband good to you?" "No! He was a drunk and he cheated on me." "Were there many women?" "Yes! Several that I know about. He lied to me all the time." "Did John ever hit you?" "No! He knew my father would kill him if he did." "But he kept cheating on you, often with women you knew." "Yeah, even when I was pregnant. When I had a miscarriage, they couldn't find the Bastard for hours." "And then much later, when you found him with your receptionist, that was the last straw, was it not?" "Your damn right! I warned him to leave her alone! She was only nineteen!" "He laughed at you! You had to shoot him!" "He kept laughing! He didn't think I would shoot! But I showed him! He stopped laughing!" "Yes he did Alice. No one has laughed at you since then, have they?" "No they haven't! Never again!" "If they did, you still had your father's gun, right?" "Your damn right! But then I lost it. Someone stole it!" "That is unfortunate. Did you realize that John was your husband in Maryland, not California? You just confessed to his murder. Alice Ferranti Wentworth, you are a fraud! I am about to file a report with the Superior Court here, stating that you are competent to face an Extradition Hearing." A W grew furious, "You Asshole! You cheated! You tricked me! This will never stand up in Court!" "This is not a Court, Alice. This is a sanity exam. You just passed." "You skinny creep! I will see that you are punished! You will all be punished!" Bill stood up, "Knock it off, Alice! The only one being punished will be you!" Simon stood and looked at her, "I had a long talk with your sister, Gloria. She told her two sons and her daughter that their Aunt Alice died in a car wreck thirty years ago. You are dead to them all. Who will mourn your passing? Who will even care?" Bill and Simon left the room. Alice Wentworth just sat there, hate in her eyes. As they walked down the Hall, Bill spoke, "That was well done, Simon. You played her well." "Bill, that is a good analogy, but she is not as smart as she thought she was. Few people are. Her needs made her vulnerable." They soon reached Wanda's desk. Bill addressed her, "Please phone the Jail and have them pick up A W. Keep her under a Suicide Watch." "Yes Sheriff." Simon offered his hand to Bill, "I think I will head for Marion's office. She said I could use it to write my report. Thanks for your assistance." Bill grasped his hand, "Simon, I want to thank you for your help with Alice. How much do I owe you for the lesson?" "No charge, Bill. Glad I could help." Bill watched Simon walk into the Lobby and on outside. Then he turned to Wanda, who was just hanging up, "Doctor Cohen found A W to be sane. She will be facing an Extradition Hearing soon." "I always thought she was strange, Bill, but I had no idea she was a killer." "Who did, Wanda? Anything come in while I was out, this morning?" "Jim stopped by with a report for

204

you. I think he left it on your desk." "Thank you, Wanda," Bill turned and walked into his office. He found a Forensic Report on his desk. Bill sat down and started reading it. It was the report on A W's car. The bottom line was very clear: There was no evidence that the vehicle had recently been on Old Mine Road. Apparently her gun was stolen from her office. So if it was not A W who killed Bob Moore, who was it? The Mine area was taking on new signif- icance: a recent murder, eight Chinese skeletons, and possible drug dealing. "I am not even sure who owns the Midas Mine, or any of the others, for that matter. How did I overlook that bit of information? The reason can be summed up in one word, Anita. I have been preoccupied. I should not have missed that." Bill picked up the phone and pushed Wanda's extension, "Wanda." "Yes, Bill." "Please contact County Records and find out who owns the Midas Mine, and also the other mines in that area." "I'll call Liz, she can get those thing quickly." "Thank you, Wanda." Both hung up. "Maybe your not the 'big pro' you thought you were," Bill thought, "Looks like you can't do your job and carry on a relationship at the same time. Or is it the nature of the relationship? Just how much do I want this woman? I am very attracted to her, is that just lust? She does things that irritate me, that demonstrates that I am definitely not indifferent to her. Do I want to be with her? Yes I do. Do I want her in my bed? In my bed, on the sofa, or on the Dining Room table, it doesn't seem to matter. I have had lovers before, but none quite like Anita. Is she the one to give me more?" His Cell phone rang, snapping him back to reality, "Sheriff Andrews." "Hello Sheriff Andrews," said a happy Anita. "Hello, Lovely Lady, what's up." "I just called to see what you were doing." Bill smiled, "I was thinking about you." "I like the sound of that. Good thoughts I hope." "Only the warmest thoughts, Anita." "Sheila and I composed a story about A W, the Network is interested." "You can add to it. A Forensic Psychiatrist found her sane. She was faking insanity. Mind you, I know she is one sick puppy." "Thanks, Bill. I'll tell your little girl." Bill laughed, ""How are you and my Daughter getting along?" "Just fine, Bill. In fact, we plan on teaming up on Dinner. Now you have something to look forward to." "With you in my home, that is already true." "Bill, you hurry home, I miss you!" "I miss you too, Beautiful!" "I'm waiting for you! Goodbye, Bill." He hung up his Cell phone and put it away. Bill thought of her smiling blue eyes.

He had such warm thoughts about her. At that moment, Bill recalled another call he needed to make. He pushed the Intercom button, "Wanda." "Yes Bill" "Please get Russ for me. Try his home number." "Yes Bill." Several moments went by before she called back. "Bill." "Yes Wanda." "Marlene says that Russ left this morning. Said he was going fishing. She said that she would let Russ know that your trying to reach him." "Thank you, Wanda." Bill was surprised by this nonchalance. He expected Russ to be foaming at the mouth, anxious to find out what was to be done with him. 'Gone fishing' was not what Bill expected from his impatient cousin. "Bill," Wanda spoke from the doorway, "Liz just faxed this over." She held a sheet of paper in her hand as she walked over to his desk. Bill took it from her. "Thank you, Wanda."He looked her in the eye, "How are things going with Jason." She smiled at him as she turned to leave,"So far, he's been a perfect gentleman. But I have hopes." Bill smiled and shook his head as she walked away. He looked at the paper, it stated that all of the mines were own by the same company: Precious Metal Inc. of San Francisco. "So that much is true. I wonder if they have a website?" Bill thought as he typed on his keyboard. They did indeed, an elaborate one. Bill found the tab for their Corporate information. He searched through the page,"A wholly owned subsidiary of World Wide Metals? Never heard of this outfit. Do they have a website?" They certainly did, and Bill found it after a short search. "Dubai, U.A.E.?" Bill said aloud. It occurred to him that the DEA might need to know about this. Bill grabbed his Cell phone and called up their number on Speed Dial. "Charlie Stevens." "Hi Charlie, this Bill Andrews." "Hello again, Bill. What can I do for you?" "Charlie, does the DEA have anything on World Wide Metals of Dubai?" "I will check, Bill, but anything in the Middle East will have to be run past Homeland Security." "No problem, Charlie, let me know if anything pops up." "You got it, Bill" Charlie hung up, so Bill hung up and put his phone away. "Why do I have an uneasy feeling about this?" Bill wondered. "You have seen too many bad things in too many unpleasant places. Still, a little fear is a good thing."

Late afternoon found Bill and Jim at the conference table, sorting papers from the AW files. Then Jim broke the silence, "You haven't said anything about what you intend for Russ."

206

"Probably a week's suspension, without pay." Bill spoke without looking a Jim, "Unless he pisses me off when I talk with him." "You know he's capable of that," Jim was bothered by Russ and his behavior, "Bill, he was drunk on duty!" "Something must have upset him. It's not his usual behavior." "Stop making excuses for him! He could have phoned in sick. Why come back drunk and sleep at your desk?" Bill was still noncommital, "I'll talk to him, then we'll see." That did not satisfy Jim, "I think you should file charges now, drunk on duty and insubordination. You could throw in public drunkenness and DUI. He drove back here, drunk!" "Jim, that was out of line! I know Russ! Right now, he is hung over and feeling bad about his actions. It will be time to talk tomorrow. Right now it would be hitting him while he is down. Trust me on this." Jim turned both of his open palms toward Bill in a gesture of surrender, but said nothing. Bill looked at Jim for a moment, but changed his mind about speaking. The two officers quietly went back to searching the files on the table. "Sheriff Andrews!" Wanda was on the intercom. "Yes Wanda" "Special Agent Charlie Stevens of the DEA is here to see you." "Wanda, please send him in." Special-Agent-in-Charge Charlie Stevens strode into the room. Bill, who was walking back to his desk, gestured to the chairs in front of it. Then he gestured toward Jim,"You know Lieutenant Bearpaw ?" Charlie Stevens nodded yes. "Do you mind if he joins us?" "Bill, that will be fine with me." Jim walked over to Charlie, shook hands, then sat in the chair next to him. Bill spoke first, "Charlie, you didn't have to come way over here. Do you have something to tell us?" Charlie's grin became a smile, "I should have expected that. Every one I talk to says your real sharp. So here goes. We followed up at the Smelter, that seems to be legit. Low yield gold ore is unloaded late at night, and processed the next day. The gold is sold and a check is sent to Washo Mining, at a PO Box in Reno. Washo Mining is okay with the IRS and Homeland Security. We have no drug ties to them. This seems to have been going on for several months." "So you came over here to tell me that?" "No Bill, not just that. I told you we were checking on the truck driver, Bob White." He saw the other two make a face at the name. "Seems his real name is Antonio Hartman, born in Mexico to a German-American father and a Mexican mother. He holds duel citizenship. That's allowed him to build a minor rap sheet on both sides of the Border. Speaks fluent

English and Spanish, which allows him to work liaison, sometimes, between the Mexican Cartel and their US partners. Our only questions are who is the partner and where are the drugs?" Bill looked at Jim, who nodded, then he turned to Charlie, "Jim and I have some information that may help answer those questions. As I explained, we have a suspect who is spending a lot of money on land here and on bribes in Sacramento. This suspect and his wife control The Lassen Land Corporation, which owns the Washo Mining Corporation, which in turn owns the Sierra Development Corporation, which is partners with locals in a large land development project. What we need to know is where is he getting this money? Why were ten or more Spanish speaking, armed men, living in tents near the Mines? Then there is the question of who killed Bob Moore, a geologist for hire? He was killed in the Mines area." "The check for the gold is never more than a few thousand dollars, not enough for the operation you're talking about, Bill. Maybe the ore comes from the excavation of one or more of the mine, it's just a byproduct. They need more space to store drugs. Why else would they haul the ore at night? Who owns those mines, anyway? Who was Bob Moore working for?" Jim responded, "The mines were all bought by a San Francisco based metals company, Precious Metal Inc., several years ago. Who Bob was working for is under investigation." Bill added his input, "Bob was surveying the Midas Mine, we think, according to the report on his Laptop. We think he was working for the same suspect we are already investigating, but we lack proof." "If your department is going to continue surveillance of the mines, we would like to participate. We can hold a helicopter on call for you. They must be moving a lot of drugs if they are spending the way you say they are." "Charlie, we run surveillance every night, coordinate it with Jim. A FLIR helicopter may prove useful. We are investigating the money trail around these corporations, but as you can imagine, it is complex. When we discover something, we will let you know." "Bill, your cooperation is appreciated. When the DEA can be of help, you let us know." Bill and Charlie shook hands. Jim spoke to the DEA agent, "Let's go to my office and look at the surveillance schedule." They started out of the office, "My boys tell me that you were a Ranger, Jim." "I still am, in the Reserve, Charlie." "Where did you serve?" "Desert Storm and in Bosnia." "Jim, I served in the same areas. When were you in Bosnia?" Bill watched

208

the two disappear down the Hall. "There they go, reminiscing about when they were 20 year olds," Bill shook his head and went back to his desk and the papers from his in-basket. He did not get very far, when a voice from the door way interrupted him. "I see you are fighting the never ending paperwork war," Jason said as he stood in the doorway to the office. "Good Afternoon, Jason. To what do I owe this visit?" "Good Afternoon, Bill. I have some information for you," Jason gestured with a manilla folder. "Is there some reason Wanda couldn't have announced you," Bill asked as he motioned to one of the chairs. Jason's smile grew larger, as he walked to the chair, "I told her you were expecting me." As Jason sat down, Bill walked back to his chair, "Perhaps I should charge you with suborning my Administrative Assistant." "I would plead guilty and throw myself on the mercy of the Court." They both smiled broadly. Bill sat down, "What have you come up with?" Jason took a sheet of paper out of the folder and slid it across the desk to Bill, "This is a report on AW's account at the Chemical Bank of LA. You will note the monthly payment coming from the Sierra Development Corp. An account in the Cayman Islands makes a monthly payment to the Lassen Land Corporation, which in turn, makes a payment to Sierra Development." "Jason, do you know who's account this is in the Cayman Islands?" Jason laid out three sheets of paper, "My people are working on that little piece of information. Who ever it is, all funds start in that account and one other. Funds deposited in Lassen Land are distributed to the Washo Mining Corp and several individuals. It also seems to be the one source for the funding deposited in the Sierra Development Corp. We are researching all funding sources for the Lassen Land Company. There is one overseas source that, so far, has defied our efforts. I have faith in my people, they will track down this revenue trail." Bill was excited, "You mentioned individuals receiving payment. Do you have any names?" "Bill, we have some names, the rest will take time. Some were direct deposits, others were by check, a few are cash payments. We are still tracking some of the checks." "Jason, this is great. This is happening so quickly. How are you doing this? Hackers?" "Bill, how I do this is a trade secret. Using Hackers would be illegal, and you know I would never do anything illegal." "Do I, Jason?" "Bill, I am hurt by your doubts," Jason said, smiling. "Jason, I am governed in this by the old advise, never look a gift horse in the mouth." "How very astute of you, Bill. And how very practical." "Jason, where is all of this money coming from?" "That question is my main focus in life, at this moment."

Bill had several things on his mind, as he drove home. What was happening at the mines? What was up with Russ? How can I keep Anita here longer? The drive home found him very preoccupied. So many things to consider! Friday, Sheila would return to LA. Anita would need to head back to Susanville. When would she return? His life was full of rhetorical questions. He was hardly alone in that, Anita had her own unanswered concerns. As she waited for him to come home, she wondered about this man she was involved with. Sheila and she had gotten along fine, the younger woman was bright and knowledgeable. She lacked the blatantly mercenary approach to things. Anita did not think it was her youth. At twenty-four, Sheila was old enough for that aspect to show, if it was in her. Mrs Garcia had been so helpful! She had started the Dinner, but the younger women carried on by themselves. Then, Bill arrived! His homecoming was a busy one! There were two attractive women to kiss. Then, there were the animals, an excited dog and cat to attend. It was their dinnertime, too! Later, he decided that Anita was in need of more attention. He was very astute in these matters. The young woman appreciated his acuity, she left lipstick as a mark of her approval. The trio ate together, talking of the AW story, and Jason's party. Bill had details from today's interview with AW, which provoked endless discussion of her state of mind. They all wondered at the existence of such a twisted mind. The Ladies added more details to their story, while Bill loaded the dishwasher. Anita took note of that. There was chilled wine in the Living Room, while the three talked. Anita and Bill cuddled on the sofa, with Susie in attendance. Sheila chose an easy chair, her Father's easy chair. Tiger quickly laid claim to one arm, for which he was briskly rubbed. It was a warm, mellow evening. All would remember tonight, for some time to come. Later, after Sheila had shut her door for the night, Anita joined Bill in his room. Anita was a Lady, in the privacy of the Master Suit, she proved to be a very health young woman. He enjoyed both sides for her nature. Anita found herself being very thankful for this night. Perhaps her luck had changed, in a very big way.

210

Chapter Fifteen

Thursday:

The Andrews household arose at the usual time. Pets were fed, and kisses were exchanged. As the trio warmed up on the porch, Sheila was still wondering about Jennifer. She had said nothing about Anita, yet she found that Bill had taken Anita to the Mines. They had viewed the skeletons, Anita and Jennifer had met there. No mention of the night her Father had kicked Jennifer out. Did she know who's car was parked out front then? Wasn't she even curious? Perhaps, Jennifer only saw what she wanted. AW may have been faking, but was Jennifer delusional? They started their run, the two Ladies in front. It was the only way they could keep his speed down. Bill relished running with his women, to him it was like they were family. Neither of the women would have minded that thought. As they ran past Jason's house, one of the Security men called to them, "Damn SEALs have all the luck!" Bill didn't mind their jealousy, he yelled back, "Skill, not luck!" Everyone waved. Back at the house, Bill showered and dressed, while the women double teamed breakfast. Sheila was sure that Anita would have like to be showering with her Father. That made her curious, so she asked Anita about 'water sports', as her Father called their activities. She found Anita very educational. Joyce (Sheila) Andrews had never indulged in 'water sports'. She wished she had someone who wished to team with her. It sounded like fun, with someone you loved. Bill was duly fed, and kissed goodby. The Ladies cleaned up the kitchen, then took turns bathing. Both washed their hair. Mrs Garcia arrived, and went right to work on the Ladies' locks. The Party at Jason's was tonight! Both cocktail dresses were pressed and waiting. Sheila's red one had been delivered from Mrs Valdez, it fit beautifully! Hair, nails, makeup all had yet to be done! Anita thought about this day. Getting ready with Sheila, with Mrs Garcia providing so much help. This was how she thought that her life should be!

In the comfort of his office, Bill had time to think about his life, and his Department. The new equipment would make them more efficient, but leadership was the key. That brought him to the topic of Russ. Through Wanda, he had learned more about what happened, two days ago. It appears that on that day, Russ had gone home for Lunch. Marlene told Wanda that while there, he was served with Divorce Papers. Gwen had him served. Russ immediately phoned her lawyer, to get the details. Marlene heard Russ repeat everything that Gwen wanted. Apparently, she asked for the House, Russ was to sign it over to her. She asked for Alimony, and child support for both children, until they were twenty-two. Gwen said he should support them through college. He was to pay off her car. The final demand was for one half of his pension, when she reached sixty-two. It was obvious, from this, Russ saw his financial ruin. There would be very little left for Russ and Marlene. Then, there was her baby. His response was typical, Russ got drunk, then came back to his office. Now, he was suspended, without pay. Russ would need money badly. He was to receive nothing from the House. "What would cousin Russ do for money? A Captain in the Sheriff's Department could sell information. He could also hide evidence, to protect those who bribe him." These were not very comforting thoughts, for a county Sheriff with a mystery on his hands. He knew that Jim was with him, but what would he do with Russ? He could keep him on suspension, until the thing with the Mines is over. What about investigating his finances? He wished to think about that, for a while. Right now, he wanted to go over the events at the Mines. It is important to plot a theory of the crime as one thinks it had occurred. "Bob Moore agreed to help Johnny Eagle with a problem at the Mines. He probably planned the expansion of one or more mines into chambers. These chambers would be suitable for storage of large quantities of something, probably drugs. The Cartel probably provided a dozen or so men to do the labor of installing the support posts and beams. They would also provided security, at least one AK-47 was seen. They were seen camping in a creek bed, nearby. Bob found out something or saw something he wasn't supposed to. Johnny felt compelled to shoot him, but the SUV ran into the gully, turning over. Nothing Johnny could do about that. It would take a large wrecker. So, we watch the Mines for drug activity, prepared to raid the area against Cartel resistance. Now, maybe

Russ is helping them, for the money. It would solve his need for cash. Is that all? Russ is ambitious, does he still want to be Sheriff? Johnny is bribing assemblymen, and state senators, supposedly to grease the skids for an Indian Casino on the Reservation. Is that what all this is about? The Drugs would finance a Casino, everything else is collateral damage." He was sure of one thing, if Johnny was in bed with any of the Cartels, then he was in way over his head. Bill would tell Russ nothing, keeping him out of the loop. Jim would be his only ally.

Wanda had taken off early, no surprise there. She had confided to Bill that Jason had asked her to the Dinner. He was sending a car for her! That left Bill on his own. Not a problem, he had plenty to think about. Jason's Daughter was one topic for consideration. Apparently, she had not mentioned Anita to Sheila. They had met at the Mines. Jason knew that Anita had visited him. Was this a refusal to see an unpleasant fact? Did Father and Daughter not communicate where her men are concerned? Jason had mentioned her anger. What would she do? Jennifer was neither dumb or shy, would she try something? It occurred to Bill that she would use her money, that was the way the rich did it. A private investigator? That would be logical, try to discredit her rival. But would she try anything violent? Bill knew to watch her carefully, starting tonight. He wondered about the Dinner, would her Father allow anything to happen at his event? That really seemed very doubtful, Jason prided himself on being a good host. It did appear to Bill that Jennifer would have to try impressing him tonight. She was a woman of impressive attributed. He figured that she would be stunningly arrayed for his appreciation. She had the money and the body. He thought a bit about that body. It was like his wife, Mary. Beautiful, desirable, but sick. He felt exactly the same about Jennifer.

The Sheriff cut his day short, leaving at 4:00 pm. At home, it was pretty much as he expected. Both ladies were preoccupied. He was afforded a kiss from both, but he knew better than touching either. Form and appearance had it all over touching and fondling today! The Master Bath was free, so he took his shower, choosing to wear a robe after. The Kitchen had become an impromptu Salon, with Mrs Garcia in charge. Bill did manage to fix himself a snack. He took it in the Living room to eat. His two Pets offered to help him with it, but seem okay when only petting

213

was supplied. Their time would come soon, Dinner at five for the Pets. He glance at today's mail, a bill, two ads, one letter from an NCIS buddy. It was a pleasant diversion, on this hot afternoon.

The evening was scheduled to begin at 7:00 PM. At 6:59 PM, Bill Andrews rang the front bell and his party was admitted by a well dressed man that he recognized as one of Jason's security guys. He noticed the man's rapt attention to the two visions of loveliness that accompanied him. "Have many guest arrived?" "No, not many, but I've only been on duty for the last 15 minutes." "Thank you." Bill moved his party away from the Front Door and into the large Entry Hall, Bill handed their wraps to the attendant on duty. It would be cool later. He saw Anita and Sheila standing there, they were both so lovely! Then a noise on the stairs caught his attention. He walked toward the stairs, to get a view of the top. There he saw a marvelous sight. Poised at the top of the stairs, dressed in a pale yellow cocktail dress, was Jennifer. Her hair was up, her long legs were on display. The abundance of exposed cleavage was very fetching. Sheila joined her Father, at the foot of the stairs. "There are days when it pays to be a woman!" Jennifer spoke to Sheila. She was beaming. Jennifer descended the stairs in a slow, stately manner, all bare shoulders, cleavage, and long legs, milking the moment for all it was worth. Her smile faded, however, when Anita joined Bill. He put his arm around her, kissing her on the cheek. Bill turned toward the Main Room, offering an arm to Sheila and Anita, "Shall we greet our host?" They each took and arm, he gave them an appreciative look, "You are both stunning! May I escort you into the Living Room?" "Only if you continue with an endless stream of such compliments," Anita winked at Sheila. Sheila took Bill's offered left arm, "It took enough time and effort to attain." Jennifer was left with only the Security man as an escort. If looks could kill! Bill entered the huge Living Room with Anita on his right arm and Sheila on his left. They heard the piano playing Chopin even before they entered the room. At the far end of the room, near the windows, sat a concert grand piano. Wanda was playing it as Jason watched her. Bill thought of the little concerts Joyce and Wanda used to give. Wanda on piano and Joyce on her violin. Jason noticed the trio as they entered the room. "Bill, in my life I have envied few men," Jason's voice boomed out, "But I envy you right now!" "I title this

214

picture as 'two roses and a thorn'," Bill said, beaming. Wanda stopped playing, "I envy the two young ladies." She stood up, and Bill noticed that she wore a floor length dark blue evening dress, revealing her bare shoulders and ample cleavage. "You look lovely, Wanda." "Thank you, Bill." Sheila moved to Wanda, kissed her on the cheek and hugged her, "You look beautiful, Aunt Wanda!" "Yes she does," agreed an appreciative Jason. He continued, "I don't believe that this room has ever held such an array of beauty. I especially include you in that remark, Doctor Davis." Barbara spoke from the doorway, on Jim's arm, "Thank you for that, Mr Saunders. Lately, I was beginning to feel rather old and faded." Sheila and Jennifer laughed. Sheila explained, "Doctor Davis allowed me to steal some of her clothes. I'm afraid I was unkind about how they fit." "Seeing how you look in them, I forgive you," Barbara graciously announced. Wanda looked at Sheila, it hard for her to believe this beautiful young woman was the same motherless toddler she had first met twenty years ago, "I wish your Aunt Joyce and your Mother could see you tonight!" Bill stepped to her side and touched her arm, "I'm sure they can, Wanda." Jason stepped up behind her, as a tear began its journey down her cheek. He gently placed one of his huge hands on her shoulder, "You are a beautiful, caring woman. You have helped to create a very capable young beauty. She gave a very sharp interview." "A very sharp interview that will be broadcast on Saturday's NBC National News," announced a proud Sheila. Bill hugged his Daughter, "I'm so proud of you! You've hit the big time!" "It's just one interview, Dad. They haven't asked me to anchor the National News." "You've been at this for just two years, and already your work is to be shown on national TV. How many others can claim that?" Jason now stood next to Wanda, "That is a good point. I have seen interviews by the best in the business, and you stack up with the finest. I have great expectations for you." Jason noticed that his remaining guests had arrived, "Welcome to you all. I would like you to join me in a toast. Everyone grab a glass." White jacketed waiters and waitresses appeared carrying trays of filled Champagne glasses. Bill noticed that many of them were Washo. Bill found Anita and slipped in beside her. He whispered in her ear, "You look good enough to eat! You are the most beautiful woman in the room." "Thank you for that," she kissed him on the cheek. Anita looked him in the eye, "You are a most convincing liar!" Bill took her hand, "I could demonstrate on my statement." She squeezed his hand and whispered in his ear, "I would like a further demonstration of your appetite, tonight, in our bedroom." She nibbled on his ear. "Drink your Champagne," he said, handing her a glass. "You'll get yours. Wait til tonight." She whispered, as she accepted the glass. Bill smiled at her, then looked around the room. He was surprised to see five members of the Board of Supervisors, including Ray Vinders, its President. He had to leave the golf course early today, Bill mused. Ray was the Father of Gwen Baker, estranged wife of Russ. Gwen was accompanying her Father, as he was a widower. Then he spotted Russ and Marlene, just coming in. "Hell!" he thought, I've got to keep Russ away from Ray and Gwen." Bill whispered to Anita, "Russ just walked in with Marlene. Gwen and her Father are here too." She looked alarmed, "Didn't Jason know about the feud between Russ and Ray?" "I don't think he did invite Russ or Marlene. Everyone knows about the split," he whispered. "What should we do?" Anita wanted to know. "Get Jim and Barbara and head toward the main door, you'll see Russ. You and Barbara usher Marlene away, Jim and I will handle Russ." Anita squeezed his hand and moved away. Bill made a straight line for Russ. Nodding to familiar faces as he walked, Bill made his way to Russ and Marlene. She was a stocky nineteen year old. She wore a pink high necked formal gown, probably her prom dress. Cute gal. Russ wore a white Dinner Jacket with black pants. Every other man wore Black Tie. He put his glass down on a side table. He saw Russ take a glass from a waiter, Marlene declined. "Good Girl!" he thought. Russ took a swig of the champagne, his movements told Bill that he was drunk, "Russ comes drunk to an event to which he was not even invited, how strange," he thought. He moved in front of his Cousin, "Hello Russ. You know your wife and Father-in-law are here tonight?" Russ slightly slurred his word as he spoke, "And why should I give a damn! It's a crock of shit! They get invited, and we get left out!" Jim came up on Bill's right. "Russ, are you packing?" Bill asked calmly. Russ drained his glass, "Bill, I'm always packing!" Bill's voice grew more firm, "Russ, give me your weapon." Russ caught the tone in Bill's voice, he dropped the glass from his right hand and reached for the gun in a shoulder holster under his left arm. His movement was not fast enough, Bill caught his right wrist and twisted the arm behind

216

his back. "Captain Baker, you are hereby suspended until further notice. Jim, get his gun and badge." Russ tried to resist but Bill cranked the arm upward, causing Russ to wince in pain, Jim removed the pistol from the shoulder holster and put it in his coat pocket. He then removed the badge in its leather case from the inside jacket pocket and put it in his other coat pocket. Marlene was half hidden behind Barbara and Anita. "Marlene, please come here," Bill requested. She did as he asked, "Marlene, please take the car keys out of his pocket." She reluctantly did so. "Russ, I'm going to let you go. Marlene is going to drive you home. I want you to stay there, until we have a nice long talk about your behavior tonight! All right?" "Okay, Bill! Just let me go home and sober up!" Bill let go of his arm and stepped back. Russ rubbed his right shoulder. Marlene grabbed his left elbow and led him toward the door. She looked back at Bill, "He was mad that we weren't invited tonight!" Bill watched the two leave the room and just shook his head. Jim was on his right side, "What set him off?" "Jim, he was not invited tonight and Tuesday he was served with divorce papers. Wanda told me, Gwen is asking for sole custody of their kids, child support, alimony and the house." Now Jim just shook his head. Bill pulled out his Cell phone and dialed a number. "Sierra Vista Sheriff's Department, Sargent Wolfe speaking." "Good evening, Sargent, this is Sheriff Andrews. I have just relieved Captain Baker of his weapon and badge. He is suspended until further notice. Please notify Dispatch that I have the Duty." "Yes sir, I will inform Dispatch." "Good evening Sargent." He put away his phone. They were joined by the Ladies. Anita took Bills left arm and whispered in his ear, "You were great, but it must hurt to do that to your cousin." Bill grasped her right hand with his left, "It hurts to see him screw up so badly." "Ladies and Gentleman!" Jason's voice boomed out, quickly quieting the crowd, "I would like to propose a toast!" A waitress found them without glasses, and they all quickly took one. "To our environment, and the great things it means to our community!" It was a toast every one present could drink to, and they did. Jason's recent Court victories was not really popular with the Supervisors. Barbara noticed Bill and Anita touch their glasses together, she touched hers to Jim's. They all sipped on their Champagne, Bill spoke to Jim and Barbara, "I want to thank you both for your help." Barbara was quick to answer, "We were glad to help. Do you have this kind of problem often?" Jim slipped his free arm around her waist and began to move her toward the piano, "No, thank God. Come with me! I want to introduce you to some people." They slowly moved away. Bill began to relax. He and Anita watched the people in the room break into small groups. "The cliques are forming," he spoke to her. She smiled at him and sipped her Champagne. Sensing that he was calmer now, she spoke into his ear, "Come with me, I want to show you something." She pulled him by his left hand, out of the room, and back into the Hall. She sat her glass on the Stairs as she went by, Bill followed suit. When she got to the area under the staircase, she pushed Bill against the wall and kissed him long and hard with lots of tongue. With her left hand, she unzipped Bills trousers and began to massage his growing Penis. When his erection was sufficient, she dropped to her knees and began to suck on it. She started to use her tongue and felt Bill shutter. A few moments of that, and he came. Bill held his special woman. Just like that, she took his mind away from the scene with Russ. "I owe you one, Lovely Lady." She looked up at her lover, "I am sure that you will meet your obligation, and very soon." He hugged her, "You can count on it."

Bill and Anita were only slightly late to Dinner. Jason sat at the head of the table, with Wanda to his left. Jennifer slipped into the chair to his right. Bill sat to her right, with Anita on his right. Only Barbara, setting across from Anita, noticed their still flushed faces. She smiled slightly, and felt a pang of jealousy. Bill, on the other hand, felt like he had been ambushed by a very wise and loving woman. He was so lucky to have found her! She was fascinating, and a bit frightening. Sheila sat next to Anita, but had two young men trying for her attention. Anita never seemed to be at a loss, she was always part of the conversation Jennifer, on the other hand, tried to control Bill's conversation at the table. She grew frustrated, as Anita kept him involved with her. Like Bill, she seemed knowledgeable on a wide range of topics. Jim and Barbara were sitting right across from Bill and Anita, which allowed them into the conversation. Poor Jennifer, she could not keep up. She was rather myopic about life, her wealth and field of study left her somewhat unaware of the world around her. The two couples were all educated, but they lived their life every day in the world. Jennifer was at a real disadvantage. They lived in the area, she did not. As the adults were drinking their coffee, a dance band started

218

up in the next room. By design, they began with a few rock tunes. The teenagers would have the first dance. And the second, and third! When Anita excused herself, and left the Dinning Room, Jennifer took the opportunity to chide Bill. "I don't like your little ploy, with Anita. If you brought her here to make me jealous, you have seceded!" Bill was amused, "Anita is not a ploy, she is my date. She is also, my house guest." Jennifer grew angry, "That is not funny! Stop throwing Anita at me! You found out about Swen, didn't you!" Bill looked surprised, then probed, "Swen who? Is he that big Blonde guy I saw at your place? Didn't he testify at the Trial?" "You know he did! At the Party that night, he got me drunk, then took advantage of me! I didn't know what I was doing!" "Relax, Jennifer. I am very glad that you have a playmate. Maybe now you can leave me alone!" Sheila had been asked to dance, when she got up to leave, so did Bill. Jennifer was left wondering, "Did I just tell him about Swen? I don't think he even knew! Now what?" Jim and Barbara witnessed the exchange with Jennifer, neither she or Bill looked pleased at the end. They had to talk about it. Was Jennifer still after Bill? What about Anita? Many questions were left unanswered.

Bill waited for Anita in the Entry. As she walked toward him, he noticed how graceful she was. Beautiful, graceful, witty, bright, he willingly kissed and held her. She really liked these spontaneous demonstration. It was very good for her ego, not to mention her confidence. A tall, beautiful, wealthy woman had just made a play for her man. Now, she had no doubt who had won the encounter. Hand in hand, they made there way to the Main Hall. Normally, the huge Living Room, most furniture had been removed. This was now the Ballroom, couples were taking the floor. Rock and Roll had made way for a slow number. Bill and Anita took their place, among the other couples. This was a first for them, dancing in each others arms. Both smiled at the ease their partner moved about the floor. They were both experienced, although it had been a few years. It all came back, so readily. Anita soon felt like she was floating! They moved on a cloud, their feet making only the briefest contact with the polished floor. All too soon, the music ended, they joined Sheila and her escort at the chairs placed around the walls of the room. Bill knew the young man, he had a passion for speed. One more ticket would most likely result in a temporary loss of his license. They passed cordial greetings, Bill intended saying nothing. He doubted that the young man would make any impression on his worldly Daughter. Some of her experience had come at her Father's piece of mind. Now, he was glad he could relax. The young man could not, however. In his haste to meet the beautiful Sheila, he neglected to note who her Father happened to be. An error he now whole heartedly regretted! A new tune, gave him an excuse to take Sheila back out onto the floor. Both Anita and Bill smiled at his obvious anxiety. Bill and Anita soon joined the dancers, they found themselves next to Gwen Baker and her Father. Both were thankful that he had handled Russ so quickly. They dreaded a confrontation with the drunken Captain. Bill introduced them both to Anita. Ray already knew who she was, but Father and Daughter were surprised to find her keeping company with Bill. Gwen vowed to find out all she could about the woman that could capture Bill's attention! Jennifer had the same idea, but for an entirely different reason! She was sure, that was the way. Investigate the Bitch, then expose her to Bill. She stood by the Dinning Room doorway, watching them dance. She fumed at the scene. "That should be me with Bill!" Her mind teemed with schemes to lure him to her room. She was sure, if she could just get him into bed with her! Anita would be forgotten Bill would lose himself in her voluptuous body. He would be her's! The pair danced on, unaware of Jennifer and her plans. Bill wouldn't have been surprised, he already knew of her obsession. But Bill had Anita, and a murder case to solve. His mind was not on Jennifer, but on the beauty in his arms. He was delighted with Anita, she was his match in so many ways. He thought that the Jennifer problem was handled. She had been told who he preferred. How could he know she wasn't listening? Jason might have noticed her behavior, but his mind was on the woman in his arms. As he danced with Wanda, he wished this night to never end. In this middle class widow, he found so much of what he was looking for. He read her signs, he was sure now, her desire for him was plain to see. Later, if he asked her to come upstairs with him, would she come? He intended to find out. He wanted Wanda, in a way that had not happened to him for many years. Yes, Jason was preoccupied. Jennifer was off her Meds and unsupervised. What would that mean? Would she be content to just spend her money to get Bill?

When Brent got to the 'dig' that afternoon, all of the females were missing, even Dr St Clair. They were all getting ready for the Saunders Party! The guys knocked off at four, by four thirty, he was alone on the site. He made his first tour, his mind dealing with routine household matters. Mona was fitting into his routine, but she had her own ideas about house cleaning. He thought that she was a bit picky. There was such a thing as being too clean! But he said nothing to her, he was aware of her life with her Mother. Her Mom had been a pig. There was no way to be nice about it. How many times had his Mother help Mona clean up? They were lucky she wasn't put into Foster care. What was he seeing now? Was Mona making up for those days? Or was she really like this, a neat freak, finally able to keep a house like she wanted? Brent completed his tour, and returned to the tent. He sat there, his mind turning to the Party. The whole Valley had gotten the word. They had heard about the Interview, the Sheriff's Daughter had done it for NBC. That was something! He was not sure about the Court Injunction that had banned work at this site. He thought of the jobs that a hotel and condos would create. There would also have been stores. That would have meant shoplifting. There could have been burglary, robberies, and vandalism. There would have been a price to pay for this progress, he was sure of that. There always was. He heard rumors about an Indian Casino. That was serious! It would have to be on the Washo Reservation, off limits to the Sheriff's Department. Would they have their own police? It caused all sorts of questions. Would it cause a lot of problems? Brent could not see how it would not. Crime would spread to the Valley, he dreaded the thought. All of the bums and deadbeats would flock here, to live off the tourist coming here to gamble. The motels would be full of low lifes and drunks. Job security for him, but an ugly way to make a living. Brent ate his lunch about dusk. Then he walked off his food with another tour of the site. He had just gotten back to the tent, when she arrived. Donna breezed in, wearing a lavender floor length dress. It had a slit up each side, showing off her bare legs. No pantyhose for Donna, no bra either. The low cut dress could barely contain her abundant chest. She wrapped her arms around Brent, giving him a sloppy kiss. He could smell the booze, he wondered if she was safe to drive! "I like the dress, Donna. You look great!" Her smile was huge, she twirled for him, "I got all kinds of men asking me to dance! A couple wanted something else! All trying to take advantage of a drunk, fat girl!" She hugged Brent, kissing him again, "I want you to take advantage of me! Come on inside, you get to unwrap the prize!" He was taken by the hand and pulled to the enclosure. Inside, she kissed and hugged him. He had some difficulty getting her dress unzipped, she was rather poured into it. But eventually, the dress was peeled off in the dark. He was nearly smothered by an amorous fat girl. He almost suffocate in her huge tits! Not the worst way to go, but he wanted to live long enough to enjoy this evening. Their couplings were monumental, Donna was a very loud and horny drunk! Eventually, the alcohol won out. Donna went to sleep after their second time. Brent quietly slipped out of bed, got dressed, then took a tour. He ran off three or four kids hanging around the heavy equipment. He didn't blame them, he had been fascinated by such things when he was a kid. He finish his rounds, then sat for a while. He needed to rest, after his labors. A session with Donna, was a workout! He was relieved at midnight. He got Donna up, and with effort, back into her dress. He escorted her to her car, telling the other Deputy that she had been sleeping it off. Another party goer who over did it. When they arrived at her car, she decided that they should do it, one more time! Fortunately, Donna could not undo her own dress. Brent managed to get her into the driver's seat, and buckled in. After several kisses, she finally started the vehicle, and headed toward her motel. He followed behind her, just to make sure. With Donna safely in her room, he was able to pick up Mona. When she complained about the lipstick on his face, he explained about the drunk girl who showed up at the 'dig' to sleep it off. He mentioned the other Deputy as a witness. Mona seemed satisfied. Handling drunks was part of his job. They had a peaceful snack, then a shower, and on to bed. Mona was feeling frisky tonight! A man's work is sometimes never done.

Apparently, Russ felt the same way. While Brent was with Donna, Russ woke from his nap, changed into his old Marine fatigues, and kissed Marlene goodby. He never said where he was going. Marlene thought that he seemed in good spirits! Odd, since he had been suspended from his job earlier. She did not understand, but she had learned not to buck him. Russ was a man used to getting his own way. He never hit her, but he was one who just left when things did not go his way. He stayed away, until you

222

gave in. Marlene was on edge, anyway. She was pregnant, a fact that Russ now knew. She had 'Morning sickness', something that Russ seemed not to understand. He seemed to treat it like it was her fault. He did not want her now. No sex in over a week. Was she being punished? None of it was really her fault. Anyone could forget to take a birth control pill, it was only one. He wanted her to get an abortion! She told him that her parents did not approve of Abortions! He said very rude things about her Parents. Didn't he know how difficult it was with them. There she was, living with a married man. A man older than her Father. Why couldn't he be kinder, like he was in the beginning? She had gone to bed with him on her eighteenth birthday. She had been a virgin. He had been rough then, she should have known what he would be like. Why did she think that he would grow to be better to her? Why had she thought that he would change? Now she was alone. Where was Russ?

Chapter Sixteen

Friday:

Bill was a little late getting to the office, Anita seemed uninterested in letting him get out of bed! He reminded her that he was the Sheriff, he had a public image to worry about, and a Department to run. Being late to the office was very bad form. She smiled sweetly, as her head slipped beneath the covers. He feared for his manhood! He needn't have worried, she gave it back when she was done with it. After their communal breakfast, Bill helped Sheila put her things into her rental car. They said goodbye to her, then she headed for the Motel. There, she would reunite with her crew. From there, the Shuttle would take them to catch their Flight to LA. She and Anita hugged, there was a friendship developing there. After Sheila left, Bill and Anita kissed goodbye. It was so hard to part, even for a few hours! Last night had been so memorable.

Later, in his office, Bill thought about his Daughter and his Lover, as he tried to handle the paperwork on his desk. Anita was proving to be rather independent, not always compatible with the job of Sheriff. Bill was not the first man with a much younger girlfriend, to sometimes feel more like a parent than a lover. Going through his in basket, he came across the invoice for the Radio System upgrades. That made him glance at the microphone on his left shoulder. He could feel the Transmitter pack in the small of his back. Every officer now had the same personal radio equipment. "Thankfully, we have a Justice Department grant to pay for it." Bill did not want to even think about going to the County Board for the money. That grant paid for several other items, Class IV body armor, more automatic weapons, night vision equipment, two new deputies, and one very long range sniper rifle. There was also the matter of Jim's new SUV. It does pay to know people in high places, especially in law enforcement. His Father had done well. "Sheriff." Wanda called from the doorway. When Bill looked, he saw that Marlene was with her. Her anxiety was apparent in her young face. "What is it, Marlene?" "Oh Sheriff Andrews, Russ didn't come home last night!" Bill waved her to approach the desk. Wanda ushered the distraught young woman to one of the chairs. "Sheriff Andrews, I'm so worried! He's never done this before! I called his Cell phone, but it just goes to Voice Mail." Now, Bill was concerned, "Marlene, under the circumstances, I think you should call me Bill. We are practically family." This had the desired affect, she paused to consider his statement. "Marlene, when did he leave and what was he wearing?" "He was wearing his old Marine fatigues, and he left about 10 pm, Bill." "The green and gray fatigues?" "Yes, and he took his old Jeep." Bill knew the vehicle well, a worn CJ5. That was what he used for fishing and hunting. "Did he take his fishing rod and gear, Marlene?" "Bill, I don't know. I wasn't paying attention. I didn't feel too well." "You have morning sickness, don't you?" Marlene's eyes lock onto his, "How do you know?" "Marlene, this is a small town. You can't keep a secret for long. How are you feeling now?" "I feel sick to my stomach." She took a small bottle from her purse. "Doctor Sarah gave me some pills to take, but I don't have any water." "Wanda, could you get our young mother to be some water for her pills." She nodded and left the office. Bill tried to buck the girl's spirits, "Try not to worry. Russ is probably just embarrassed about last night. He is a proud man. Camping out for a few days will be good for him." "But we didn't have any camping equipment, Bill. It was all over at his wife's house." Bill's furrowed brow told Marlene that he was worried, that made her more anxious. Bill picked up the phone handset and dialed a number from memory. "Hello," said Gwen Baker "Hello Gwen, this is Bill." "Oh hi Bill, what has you calling this bright and shining morning?" "I am trying to locate Russ. Has he been by your place recently?" "No Bill, not for several days. Not since he took the dog to the vet." Wanda returned with a glass of water, which she gave to Marlene. Marlene then took two pills out of the bottle and swallowed them. "Gwen, Russ is missing. He said he was going fishing yesterday and did not come back last night. Marlene is in my office right now." "Bill, is it true. Is she pregnant?" "Yes Gwen, she has morning sickness right now." "The poor girl. And the Bastard runs off and leaves her alone. Who is taking care of her?" "Right now, Wanda and myself." "Bill, you tell Wanda I'm coming over to pick Marlene up. Her first baby! Somebody's got to look after her." "Okay, Gwen. I'll tell her. Just one more question. Did Russ pickup any camping equipment from you?" "No Bill. Its all still in the garage." "Thank you, Gwen. See you later." "You sure will, 'bye." He hung up the phone, and addressed the two women, "Gwen has not seen Russ for days. He pickup no camping equipment. By the way, she is on her way over here to pick you up, Marlene." Marlene was startled by this information, "Why is she doing this? I thought she hated me!" Wanda put a hand on her shoulder, "Relax, Marlene. Gwen only wants to help you and your baby. I think she blames Russ for everything. Are you feeling any better?" "A little. Now I'm more worried about Gwen. What does she think of me?" Wanda offered her a hand, "Why don't I take you over to the Ladies Room. You can lay down there." Marlene got up without assistance and followed Wanda out of the office. Bill watched them leave, and thought about the girl. "Nineteen years old. She got involved with a married man old enough to be her father. An irresponsible man, unfortunately. He left his wife, but will he divorce her? When will he marry his young, pregnant mistress?" Bill thought about Russ and his actions to date, he did not like much of what had occurred. "He had only two things worthwhile, his marriage to Gwen and his career with this Department. Now, he seems to be destroying both. Where will it end?" He wondered, "Russ can take care of himself, but can Marlene?" He grabbed the phone and punched in a number, "Dispatch, Officer Jones" "This is Sheriff Andrews. Please put out an APB on Captain Baker. Get the information on his Jeep from the DMV. Instruct all officers to just observe the Captain and report his whereabouts." "Roger, Sheriff. I'm on it." She hung up and so did Bill.

Bill shifted his focus to the Bob Moore murder. "Was he working with Johnny Eagle? He had Johnny's card in his room. Johnny would need expert assistance in enlarging the mines. Bob was already working in the area. Why would Johnny kill him? Why was it done so clumsily? It does not appear to be well planned. Perhaps it was not planned at all. Did Bob do something to make Johnny shoot him? Did Bob discover something he wasn't suppose to? If so, in which mine? We need to find that gun! Does Johnny have it?" His attention was drawn to Jim in his doorway, "Bill, I just got word. Senor Hartman took off earlier this morning

227

with a Semi. He's pulling a 45' trailer." That made Bill ask, "Does any one know where he is headed?" Jim walked over to the desk, "No, but I let the DEA know. Maybe they can track him" "Jim, we need to know where he's going. But we know he won't deliver it before tonight. Who's on duty at the Mines tonight?" "Sargent Yeager and myself." "I didn't know Yeager was part of your team." "He wasn't, but he came to me and volunteered. Did you know he was a Ranger too?" "No, I did not. But it doesn't surprise me. Only Rangers are dumb enough to volunteer." Both men smiled at that. "I thought that SEALs were all volunteers, Bill." "Touche', Ranger. What time are you two going to be at the Mines?" "I thought that we would slip in about ten tonight, slip out before dawn." "Okay, Jim. What did the Doctor say about this?" "She doesn't like it, but she is a professional." "She is also a woman. Try not to forget that, ever." "Bill, I never forget Barbara's gender. I find it very hard to forget her female form." "Kid, I find that entirely understandable. I find that I have the same problem with a certain Beauty." "I think I should report you two for all of this sexist talk," Wanda spoke up from the doorway. "I believe you can only report us if we were talking about you, Wanda, would you like us to? " "No thank you, Bill Andrews. I'm the topic of too much conversation already." Jim could not resist, "By the way, how is the romance with Jason going? You will keep us informed, won't you?" "That will be the day, Jim Bearpaw! I will have to report you to Barbara Davis, she needs to keep you on a shorter leash." "Jim," said Bill in a conspiratorial manner, "Perhaps we should discuss Wanda's female form." Wanda grew indignant, "You wouldn't dare!" Bill saw the hint of a smile on her face as she stomped off to her desk. "I am glad you stopped by, Jim. Russ is missing. He went out last night and is still missing. Marlene is worried. To tell the truth, so am I. Gwen hasn't seen him either. He disappeared in his old Jeep CJ, wearing his old Marine camo fatigues. I put out an APB on him. It could be him just being bullheaded, but I have a bad feeling about this. He apparently did not have any camping gear with him. That is not like Russ, he likes his comfort. I can't see him roughing it out there all night, not when he had Marlene waiting at home for him." "Bill, I'll put out the word on Russ and his Jeep." "We need to talk about one other thing. I want to bring in Linda Littlewolf for questioning. We need to know if the murder weapon did disappear

228

from AW's office and when." "Bill, I doubt if Johnny will allow his Wife to be questioned outside of his presence." "If we bring him in for questioning about his connection with Bob Moore, he won't be able to be with Linda. She is not a suspect, so she has no need for a lawyer. You could handle Linda, you know her better than I do." Jim acknowledged his statement, "That could work, if we spring it on them. We can't give them a chance to plan anything." "Why don't you set it up. I'd like to see them as soon as possible." "You got it, Bill!" Jim left the office. Bill went back to the Justice Department Grant paperwork. Do we have everything we ordered?

Jim and Bill came back from lunch. They delivered lunch to Wanda, by special request. Mama Castro's Chile Relleno was not to be missed. She thanked them loudly, grabbed the package, and headed for the Lunch Room. She would have preferred the red sauce, but that had started giving her indigestion. The green sauce was a concession to age, along with her increased waistline and half-glasses for reading. She smiled to herself. Lately, she found that there was someone that liked her crows feet and ample figure. Things had progressed to the point where there had been many increasingly passionate kisses. Jason was too much a gentleman to "grope" her. But she could tell that he wanted to. A ladylike hint or two should over come that hesitation. He was large, but gentle. Wanda had no doubt that those big hands could be very nice on her body. As for that "other part" of his anatomy, she assumed it was large. How large did not concern her. Nature, and the birth of two children, had seen to it that she could accommodate virtually anything Jason had to offer. Her thoughts, however, were always touched by caution. She tried not to count on too much. Men had disappointed her before. Her husband had been a drunk, who always complained that she was "too large down there". And affairs had also been unsatisfactory, for a variety of reasons. This time, Wanda hoped she had hit the lottery.

As Wanda ate her lunch, the object of her affections came sauntering toward her desk. Disappointed by her absence, Jason moved on into Bill's office. Bill, sensing his presence, looked up, "To what do we owe the pleasure of this visit? Wanda is at lunch, I know she will regret missing you." "Bill, she deserves this break, you work her too hard." "Jason, I would not dare to work her too hard. See knows where all the skeletons are buried." Both men were now smiling. Jason's face grew more serious as he drew a sheet of paper from the folder he carried. By the time he handed the paper to Bill, his expression was very serious indeed. "Bill, this is the list I promised you of those receiving money from Johnny Eagle's companies. It will not give you any joy." Curious, Bill studied the page. On the list, he saw one State Senator, two State Assemblymen, two members of the State Gambling Commission, and Bob Moore. The next names saddened Bill, but did not surprise him, Frank Lovejoy and Brian Culpepper. Both were County Supervisors. Bill's phone rang, "Sheriff Andrews." "Sheriff, this is Dispatch. Deputy Horner reports sighting Captain Baker's Jeep at Judy Johnson's house. He observed the vehicle leave and the Captain drove to his residence and parked. Officer Horner observed the Captain enter his residence at 1:12 pm." "Thank you, Dispatch. Please give Officer Horner a 'well done'." "Will do, Sheriff. Bye." Bill pushed the button for an outside line and dialed a number from memory. He spoke to Jason while he waited for someone to answer, "Russ has been missing overnight, we just found him and I need to tell his women." "Hello," answered Gwen Baker. "Hello Gwen, its Bill Andrews. We found Russ. Tell Marlene that he just got back to their house." "Where was that Bastard, Bill?" "At Judy Johnson's place. I assume he went to Monty's, got a snoot full, and went home with Judy." "Yeah Bill, you're probably right, he's done it before. He's one old dog that sure uses the same old tricks." "Gwen, did he always tell you that he was going fishing?" "Or hunting. Yeah, that was his usual method. But he usually made it home before dawn. Usually, still horny." "Did he avoid sex with you when you were pregnant?" "No Bill, I usually had to cut him off when I got too far along. Why?" "I am just curious about why he left Marlene alone and ended up with Judy?" "Morning Sickness, Bill. He could never stand a nauseous woman. He would always leave me in the morning when I was sick and come back later." "Not exactly a 'Help Mate' was he." "No Bill, he wasn't. I wish he had a better relationship with his kids." "Well Gwen, neither he or his sister had a good relationship with their Father. Do you still hear from DJ?" "Yeah Bill, she is now working at Children"s Hospital in LA. Those kids really seem to relate to her. She's had some of the same problems that they do." "Yes, she has seen more than her share of

230

Hospitals and Operating Rooms. How is she doing?" "Well, she says things are about as good as they are going to get, psychically. But, things are looking up emotionally. She met someone." "That's great. But Gwen, what is he like?" "She said that he is just like her, exactly the same. He is a psychotherapist at her hospital. " "That is great. Please tell her hello next time you talk to her." "Will do, Bill. Goodbye" Bill hung up. He thought for a moment of his cousin, DJ. Dwarfism is no picnic, regardless of what type you have. The surgeries and physical problems have to compete with the emotional isolation and social limitations. Della Jean Baker is just over four feet tall. Life has been a great challenge for DJ, for neither her Father or Brother wanted anything to do with her. Dr Sarah came to her rescue all those years ago. She arranged for DJ to be helped by a charitable organization. First with her surgeries, then with her education. DJ was now an Orthopaedic Surgeon, helping those with problems like herself. But it all meant largely doing without her family, only rare visits with her Mother were possible. He could never understand why Russ could not help his Mom go to see her only Daughter? That reminded him, "My Daughter should know about Doctor Della Baker, it will make a good story." Suddenly, Bill remembered that Jason was in his office, "You'll have to excuse me. It seems that Russ has returned home, but not before doing something to further lowering my opinion of him." Jason managed a slight smile, "Today seems to be a day for such discoveries." "Jason, I suspect Russ is one of those getting cash. A man like Russ, supporting two households, should have money problems. I want to know what he spends and where. Have you seen the car Marlene is driving? I figured he had to have another source of income, and now you need to confirmed it" "I am sorry to be charged with this task, I believe that he is your cousin. I imagine that makes it much worse." "Jason, Russ is family. That makes it personal. It is another slap in the face, far from the first from Russ. I can't take any action against him any way, not until after we unmask this operation. It looks like Mexico and the Middle East are involved. Are your people finished with the investigation of the finances?" "No, it is very complex. We have traced the money from the Caiman Islands to Mexico, but it was transferred from bank to bank in order to hide its origin. It will take time. The other funding was routed through Germany, but we tracked it back to a precious metals company in Dubai." "What precious metals company? The Mines are owned by Precious Metals Inc. of San Francisco, a subsidiary of World Wide Metals of Dubai." "We have traced payments back to World Wide Metals." "Jason, have you seen any payments from any of Johnny's companies to either of the Metals companies? He should be making lease or royalty payments for mining and removing ore from the Mines." "No Bill, the only payments we have document-ted are to the individuals I have mentioned. Does he even have permission to use the Mines?" "I wish I knew, Jason. This deal is getting strange. The Dubai connection casts this thing in a whole new light. I need to get this information to Homeland Security. There will be hell to pay if they don't hear it from me first. The problem I have is how to bring this to their attention without revealing your part in this discovery." "Bill, if Homeland Security or the CIA starts sniffing around this operation, they could blow the whole thing. Neither of us want that." The Sheriff was concerned, "I have already pointed them to the Dubai connection for Mine ownership. I could just leave them to follow that lead at their own pace. They don't need to know that we knew anything more." Jason considered that, "That sounds like one possible plan. I believe that discretion is the path to follow at this point in time. We might have to give them a hint along the way, but I think they can be trusted to ferret out the facts in this matter, soon or later." "Yes, they're nothing if not dogged. This anti-terror stuff can get so complex, everything is a fight for jurisdiction. It's one big turf fight between Homeland Security, the ATF, the CIA, and the FBI." "Bill, I may have a solution to your dilemma. I could run this information through my Brother. A three-star Admiral could present information to Naval Intelligence with out too much inquiry, at least not immediately. Did you know that he is now in charge of Special Ops. I believe that includes the SEALs." "Yes, it would. I did not realize that new Department was his command. You could approach him with this information, but he might not want to hear it. Even if he did, how long could he hold off inquiry into the source of this information?" "My little Brother is quite capable. He could site an undercover source, or a turncoat. Secrecy would be required in either case." "Your little Brother is not the only one in the family with capabilities. That approach could work, if he is willing to help us." "Bill, this could be helping the Country. He will know that. I think he will see the benefit of helping us." "Right now, speed is of the essence. You need to get this to him a quickly as possible. Jason, how are you going to do it?" "As soon as I get back home, I am going to be on a Secure Line to him." "Leave it to the famous Jason Saunders to have a Secure Line at home. I should have known." "I must be off. Please give my apologies to the lovely Wanda. Tell her I will call her. Goodbye." He started to leave, then stopped, "I think I should warn you. Jennifer is quite upset with you, I do not know what she will do. Someday, you will have to tell me what happened between you two." "Jason, let's just say that I prefer to date adult women. Not spoiled rich girls." "That is harsh, Bill, but I am sure that she deserves it." With that, Jason was gone. He left Bill wondering what the Amazon had in store for him, and when. He caught himself frowning at the thought of this beautiful woman trying to push her way into his life. "She doesn't even live here!"

Bill was putting together a training schedule for the Department. There were several courses available at the State Law Enforcement Academy in Sacramento, even one opening in the FBI course at Quantico. Bill had Jim slated for that one. "Sorry Barbara," he thought, "you and Jim will have to do without each other for thirty days. Absence makes the heart grow fonder." That was certainly true for Bill. It had been over seven hours since he had left Anita. He found that he did miss her. What's worse, he found he wanted to talk to her about some of his plans. Not the sort of thing he was use to, not with a woman much younger than himself. The change both excited and frightened him, like the woman herself. He wondered if he was reading too much into this relationship. She seemed very committed, but was he? Fortunately, that was a rectorial question, for Wanda interrupted his thoughts, "Johnny Eagle and his wife just came in the front door," she said from his doorway. "Does Jim know?" "I phoned him, he's on his way." With that, Wanda went back to her desk. Bill grabbed a fresh tape for the audio recorder and put it in his pants pocket. He then rose and went to the door. From the doorway he saw Johnny and Linda approach Wanda's desk. Linda was a petite woman, five three or four, maybe 110 lbs. She was in her early thirties, with jet black hair and dark eyes. Her appealing, but rather flat face was filled with anxiety, Linda obviously did not want to be here. When the couple saw Bill, their responses were markedly different. Linda seemed to grow smaller, her face became even more contorted with fear. While her husband's face took on the large smile of a used car salesman or a political candidate on the stump. Jim joined him as Johnny and his brilliant smile approached them, Linda trailing behind. Johnny was perhaps five inches taller and fifty pounds heavier than his wife. He thrust out his hand as he came to the Sheriff, "Ah, Sheriff Andrews, we are happy to help you in your inquiries." Shaking his hand, Bill responded, "We are glad to hear that, Mr Eagle. Now, if you and your wife will follow us down the Hall, we can get this questioning out of the way." "Of course, Sheriff. You lead the way," Johnny smiled brightly and gave a sweeping gesture down the Hall. With Bill leading the way, the quartet walked toward the Interview Rooms. Johnny Eagle walked behind Bill, smirking smugly. Linda followed anxiously behind him, while a serious looking Jim brought up the rear. Bill opened the door to Interview Room One and gestured Johnny in. Entering the room, Johnny turned to his wife, only to see Jim grab her arm and escort her toward Room Two. He tried to push his way past the great bulk of the Sheriff, "Stop! You can't do this! I must be with my wife!" "Why is that, Mr Eagle?" responded Bill, as he pushed Johnny back and shut the door behind him, "She is not a suspect. Lieutenant Bearpaw will only be asking her questions about A W and her gun." Bill saw a noticeable crack in Johnny's facade, "But I must be with her during her questioning!" "Mr Eagle, your wife is not a suspect, she does not need a lawyer. While you, on the other hand, are a suspect in the murder of Robert Moore." "This is a setup! You lied to me!" "Mr Eagle, I was not the one that talked to you. Now, sit down, Mr Eagle!" Unwilling to confront the large and capable Sheriff, a now sullen Johnny Eagle sat down. "Now then, shall we get started?" Bill took the new tape from his pocket and placed it in the recorder. He pressed the Forward button and watched until the white Leader tape was past the Record Head, then he spoke; "This interview is starting at 4:04 pm, present are Mr John Eagle and Sheriff William Andrews. Mr Eagle, what was your relationship with the Geologist, Robert Moore?" "Sheriff Andrews," Johnny said, regaining some of his cool demeanor, "I never met the man." "Then please explain why your business card was found in his motel room." "Someone must have given it to him," Johnny spoke, his smile returning. "Please explain to me, if that is true, then why are there no other fingerprints on the card but Mr Moore's and yours?"

Bill's voice was penetrating and his eyes seemed to Johnny as if they could see right through him. "How much does he know," Johnny wondered, "He only asks about the murder." Johnny smiled again, "Sheriff, they were probably wearing gloves, whoever gave him the card." "I see, you think that he was given the card earlier in the year, during cold weather. Bob Moore didn't arrive in this area until early May. I don't recall any cold weather any time from mid April on, do you?" "It is often cool at night, Sheriff Andrews, perhaps that is why they were wearing gloves." "Perhaps" Bill paused, then spoke again, "Mr Eagle, what is your relationship with Captain Russell Baker of this Department?" "I believe I have met the man, when I arranged bail for some of my clients, for instance." "Is their any reason why any of the companies that you're involved with would be making payments to Captain Baker and Mr Moore?" "What a peculiar thing to say, Sheriff." Johnny's smile was getting thin, Bill noticed the worry lines around his eyes. "There is no reason that I can think of, unless they were doing some sort of work for one of them. Which company did you have in mind?" "Mr Eagle we both know that it is the Sierra Development Corporation that I mean. Your Wife, Linda, oversees that company, does she not?" "Yes she does, Sheriff. I am her advisor in business matters, but I do not deal with the day to day matters." "Then you wouldn't know why she would be paying these two men, except for the possible purpose of some "sort of work"? What "sort of work" did you have in mind?" "I have no experience with these matters, but it does occur to me that all of that expensive construction equipment that was at the Condo site needed guarding. A Geologist would be needed to check the soil." "Mr Eagle, could you tell me why your wife, a high school graduate of average ability is President of a company, while you, a cum laude graduate of Harvard Law is just her advisor?" "Sheriff, my wife is a late bloomer. She really is quite capable." If she is so capable, why is she working as a low paid secretary for A W Fairbanks?" "It is a matter of convenience, my wife's company does business with A W. She does draw a salary from the company, as well. "He really is glib," Bill thought to himself. "Mr Eagle, you seem to have an answer for everything. So I will have to keep asking question, until I find one you can't answer. Right now, I need to check on something. Please remain where you are until I return." Bill rose, stopped the tape, and started for the door.

"Wait a minute, Sheriff, I think you have asked enough questions."
"That is not your decision. Are you invoking your right to counsel? If you are, then you can wait here until your lawyer arrives." Johnny's bluff having been called, he decided to back off, "No Sheriff Andrews, I do not need a lawyer, I have nothing to hide." Bill opened the door with his key and turned to Johnny, "We will see about that." Bill left the room and closed the door behind him. It locked automatically. Johnny Eagle was very upset, but did not dare show it. "How much does this Sheriff know?" "How did he get a Court Order for the bank records? Which bank records did they get?" Johnny Eagle continued to stew in his own juices, as was intended, while Bill walked next door. He knocked on the door of Interview Room Two. Jim opened the door with his key, "What is it, Bill?" "Could you step outside for a minute, Jim?" Jim exited the room, closing the door behind him. "Jim, how is it going with the Linda? Do we know any more about the gun?" "Plenty, Bill. She took it out of A W's desk after A W waved it around in a fit of anger. Linda was afraid of what A W might do with it. She then took it home and hid it in the bedroom, in her dresser." How did it get out to the Mines to kill Bob Moore?" "She doesn't know." "Jim, I want you to ask her why her company is paying Russ Baker every month." "Is Russ corrupt?" "I think that he is." "Is that why you wanted him kept out of the loop about the Mines? Did you know about him?" "Jim, I suspected that he was taking money, but I have not received conformation, yet. Now, I want you to pump her about any payments to Russ." "Okay, Bill. But I intend to be gentle, she is on the verge of panic. She really expected Johnny to answer for her, I think." "Handle it as you see fit. I trust your judgement." Jim managed a weak smile, "Thanks, Coach." He used his key to open the door, and went back into Room Two. Bill headed back to Room One and used his key to reenter. He noticed that Johnny quickly closed his Cell phone and put it in his shirt pocket. "Calling your attorney. Mr Eagle?" "No Sheriff, I received a call from one of my clients." Bill returned to his seat, and started the tape again, "this interview is resuming at 4:13 pm "When we have your phone records pulled, we will see about your phone call." Johnny's smile faded for a moment, but quickly recovered, "I welcome your investigation, Sheriff. As I have stated, I have nothing to hide." "That is good, Mr Eagle. Then you won't mind telling me when did you remove A W's gun

236

from your bedroom dresser?" The smile on Johnny's face froze for a second, his mouth twitched. Bill saw both clearly. "Sheriff," Johnny began, recovering his smile, "Perhaps my wife told me about the gun, I really do not recall. But I swear to you, I did not remove the gun from the dresser." "Do you think it was taken in a burglary?" "Neither my wife or I have noticed anything missing, but we could check." "I will send an Officer to investigate the loss of the gun. He will check for signs of a break in. Perhaps I'll send a forensic team. After all, we want a first class job done, don't we?" Fighting his growing anxiety, Johnny sought to delay events, "I must ask, Sheriff Andrews, why is this gun so important? How do you know it was the gun that killed Mr Moore?" "The FBI matched it for us. You see, A W killed someone with that gun thirty years ago in Maryland. The FBI documented the bullets from that case. The bullets taken from Bob Moore matched. Now, I think you can see how important it is we find that gun." Indeed Johnny could see. He saw how stupid he was to assume that the old gun was untraceable. It was anything but. Johnny Eagle was so glad he had time to make a quick call, he had started the wheels turning on a little plan that he hoped would stop this Sheriff and make Russ head of the Department. "Then they could do business," Johnny thought. "Sheriff, I welcome your search for the gun. My wife took it for her own protection. Perhaps she was wrong about where she put it. I will help your men search. Could we not postpone this search until tomorrow morning? It will require some time." "Perhaps you're right, Mr Eagle," Bill detected Johnny's relief, then he dropped the bomb, "I will, of course, place an Officer outside of your home tonight." It was as if a knife had been thrust into Johnny Eagle's heart. Bill saw the flicker of a grimace. "No problem, Sheriff, I understand perfectly," Johnny understood perfectly that he was now going to have to sneak out of his house tonight. He knew that someone would have to pick him up. He also knew that this Sheriff would have to go, along with whoever was giving him information. "If that is all, may my wife and I leave?" "I will need to check on one thing first. This interview is terminated at 4:19 pm." Bill used his key to open the door. He stood in the doorway and looked down the Hall. Linda was just sitting in a chair opposite Wanda's desk. Jim stood beside her, looking at Bill. When he had Bill's attention, he gestured okay. Bill acknowledged and looked back into the room,

237

"Your wife is waiting for you down the Hall. I hope you both have a good evening." He held the door open for Johnny to exit. "Goodbye Sheriff," Johnny smiled as he left the room. Bill followed Johnny down the Hall, gesturing to Jim to meet him in the Sheriff's office. Johnny just kept walking down the Hall, toward the lobby. Linda hurried after him with an anxious face. "Chauvinist," snapped Wanda. Johnny did not seem to notice. Wanda stared at the couple until they were out of sight. In Bill's office, he and Jim walked over to the desk, and sat down. Bill picked the sheet of names he had received from Jason and showed it to Jim. He looked at it and shook his head, then looked across the desk at Bill, "What are you going to do about Russ?" "I can't do anything right now, our information is illegal. I will have to get the DA's office to investigate, I just have to get them enough probable cause to get a Court Order for their financial records." Jim handed the sheet back to him, "What are you going to do about the other men?" "Jason will give the word to his pal, the Attorney General, then there will be an investigation. What happens after that, we will see. Right now, we need to take care of Johnny Eagle. What did Linda say about payments to Russ?" Jim sat back in his chair, "She said she knew nothing about it, Johnny took care of all company business. He just had her sign the papers. This guy doesn't leave too many things you can tie to him." "If she testifies against him, I bet she knows where the bodies are buried." "You mean more murder victims? I thought that a wife couldn't testify against her husband." "No one can be compelled to testify against their spouse, but they can choose to. I bet Linda will choose to if it means escaping the trap he set for her. I meant that she knows a lot of details about the Mines, most she probably doesn't know she knows. I hope there are no more murders." "Bill, what are we going to do about Johnny?" "Jim, I want you to send a Forensic team to his house in the morning. He is expecting it. Have them look for the gun and for signs of a break in. I want his Cell phone records for the last month pulled. I also told him I would place a car in front of his house. So please set that up. I also want you to assign one Officer to watch the back of his house. I expect Johnny to sneak out of his house and be picked up by someone. I want that information transmitted by phone to me through Dispatch. After you set these up, I want you to go home and get ready for tonight. I think something is going to happen at the Mines." "What do you think will happen?" "Jim, if I were Johnny and his Mexican pals, I would be packing up my drugs and getting the hell out of Dodge!" "I think Yeager and I will pack extra ammo. Do you want us to pack flares?" "No, let the DEA helicopter provide that. Their parachute flares are better than anything we can provide, if it comes to that." "Okay Bill, I'll handle these little chores, then head out. A certain Doctor is fixing dinner for me tonight." "It is a shame you're going to have to cut and run after dinner." "Duty calls, my leader." "Next thing I know, you'll wrap yourself in the American Flag and run for office." "Fat chance." "While you hold down the Fort, I'm going over to Monty's to check on where Russ was yesterday. Then I'm heading home." "To have dinner with a certain Publicist?" "You can never tell about those things, Jim. I may be surprised tonight." "Good luck." "You too." Bill had no idea how prophetic his words were.

One hour later, Bill was driving home from Monty's. The old tavern was tired and dirty, just like most of its patrons. His questions had revealed a few things about Russ. He had not arrived there until after 12 pm. Where was he for those two hours? He bought the house several rounds, almost got into a fight with one of the out of work lumberjack, and after the place closed, went home with Judy Johnson. Judy Johnson, there was a sad story. At seventeen, she married into the Johnson family only to find that her 'Husband' was already married to someone else. She was left pregnant, with the baby's Father in jail for Bigamy. She gave birth to a health baby boy, six months later, the baby died of SIDS. The Johnsons think she smothered the baby, so they have no help for her. They think she uses the Johnson name just to embarrass them, but she used it because her own family had disowned her when she left them to marry a Catholic. For her, there was only working at Monty's and sleeping with the likes of Russ. Bill thought of other young women who life offered little, so many with so little hope. Faces filled his mind as he drove over the familiar road toward home.

Juan Carlos Calderone was a small Mexican National of twenty-five. At five foot six and one hundred forty pound, he was not an impressive specimen, but he had been born into a lesser Mexican Cartel. Even though his Father was high up in the organization, Juan Carlos was still expected to start at the bottom, like his older brothers had done. Starting as a "Coyote" along the Arizona border, he had guided 'mules' carrying backpacks full of drugs. After that, he worked his way up to bigger operations. This current operation could mean transportation of drugs by the ton, if they could get rid of the local Sheriff. He had been chosen to kill the man. It would be the first time for him, but this was an important step if he was to rise in the organization. To kill the enemies of the organization was an important part of any member's life. He had been dropped off at the main road, to work his way to the rear of the house. He had been watching the house for several minutes, there were no signs of people. The carport where the Sheriff parked his car was empty. The gringo policeman, who gave him instruction, was very good, everything was like he said. Juan moved closer to the house. On this side of the house was a brick chimney. Behind it, there was a place in shadows. Juan Carlos decided that this was to be his hiding place. When the Sheriff arrived home, he would surprise the man and kill him with the 9 mm, Beretta 92 he carried. Then he would put the body in the Sheriff's car, and after dark, he would drive it to the Mines, where it would be hidden in one of the unused shafts. As he settled himself into the bushes next to the house, he knew that now he must wait. Juan Carlos was very nervous. This was the most important task he had ever been given. The call today had surprised him. The task came sooner than he expected. If he succeeded, it meant much to his career. If he failed, the very dangerous Sheriff would kill him. Juan Carlos had to wait for over one hour, the Sheriff was running late. But eventually he heard a car coming up the driveway. Tiger heard the car coming long before Juan Carlos, he decided to saunter over toward the carport to greet his human (what cat really has a master). It was past dinnertime. As Bill drove into the carport, Tiger walked toward him. Then, Tiger discovered Juan Carlos. Tiger didn't know who was in the bush, but it reminded him of the Mexican Gardener in his old San Diego neighborhood. The same smell of dirt, sweat, and Mexican food. He hated that Gardener. Bill opened his car door and got out. Juan Carlos drew the Beretta and burst out of the bush, running right into Tiger. Tiger responded by sinking his teeth and both sets of front claws into the left leg of Juan Carlos. The very surprised Mexican yelped and fired a shot at Bill, it just clipped his left ear lobe. Bill did not yelp, but drew his Glock 22

240

and fired twice. Two .40 SW/180 grain JHP slugs hit Juan Carlos, the first destroyed his Aorta, the second turned his left Ventricle into mush. Juan Carlos Calderone, pride of his Mother and Father, was dead before he hit the ground. Tiger stood glaring at the fallen man, the hair on his back standing straight up. Bill cautiously approached the prone figure with the Glock still held in his right hand. With his left hand he felt for a pulse, there was none. He holstered his gun and looked at the enraged cat, "Well Tiger, I owe you one. I only asked you to get a mole." Bill pocketed the Beretta, then pushed the talk button on his shoulder Mic., "Dispatch, this is Unit One." "Roger Unit One. Over." "Dispatch, please send a unit to my home. We have a Homicide. Notify the Coroner. Notify the DEA, I shot and killed an Hispanic male, who attempted to kill me. Over." "Unit One, should I notify Unit Three? Over." "Dispatch, Please notify Unit Three, but his presence is not required. Over." "Roger, Unit One. Out." Despite his adrenalin rush, Bill calmly went through the dead man's pockets. He found a small flashlight and a map of his land and house. He thought that the handwriting looked familiar. He stuck the map in his pocket for later. Bill found two full magazines for the Beretta, but no ID. He walked back to the car and got his notebook. Bill knew it was important to get the details down quickly. He was busy writing about the incident, when he heard a car on the driveway. He was sure that it was the duty patrol car. He was wrong. A white Honda came up the driveway. It skidded to a stop, then Anita hopped out and ran toward Bill, "Oh Bill! Are you alright?" She saw the open car door. She hugged him, then noticed the blood on his left shoulder, "Bill, you're wounded!" She grabbed a tissue from her pocket and placed it on the damaged ear. Now Bill felt the pain of the ear lobe, but he was more interested in how much Anita knew of what had happened. "Beautiful, I appreciate your nursing, but something serious happened here!" She looked anxiously at the prone figure, "Did you kill him?" "Yes, Anita, after he fired on me." Further conversation was squelched by a bear hug from the Beauty, followed by a big, juicy kiss. They held the kiss for a while, then they embraced, "I'm okay, Anita. Tiger helped me." She stepped back and looked at Bill, "Tiger did what?" "Tiger bit the guy in the leg, it threw off his aim, and then I shot him." She followed his gaze to the calm Cat setting near the body gazing back at them. "It is past feeding time for the Animals. Anita, could you do the honors? I have to remain here." He offered her his house key. She had her own key in her hand. She kissed him on the cheek, "Yes, Sir." And then the now smiling Beauty was gone. When Tiger heard the key in the front lock, so was he. "Eat well Tiger, you earned your keep today." It was only a minute or two later that Bill heard a vehicle traveling at high speed up his driveway. Shortly, a Sheriff's car came speeding up to the house and stopped. It was Sgt. Yeager that got out of the vehicle. "I understand you had a problem here," Yeager said, smiling. "Nothing major. Just an attempted hit by the Mexican Cartel." Yeager quickly got serious, "How do you know it was them?" "Sargent, do you see those tattoos?" Bill pointed to the body's arm, "Those are Mexican Cartel tats. I first saw them in San Diego." "What is a Mexican Cartel member doing this far from home, Sir?" I think you and Lieutenant Bearpaw may find out tonight. I think that something is going to happen at the Mines tonight. The Lieutenant will fill you in. You shouldn't stay here too long, you need to get ready for tonight." "We were just on the way home when I heard the call." "Is that your wife in the car, Sargent? That's Hilda from the Bank" "That's right, Sir. I met Hilda when I was stationed in Germany. She's a distant cousin." "What does she think about you going on special night duty." "I don't think it's her favorite, but she's a pro. Her Father was in the East Germany Army, and we got married shortly before my year in Afghanistan. She's okay with it." For both their sakes he hoped she was. He remembered the blonde, buxom Hilda, a large boned woman of Wagnerian proportions. "I hope you both are happy with your situations." "Thank you, Sheriff Andrews. We both like it here. My family is here and Hilda is part of my Mother's family. Hilda speaks good English, sometimes better than me." "Do you have any kids" "Not yet, Hilda had two miscarriages, so we're taking a break." "I'm sorry to hear that. What does Doctor Sarah say." "She says to keep trying, so I guess that's what we'll do." "Good luck, then. Why don't we get some his paperwork done while we wait for the Coroner?" The two Officers used the hood of Bill's car for their forms and reports. They were engrossed in their work when Anita reappeared from the house. She saw the Sheriff's Department car next to hers, she then recognized Hilda and waved. Hilda waved back and got out of the car. The big Blonde had recently helped Anita cash a check. "Hello Ms. Brubaker. I did not know you knew the Sheriff." "Please Hilda, call me Anita. Yes, I know the Sheriff very well." Both women smiled knowingly, glancing at their men. Bill was taken by the sight of the two women. Anita looked so small and thin by comparison, and Bill knew she was neither. The two young women talked and the two men filled out their paperwork. Then another vehicle came up the driveway. There is one good thing about being a Coroner, there is no need to rush. A Coroner's clients are not going anywhere. Barbara pulled up in the Coroner's newly converted hearse, Jim Bearpaw was a passenger in the glossy black Cadillac. The pair exited the vehicle and walked toward the body. "Hello," offered Bill, "Sorry to have interrupted your evening." "We were having dinner when the call came in," replied Dr. Barbara Davis, "our evening was already short." "I volunteered for the duty, Barbara," Jim replied to her comment, "don't blame Bill for this." "Sorry, Bill," Barbara spoke without looking at him. Her eyes were on the body. She knelt beside it and felt for a neck pulse. Feeling none, she took the Stethoscope from her neck and put the earpieces in her ears. She listened to the chest for a heartbeat. "Death pronoun-ced at 6:27 pm," Barbara announced to Jim, who was taking notes for her. She opened the small case she now brought with her on Coroner cases. She took out the digital meat thermometer in its case, removed it, and inserted it into the liver of the late Juan Carlos. After a moment, she read it, "Dead for less than one hour." Jim noted the temperature, then she removed the thermometer, wiped it clean, and returned it to its case. She then took the small Digital Camera from Jim, and proceeded to photograph the body and the area around it, from several angles. Jim, now free of his secretary duty, walked over to the other Officers. As Bill turned to greet him, Jim noticed the tissue on Bill's left ear, "Barbara, Bill's been injured!" Barbara rushed over with the camera hanging from her neck. She examined the damaged ear, removing the tissue. "Jim, could you get my bag from the car." He obediently went to get it. Bill noticed the action between Barbara and Jim, "He sees this as her domain, it is his job to help her. They have worked this out very quickly." He then glanced at Anita and wondered if they would ever reach that level of cooperation. Jim brought back the medical bag, and Barbara treated the ear with antiseptic and bandaged it. "You were lucky." That was Barbara's only comment as she examined her work. "Thank you, Doctor Davis, for your professional care. And since, as the shooter, I cannot be involved further in this investigation, I leave this in the capable hands of Sargent Yeager and our efficient Coroner." He turned to Yeager, "Here is the shooter's gun. Any more question, I'll be inside." He nodded toward his house. Yeager nodded his acceptance, so Bill headed toward the two Ladies. They both turned to greet him. Anita reached to touch the bandaged ear, "I'm glad that was all Barbara had to fix." Her expression was concerned and serious. "I'm headed into the house. I need dinner," Bill spoke as he turned to go. Anita seized his arm, "Wait! I've got dinner in the car. I almost forgot. Help me get it!" Hilda wandered over to her husband, probably to ask about when they would be having their dinner. Bill and Anita each carried a box of food containers into the house. Anita had picked up Dinner, with some help from Mrs Garcia. She had mentioned Mama Castro's. Bill was pleased by her choices. Later, dessert was served, a selection of carnal delights. Anita was pleased by his choices. A call came in from Despatch about 10:30 pm, Johnny Eagle had snuck out his back gate and was picked up by a Jeep CJ. Russell Baker's CJ. Bill knew that something was a foot, probably at the Mines. Jim and Sgt Yeager should be on site. Bill was sure that the team at the Mines would have something to report.

Chapter Seventeen

Saturday:

Bill lay awake in bed, the clock read 12:20 am. He could hear Anita's steady breathing. Their lovemaking had held some aspects of joy and desperation. Both of them knew how close death had come. Bill knew it was an occupational hazard, but he was not about to belabor the point. Not tonight anyway. That was a discussion for later. He did not know what woke him up, he never did. The proper term was premonition. It was part of what had made him an exceptional SEAL officer. It was now part of the equipment he brought to law enforcement. It was active tonight. He thought he knew what was the cause. Something was happening at the Mines. Something involving Russ. The map carried by Juan Carlos had been written by Russ. "He tried to have me killed," Bill thought, "he almost succeeded." His Cell phone rang. He grabbed it after one ring, "Sheriff Andrews." "Sheriff, this is Dispatch. Lieutenant Bearpaw called me on his Cell. There is a Semi arriving at the Mines. He sees about a ten suspects active." "Dispatch, stay off the radio for anything but routine patrol stuff. I will contact the Lieutenant." He hung up and redialed. "Jim!" "It's Bill. Report." "A Semi with a forty-five foot trailer pulled in about thirty minutes ago. They are unloading the trailer with a forklift. Pallets of 'bricks' are being taken into the Midas Mine. I count ten men, some with AK-47's." "Very good. Just observe. I'm going to play dead for a while. Let them think they killed me." "Okay, Bill. What about the dead shooter?" "Maybe they will think that we got each other. Tomorrow, get on the radio. Tell them that with me gone, and Russ suspended, you are taking charge. I will hide out here. Use the phone or email to reach me." "Okay, Boss! Talk to you in the morning." Bill hung up. "Are we going to hide here all day?" Anita's voice came out of the darkness. "I am. I think you should go through with your plans to return to Susanville. It may not be safe here." She moved against him, "I want to stay here with you!" He put his arm around her, "I know you do, and I love you for it. But it will only be for a couple of days, then this should be over." He kissed her, they made love. It would have to last them for a while.

She wanted to be held, it suited Bill to do so. There was mutual need, between the two lovers. Breakfast was slow going, it took second place. Eventually, Anita got her things into her car. They said goodbye in the house, Anita understood. Bill was pleased with his lover, she was very bright. Bright, loving, and beautiful, he was so glad he had found her. She feared losing him. She quaked inside, but for his sake, she put on a brave face. He watched her drive away with dread. Jim had made his radio broadcast, so Bill hoped that bad guys now thought that the way was clear. He spent some time loving on his animals. They liked it, and it did him good as well. With no intention of remaining dead for long, he eventually used the computer. He had Jason Saunders' email address, his private email address. A brief request for an update on the Johnny Eagle matter, produced a quick response. "I am so glad to find that you are still among the living. I take it that there was an attempt was made, obviously unsuccessful. So glad that you prevailed. Does Wanda know of your deception? We are now sure that one source of the money is the Juarez Cartel. Brother Roy has done his part. So far, no noise out of Washington. In Sacramento, the Attorney General has started a bribery investigation. He is focusing on the members of the Legislature we discussed. I hear that AW faces an extradition hearing. I hope she is soon returned to Maryland. That is all for now, please keep me updated. Jason." Bill acknowledged the message, and promised to continue communication. Next, he use to email address off of Charlie's card. He wanted to know what information the DEA had for him. He passed on what he had. He knew that the DEA would receive everything it could about the would be assassin. Last, but not least, he emailed his Daughter about the attempt on his life. He was sure to mention Tiger's part in the incident. There was no immediate reply to either. He was not surprised.

Bill was just getting up from the computer, when there was a knock on the front door. More properly, it could be called an assault! Using the security peephole, Bill saw a very anxious Jennifer on his front porch. Was her revealing sun dress for him? He hadn't heard a car, she must have walked over, or run. She pounded again, "I know you're in there! You just emailed Dad!" His first instinct was to ignore her, but it occurred to him that she would probably attract too much attention. Reluctantly, he opened the door. She rushed in, giving him a bear hug, and a big kiss. "I need to start locking the screen door," was one thought that occurred to him. "Oh, Bill! I thought you were dead!" He received another crushing hug. "Jennifer, I'm trying to stay out of sight!" How can I do that with you barging in here, unannounced!" "I was worried about you! I heard about Jim's radio broadcast. Then, Dad told me about you email. I just had to come over to see you! I don't care about your affair with that whore!" Bill slapped her face! Jennifer was stunned! "Jennifer, the affair was with you. I have a relationship with Anita. She is not a whore, any more than you are. Don't you ever call her that again!" She was amazed, "How can you say that about us? We have a relationship!" He shook his head, "Jennifer, you wanted to have sex, remember? You wanted to sleep with me. I did not pursue you! Then you got busy and forgot about me!" She remembered her night with Swen. "I contacted Anita about an article she wrote, she was on her way here, on business. We had dinner together. Since then, we have found that we are very compatible, in bed and out." She was pouting, "How can you prefer her to me? What's so special about her?" "That's an easy one, Jennifer. She cares about me. You only seem to care about yourself. When you got busy, you forgot all about me. Now you are all concerned about your territory. Did you ever consider my feelings?" Her lips quivered, "I love you! I care about you!" Bill got a disgusted look, "You only care about your happiness! Having me would make your little fantasy come true. I've played this game before!" She lost her pout, "What do you mean, 'played this game before'? I'm not playing a game!" "My wife, Mary, was a lot like you. She wanted things, then lost interest when she got them. You wanted me, then lost interest when you had graves to examine, and a Trial to attend. When you and your Father won your big Court Case, you never even called to tell me! I needed you that day, but you weren't there. I called Anita about an article she wrote. She was there for me. I can count on her, but not you." Jennifer embraced him, "Give me another chance! We can work this out!" His arms were at his sides, "Jennifer, why do you use a diaphragm? Most women chose the pill." She let go of him. Bill saw her stiffen. "I got pregnant on the

Pill. I had a miscarriage. I was five months along." "How sad for you, I imagine the baby's Father was upset." Her mouth curve down at the corners, "I don't want to talk about him. He wasn't what I thought he was." "I see. Did you leave him, or did he leave you? I understand that a miscarriage can be traumatic. So can an abortion!" She jerked open the door, and rushed out. Bill closed the door, shaking his head. "So she had an abortion at five months. Did she make a poor choice, or did he?" His thoughts were interrupted by the beeping of his computer. Entering the Den, Bill saw that he had an email message! "Senor Hartman left Susanville with the same rig. Heading south. Thanks to your Coroner, DEA Intelligence has identified the assassin as one Juan Carlos Calderone. His family is high up in the Cartel. He has several older brothers, so watch your back! Anita send her love. Charlie." Bill smiled at the highly improper message. He knew she used that word on purpose. It did not disturb him. Anita was an emotional person, Bill sensed the depth of her affection for him. This beautiful, intelligent woman loved him. How did he feel about her? He went upstairs and changed into his sweats. He wanted to take a long run, but the treadmill would have to suffice. As he began his warmup, he thought about Jennifer. Losing a baby in the second or third trimester would be hard for most women, whether it was intensional or not. He was sympathetic, but he could not help himself, his mind went back to Anita. Even her blue eyes seemed to smile! He loved her touch, he loved to touch her. The future looked rosy for them. They just had to get through this drug business!

Anita sat at her desk. Her DEA office was small. Her job was part time, after all! She had gone through the memos and press releases from her In Basket. She had called the local radio station about their needs. Now, she just sat there, thinking of Bill. Actually, she thought of herself with Bill. She refused to think of herself without Bill. They would get through this problem at the Mines. Then they would spend more time together. She would talk to him about taking a vacation together. The Hospital in Sierra Vista was talking to her about a position. If that came through, she could ease out of her work here. She was sure that Bill cared about her. He was very kind and thoughtful. Her nights were heaven! She did not expect him to commit to her easily. Men like Bill usually did not move too quickly, where women were concerned.

248

Bill had baggage, the experience with his wife had left him cautious. She knew what some of her Georgetown classmates would say, "You don't need a man to validate your dreams." Anita wondered what they did at night, or how they dealt with the boredom? The sad fact was, until Bill, none of her lovers had been as bright as she. That had always left a hole in her life. She felt no such hole with Bill! She could exist without him, but why would she want to? He had a grown Daughter, would he want more children? She wanted a child, with Bill as its Father. She was sure that their child would be loved, just as she was sure that they would love each other. God would not deny her this happiness, she had waited so long!

Jim Bearpaw found that his day was busy. Wanda shielded him from some of the calls, but there were still enough to eat up his time. Everyone wanted to know about the Sheriff, or where was Captain Baker? He gave Sgt Yeager the afternoon off. At least one of them should get some sleep, before tonight. Barbara had been in his bed, when he got home last night. She was so glad to see him. He really liked that. There had been requests from news people. He thought better of granting an interview. In a day or two, they might really have something to report! There might be another drug shipment tonight! Two Semi loads of drugs, what a haul! He would take the Sniper rifle with him. Yeager would have an M-16, he would spot for Jim, and ride shotgun. The night vision scope worked well last night, he could have hurt them badly. Tonight would be soon enough to kill the men who tried to kill Bill. The Sheriff was like an older brother to him. "The enemies of my brother are my enemies." It was the Washo way. The map Bill found on the assassin was examined, it looked like Russ wrote it. Jason had found an account Russ had set up under Marlene's name. It had just received a $50,000.00 deposit. A lot better than thirty pieces of silver. Bribery, now attempted murder, Russ was really bad. If he was at the Mines, he would die. Jim had received notice of AW's extradition hearing. The DA would not be contesting it. She would go to Maryland, the Cartel's operation would be smashed. Then he and Barbara could get to know each other. Perhaps, she would move in with him. He liked that idea. Barbara was beautiful, intelligent, and highly sexual. He was strongly attracted. He had never felt like this before. Together, they were electric! Maybe it was time to end his solitary existence. He did not mind the idea at all. He was sure it would mean change. The Washo knew, life is change.

Dr Barbara Davis looked at the Hispanic male on her table. She had removed two bullets from his lower chest. His heart was like mush, his Aorta completely separated from the heart. She knew that death had been immediate. "What had this young man thought of, as he tried to kill Bill? Bill killed him so quickly. Was he married? Did he have a family? Did they know he was dead?" She sewed up the 'Y' incision, it was the standard cut used in an Autopsy. She thought about what Jim had said last night. There was a big drug operation at the Mines. She knew what that meant. Jim, and the other Deputies, would be going there to arrest the Cartel members. There would be a lot of drug to seize. Maybe Russ Baker was with them. That made her think of Marlene, nineteen and pregnant. Now, she was faced with Russ missing. Another foolish young woman, like she had been. Another betrayal, of another trusting female. Another pregnancy, born of lust and ignorance. Marlene did not know enough about birth control. There were too many like that. They operate on optimism and old wives tales, then they end up expecting a child their man does not want. So they either abort the baby, or bring it into an unfriendly world. Either way, it left scars. Barbara thought about having a child. It would be inconvenient for her Practice, but she was sure that Aunt Sarah would not mind. Not if she got to deliver it. Would Jim be the Father? She certainly hoped so.

Johnny Eagle felt tired. It was noisy in the mine where the men slept. The place stunk! The tents had been hot, but at least they were out in the open. Then, there was the problem. They were glad about the Sheriff, but where was his killer? According to Russ, the radio report said nothing about that. Later, he would make some discrete inquiries. The insistent Mexican would just have to wait. Apparently, the young man was his cousin. Then, there was Russ, asking about what was in the Molly Bee Mine. He had no need to know. A patriot like him might have a problem with the contents. The gentlemen storing things there might upset him. He did not understand, ignoring the contents of the Molly Bee, made all the rest possible. If he nosed around it, he would die violently. That would bother Johnny, for then Russ could not become Sheriff. He hoped nothing interfered with that. Soon, he would take over the Department! Times would be good! This business at the Mines could finance a Casino. He envisioned his company managing it, with him as its Director. Linda, his wife, did not fit with these plans. Perhaps she would just disappear, some-day. He would like a blond companion. No marriage, without a prenup. Yes, life would be good, after the Casino opened. He supposed that some day, Lieutenant Bearpaw would have to be dealt with. He was so self-righteous! If he could not be bribed, then he would have to go. Perhaps, he and Linda could die together. It could look like an affair, then a car accident. How nice that sounded! Johnny lay on his cot, lost in dreams of his Casino.

Jason Saunders did not know what to make of Jennifer's behavior. She came rushing in, then went straight upstairs to her room. She was up there now, with the door shut. Questioning his security staff, had revealed that she had been informed of Jim's radio broadcast, and of Bill's email. She had apparently left the house. Did she go to see Bill? If so, her reception was not to her liking. She never had been good at handling rejection. Now he would have to bring back her good humor. He knew this had to happen. He had seem Bill and Anita together, the connection was obvious. He knew Jennifer would need time to get over this. In a few days, she would return to LA. She was to work on a project in Mexico, starting in two weeks. That would take her mind off this disappointment. It was all so much like his late Wife. The mood swings, the fixation on unattainable things, Jennifer was like her Mother. Jason hoped that she was still taking her medication. He hoped in vain.

Bill received an email from Charlie at the DEA, "Senor Hartman drove to a warehouse in Vacaville, just off Interstate 80. The Trailer is being quickly loaded, at this moment. I will keep you informed about his location. If he returns to the mines, I want to raid the place. What do you think?" Bill emailed back, "Sounds good to me. Two Semi loads of drugs will make a hell of a haul." Charlie wanted to know what manpower Bill could provide. Bill replied, "I will have one sniper and his spotter in place on the Ridge across from the Mines. I will bring a total of eight more Tactical Squad members with me." Charlie wanted to know about their equipment. "All of us will have Class IV armor with helmets, M-16's, and sidearms." Charlie emailed back that his eight would be similarly equip. He mentioned that he would be bringing a surprise. Bill did not appreciate this secrecy, he thought it was childish. With Charlie on board for the Raid, Bill next needed to communicate with Jim.

Charlie sat at his computer, after signing off. He was deep in thought. If the drug warehouse in Vacaville was a surprise, what else did his superiors not know about this operation? Large quantities of drugs seemed to be getting to the warehouse. How were they getting there? Where were they coming from? Charlie felt more than just a little bit out of the loop. Charlie did not like feeling that way. When he did, it could mean surprises. Nasty surprises. But then, he did have the new toy, even if it was only on loan. It could even the odds. They were dealing with the Juarez Cartel, one of the smaller ones, but still dangerous. It occurred to him, that a suc- cessful operation could mean much credit for him and his team. Having Anita there, after the fight, could mean a great deal of positive press. But she would need a place to work. She would need a computer, a fax, plus good phone communications. There was nothing near the Mines. He knew what that meant. He made a call to his Boss. The advantages for the DEA were pointed out, if they had good, on the spot Press Coverage. Charlie was nothing, if not glib, he got his wish. He was told that the Mobile Command Center would be driven to Sierra Vista tonight, and held there until needed. When the site was clear, it could be driven over. Charlie thanked his Boss, and silently cheered! Next, he obtained permission to park the vehicle in the Sheriff's parking lot. He then put Anita on alert for the follow up. With that done, it was now time to ready their equipment for the Raid.

Corporal Denise Deertail was working on her equipment. She had her M-16 field stripped for cleaning. It made her smile, to clean the weapon. Many of her male teammates had problems with this task. Their huge hands were not suited to handling the small parts. Her smaller hands handled the task with great speed. She, the only woman on the Tactical Squad, held the speed record for tear down and reassembly of an M-16. When she was asked to tryout for the Team, she thought that it might be because Lt Bearpaw was interested in her. But his interest seemed to be only professional. That was the way he was. Someone told her that he was seeing Dr Barbara Davis. Denise thought that she was very pretty. She had a beautiful face, not a flat Indian face like her. Denise knew that she was not beautiful, not by white standards.

She had a flat, plain face. But it belonged to a strong, stocky body. She was five foot six, and one hundred forty-five pounds. She could out run or climb most of the men on the Team, except Jim Bearpaw. He was in great shape! The Sheriff was also in great shape. Although he was in his forties, she had seen him take the Team members in all contests. Her girlfriends talked about what he would be like in bed. She knew that she would never find out. His Grandmother had been of the Lee clan, same as her own Mother. That was not the Washo way. Incest was a taboo. She had heard that he was seeing the tall, blonde Saunders woman. She was rich and beautiful. It somehow fit that he should mate with someone like that. Denise finished cleaning, and started reassembly of her M-16. She thought of the Raid on the Mines. It could be tonight, no one was sure. When it did happen, she would wear the heavy armor, with it's helmet. It was hot and uncomfortable, but it could stop an AK-47 bullet. Word was that the Mexican Cartels all used the AK-47. That was no surprise, there were million of them around. She had five years in with the Department, and a degree from Chico State University. Hard work had gotten her this far, but making Sargent was a much tougher proposition. There were fewer openings, for one thing. Each one entailed more responsibility, for a start. She did not mind that, her social calender was no impediment. Her cat was low maintenance. Would they trust her with the position? She knew she could do well on the test, but would she get fair treatment in the selection process? She nodded to Sgt Yeager. He went to the gun room, soon coming back with his M-16. He had similar thoughts about being prepared for the Raid. He began the cleaning process, as Denise finished hers. Her M-16 went back into the gun room. She put away her cleaning kit, then nodded to the Sargent, as she left.

Jim had a long talk with Bill. Their plans for the Raid were set. Except that you could not be sure when or what would happen. You never knew, for sure. Combat had taught him that. Still, you had to start with a plan. He and Sgt Yeager would slip onto the ridge tonight. If the truck showed up, there would be a Raid. That would probably mean a fight. Both sides would have automatic weapons. Jim was thankful that he would be on the ridge, in the dark. The night was his friend. It was so for most snipers. He would be laying on the ridge, with his big rifle. The night vision goggles would let him see the enemy. So would the Infrared Scope and laser. It would allow him to see their body heat. It would be their death warrant. He would not tell Barbara about that part. He would spare her from that. But he hoped that she was waiting for him, like last night. He came home to find her in his bed. What a joy, to lose himself in that loving, voluptuous body! He had grown to need her with him. Did this mean that love had found him? It had taken long enough. He would call his Mother, then Barbara. Jim would go home about three, he needed sleep before tonight. Before then, he would check his weapons. A craftsman always took care of his tools. Jim was a true craftsman, with six kills as an Army Sniper. Six kills were no accident, that was skill born of preparation. The Mines could mean more kills. How would Barbara take that? What would it do to their relationship?

She stared out of her window, across the lake, at Bill's house. Jennifer had made the first move. She had hired a Private Investigator to dig up dirt on Anita. She was sure the woman was a slut! There would be a lot of dirt, she was sure. Bill would come to see that Anita was a phony. Then he would come back to her. He had to, she had plans! She knew that Bill and she could have a fine life! She would have to return to LA, she would finish her PhD. After that, she would get a position with a large museum, maybe the Smithsonian! Then, Bill would join her. Maybe he would work with their security. It would be so good, especially the nights! She knew that he would be the one. He would help her with her problem. With Bill, she was sure, she would not have to go back on her medication. She hated those pills, it was like looking at life through a veil. She had lied to her Father, when he asked her about her Meds. Life with Bill would cure her! No more drugs! The Doctors were all wrong, this was not a permanent problem. She would be cured! "Bill was so much more understanding than the others. He would see that Anita was a mistake. Then, he would concentrate on me!"

At that moment, Bill was concentrating on a small blonde dog, and a large, striped cat.They were both in need of attention, he didn't mind. Plans for the Raid were set. If the truck came back tonight with a load of drugs, they would raid. He would reappear, as part of the Tactical Squad. That pleased him greatly. If something big was going down, he wanted to be there. He was not at the point in life where he wished to command a desk. Not yet! He rub and patted his little friends, his mind filled with another friend. A wonderfully shaped, blue-eyed friend. Anita was on his mind, she was lovely, all tanned and toned. She always seemed to be aware of where she was and what was going on. He was sure that she had her dreams and fantasies, but she kept firmly grounded in now. Jennifer was a dreamer, Mary had been one too. They floated, lost in fantasy. He had his fill of that life style. After this was over, there would be time for he and Anita. Perhaps he could get her to move in with him? She was delight to find waiting when he got home. Her warm kiss and embrace were so welcoming. She talked about her day, then listened to him talk about his. She was his equal, his partner. Mary never really was. He doubted that Jennifer was ever interested in his work. She seemed so self-absorbed, just like Mary. Was Jennifer ill? It was not his problem. Let Jason take care of his own. If she was sick, wouldn't he know? He seemed on top of most things. Perhaps she was his blind spot? Such things had happened before. That made him thing of his cousin, Russ. Was Russ sick? His aggressive behavior, greed, stubbornness, all seemed excessive. He and reality had a only a fleeting relationship. About like he had with his kids. Bill had observed his illogical actions time after time, over the years. Bill could not see him fighting to the last man. He was not the surrendering type either. In the end, he would flee. He could not be counted on to do the honorable thing, eat his pistol. He would fight, then try to run away. He would try to lie his actions away. Then, he would be tried and convicted. Russ did not possess the kind of temperament that would do well in prison. And the Inmates would not take kindly to the ex-cop with a bad attitude. Bill wondered just what would cousin Russ do? Bill owed him something very personal. His resurrection would come as a big surprise to cousin Russ.

Anita packed a small bag for after the Raid. She gave thought to what she would wear. It would be a very warm day, and the Mine area lacked many shade trees. The DEA van was parked out front of her Dad's house. She had it filled with cases of bottled water and folding cots. It was just a start for the supplies that would be needed, after the Mines were seized. They would let her know what else was needed. Fred, her ex-boyfriend would be there. She hoped that he was not going to be a problem. He had made it obvious that he was still interested. She had made it clear that she was not. He was a simple minded redneck, she had no time for the type. He had been a mistake in judgement. She must have been desperate to even consider dating the DEA agent. Charlie had let her know that Bill would be there, which made her feel so much better. Charlie and Sally, his wife, had become her good friends. Could they be pushing Bill and she a bit? That brought a smile to her face. Thinking of herself with Bill, usually did. Her Father had asked her about her many trips to Sierra Vista, so she told him about Bill. He was happy for her, and told her about Marge, his neighbor. She had been a widow for five years. He told Anita, that they were seeing each other. When she reminded him that her Mom had only been gone for six months, he pointed out that she had been ill for two years before her death. He had a long time to grieve for her. She knew that he was right. Marge joined them for Dinner. Anita made her feel welcome, she did like the retired nurse. Watching the old folks together, she knew that it was right. Secretly, she was glad. If she moved in with Bill, her Dad would have someone. He did not deserve to be alone. Who did? Then, she remembered Fred!

Russ Baker lay on his back. His cot was in a corner of the mine, somewhat removed from the loud Mexicans. He did not like them, and they did not like him. No matter, he would return to Sierra Vista tomorrow. He would find out about Bill, he had to be sure. If Bill was dead, he would become the Acting Sheriff. They had two bought Supervisors who would see that it happened. He had talked to them today, they were not happy, but they knew that the money they took made them dirty. Too bad about the kid, Bill must have got him. They probably got each other. He would enjoy sitting in the Sheriff's Office. He would see that no one bothered the Mines. Johnny could build his Casino. Russ was sure that he would get his cut, he knew about too many skeletons. Even a shark like Johnny Eagle, would have to take care of Sheriff Baker! Of course, he would hide his side money, he had already started. No sense in giving any to his wife, in the divorce. He would have to take care of Marlene, too bad about her getting pregnant. She would not hear of an abortion! He had no intension of marrying her, maybe he could pay her to leave, with the child. Then, everything would settle down. The troublemaker AW would be gone. She had stirred up too much, people got nosey. Jason Saunders seemed content, maybe he found another project. Maybe something in South America? Wanda could keep him busy. It was

256

a good thought. Like Jason's Daughter, Jennifer. He wondered if Bill was still seeing her. With Bill gone, maybe she would be interested in the new Sheriff. What a body! He suppose that Jim Bearpaw would want to investigate Bill's killer. He would tell him to let the DEA pursue it. They could chase the Mexicans. He hoped the DEA and the Cartel took care of each other, in another County, of course. He wanted no trouble in his County. The Mexicans were settling down, the lights went out. Russ smiled and closed his eyes. The future would answer so many questions. He was sure, this was his time to win.

She read, at least she tried to read. Barbara was sitting up in Jim's bed. She knew that Jim would be at the Mines tonight. Would there be violence? If there was, there would be killing. Jim would be involved, if there was. She had to consider, "How did she feel about that?" She knew that it was his duty. It was necessary for a Raid on the Mines. It occurred to her that more law enforcement officers would die without Jim and his rifle. The irony was not lost on her. Then there was Jim's reticence to speak about his sniping. There was no bragging, no war stories. It appeared to be just part of his duties. That made it bearable, for a dedicated Doctor. When she was with him, Jim made her feel like she was the center of his world! She knew that she longed for those nights with her man. Was this a betrayal of her oath, as a Doctor? She did not aid or encourage him, she simply forgave him. She accepted the idea that the World was better off with Jim and his rifle, then without them. Her thoughts went to ones of her in bed with Jim. So much for her reading.

Bill received a late night email from Charlie, "Semi still in Vacaville. Driver and mechanic working on engine. Looks like no shipment tonight!" Bill loved his animals, then took a shower. It looked like tomorrow would be a day of waiting.

Chapter Eighteen

Sunday:

Russ listen to them argue, Senor Calderone and Johnny Eagle. He figured that the Semi breaking down had everyone on edge, even these two educated men. The Mexican spoke good English, which was fortunate, Johnny spoke no Spanish. The Mexican demanded to know about his kinsman, the assassin. Johnny feared that the Cartel was reneging on their deal. Did the Semi really break down? The second shipment marked the Phase One completion of their plan, the Cartel could begin shipments from the Mines. Johnny was to receive a large sum, which Russ was sure, would allow him to pursuit his Casino. He could never forget that there were at least ten men with AK-47s nearby, in case this disagreement got hot. Nerves! He had seen them ruin missions and men. But not him, Russ was made of sterner stuff! He told both men, that he would go into town. He would find out about the kid. Privately, what worried him was the health of cousin Bill. Did the Sheriff still live? If he did, Russ intended to put him down. Russ would be the new Sheriff. He would have his day, not Bill. Neither man could find fault with his plan, so he received reluctant permission. Russ thought that this was the height of ego, he was a better man than either of them. When he was Sheriff, they would learn just who was in charge. He could call the DEA at any time, claiming to have infiltrated the plot. Russ could then take credit for the arrest of the men, and the seizure of all their dope! As he drove away, Captain Russ Baker knew he could play it either way. He was not a man that often recognized that he had options.

Russ uncovered his Jeep, he had it stashed in the Red Dog Mine. As he had walked past the Molly Bee, he wondered. He was sure that there were at least two men hold up in there. Why did they keep apart from the rest? Russ considered what they might be up to. Too much speculation, not enough facts. He decided that when he got back, he would pick a time to snoop. No way he was going on without knowing what was going on here. Everything that was going on here. As he drove into Sierra Vista, Russ mulled over how to proceed. He needed to do a bit of reconnaissance, that meant a base of operations. He had just the place! Avoiding the main streets, he slowly maneuvered the noisy old Jeep through back allies. Judy was not expecting a caller quite so early, she worked nights! She let him park in her garage. Russ made it worth her while, he always did. A wake up romp in her bed, a fifty dollar bill, then Russ got on the phone. The two Supervisors were good for some information. The DEA had picked up something from the Morgue. That could be the assassin! What about Bill? No real facts. He had not been seen since Friday. No sign of him at the Hospital, but they knew he was friends with Dr Barbara Davis. Russ pondered, what did this mean? The assassin was apparently dead. Was Bill only wounded? Russ knew what he must do. After dark. He would scout Bill's place! If cousin Bill was alive, he would have to be disposed of. Better he be at home, than in the Hospital. At home, and totally unguarded, that would be best. Russ smiled, to himself. Things would be clear, tonight!

For Jim and Barbara, last night had been something of a let down. Not the sex, after Jim found her waiting in his bed. What a joy, after the disappointment at the Mines, to have her warm reception as compensation. They made passionate love, but over breakfast, they both realized that they still did not know if Barbara could weather the storm. How would she react, if Jim had to use his Sniper rifle? As Coroner, she would view his handiwork. What a .408 caliber bullet did to the human body, was not pretty. It was the kind of thing that would leave a lasting impression. Jim dreaded it, Barbara had no idea how bad it could be. They ate breakfast, held hands, and tried to plan something pleasant. Both tried to forget, that tonight the Raid could occur. Tonight, Jim might be called upon to kill. It would be at long range, he would not touch his victims, but they would be very dead. Their remains could be very ugly, shattered pieces of human beings. He would give anything to shield Barbara's eyes from such things.

Bill was late rising, he slept in after last night's email. Everything was on hold for another day. He thought of his Cousin, waiting was not for Russ. Bill fed his animals, made his breakfast, and tried to stay out of sight. Anita had left him with a well stocked kitchen, one more thing to her credit. Her account was

260

already full of positive things. It sometimes amazed him, that she was unattached, and interested in him. Beautiful, intelligent, accomplished, and a good lover, her list of attributes was long. He imagined her face, her blue eyes, her wonderful body, so delightful. Then his mind went back to Russ, and the Cartel he was now involved with. He had been told that Russ had received fifty thousand for helping with the attempt on his life. Would they lay low, until the Semi returned? Then they would be raided, the drugs seized. How many would die, over those tons of profitable poison the Cartel was bringing to the Valley? He thought of it as his Valley, he was sworn to protect it and enforce the laws. How very hard that could be sometimes. Would Russ be content to wait, or would they manage to restrain him? Would another Calderone brother come for revenge? The DEA said that there were several, probably some older. The dead man was young, early twenties, he may have older brothers. Brothers who may come looking for his killer. The Cartel can't take kindly to have one of their leaders killed, no matter how young he was. "I wonder if there is a price on my head?" Then he thought, "If not now, certainly after the Raid. They will be very unhappy." After breakfast, Bill fired up his computer, an email check was in order. There were several, four were random porn offers. One from Charlie let him know that the Semi was still down, but parts had been obtained. Would it be repaired today? His Daughter wanted to know more details about the attempt on his life. He told her that there was a bigger story here, but give him another day for things to play out. He assured her that he was okay, so was Anita. Anita sent copies of her Press Releases, and an inquiry asking when could she return? He wanted her here, right now! He had to ask her to wait, until after the Raid. He warned her about possible Cartel retaliation. He did not expect it to deter her to any degree. By now, he figured that he knew her that well. "After this is over, we can get to know each other better." Susie wanted attention, so she was brought into his lap. His hand on her head was all she asked. Bill found it easy to comply.

Jim Bearpaw had conversations with most of the County Supervisors. Two asked about Bill's funeral, they wanted details. He knew from Jason, those men were dirty. They got a story about Bill's body awaiting his Daughter's decision about the burial. Ray Vinders confided to him that he had five votes lined up to make him Interim Sheriff, the other two wanted Russ. Jim did not have to ask who supported the rogue Captain. He had a two man team checking the Eagle home. No sign of the AW's pistol, but they found only Linda at home. She said that her husband went out. Both of their vehicles were in the garage. But Jim knew, Russ picked up Johnny last night. Jim was told that Linda seemed very nervous, even though they found nothing a miss. He was informed about one file cabinet in their Den, one drawer held foreign language documents. The Deputy thought that it was Arabic, she had served in Iraq. The Search Warrant did not allow them to take it, so it was just noted, for future reference. Jim though about what it could mean. They were using the Mines, which belonged to an Arab company. Perhaps they sent English translations with the letters in Arabic? There was nothing there for the moment, but Jim though that it deserved further investigation. There were a lot of things that fit that description. Jim received a phone call about the two wanted Meth 'cooks'. Santa Cruz County was holding them. They had been stopped for a traffic violation, then held on the APB from Sierra Vista. Jim would have to send two officers down there to pick them up. He wondered if they would talk about who bank rolled their operation. Two small time operators could not have rented the Mansion, and bought all of their equipment. They had 100 pounds of Crystal Meth in production, and that was just one batch. Could this be like the Marijuana field? Was this the same group? Was it Johnny Eagle? There were still a lot of questions to answer.

She woke slowly, last night had lasted into the wee hours. Jennifer had fallen asleep on her window seat, staring at Bill's house. The cool morning air had driven her to bed. "How long would it take, for her man to get the dirt on Anita? Had she been with Bill last night?" Jennifer had not seen any arrivals or departures, last night. Had he broken up with the Bitch? The big Blonde got dressed, and went downstairs. The coffee was on, but Maria was missing. Probably at Mass, with her Parents. Jennifer poured herself some coffee and orange juice. That gave her time to assess her appetite. She found that she seemed to eat more, off her Meds. Dry cereal was a safe choice. The pantry held many varieties, she grabbed four or five. With no audience, she chose a large bowl. Three different cereals went into the bowl, plus milk, and a sliced Banana. She dug in, part of her binge and abstain roller coaster. Yesterday, she forgot to eat. Maria and her Dad had to get on her. She was upset, Bill was being difficult. She felt better now, she had a plan. With the dirt on Anita, she could reclaim Bill. She was sure of her plan, how could it fail? But how long would it take? How long should she stay away from Bill? Jennifer ate her cereal with relish. She felt very positive today! She thought of visiting Bill! What should she wear?

Brenda was back at work, wild horses couldn't keep her away. The Sheriff Department had her statement, she had been assured by the District Attorney that Jake would serve many years for his unprovoked attack. DA Van Cleef reminded her of a used car salesman she had met once, a bad used car salesman. Everyone else had been so kind to her. Danny and Sally had visited her, the day after. Sally was so sweet. The way the young couple clung to each other, Brenda was sure that they were doing it! And why not, they were both adults. She hoped they were using condoms. Seeing them had reminded her of her own situation. She was sure that Stan would welcome her into his bed. Would that make her happy? She had to admit, the idea did appeal to her. What would it mean, long term? Stan had gotten permission to offer a temporary position to one of the Volunteers. The one chosen was one Eugene Wagstaff, a twenty-nine year old former Air Force firefighter. Gene was a burly six footer, who always seemed to be smiling. He showed everyone photos of his six month old son. He was their first, they planned on at least one more. That would be, if Gene found work. He was laid off from his firefighting post when the Mill closed. He so hoped that his application to Cal Fire was accepted, they knew that he was ready to work, little schooling would be needed. He seemed to be working out, Brenda had noticed that he and Danny got along. Gene was a real worker. No friction on the Engine, meant that Brenda had more time to consider her needs. Maybe the assault had been a wake up call. None of her relationships had worked out. Why was that? Was it the men, or her. She had to admit, she had made poor choices. What about Stan? Solid and reliable, she knew she could depend on him. Would he want children? Would the age difference create a problem? They were of different generations, but she saw how well they got along. So far, it had been all right. Would it stay so? If she shacked up with Stan, no one needed to know. She reported to Gary, he did her review. No rules were violated, but Cal Fire would not be happy. What if she wanted to be a Captain? Would it mean leaving the area. Would they let her serve under Stan? What would happen if they married? So many questions, but they were important to the young firefighter. Vital to her future, and her heart. Bottom line, Brenda was not sure about living with Stan.

Sargent Wolfe had new orders for Brent. He was to leave the 'Dig' at the usual time, but he was to go on overtime, driving to the Station. There, he was to pickup a patrol car, one would be waiting for him with a trunk filled with traffic barriers. "We will tell you when to head out." Brent was assigned to setup a roadblock on Route Five, just below Route One. He was told about the Raid on the Mines. "It will be your job to keep civilians out of the Mines area. There will be another roadblock on Route five, to the North, above the Mines." Brent promised to take care of it. When Mona entered the Kitchen, she wanted to know, "Who was that on the phone?" Brent told her about the extra duty, but not about the Raid. "The Tactical Unit is conducting a night drill. We need to keep civilians out of the area." Brent held his breath, watching for Mona's reaction. She frowned, "Can you still take me home tonight?" Brent wasn't sure, "I might be sent out before one. But if not, I can still pick you up." She smiled, as she crossed to him. They shared a big kiss. "You be careful out there! I want you safe with me. We have things to do, tonight." He hugged her compact young body, remembering last night. He was aroused by the memory. He whispered to her, "Why wait for tonight?" She giggle at his suggestion, but reminded him that they needed to fix dinner. They shared another kiss, then got busy on the planned meal. Brent had time to consider tonight. It was not only civilian travelers he could be dealing with. What if one of the Cartel gets close? He knew that they could be heavily armed. Would he try to stop them? The thought dampened his appetite.

Jennifer was back at her window, staring at Bill's house across the lake. No activity, no sign of visitors, or of the owner. She was frustrated, it made her restless. She wanted to do something! The more she thought about it, the better that seemed. After dusk, she would visit Bill! Now, she needed to figure what to wear. She considered many dresses, she wanted him to see her long legs. But then, what about her bust? She knew just the dress! It was a short white one, that buttoned down the front. It was quickly out of her closet, undergoing inspection. She was sure that

264

this one would do the trick! She envisioned Bill opening the door, she would be there on the porch. The dress would be unbuttoned, she would throw it open! Bill would embrace her nude body, they would quickly be in his bedroom. Anita would be forgotten. She could see it all, how Bill would be her's! Suddenly, she felt hungry! The dress was rehung, then the big Blonde headed downstairs. No Maria in the Kitchen. She must have taken the day off! Jennifer knew that her Father was out with Wanda. No matter, she would feed herself. Soon, her head was in the refrigerator, containers were set on the counter. She grabbed a beer, no worry about its affect on her, she had not taken her Meds for several days."I never want to take my Meds again! They will just have to accept the real me!

Bill had a good workout. He took a shower, ate, then took a nap. Jennifer never crossed his mind. It was Anita, all the way. He knew that he wanted her to move in, after the current difficulties were over. He saw her face and form, in his dream. He dwelt on her, it saved him from thinking about the firefight that could develop tonight. Bill had learned all about the futility of wondering why something happened. The Cartel chose his County, now he and the DEA had to deal with it. He and Charlie had emailed each other, the plans were set. He had gone over every aspect, adding roadblocks, calling for an EMT unit on standby. It was now time to relax, to prepare the mind for tonight. Bill was sure that there would be a Raid at the Mines. The Semi would return, the drugs would be seized, and the Cartel in his County would be smashed. The power of positive thinking. He was currently feeding the pets, and thinking positively about Anita cohabiting with him and the animals. Tiger seemed to miss her, almost as much as him.

With the approach of dusk, Russ got active. He was alone in the house, Judy was at work, carting drinks and dodging horny hands. She was not particularly pretty, but she had a nice bod, and she lived alone. Just what was needed by a cheating husband, looking for something on the side. Some women did not think they should lower themselves to perform certain sexual acts, "Only whores did that!" So their spouse got it somewhere else. Some men, like Russ, had other women no matter what their spouse did or didn't do. After a romp with an experienced woman like Judy, Russ was thinking that he needed to move on from Marlene. The novelty of having a virgin had definitely worn off. Her pregnancy clinched the deal, she needed to be gone! Russ took his things to the Jeep, but not before leaving Judy another crisp fifty dollar bill. With the fading light, he put his vehicle back on the street. He kept to the side streets, avoiding the main roads. There were too many eyes on the busier routes. Eventually, Russ made it to Bill's place. Every time he came here, it rankled. This should be half owned by his Mother! It was so unfair, his Father did all the wrong, why punish her? When Bill was gone, it will pass to his Daughter. What will she do with it? Her life is in LA, will she sell it? Would he want to buy it? He hid the Jeep in the woods that covered the front of the property. He quietly walked toward the looming hulk of the house. Best to skirt it, he silently crossed the driveway well away from the house. Russ entered the woods, beyond the paved area. He could watch the house for signs of life from there. He saw no lights, only Bill's official vehicle parked off the driveway, yellow tape blocking it's car port. He found a spot opposite the house, behind some bushes. Everything looked dead, no light, no sound. Russ sat on a rock and waited. Nothing but the night sounds. Those he had heard since childhood.

With darkness descending, Jennifer sprang into action. First thing, was to insert her diaphragm. She put on the white dress next. Just the white dress, nothing else. Bill was going to have easy access! Leaving the house, she told the man on duty, that she was "just going for a walk around the Lake." She had done it before, so no problem. It was obvious that this one wanted in her pants, but she was not interested. She left the Estate, following the familiar path. She was very positive about this. Bill would fall over himself to have her voluptuous body! He would take her, right there in the entry. How glorious it would be! They would make love all night. Anita would be forgotten, Jennifer would be all he wanted! The young moon had risen, casting its pale light over the still Lake. But she never noticed, her mind was filled with fantasies of her and Bill. Her body ached for Bill! Her pace increased.

Russ heard someone on the Lake path. Someone walking fast, not at all cautious! Russ hid himself and watched. He saw the dress and pale hair. The hair and build were easy to identify. He had seen Jennifer Saunders a few times. Was she coming to see Bill? He would have to take her out, Bill must be alone! He saw her silhouette. What a body! He wanted her! His mind was busy. He would take her, kill Bill, then enjoy her at his leisure. What a

266

plan! She stopped before the house, he saw her unbuttoning her dress. She did not stop with showing her cleavage, but undid it all the way! She was so intent on Bill, that she never heard the slight sounds of boots on the asphalt. Then, a hand went over her mouth. The other arm came across her throat. The forearm shut off her air! Her vision grayed, then Jennifer slumped unconscious in his arms. He drug her backwards, leaving her sandals behind. Russ laid her on the grass at the edge of the pavement. The loose flaps of the dress were flipped aside, exposing Jennifer. His small flashlight illuminated her form. "Wow, look at those Tits! Those long legs!" Russ was seized by overwhelming lust for the big Blonde. Russ didn't hesitate, he lost all control. He put the light away, then grab her Tits with both hands. He fondled, he squeezed, he licked. Quickly, he unzipped himself. He could wait no longer. His rape of Jennifer Saunders, Bill's lover, began! The idea that she was Bill's, sealed the deal. His vigorous thrusts began to wake Jennifer. At first, her confused mind thought that Bill was on top of her. She smiled, then opened her eyes. It took her a moment in the dim light, but the smell wasn't Bill. Then she saw him, "Who are you?" "Your new lover! I'm going to kill Bill, then we can have some good times." Russ groaned, then came. He became totally focused on pumping sperm deep into her body! Jennifer screamed! Bill was on the front porch, then on the asphalt, gun in hand. A neighbor had warned him of a 'visitor'. He saw Jennifer's sandals, then looked up. He saw the white of her dress. Russ had some trouble standing. "You raped me!" Jennifer wailed. Russ reached for his Beretta, but too late! Bill's first bullet entered the open mouth of Russ Baker, exiting at the base of his scull. Meanwhile, a second bullet hit him in the left eye, and a third bullet caught him in the forehead. The corpse of Captain Russell Baker crumpled on the grass, oozing blood and cerebral fluid. Bill cautiously checked his pulse, nothing. Then he checked for a ballistic vest, there was none. "Russ, you were such a fool!" Bill just stared and shook his head. He had fired at his Cousin's head, on the chance he wore a vest. "Macho to the end, did you have time to realize your foolishness?" As he picked up the dead man's Beretta, Jennifer moan, "He raped me, the Bastard raped me!" Bill engaged the gun's safety, then stuck it in his belt. Reaching Jennifer, he bent down and covered her. Her eyes did not follow him, but stared straight ahead. "Jennifer?" She made no response. He waved his hand in front of her, no response. "Maybe shock." He said aloud. Then used his Cell, to call in the rape and shooting. "He raped me!" She kept saying, like she was in a daze.

First one on the scene was the head of Jason's Security Team. Bill thought that now was not the time to chide him for his monitoring Department radio communications. The man was distraught, his employer's Daughter had been raped, on his watch! Bill got him to contact Jason Saunders, he could be at the Hospital when they brought Jennifer in. Twice, the former Green Beret tried to comfort the victim. Bill had to remind him about crime scene protocol, "Beside, she is in profound shock. I doubt she even knows we're here." The EMS unit was next to arrive. Bill reminded them about a rape kit, and preserving evidence. He did not think that it would matter much. The perpetrator was dead, the victim was out of it, unable to testify. He held little hope for her rapid recovery. As the EMTs put Jennifer into the Ambulance, Sargent Wolfe and the two person CSI team pulled up. After a quick survey of the scene, with Bill's narrative, the two Technicians set up lights. Bill showed them where to find power. They photographed the crime scene, while Sargent Wolfe took his statement. Soon, Dr Barbara Davis pulled up, in her black Cadillac. The former hearse now had red roof lights. Did it have a siren? An irritated lady coroner march right up to Bill and the Sargent, "All right, Bill, who did you kill this time?" He pointed toward the body, "Russ Baker, he was raping Jennifer. He tried to draw his weapon, I had to shoot him." She was instantly sorry for her attitude, "Raped Jennifer? Wasn't Russ your Cousin?" He was stoic, "Yes, he was. Russ has gone totally bad, he arranged for the assassin I killed. He was paid $50,000.00 to set me up." Barbara was stunned and contrite, "Excuse me, Bill. I didn't know! I apologize! Me and my stupid mouth! Let me get to my work!" She began her examination of the body. Bill watched her and wondered, "Is she mad at me for sending Jim out tonight, or is she worried what might happen? Probably both." Bill turned over the Beretta to Wolfe, "If you need anything else, I'll be inside. Wolfe nodded his acceptance, then watched Bill walk away. "He just killed his own Cousin, a murdering rapist. What is going through his mind?" Wolfe had no answers to his question. Barbara called Wolfe over to help her roll Russ on his back. His damaged face made both of them queasy.

268

There had been that one burst of activity, then Dispatch grew silent. Brent was concerned, he wished he knew what was going on. He now wore a radio, like all of the Deputies. He heard the report of a shooting, but didn't recognize the address. This was beginning to be too regular a thing. First, the attack on the Sheriff, then this. Would it affect the Raid? How about his later duties? Mona had been worried tonight, he had a difficult time getting her to let go at the Motel. "She was young, she worried over everything that might affect our life together." She looked paler than usual. Brent did not blame the little redhead. He had already done his first tour of the site, but he knew another would not hurt. It was on the return half that Brent heard the car. He was pretty sure he knew who it was. Sure enough, Donna sat at the table under the tent. She smile when she saw him. "Hello, Donna. Long time no see." "Well, I was really hung over! Got sick all over the place." He looked her over, short sleeve blouse and shorts. "You look good now. How do you feel?" "Good! I lost five pounds!" This surprised him, "Five pounds! I didn't know you were trying!" She looked a bit sheepish, "Well, I wasn't eating too well for a couple of days, so I decided to start." He hugged her, "I think it's great! How much do you intend to lose?" She looked into his eyes, "Forty or fifty pounds, does that sound like too much?" "Maybe you should do thirty, then see what still needs to be lost." She thought that sounded good. She also had a suggestion about what would help her diet. They met in the enclosure. Brent insisted on undressing her. She liked that a lot! He still preferred doing it in the dark. They took turns pleasuring each other. Brent made the most of her generous chest. That was okay with Donna. Both of them did wonder what weight loss would do to those two beauties? Oh well, enjoy them while you can!

There were no lights on in the house, no creature stirred. Bill lay on his bed, half asleep. Images of Russ, Anita, and Jennifer floated through his head. Greed and lust had killed Russ, he had just been the instrument. Bribery, rape, conspiracy to murder, what other crimes has he been involved with? Drug transportation and storage, with intent to distribute? "You really out did your Dad, Russ! He was small time, compared to you. You wanted to be rich, to be Sheriff, and to rape Jennifer. Did you plan on a relationship with her? That was foolish! She was deluded, but then, so were you!" His body was taken to the Morgue, Barbara

269

was appalled at the damage to his head. She had much to learn about law enforcement, and staying alive. Anita had emailed him today. Bill wondered if it qualified as soft porn. She was a bright, sensuous creature. He had no doubt about her, he had less doubt about his own feelings. He wanted her with him, the sooner the better. But it would have to wait, this thing at the Mines would have to be dealt with. Or did it? Could this end peacefully? The question had to be asked. Could the fight be avoided? No matter what Bill wished, he knew the answer. When the law enforcement personnel showed up at the Mines, the Cartel would fight. With AK-47's, they would resist. They had so much to lose, surrender meant death to a Cartel member. They could be assassinated for what they knew, and as an example to others, Cartel justice had a long arm. When the Semi came back tonight, there would be war. Charlie had told him that it was on its way. What could he do about that? Having exhausted the topic, Bill turned to Anita. Would he ask her to move in? As soon as he could, they could start building a life together. How good that sounded, to the long alone Widower.

Gwen and Amy comforted a distraught Marlene. "What will I do!" Wailed the teenager, "Where will I go?" She sat on the sofa, between the Mother and Daughter, wringing her hands. "What's wrong with staying right here?" Gwen asked. Marlene blinked, while she considered that. It was the first peaceful moment since Bill had called about Russ. Gwen saw possibilities, her house would accommodate the pregnant teen. Amy would be a senior in high school, then off to college. Marlene and the baby could live here. She would need some work to do, after the birth. She would talk to her Father. He knew all sorts of business people. Maybe one of them could hire Marlene. Gwen and Amy could baby sit. "Could I really stay here?" The young woman had stopped crying. "My folks didn't approve of Russ and me! He want me to have an abortion, but I said no." Gwen nodded, "I know, you can't think of destroying your baby! We will have to make sure you see Dr Sarah regularly. We want your baby to be health!" Marlene quietly contemplate her future, while Gwen and Amy discussed taking her to pick up her things. Marlene knew that Russ was dead, but not how he died. She knew nothing about the rape.

The rape set off a chain of events, culminating in the Intensive Care Unit at the Valley Memorial Hospital. Dr Sarah Davis stood before a bed in the ICU, her hands were in the pockets of her white lab coat. She was concerned for her patient, Jennifer was not responding to treatment. Sarah was sure, there was something more here than shock! In order to find out what, she turned and made her way to the small waiting room nearby. Jason Saunders sat there, holding hands with Wanda. Both were drawn and pale. They both studied the Doctor's face for a sign of anything. Her look was grim, "Mr Saunders, I need all details that you can supply about Jennifer's past health. Is she currently on any medication?" Jason, hesitated before withdrawing a paper from his jacket. "Doctor Davis, this is a list of her currant Meds." Sarah took the list, then studied it for two or three minutes. "Mr Saunders, these are powerful antidepressants and antipsychotics. What was her diagnosis?" "After her rape in Mexico, they found that she was a Bipolar, Type II. The phone number of her Psychiatrist is on the paper." "Is she currently taking taking these medications?" Jason was very unhappy, "I don't believe so. I believe that she has been lying to me." Sarah raised her eyebrows, "I see. Doesn't sound unusual to me. Most patient like your Daughter try that regularly. I know she is not a child, but you will have to treat her like one. It is for her own good! We will check her blood, then start her on a drug regimen. I suggest you make arrangements for her to treated by her own Doctor." A grim Sarah returned to the ICU. Jason had some explaining to do. Wanda had many question about the family secrecy. She was not please with her lover. Was he ashamed?

Chapter Nineteen

Monday:

Bill was awake early again. His heavy workout yesterday let him fall asleep, but his senses were now fully awake. The clock read 12:30 am. His 'gift' always made him ready for what life had for him. He lay there, waiting for the phone to ring. He assumed that Jim would be calling in. That was the problem, he knew that something was happening, just not what. He was glad that Anita was not there tonight. That would have been an emotional goodbye, it would not have been good for either of them. He was thinking of the lovely Anita, when his bedside phone rang, "Sheriff Andrews." "Sheriff, this is Dispatch. Lieutenant Bearpaw called me on his Cell. The Semi has returned to the Mines. He sees about ten men with AK-47s. They are unloading the Semi with a forklift." "Dispatch, stay off the radio for anything but routine patrol stuff. Call all members of the Tactical Team. Tell them to meet me at the Team Room. Draw full combat loads, full armor. Sargent Yeager is with Lieutenant Bearpaw." "Roger, Sheriff. I take it that the bad guys may be monitoring our radio." "Smart Girl, Betty! Now get cracking!" The phone went dead and Bill hung up. He heard a movement, then turned to see his two animal. Their eyes were large as quarters. Okay, you two! "Come here!" He patted the bed. Both animals came to him. He hugged and petted them both. He had been doing a lot of that lately. Irregular events upset the animals. They did not understand this stuff. Sometimes Bill wondered if he did. Then Bill grabbed his Cell phone from the night stand. He picked a number from speed dial. "DEA Operations." "This is Sheriff Andrews. I need to report a large drug transfer at the Old Mine Road." "I have been briefed on that operation, Sir. What is your response going to be." "I will have a ten man Tactical Team. We can meet your team by the old logging road at marker 54 on County Road Five in ninety minutes. Use my Cell phone." "Got it, Sheriff! I"ll pass the word!" "And

273

hurry! Bye." He hung up. Time to get dressed! He did not want to storm another position against heavy resistance. The Cartel could field an army of their soldiers, was it really only ten at the site? Duty called, if not him, then who? Once again, he was simply the best man available for the job. Once a SEAL, always one. Bill finished dressing, and went downstairs.

Charlie alerted his men, Anita got the word for the follow up. She made one call, to Dr Barbara Davis, who was informed that the Raid was going down tonight. "Thank you, Anita. I owe you one!" She lay in bed for just a moment. Then, it was up and at them! She dressed, jeans, a blouse, and a sweater. Coffee was brewed, while she retrieved her food from the 'fridge. A quick brush of the hair, some lipstick, then back for the coffee. She had this all planned. She drove the Coroner's converted hearse, the black Cadillac would serve her purpose tonight. Barbara drank her coffee and ate her breakfast as she drove. Off of Route Five, she found the old fire road. She pulled in, then turned the Cadillac around. She parked, with the lights off, facing Route Five. "Now, if the posse comes along, I can joined the parade. As Coroner, I have a perfect right to be at this Raid. It is in my County!" It all sounded so hollow to her ears. Bill and Jim would be very upset by her presence, and she knew it. "Besides, they might need a Doctor on site!" That sounded a bit more convincing.

Bill arrived at the Sheriff's Department to find that all of his team was there, in various states of dress. The uniform for tonight was dark green fatigues, over which was placed upper body Class IV Armor, Class III Leggings and a cartridge belt with spare M-16 magazines and a holster for their service pistol. They wore black paratrooper boots, black gloves, and a Ballistic helmet with ear pieces. They would not be using the face shield with the helmet, because it interfered with their night vision goggles. In the Locker Room, Bill changed into his fatigues, everything but the helmet. Back in the Team Room, he banged the butt of his M-16 on a wooden bench, "I want everyone's attention!" The chatter subsided. "This is not a drill! We are joining a DEA team in an assault on a suspected drug storage site. At least ten suspected members of the Mexican Drug Cartel have been spotted at the Mines. There may be more. Assume them to be heavily armed. They have nothing to lose by fighting us. They will probably try to shoot their way out. Sargent Wolfe will be second in command,

274

Lieutenant Bearpaw is already on site. Stay off your radios until the fight starts. They are probably monitoring our channels. Everyone switch to Channel two. Earlier this evening, I shot and killed Captain Baker, while he was raping a neighbor woman. I have proof that Captain Baker has been in their pay. Meet you at the vehicles in five minutes." The room was alive with talk as they finished suiting up. And then they began to filter out into the parking lot, seven men and one heavily armed woman.

Bill rode in the passenger front seat of the Sheriff 's SUV on County Road One. Twice he had talked to the DEA by phone. Charlie Stevens was coming with a ten man team. He had three more in a FLIR equipped helicopter. They could drop flares, if needed. Bill hoped his team's night vision goggles were enough. Soon they came to County Road Five. They saw no sign of the DEA convoy. The column turned left on to Road Five and headed for the rendevous. A few minutes later, Bill got a call, "Sheriff Andrews." "This is Wolfe in the last car. We have a column of vehicles on our tail, about a mile back." "Roger, Wolfe." Bill hung up. "The DEA convoy is about one mile behind us," he informed the men in his vehicle. A few minutes more, and they pulled off onto the shoulder of County Road Five, just past the old logging road. Each vehicle switched off its lights as planned. Bill got out and walked along the shoulder until he came to the end of his convoy. He could see the row of vehicles headed his way. Shortly, they pulled off of the road behind the Sheriff's vehicles and switched off their lights. DEA Special Agent-in-charge Charlie Stevens got out of the first vehicle, and Bill headed to him. He was dressed similarly to the Sheriff. "Welcome to the party, Charlie." "I just wish you had scheduled this little get together for some later hour." "Charlie, we got the best seats at the Three am seating!" "That's what I was afraid of, Bill." "Hang on a minute, let me make contact with my scouts." Bill slipped on his radio headset, he clicked his 'Talk' button twice. In his ear piece, he heard the two clicks. A moment later, he heard one click in response. "What is the situation?" Bill asked. Jim responded, "Bill, their sentry has been eliminated" "Okay Charlie, my guys are in position. What's the plan?" "Bill, my second vehicle is an M1117 Armored Vehicle. I think it should lead the way. It has Infrared headlights. When we get to Old Mine Road, all other vehicles should block the road to the mines. We can form our assault group behind my vehicle. It has a .50 caliber machine gun, grenade launcher, and an infrared spotlight in the turret" "You Feds have all the toys. Do you have our radio frequency?" "Yeah, Bill we're set on that. With us on the ground, and your team on the ridge, we look to be set." "Okay Charlie, you take the lead with your 'tank' and we will follow." "Sounds good, the rest of my boys will take the right, when we attack. We need a minute to pass the word." "So do I Charlie" The two men split up and headed in opposite directions, stopping at each vehicle to spread the word. That done, everyone climbed aboard. The Armored Vehicle swung onto the road and slowly moved to the front of the column, the infrared lights unseen to anyone without the proper eye gear. The Sheriff and his convoy pulled out behind it, and the DEA convoy brought up the rear. That is, almost brought up the rear. As the last DEA vehicle passed by the old logging road, a black Cadillac Hearst pulled onto the road behind it. The DEA guys thought it was just the local Sheriff's idea. Barbara was wondering what the Sheriff or Jim would think if he knew where she was. "Too late now. I am committed!"

The Convoy drove slowly along the road, trying to keep the noise down. When they reached the Old Mine Road, the M1117 turned onto it and stopped fifty feet in. The Sheriff Department vehicles formed a line half way across the road mouth, then the DEA vehicles pulled in behind them, completely closing off the road. The Black Hearst pulled up next to the gully and stopped. Then all Officers exited their vehicles and formed up behind the armored vehicle, many just putting on their helmet. Bill had his helmet and night vision goggles on. The goggles allowed him to see the other men, one of the DEA agents had a M203 grenade launcher underneath his M-16. "I hope he knows how to use that thing," he reflected. More signs of the benefits of working for the Justice Department. "Sheriff, are we ready?" "Move out!" The engine of the Armored Vehicle revved, Bill hoped the bad guys didn't hear it. Then they started moving. "Warning! The Semi is getting ready to go!" The radio came alive! It was Yeager's voice. They could hear the roar of a truck engine above the sound of the M1117. As they rounded a curve, they suddenly saw the Semi turning toward them, a half mile away. There it was heading right for them, its forty-five foot trailer throwing up a cloud of dust. Its headlights turned on, illuminating the entire law enforcement

276

group. "Charlie, now would be a good time to kill that thing." "Your wish is my command." Immediately, the .50 caliber opened up. The semi lost both headlights and the windshield blew out, as sparks flew. Bill slipped his night goggles back on and saw the truck's radiator had six or seven fast leaks. Its roar subsided and it coasted to a stop, fifty feet away. Bill saw no burning, "DEA doesn't use Incendiary rounds," Bill observed. The M1117 swung to the right, around the Semi. Bill could hear the familiar sound of an AK-47, then another. Soon there were three or four firing at them. He could hear rounds hitting the armor of the vehicle. "The Semi driver is dead." It was Wolfe's voice. As they cleared the rear of the semi trailer, a white streak emerged from the Molly Bee Mine. The RPG hit the left front wheel of the Armored Vehicle with a brilliant flash and boom. The blast destroyed part of the tire and rim, stopping the vehicle. Bill sat up and checked himself and those around him, "No one hurt, just knocked down by the blast." Then he hit the 'Talk' switch, "Yeager, get the RPG in the Molly Bee Mine." "We're on it, Sir." Jim could see through his infrared sight, a figure emerging from The Molly Bee and stop. Jim fired. The figure flew backwards, as the four hundred nineteen grain bullet hit him at two thousand feet per second, going right through his Kevlar vest and him. He slammed against the wooden barrier across the mine opening, then laid still. Yeager was spotting for Jim, "One down, Sir." "Now the AK-47s," Bill ordered. The deputies and DEA Agents spread out and the M1117 limped backwards, leaving Charlie standing there, pissed. "Did they get that Bastard, Bill?" "Yeah Charlie, they got him. Now they're going for the AK's" "Good" Bill could now see three AK's firing from the gully and perhaps one from the Midas Mine. Jim saw all four clearly, plus he saw other figures around the Midas Mine. The Mine was his first target. He saw the form firing from the mine opening, the stooped form firing at his friends. He aimed at the chest and fired. The silencer allowed only a whoosh of air, then the shooter flew back and fell. He did not move again. "That's two, Sir." Fire continued from the gully, one deputy went down with leg wounds. "Give me forty millimeter frags (fragmentation grenades) along the gully." "Yes Sir." Answered the DEA agent. The first grenade burst short of the closest shooter. The next one burst close enough to make the shooter duck. The third one spattered him all over the ridge behind him. Fire now started coming from beyond the Midas Mine. The farthest shooter in the gully suddenly lost his head, it just exploded. "Three down!" yelled Sgt. Yeager. "There is one bandit coming up the ridge from beyond the Midas!" "Thanks, Sir!" yelled Yeager. A DEA agent went down with a leg wound. Bill saw it was the one with the grenade launcher. He saw the bandit climbing the ridge, almost to the top. Then he pitched back, his body slid down the slope into the gully. Yeager yelled, "One for me, Sir!" The shooters beyond the Midas was getting better, one bullet bounced off Bill's shoulder. The impact made him stumble. When he looked back that way, there was no gunfire. "Four down, Sir." Jim had nailed another one. Bill picked up the rifle with the grenade launcher and got the bandoleer of grenades from the wounded agent. Loading the first projectile, Bill felt very comfortable. "Just like old times." His first shot fell just short of the last AK-47 shooter. He immediately dropped his rifle and threw up his hand. Bill put out a radio broadcast, "We need to find Johnny Eagle. Be careful, this may not be over!" Two men disarmed the shooter and marched him over toward the Midas Mine. Men checked the Midas and Red Dog Mines, no sign of Johnny. They brought the bodies from all over the area, and laid them out before the Midas Mine. One man was found cowering inside the Midas. He was disarmed and handcuffed to the shooter. The shooter seemed disgusted with the older man. Charlie seemed very interested in the man. Bill noticed that one of the bodies was markedly different than the others, more Middle Eastern. "Bill, we have a runner, up the hillside beyond the Midas. The FLIR found him." Bill was sure that at least one man would try to flee over that mountain. "Where is he, Charlie?" "The boys say he is near the crest. He has stopped moving." That gave Bill pause. He thought about someone setting up there, "I bet he is waiting to kill anyone who follows." Then he knew what he must do. The man was not stupid, he had all the advantage, with his AK-47. He was shooting down hill. Bill found an AK-47 and three full magazines, he stuffed them into his pockets. He picked up the rifle, it had part of a mag. It was time to finish this operation. He started walking toward the slope. At the base, Bill pulled his night goggles down over his eyes. Then he looked up the hillside. By adjusting the goggles, he could just see the outline of a man. Did he have night goggles too? The veteran Cartel soldier saw a form at the base, "I bet that fool is after me. If he has an M-16, I've got

278

him!" Bill raised his M-16 and fired. There were six rounds left in the magazine. They hit just below the Mexican. "I'll kill him!" The man yelled. Bill dropped the empty rifle, picking up the AK-47. Bill pushed his talk button, "Charlie, I could use a flare about now. The man raised his rifle. A magnesium flare burst above the Mines. The sudden glare blinded him. Bill, who had already removed his goggles, snapped the rifle to his shoulder and fired. Three rounds hit the Mexican in the face, he died knowing that somehow he had blown it! His body pitched forward and slid partway down the slope. "Nice shooting boss." It was Jim's voice. Bill thought about this, "I could have had Jim take him out. Why did I think that I needed to do it myself?" He suddenly remembered his men,"How many wounded do we have?" He asked, over the radio. "Three total." It was Wolfe's voice. Bill was on top of things again, "Get stretchers from the vehicles. We need one or two vehicles to take them to the hospital." Wolfe and three others headed back to the vehicles. Wolfe had his night goggles on, so he had no trouble seeing the Black Hearst and the woman beside it. Curious, he walked over, "Who are you?" Barbara quickly answered, "I am Doctor Barbara Davis, County Coroner." "Hi Doctor Davis, it's Tom Wolfe. We need you at the Mines, we have three wounded." "All that and only three wounded?" Barbara asked as she got her bag. "The bad guys have eight dead." Wolfe and his men accompanied Barbara to the wounded, they had three stretchers. Barbara's outfit did little to hide her "assets". It was strange enough to have a civilian female appear in the area after the carnage they had been through, but one shaped like Barbara drew every eye. Barbara was up to it. She didn't hesitate a step, just march with her escort to the first wounded, and went to work. Bill was walking to the weapon pile. When he got there, he laid his AK-47 on the pile with the two Magazines. One of his Deputies walked over to him, "I found your M-16, Sheriff." He handed the weapon to Bill, "Thanks. There is one more body up that slope." He pointed beyond the Midas," Grab three others and a stretcher. Please bring the body down. Call EMS for our wounded." "Doctor Barbara Davis is already here, helping the wounded!" He wondered what the hell she was doing here. Did Jim know? "Sheriff. Please come to the Midas Mine." It was Charlie's voice in his earpiece. Bill left the Deputy and headed for the Mine. Fatigue was starting to set in, always the aftermath of prolonged exposure to Adrenalin. When he got to the Midas, he found Charlie and another DEA agent waiting for him. Charlie spoke, "Wait till you see what we found." He motioned Bill into the Mine. Through the partially ruined wooden gate that used to inclosed the Mine. There sat an a Jeep, the Washo Tribe's Jeep. "That belongs to Johnny Eagle, or it did." He noticed that it did have a police scanner. Charlie acknowledged this information but continued walking in the darkness. Only the flashlight Charlie held lit their way. Suddenly, there were several pallets containing wrapped kilo 'bricks', they surrounded the trio. "My God!" Exclaimed the DEA Agent. "I second that, Fred." Charlie was shocked, "This is more dope then I have ever seen, in one place!" Bill was on top of it, "We need to inventory this Mine, Charlie! What about the Semi, was it unloaded?" This snapped Charlie back to reality, "You're right. Fred, post two guards on this mine, restrict access. Then you and I will begin a quick count of this haul for my report." Fred ran off to comply. Bill was no longer needed in the Midas Mine, so he used this opportunity to visit the Molly Bee. Why would an Arab be here, and are there more? Is Johnny hiding there? Bill held his pistol and his flashlight, as he stepped through the open entrance. The mine had been excavated into a large room. A long, tarp draped form filled the room. He could see a Semi type hitch on the end near him. He started to pull off the closest tarp, he sensed movement, above him! Something hit him, knocking his Glock and flashlight away! The light shattered on the stone floor, plunging the room into darkness. Bill had rolled away from the blow, he was now on his feet, the knife in his hand. His breathing was controlled, not so, his attacker. The man was to his left, neither man moved. Bill could hear him breathe. Silently, Bill got an M-16 magazine out of it's pouch on his belt. It was tossed under the Semi trailer. The man fired at the noise! Bill was on him in an instant. His pistol clattered to the floor, he grunted, then reached for the knife on his belt. Too late! Bill's knife sliced the man's belly wide open. Bill found the man's knife, then checked his pulse. He still lived, so Bill stepped to the entrance, then keyed his radio, "Sargent Wolfe, please bring Doctor Davis and a stretcher to the Molly Bee. We have one more prisoner." Wolfe came running, "What is it?" Bill directed his light into the Mine. "Who is that?" Bill took the light, "I believe that he is Arab, beyond that, I have no idea." Bill picked up the two pistols, then

280

checked the man's pulse. Barbara Davis appeared in the opening, Bill heard her, "Over here, Barbara. He has a knife wound. Bill held the light for her. "This is a bad wound! Did you do this?" "Yes, Barbara. He had a gun, I had to use my knife. It was my life or his." It was a statement of fact, Barbara said nothing, just worked swiftly to stop the bleeding. "Bill, I need to get this man to a hospital, and surgery! He needs a transfusion." As if they heard her, two Deputies appeared with the requested stretcher. "In here, assist Doctor Davis." Bill gestured to Barbara, and the wounded man. In short order, the man was on the stretcher, being carried out of the Mine. Barbara hovering over her charge. "Please get Doctor Davis the plasma from the Team medical kit," Bill called after them. "Will do, Sir!" One Deputy answered. With that handled, Bill used his radio again. "Charlie, please come to the Molly Bee. There is a surprise for us." Then, he spoke to Wolfe, "Help me pull off this tarp." With the plastic tarp gone, Bill shined the light on a pallet loaded with a large bag of something. He was examining the bag, when Charlie walked in. "What have you got there?" "Something that two Arabs were willing to die for," Bill said, without tuning. Charlie's light was on the large bag, "What is that?" Bill turned to him, "Ammonium Nitrate, in a one thousand pound bag." "Are you sure?" Charlie jumped on his verdict. "I've a degree in Chemistry and years of experience with explosives. You put this stuff with some diesel oil and you can take down a Federal Building, just like Timothy McVeigh." "Maybe that is what is under the tarp, diesel oil." Offered the DEA agent. Bill helped him pull the next tarp aside. The huge, round container revealed was bright yellow, with large red letters, DANGER! RADIOACTIVE WASTE. Charlie yelled, "Let's get the Hell out of here. All three men beat a hasty exit from the Molly Bee Mine. Charlie looked back at the Molly Bee, "I've got to call ATF and Homeland Security about this." He got on his Cell phone. Bill looked at the DEA Agent with them, "Maybe we should put two men on this mine. Has anyone looked into the Semi trailer? "I'll get right on it, sir." "See Sargent Wolfe. He can help with the manpower. The Agent nodded, then rushed off. Bill decided to have a look in the trailer, was it empty?

Barbara accompanied the stretcher to her vehicle. The two Deputies followed her instructions, setting the victim in the back compartment, using the casket tie downs for the stretcher. While she checked her patient, one of the men retrieved the plasma kit from the Team vehicle. The pretty Doctor was very thankful, quickly starting the fluid flowing into the sedated man. One Deputy went to check with Bill, while the other stood by. With the IV going, Barbara thanked the Deputy for his help. He left, as she started the Cadillac, and got ready to leave. She was fastening her seatbelt, when the passenger door opened! A smiling Johnny Eagle appeared, holding a gun, "Ah, the lovely Doctor Davis. I am afraid that I will need you to drive me back to town." He slid onto the bench seat, closing the door. "How the hell did you escape?" The angry Doctor inquired. Johnny seemed almost apologetic, "I was necessary for me to use the drainage ditch for my exit. I did not like the odds." "You may not like the odds from here on, I heard the Deputies talking, they know you are missing." His smile returned, "Thank you for that bit of information! Now, shall we get going!" Reluctantly, Barbara put the Cadillac in gear, and headed onto Route Five.

Deputy Brent Carter had been able to take Mona home this morning. She had insisted that he take some food with him. He also took several juicy kisses. Mona made him feel very important, something that a rookie Deputy needed. He left for Route Five, with a hug and food. On the drive, Brent thought again about what might be in store for him. He liked driving the Patrol Car, it was powerful and fast. A real threat, after his econo car. He decided to park off the road, he would use the barriers to build a roadblock across Route Five. As he setup his roadblock, Brent heard the sound of a Helicopter to the South. The Raid! He hurried his task, completing the barrier in a few minutes. The young Deputy wanted to be ready! He thought about grabbing the shotgun from the car, but soon realized that he needed both hands to shift the barrier for emergency vehicles. He no sooner had that thought, then her heard a siren on Route One, then another! Soon, two EMS vehicles passed through his roadblock, headed for the Mines. "Many wounded," they yelled to him. Then there was a radio broadcast! "Johnny Eagle is wanted for his part in multiple felonies. Consider him armed and dangerous. He is the suspect in one killing already." Johnny Eagle, Brent had seen him before. Always smiling, he was a real cocky type. Brent did not like that type of person. Would he come this way?

At the rear door, Bill found that there was no padlock. The door easily retracted upward, when unlatched. The flashlight revealed more pallet loads of drugs, almost to the rear! "Charlie, you better inventory the Semi trailer. Looks like it wasn't unloaded." "Be there in a minute. We count fourteen pallets of drugs in the Midas Mine!" Others started clustering around the Trailer. "Don't we get a finders fee, Sheriff?" Asked Sgt Wolfe with a smile. One of the DEA agents had a different idea, "Man! That stuff will burn for a week!" Charlie came walking up with a worried expression, "Now what was it you wanted to... Holy hell!" He lost his worried look. His mouth dropped opened and his sleepy eyes were suddenly wide open. "Bill, with what is in the Midas, it is more dope than I have ever seen in one place! Wait till I tell my Boss. He'll shit a brick!" "I'm glad you like it Charlie. But I've got to ask, do you have someplace to lock up this much?" "Frankly, no. Bill, we have to hold it here until I can arrange transportation to San Francisco, or maybe LA. They're the only places with enough secure storage." "If I might suggest, you could set up a camp here. You need security, and it will take some time to document everything on site. You could use some help, Charlie." "Okay, you got me there. What do you have in mind?" "A joint effort, my Department and the DEA. We set up a camp here, put out security, get teams inventorying what we captured. Right now we need to feed these men. Then they will need some sleep. Work parties need to be assigned." Charlie looked very weary when he turned to Bill, "We are going to be flooded with DEA and Homeland Security brass. We not only busted a big drug operation, but also a terrorist plot. The radioactive stuff and the ammonium nitrate were, apparently, part of a plot to make a "dirty bomb". Their target was probably San Francisco, and the South bay, Silicon Valley. I got my hands full, I need your help. Will you set this up for me? I mean for both of us. I'll make sure you get whatever you need to do the job." "Aside from good publicity for my Department, what's in this for me? Sounds like a lot of scut work." "Okay, Bill. You will be with me and the brass during their tour. And you may get to keep certain items of equipment, like the grenade launcher. I would appreciate your help in writing my report of this action. I will give you one of my men to assist you. Fred!" The stocky redhead from the Midas Mine moved to the front "What's up?" Bill look at Fred and thought for a moment.

"Okay, Charlie. You got yourself a deal. We will discuss payment at a future date. Fred, come with me!" The two walked away from the group, toward the Molly Bee Mine, "Fred, have you ever handled the logistics for any operation?" Bill asked warily. Fred was quick to answer, "Not exactly, Sir! I served in the Army in Iraq. As a First Lieutenant, I had some responsibility for suppling my Company. I do the same thing in the Reserves." "Then you have some idea of what we need here. First, we need to feed these men. I don't have much budget for this kind of operation, so it's going to be on your dime." Fred nodded. Bill continued, "We're going to need around the clock security here, for the foreseeable future. That means our men will need somewhere to sleep and shower. We need communications, phone, fax, and radio. We are going to be swamped with Big Shots from Washington, and that means lots of news people. I hear you have someone to handle PR." "Sir, we have a restaurant on call for meals. I can call them. DEA Sacramento has a mobile Command Center we can use. It has a shower and a Communications Center. PR is handled by a local woman in Susanville." "First of all, stop calling me Sir. My name is Bill. Secondly, get going on your phone calls to get those things here. Thirdly, how capable is this PR woman?" "Well, Bill, she was a Congressional Page for two years, so Big Shots don't impress her. She handles fund-raising for the United Way, so she is used to arm twisting. And she handles ad sales for the local radio and TV stations, so she knows about news people." "She sounds very capable. How is she to look at?" "A stone cold fox. But then I am prejudice, I asked her to marry me." "I see. Well then, please ask your fiancé if she would consent to handle our PR." "I'm on it, Bill!" As Fred walked away, with his Cell phone in his ear, Bill reflected on the enthusiasm of youth. Fred had no idea he already knew Anita. Bill now knew that Fred could be a stone cold liar. He would have to keep a close watch on Fred. Lost in thought, he didn't hear the men walk up behind him. It was Jim Bearpaw and Sgt Yeager. Jim was first to speak, "It was a good plan, Bill. We smashed this operation good." "Thank you. It would have been a hell of a lot harder without you two on the Ridge. Yeager, I want you to find Sgt. Wolfe. Tell him that we need to have a Pow Wow about this site. Jim, I want to check out the Red Dog Mine. Any contraband found should be inventoried and turned over to the DEA. I would like to make that mine our dormitory. I'm working on food, cots, and water. It's going to be a hot one today, get two men to collect all armor and helmets, when the Mine is open to receive them." "Don't forget toilets, Bill." Bill smile ruefully, "Thank you for reminding me of something so basic. I will get toilets." "Okay, I'm off to find Wolfe." As Bill watched Yeager go, he turned to Jim, "The Molly Bee is full of Ammonium Nitrate and Radioactive Waste. Charlie tells me it was part of a Terrorist plot against the Bay Area. Who can we get to check this stuff!" Jim was stunned but not speechless, "Cal Fire has the Haz-Mat responsibility in this County. I'll give them a call, if you bring me up to date." Bill smiled, "You got a deal." Jim got on his Cell. "Fred rushed up to Bill, "I've got scrambled eggs and bacon on their way by 'copter! Plenty of coffee and rolls too! The mobile unit is on its way from Sierra Vista!" "Good work, Fred. Next we need plenty of drinking water, cots, and toilets." "I'll have Anita bring as many cots and cases of bottled water that she can fit in the van. Toilets I can get from a construction outfit I know." "So far so good Fred. We will headquarter in the Red Dog Mine, if is clear. Where will the DEA camp out?" In the Midas Mine, that is where the Cartel were living. We will have a small generator for lights. At least these old Mines are cooler then out here will be." As Fred walked off, Bill wondered about the DEA Agent.

Barbara drove, worried about her patient, and wondered if she would live to see the sunrise. Johnny did not help, with his nervous chatter. She figured that the man was ad-libbing now. The Raid had killed his plans, in a very spectacular fashion. Two EMS vehicles passed them in a hurry, headed for the Mines. She knew that the wounded would be picked up. The doctor in her was glad. Now, what was she going to do? She had a preloaded syringe in her bag, the sedative would take care of him. But would she have an opportunity to use it? What was this! A roadblock up ahead. That was a Sheriff's car with its lights on. What will happen? Barbara slowed down, then stopped at the barrier. She had been warned not to try anything. She rolled her window down, "Deputy, I'm Doctor Davis. I have a wounded man in the back, I need to get him to the hospital." Brent found nothing amiss, "Sure thing, Doctor Davis. It will take me a minute to remove the barriers." He pickup the one nearest the centerline, carrying it to the shoulder. Placing it off the roadway, gave Brent a chance to see the passenger. The light from his patrol car illuminated the man just enough. It was Johnny Eagle! No mistaking that face. The young Deputy had been on the Front Desk when the arrogant lawyer had visited the Sheriff's Department. Johnny looked his way, then turned to respond to something that the Doctor said. Brent drew his Beretta, moving to the side of the Cadillac. Johnny looked back in time to see this move. The revolver was thrust out, as Johnny open his door. Wap! Brent knocked Johnny's gun on the ground! Johnny yelled in pain, then tried to reach for his gun. Thump! Brent caught Johnny at the base of his skull with the Beretta! Johnny fell out of the car, onto the pavement. Brent picked up the revolver, then handcuffed the fugitive. He drug his prisoner to the shoulder, then came back to the Cadillac. "Are you all right, Doctor Davis?" She smiled at the young Deputy, "I am now. Can I go? My patient needs surgery." "Sure thing!" Brent slammed the door, then removed the remaining barrier. The Cadillac peeled out! Dr Davis waved, and was gone. Brent put his prisoner in the rear of his Patrol Car, then used the radio to call for pickup of Johnny Eagle.

Ambulances arrived for the wounded and they were transported to the Hospital. The word went out about Johnny Eagle. Captured by a young Deputy, at a roadblock! Jim only found out later that he had car jacked Barbara. What was she doing there, anyway? Fred was true to his word. The DEA helicopter brought in breakfast, then made a second trip for water. Anita made it in the DEA van, loaded with cots and bottled water. A lovely face, nice figure, and great legs, shown to good advantage by her shorts. With her blue eyes, light brown hair, and a smile that would melt glass, Anita Brubaker had no trouble charming three men into unloading the van, and saw to it that Fred handled the distribution. Charlie told Bill that the Brass would be here about nine am tomorrow. The Midas Mine became the DEA dormitory, the Deputies used the Red Dog, as Bill had planned. A Fork Lift, a Bobcat, and fourteen pallets of drugs were in the Midas, plus various personal items. The bad guys had been living in it. Bill commandeered the cots from Anita. It cost him a hug and kiss. She made sure that he was in one healthy piece. They were set up in the Red Dog Mine. He made sure that Jim and Yeager were two of the first to sleep. Their night had been longer than the others. Wolfe and Fred took charge, both arranged to be relieved in the afternoon. Bill conferred with Charlie. The mobile unit would be here in the afternoon. It would bring the communications gear for tomorrow. Toilets were on the way. They agreed that Bill should take off for the hospital. Charlie thanked him profusely. Bill said goodbye to Fred, Anita, and Sgt Wolfe, and walked to his SUV. On the way, he switched his radio back to Channel One, "Dispatch." "Dispatch!" "This is Sheriff Andrews. I am leaving the Mines and heading for the Hospital." "Roger, Sheriff. Heading for the Hospital. Congratulation on the raid. Over" "Thanks. Anything to report? Over." "Nothing unusual. Out." The sun was over the eastern peaks, as he drove away. It was morning.

Chapter Twenty

Page after page went through the fax. Deputy Wayne Quest was sure that Homeland Security would be able to translate the Arabic. He was sure that it was some sort of Arabic. Two tours in Iraq had taught him that much. Wayne had been assigned to watch Linda Littlewolf, A.K.A. Mrs Eagle. It had been largely boring, except in the wee hours, when she slipped out her back door with a stack of papers. She had placed them in a fire pit, a circle of stones. They were lit them on fire, then she went back inside. Wayne quickly put out the fire, most were barely singed. Linda knew nothing about lighting a fire. Besides, open fires were illegal this time of year. Too much danger of grass fires. He had seen the foreign language, so the papers went with him. After he was relieved, Wayne had grabbed a phone at the Station. It sure was the shits, not having any management in house. With Captain Baker dead, the Sheriff and Lieutenant Bearpaw at the Mines, he felt very much alone in this. The only Sargent around was old Sumner, over in the Jail. Wayne knew better than ask that old fossil for advise. The phonebook had gotten him an 800 number for Homeland Security. That had gotten him to a nice young woman who was very interested, when the Deputy had explained the involvement of drugs, and a terrorist plot. She supplied a fax number, and now he was sending her the documents. He now had something exciting to tell the wife. It really angered him, not being involve at the Mines. Maybe now, he was.

Danny and Gene helped her load the pickup. It was several wears old, but it had a utility body. Lots of compartments for the Eco-Hazard equipment and materials. Brenda was excited when she got the call from the Mines! But reality was now sinking in. Radiation! Explosives! This was for more than a few gallons of solvents! In the store room, she found the Geiger Counter and Anti Radiation Suit. It did fit the big Brunette, one benefit of being an Amazon. This could be so dangerous, and yet, she found herself impatient to get going! She who had known change since her childhood, found that she relished change. She was heading into a new adventure! Stan was there to see her off. Brenda thought that he looked worried, she knew that he cared about her. Brenda fought to keep her speed down, chill out! The Roadblock was a sobering experience, especially when the Deputy told her what had happened there on a previous shift! There was more security at the entrance to Old Mine Road. She was not surprised, she knew about the drug bust, and the contents of the Molly Bee. Asking about the mine, got her directions to it. Inquiries about Lt Bearpaw were met with a shrug, until Sgt Wolfe told her that the Lieutenant was asleep! After the initial shock, she had to allow that he had been busy last night. Reluctantly, Brenda suited up. The Anti-Radiation Suit was not air conditioned, and the morning temperature was already in the 80's, with a high of 95 degrees expected!

The drive from the Mines gave Bill time to think about Jennifer. There had been precious little time for that. He saw things clearly (such an over used word), he felt a great deal of sympathy for Jennifer and her Father, she obviously was in a bad way. Just how bad, he would find out after he reached the Hospital. First thing, he talked to Barbara about the wounded Terrorist (who was recovering from surgery) and the other wounded. Barbara told him how Johnny Eagle had kidnaped her, and how Brent had captured him. Bill made a note to learn more about his Deputy, he sound like a bright lad. Barbara then talked to him about the corpses at the Mines. How could they be trans-ported? Bill suggested that she contact the School District for the use of one of their buses and a driver. Jason was snoozing in the ICU lounge, when Bill got there. Wanda had gone home earlier. The two men talked about Jennifer's condition. He was curious as he went with Jason and Sarah Davis to see Jennifer. His disregard for her, suffered a serious blow when he saw her sleeping face. He wanted to hold her, to tell her that everything was going to be all right, and to protect her from all evil! But he knew she had been deluded, now changed to something worse. Sarah told him that Jennifer should wake sometime in the early evening, her condition could be further assessed, "Get the hell home! Get some sleep, then come back." It was sound medical advice, which Bill reluctantly took. Charlie contacted Barbara about the corpses, she told him of her plans. Charlie had all bodies in body bags with tags. He asked her to email a photo of the Arab that Bill had wounded. His Communications Center was nearly operational. Barbara went to the Surgical Ward to comply.

The Geiger Counter showed minimal background radiation. The containers did their jobs, lead lined? The flatbed trailer was completely uncovered, revealing four cylinders of Radioactive Waste, surrounded by ten big bags of Ammonium Nitrate. Brenda wasted no time in shedding the heavy suit. She carried it back to her vehicle, along with the Geiger Counter. What she broke out, was a hand held chemical 'Sniffer'. In the glare of the two flood lamps she had set up, Brenda read the manual for the Sniffer, then put it together. She was about finished, when Lt Jim Bearpaw joined her in the mine. Fatigue pants, jump boots, and a dark green T-shirt. She was taken by his relative youth, and dark good looks. He was surprised by her age, height, and beauty. She was fetching, in a Tee shirt. "You, are the Haz-Mat Specialist?" Jim inquired. Brenda turned to him, smiling, "Brenda Dawson, from Cal Fire. You must be Lieutenant Bearpaw. I don't think anyone else would be brave enough to stick their nose in here." "The Cal Fire blue pants gave you away. I take it that the radiation level is safe." Brenda got serious, "Normal background level, the containers appear to be lead lined. I was just about to identify the chemicals in the bags." Jim was curious, "What have you got there?" She smiled, holding up the assembled device, "This is a Chemical Sniffer. Most compounds give off vapors, fumes from the chemicals in the mixture. This device analyses the fumes." "How can it tell them apart?" "According to the manual, it compares each one to a library of compounds in memory." Satisfied, Jim gave Brenda a good looking over, "I don't recall seeing you in the Valley. New to the area?" She knew when a man was attracted, "Yes, I joined Station One recently. I'm their new Engineer." That got a raised eyebrow, "Engineer and Haz-Mat Specialist, talented and ambitious. Next, you want to be Captain, right." She gave him a wry smile, "Some day!" Brenda switched the device on, then held it over one of the bags. After a moment, it buzzed! She looked at the display panel, "Ammonium Nitrate. Looks like you boys were right." "Not us boys. Sheriff Andrews is a chemist with military experience with explosives. All he had to do was take a look and a sniff." She 'sniffed' each of the other nine bags, all with the same results. She knew that Jim was watching her, it did not make her unhappy. Brenda got a serious look on her face, "I have to go back to my truck for some warning signs. Protocol requires them." She put the Sniffer away, then the pair walked outside. They saw that the DEA Mobile Command Center had arrived, they were setting the jacks to level the unit. Brenda spotted Anita standing nearby, in shorts. "Isn't she out of uniform?" Jim smiled, that is Anita Brubaker, PR person for the DEA and this County. Anita chooses her own uniform." That surprised her, "PR for both? How did she manage that?" "Would you like to meet her? I think that Mobile unit will be hers to control. I hear it has air conditioning." Wiping the sweat from her brow, Brenda said that she would. Anita was all smiles, "Hi Jim, who's your friend." The two were introduced. "I envy you the shorts." Anita laughed, "I decided to dress strictly for comfort. When they get the generator running, we can go inside. They tell me that this unit has excellent air conditioning!" They both smiled, "Anita, I need to put up some warning signs around the Molly Bee Mine. Then I need to dig up some lunch." Anita had an invitation for her, "Brenda, come back here when you are finished. We can have lunch, and get cool! You come too, Jim. The helicopter is on it's way with the food!" and so it was agreed, Brenda handled her signs, while Jim checked with Sargent Wolfe.

Bill went home to find Mrs Garcia there. Rosellinia Garcia was a formidable woman, five feet nine and two hundred fifty pounds. She had already raised four sons and three daughters. And buried two husbands. She took one look at Bill, fixed him a good lunch, and insisted that he go to bed. Charlie let him know that the mobile command vehicle had arrived and was set up. Thing were going according to plan. The animals followed him upstairs, Mrs Garcia had fed them. He loved on his pets for a bit, then laid down on top of the bed spread Mrs G. had so recently put on the bed. He was just going to rest his eyes for a few minutes. He woke up about five pm, took a quick shower, and put on a fresh uniform. He would have to stop by the Department to pick up his gun belt and other items. He did that first. There were congratulations from the Officer on the desk. Wanda had left him several notes, none that needed his immediate attention. He walked on down to the Team Room and picked up his things. Seeing the mess reminded him, "I've got to start rotating men out of the Mines." Bill straightened his badge in a mirror, then headed back out the front door. The drive to the Hospital was a short one, then he was in the lobby. It was deserted as he walked toward Jennifer's room. The guard at the desk nodded. Outside her room, Bill found Jason and Sarah talking. Sarah looked tired, "She's awake," the veteran physician said quietly, "but she doesn't remember much past dusk, the day she was raped." Jason then spoke to him, "Go see her, it may do her good. Please don't mention what happened!" Bill looked pained. Jason quickly apologized, "Sorry Bill, I don't have to tell you that." Bill tried to comfort him, "It's all right, Jason. I know you're worried. I'll talk to her for a few minutes. She can talk about whatever she wants. Sarah can come with me. She can keep me from saying the wrong thing." Bill open the door and walked in, trailed by Dr Davis. Jennifer's big blue eyes were staring at him, "Bill! You came to see me!" She was wearing a short sleeved hospital gown. Her arm were extended to Bill. He moved to the side of her bed and leaned toward her. Her arms wrapped around him in a hug. She gave him a big kiss. "Hi beautiful! I was here earlier, but you were asleep. How do you feel?" "Sleepy! Doctor Sarah must have given me something." "That's right Jennifer, she gave you something. Sleep is the best thing for you right now." "Why is it the best thing for me? Is there something wrong with me?" Sarah was quick to respond, "We don't really know. You passed out at Bill's house. Mrs Garcia found you this morning and they brought you here to see me." Bill picked up the lie, "You worried me when I found out. I came back to see you." "Came back from where, Bill?" "I've been tied up with a drug bust since last night." "Did everything go well? I hope no one got hurt?" "No Jennifer, it was a piece of cake. Now, I'm going to talk to your Father for a while. I think Sarah needs to talk to you right now." Dr Davis had been nodding her head in agreement, now she began to ask Jennifer questions about how she felt. Bill kissed her on the cheek and slipped out the door. Closing the door behind him, he sought out Jason. Bill found him sitting in the lobby, on his Cell phone. Wanda was sitting close by him on the sofa, very close. Wanda's body language told him one thing, the two of them had slept together. Probably night before last. Wanda had that relaxed and confident manner of a mature woman who is sure of herself and her man. She wore a serious expression as she motioned for Bill to sit in the chair opposite them. Jason was obviously talking to a Psychiatrist, one who knew Jennifer. "Probably the one who treated her for rape," Bill observed. Arrangements were being to take Jennifer to LA for treatment. So there it was. Jason would take good care of his Daughter. She would be wrapped in a safe little cocoon, complete with a resident Psychiatrist. After Jason got off the phone, he told Bill of his plans for Jennifer. There were no surprises for Bill. She would be bundled off to LA, living in her fantasy world where nothing bad ever happened. They all stood to say their good byes. Wanda touched Bill's arm in sympathy. Jason patted him on the shoulder. Jason and Wanda went back to Jennifer's room. It was the last time that Bill saw Jennifer, for a long time.

Mona first yelled at him for taking chances, then she hugged him so hard that he could not breathe. She wasted no time in going back to bed, with her lover. Brent did not think he took too big a risk. He had his gun drawn, Johnny would have gotten shot, not him. The Deputies at the Station knew, he was just doing his job. Some told him that it was a big deal. He would be rewarded for what he did. All Brent wanted was his job, and a chance at Corporal in three or four years. The higher ups seemed to have noticed him. He already had a new assignment, take fresh clothing to some Deputies, then pull duty at the Mines. He had not told Mona about that part, they had not spent a night away from each other, since her Mother died. He was sure that she was not going to like it. He didn't care much for camping overnight either.

Jim said goodbye to the two women, he had turned over the Deputies to Sargent Wolfe. He was senior. He drove on back to Sierra Vista, with a desire to know more about Brenda Dawson. He knew that Barbara was no sure bet. That made him wonder what Brenda would think about his sniping. Brenda was just as interested to know more about Jim Bearpaw. Anita told her what she could. His relationship with Barbara was mentioned. Brenda acknowledged the warning, but wondered if Jim was really 'taken'. When Anita found out that Breda planned on spending the night in the Molly Bee, she went to work. She saw no reason why Brenda couldn't share the Command Center, there were two bedrooms. She did not have to work very hard. Brenda moved her things into Bedroom two. Anita showed her a few goodies that had been snuck into the kitchen, from a cooler that made it here in her van. The ladies would dine well, tonight!

Bill left the Hospital headed for home, on the way he stopped off at Monty's to pick up dinner. He told Monty what happened to Russ. Monty said he'd pass the word. There had

294

already been a rumor. Bill headed on home. Crime tape blocked off his normal parking place, so he parked in front of the house. Inside, he fed the animals while his dinner warmed in the microwave. He remembered to call Wanda's Voice mail, "Please cut a memo promoting Jim Bearpaw to Acting Captain, and Sgt Wolfe to Acting Lieutenant. CC the Board of Supervisors. Thank you, Wanda and good luck." He ate his dinner in peace, only Susie's wet nose and tongue to interrupt his eating. He was cleaning up the kitchen when Charlie called him, "Hello Bill. I've got lots to tell you. The assassin you killed the other day was Juan Carlos Calderone, youngest son of the number three man in the Mexican Cartel. The older prisoner we have is a cousin, Geraldo Calderone, a mid level manager in the Cartel. He was probably in charge of the operation." "Well Charlie, I bet the Cartel is not happy about losing all that dope and the son of one of their big boys." "You are so right Bill. Word out of Mexico says there is a bounty on both our heads. Much more on your head. San Francisco DEA is sending two trucks over tomorrow to pick the dope up and take it back. They'll weigh it and analyze it there. The figures should be real interesting. Is your Coroner that the Babe that was here this morning? I hope she's single." "Yes, Doctor Barbara Davis was there this morning and she is single, but lately she's been keeping company with Jim Bearpaw." "I think I'll tell my boys to pass on the lovely Doctor, I do not want the Sniper mad at my people." "Probably a wise choice. I will see you tomorrow morning for the big tour." "You better Bill. I don't want to face those Homeland Security guys by myself, old buddy. " "Neither do I, old buddy. See you tomorrow." "Bye Bill." Bill hung up the wall phone. Then he called Jim. "Hello." "Hello Jim." "Hi Bill. How are you? Barbara told me about Jennifer. I'm sorry to hear it. Jason has been a big help to us." "I concur. What I called about, is I want you to take charge at the Office tomorrow. I'm going to be over at the Mines entertaining some big shots from Homeland Security. Charlie has some DEA brass to escort. We need to start rotating men out of the Mines. Start with Sargent Wolfe. He's going to be an Acting Lieutenant." "An Acting Lieutenant, won't that make things a bit crowded, Bill?" "Not really, Jim, since you will be an Acting Captain. Congratulations!" "I don't know what to say, except to say thanks." "You earned it, Jim. So now you can take charge tomorrow. Maybe you should tell Barbara. Good night,

Jim." "Good night." Bill hung up, then finished in the Kitchen. He poured himself a glass of wine and headed for the Living Room. He turned on the Stereo system, choosing a CD of Ashkenazy playing Chopin, The Etudes. He sat in the big old easy chair that had been his Father's. Susie soon jumped into his lap, licked his face, then laid down and made herself comfortable. Bill petted her, to her great joy. He sipped his wine and counted score, "Let's see, a price on my head, a crazy ex-lover, and Homeland Security about to crawl all over my county. Let's not forget killing your own corrupt Cousin. I'm responsible for more deaths. That's how many over the last twenty years? The score just keeps increasing. But then, it's better than the alternative." He patted the little dog in his lap. Tiger jumped up on his chair arm, he wanted his share of the attention. Bill readily complied. "Russ, we knew what you were by the time you were eighteen. Ambitious, impatient, and greedy. We always hoped you would change. You never did. Now you have left us to pick up after you. You always wanted someone else to pay the bill. Russ, this time it was your turn." Bill sipped his wine, loved on his pets, and contemplated the future. Jennifer was lost to him just as Mary had been. He had been made to jump through the hoops with Mary, receiving a crash course in Mental Illness. He had not been not ready for another lesson. "Sorry, Jennifer. I've already given." Johnny Eagle rested in the County Jail. Tomorrow, he would be arraigned. Bill was sorry that he could not be there to see Johnny's face. The BS would probably fly, as the liar tried cover his tracks. His home phone rang, it was Anita. She took advantage of the Communications Center phone system to call her lover. She was warmly welcomed. The lovers talked about their plans. Bill would be with her tomorrow, then they would make time for each other. Two working Professionals.

Jim stopped off at home for a quick shower, and a fresh uniform. His fatigues were becoming a bit 'ripe'. When he got to the office, Wanda made a big deal of handing him a set of Captain's bars. A present from Jason, to commemorate his promotion. "It is temporary, Wanda. Please remind your friend of that fact." Wanda just smiled, then reminded the new Captain to check his In Box. It was loaded. Much of it was addressed to Russ, put off by the preoccupied former occupant of this office. Undaunted, Jim dug into it. After a few minutes, he put in a call to Barbara. The call was brief, she was busy with several wounded. He was congratulated for his promotion. Jim thought the call was a bit curt and impersonal, but she did have responsibilities. No plans were made for tonight. Jim knew that she had autopsied Russ, the bodies from the Raid were still at the Mines. All were in body bags, stacked in the cool interior of a Mine. He went back to the paperwork. There were interruptions for phone calls. Two Board members calling to thank him for his performance, and to wish him well. They were good men, he knew they were sincere. He spent sometime arranging his things. He supposed that Wanda had removed the previous contents. Nothing of the previous occupant of this office remained. He did ask for his display cabinet to brought over. Some items went best in that display case. The sound of a distant siren made him think of Cal Fire, and a tall Brunette. Brenda had a pretty face, and a nice build to go with it. He recalled some of their time together. Part of him wished that it had been longer. He tried to picture her in fire gear, tending to her Engine. Fire House One was her Station. That was less than a mile from his house. His mind wanted to picture her out of fire gear, or any other type of apparel. It made a pleasant picture.

Brent made it in about five. His cargo was very welcome. Wives, Mothers, and girlfriends had sent clean uniforms and personal items. Some packages even had a personal note. Very welcome, indeed. Sargent Yeager gave him a tour of the site. The sheer amount of dope blew the young Deputy away. He was very wary of the Molly Bee, all of those warning signs; Radiation, high explosives, their tour was a short one. Brent had assured Mona that there would be only a bunch of guys on site. A tour of the Mobile Command Center, proved him wrong. The two Ladies were cordial, especially when told that this was the captor of Johnny Eagle! Anita knew what this meant, she made a mental note to mention Brent to Bill. After the tour, Yeager took him out to the entrance of Old Mine Road. He was to join another young Deputy in guarding the only road into the site. Left alone, Brent and his cohort talked about what a raw deal it was, not being eligible for the Tactical Squad. Neither man had military experience. The two macho young men were sure that they could handle an M-16. If only they had a chance! As darkness descended, both men wished that they were somewhere else.

Anita found that she liked the young firefighter. Brenda was impressed by the smaller woman. They had a lot in common, brains, beauty, and ambition. They combined their efforts on dinner, it gave them time to talk. When Anita wanted to shut herself in the Communications Room, Brenda found out about Bill. While Anita talked to her love, Brenda took a shower. After Anita was through talking, they reversed rolls. Brenda talked to Gary and Stan, while Anita showered. The two ladies had time for conversation, before hitting the sack. It had been a long day for both of them. Anita went right to sleep, with dreams of her lover. Tomorrow, they would be reunited! The drug business was over, they could get on with their lives! Brenda had one chapter to read on her 'Sniffer', there was quite a lot to the little device. Someone enter the Mobile Center, no surprise there, the door was open for the DEA staff. She heard her door knob rattle, someone was trying to get in! She quietly got up, put on her robe, and grabbed her can of Pepper Spray. This was a new one, the one she used on Jake was held as evidence. She heard the knob again, then he spoke! "Come on, Honey," He spoke softly. "You can't stay mad at me for ever." "Go away! Stop bothering me, or I'll call the cops!" "Very funny, Anita. Come on, let me in." Now she wondered who this was? "My name is Brenda, not Anita. Go away!" "You can't fool me that easily! Come on Anita, open up." Brenda thought that sounded like a good idea. She had just about had enough. Pepper Spray in hand, Brenda unlocked the door. Fred had just enough time to see the tall Brunette, before the Spray hit! "Yeow!" He screamed, then started bumping into things. Anita peeked out of her room, just in time to see Brenda throw the blind Fred out of the Mobile Unit, yelling Rape! Deputies and DEA Agents came running. Blind Fred was handcuffed by two Deputies, although both were quite taken by the tall Brunette in her bathrobe. Those long legs were quite fetching. She was soon joined by Anita, in her bathrobe. Charlie quickly arrived, he had the whole story quickly out of the bleary eyed Fred. Anita got them something to wash his face. Sargent Yeager wanted to hold Fred for the Sheriff's arrival, tomorrow. Charlie talked him into releasing him into his custody. Seeing the look in Charlie's eye, told Yeager that this was just the ticket. He had the pleasure of hearing Charlie tear off a big piece of the arrogant Fred, "What in Hell did you think you were doing? Anita told you no, she broke up with you, she moved on! Did you know that she is seeing Sheriff Bill Andrews? What if he found out?" Fred had a whole lot to think of. What if the big, Ex-SEAL

298

Sheriff did find out? He had killed men with guns, knives, grenades, his hands! What was going to stop him from finding out? DEA Agent Fred had a whole new field of concern. He forgot all about what Charlie now thought of him. He would wait a long time for a promotion.

Anita ushered Brenda inside, where she explained about Fred. She was so sorry! Brenda then explained about Jake, and his attempted rape. Anita was very comforting for the younger woman. Anita had never been raped, but there had been a close call in college! The pair talked for a while. Brenda admitted that she was lonely. She told Anita about Stan, how they went back a few years. She was on the fence, about a relationship. Anita asked her how she felt about Jim Bearpaw? Was it the same as Stan? This caught the big Brunette cold. She had to think about it for a minute. How Jim made her feel was much different. It was very sexual, all lust and sex. Stan made her think of stability and safety. She did not tell Anita all of her self analysis, they were not all that close. Anita did not expect her to divulge everything. It was important that she think. Relationships were tough enough, without jumping into them blind. She should know, that's how she began dating Fred. Not thought through, and very unsatisfactory. She was still paying for that one! She pointed that out to Brenda. Brenda related a couple of her own mistakes. Later, as she lay in bed, Brenda thought again of how she felt with Jim. She knew he was interested. She had enough experience for that! What would he do about it? What would she do if he does ask her out? Brenda knew that she wanted to find out! But what about Stan? Brenda, the foster child had never known her Father. Foster Dads can be all right, but it was not the same. You could feel it. She had to admit, Stan was what she would want in a Father, for a young woman of twenty-five. Was he her Father substitute?

The two Deputies got relieved at Midnight. They had to walk all the way to the Midas Mine area for food. A mess tent had been set up in the roadway, a generator keeping things cold. Meals came in by 'Chopper', but plenty of snacks were available. DEA guys drifted in, as they got off their duty. Brent noticed that the Deputies hung to themselves. The DEA weenies did likewise. Brent knew that something was not right, so he asked Corporal Deertail about it. Denise had no problem telling the young Deputy how the DEA lorded it over the Sheriff's Department, taking the best jobs and the best times. He did notice that the night crews were mainly Deputies. Why was that? It messed with his belief in fair play. Denise had no legitimate reason for this situation, other than that was how the DEA wanted it. She did have a explanation for the upset that happened earlier in the evening. The sorry tale of Fred was told. Since he was a DEA honcho, the young Deputies found it very funny. Brent was still chuckling to himself, as he got over to the Mobile Center. The door was unlocked, so he quietly made his way to the Comm Room, and closed the door. No trouble getting an outside line. Mona answered on the second ring. He was anxious about her driving. He had left his car for her, she had a license, but had just started to drive when her Mother trashed their car. He shouldn't have worried, Mona and the car were both fine. Except, Mona was lonely. She missed him. He had to admit, he missed her. The lovers talked for about fifteen minutes, before Brent thought that he should get off the phone. He went to his cot a sadder man. He missed his petite lover.

Chapter Twenty-One

Tuesday:

Next morning, Bill arrived at the Mines to find things changed. There was more order, more organization. The repaired M1117 had pulled the Semi off to the side, creating a larger helicopter landing pad. Sentries guarded the entrance to Old Mine Rd, the two mines involved, and Bill saw two on the ridge opposite the Mines. He got there just in time to see Barbara pull out with her bus full of corpses. She did look somber. The Mobile Command Center was impressive. It had a kitchen, conference area, communications room and two bedrooms with a full bathroom. Charlie was in the conference area, going over faxes with Anita. Charlie was in slacks and a sports coat, he had a tie on. Anita was lovely in a pale blue pants suit and blouse. Charlie was facing the door, he saw Bill first, "Welcome back, Bill. We're just going over the schedule, grab a seat. Anita turned and smiled at him, "Good Morning, Bill. Why don't you sit here." She indicated the chair at the table head, between Charlie and herself. Bill sat down. "Bill," Charlie began, "the DEA brass will be in by nine forty-five. Unfortunately, the Assistant Secretary of Homeland and his entourage will be here about ten or so. I need to take my people through the drug bust, Homeland Security will be interested in the terrorist plot. I need you to take care of that." "If that is the way you want it. The Assistant Secretary is the bigger fish, you would make more points giving him a tour, Charlie." "Bill, how many point would I make talking about something I know nothing about? You're the one with the Special Ops background. The drug business is what I know." "Point well taken, Charlie. Okay, I'll be the tour guide for Homeland Security." "Good! I'm going to leave you with Anita. She needs to go over some items we've found. I need to get my troops ready for our 'guests'. Charlie got up to leave. Bill delayed him, "Charlie, could you send Sergeants Wolfe and Yeager to me?" "No problem Bill," Charlie left the room. Bill heard the front door open and close. Anita seemed a bit tentative, "You know, Bill, dealing with Homeland Security could be a political minefield." Bill looked at her thoughtfully, "I am aware of that. But thank you for warning me. You do look lovely, Anita. I forgot to congratulate you yesterday." Anita's warm smile turned to a puzzled look, "Congratulations for what?" "Why your engagement, of course!" "Bill, I am not engaged to anyone!" "Your friend Fred told me he had proposed to you. The way he acted, I assumed you had accepted him." "I turned him down. We broke up. What's wrong with him?" "Anita, Fred probably thinks that you will 'come to your senses' and accept him, I have seen this before." "This just proves how little he knows me! He is a chauvinist! His idea of 'quality time' is drinking beer and watching NASCAR racing! He may have a college degree, but he sure didn't learn anything about how to please a woman!" She realized that she was getting loud, she grew a bit selfcon- science. Then she saw Bill smiling at her. She was reminded that he was a very attractive man. "Excuse me. I got carried away. Fred got me mad." "You have every right to be mad. Fred did a dishonest thing. Your complaint about 'quality time' is one I have heard before from other young women. My own Daughter among them." Anita looked coyly at Bill, "I bet you don't drink beer and watch car racing." "No, Anita, I don't," he said, smiling back at her, "Its wine, and entertaining beautiful PR women in my bedroom." This caused her to blush, something she had not done for a long time. "That blush is very becoming. I am glad you can still blush." She smiled at him, "It surprised me. At thirty-four, I thought nothing could make me blush anymore." He thought that she was a young looking thirty-four. She thought that it was someone, not something that made her blush. "Bill, you should look over this inventory of the Molly Bee Mine," she handed him a sheet of paper. Bill studied it for a bit. It interested him, although it demonstrated how little detail he saw yesterday. "Thanks, Anita This may come in handy during my 'tour'." "No problem, Bill. If you have any other questions, just ask." The entrance of the two Sergeants took Bill's attention. Sgt Wolfe stepped up to the table, "Welcome back. We need some help with these DEA 'weenies'. They have us pulling most of the duties around here." "Who is doing the duty assignments, Lieutenant?" "This guy Fred, Sheriff. What do you mean, Lieutenant?" "I mean that Wanda is cutting a

302

memo for my signature making you Acting Lieutenant and Jim Bearpaw Acting Captain. Congratulations." "Thank you, Sheriff. What happens next?" "You are relieved of duty here and are to report to Captain Bearpaw tomorrow for your new duties. Get going!" "Yes Sir," he saluted with a big smile, turned and marched out. Bill looked at Sgt Yeager. He and Anita were smiling at him. "I am sorry Yeager, your time will come. What about the duty assignments?" "No problem, Sheriff. Tom has a lot more experience than I do, and he finished above me on the Sargents' Exam. Fred doesn't discuss assignments, he just hands them to us." "That is his style," Anita added sourly. "We are going to see about this. Please ask Fred to see me, when you go back. Who do you want as your No.2?" "Corporal Deertail, Sheriff." "Okay, Denise Deertail it is. Now go tell Fred." Sgt. Yeager left, smiling at what he imagined was going to befall Fred. Anita was enjoying the proceedings, "You run things like a military outfit. Sharp." Anita, I am a Commander in the Naval Reserve. I was an active SEAL officer for over twelve years. Fred is just about to discover this." "I have to see that," Anita was obviously enjoying the show. "Did I hear correctly, he asked for an Indian officer, a female Indian as his No. 2?" "Yes, Anita. You heard correctly. My No.2 is an Indian. I'm part Indian myself. You know there is a Reservation nearby. They are an important part of this County." She saw his dark hair and eyes, his high cheekbones. "I was just surprised Bill, around home the Indians seem to keep to themselves. His dark eyes were on her and she felt self conscience. "When was the last time a man made her feel this way?" Confusion filled her mind, she wanted to be held by her lover. Then she heard the fax machine and left the room to see. She came back with a sheet of paper, "It's for you, from Wanda." Bill took it and looked it over, "This is the memo I was talking about." He signed and offered back to Anita, "Could you please fax this back to her?" "Sure Bill." Their fingers touched. Anita felt herself blushing again, so she took the fax and left. "You are a very young looking thirty-four." He called to her. "Today, I feel younger than thirty-four. Try seventeen!" "Stop!" Bill yelled, "That would make you younger than my Daughter!" "When do you think we will see Sheila again?" She said, from the Comm Room. His face betrayed a wry smile, "You can never tell about our intrepid reporter!" Bill's Cell phone rang, instantly changing the subject, "Hello, Sheriff

Andrews." "Hello yourself," said Joyce / Sheila Andrews. "Hi Sheila." "Hi Dad, could you stand some company?" "I take that to mean you're coming to visit." "Yes Dad, I'm coming to visit and work. I'm one of the press party coming to cover the big drug bust at the Mines" "I'm at the Mines right now, Joyce. I'll see you later." "You called me Joyce, is there something wrong Dad?" When you get here, we'll talk, all right?" "Okay, Dad!" She hung up or was cut off. "Damn Cell phones, so unreliable up here." Anita reentered the Conference Room, "Who was that, Bill?" "Anita, you wanted to see my Daughter. She'll be with the press party today." Anita picked up the Press roster from the table, "Yes, Sheila Andrews is listed for the Press party. That is pretty good for a "rookie" out of LA!" "She has her Mother's beauty, and enough nerve to get in serious trouble." Anita saw the pride and concern for his Daughter in Bill's face, "I bet she has her Father's brains to get out of trouble as well." Bill laughed softly, "I believe that she thinks her way into trouble and then charms her way out." "I can't wait to see her, again." "Later today, I think we can arrange that," Bill said with a smile. Anita thought she saw a twinkle in his eye. Fred came sauntering in, and sat down next to Bill. Anita saw the change in Bill's face. Suddenly, there was a stern, cold countenance where a moment ago there was a smiling face. "Special Agent Fred Peterson," Bill began coldly, "who asked you to set down?" Fred grew confused, but Bill's face told him that he had screwed up bad. Fred got up and stood by the table in a half-ass attempt at attention. He was sure that last night was going to be mentioned. Bill held up the duty schedule, "Can you tell me, Special Agent, why my Officers are doing most of the work around here while you and your men sit on your tail feathers and drink coffee?" A shaken Fred tried to respond, "I, ah, wasn't aware there was any, ah, problem with the schedule. Sir." Bill jumped on that with cold disdain, holding the schedule up to Fred and pointing to the signature, "Is this not your signature? Or did some passing sheepherder slip in here, make up this schedule and forge your name to it?" "Ah, no, Sir. I mean yes, Sir, that is my signature." "Now that we have that established, I tell you what I'm going to do. I am going to give this document back to you and you are going to change it to a more equitable schedule, sign it, then bring it back to me for my approval." Out of the corner of his eye, Bill saw a smirk on Anita's face. Fred looked pale, like a little boy

304

caught with his hand in the cookie jar. Then Fred seemed to stiffen, "I don't think I want to do that, Sheriff. I have already published that schedule." Bill's eye seemed to bore through the hapless DEA Agent, "So, you're worried about losing a little face? That is the least of your worries. If you do not fix this, Charlie and I are going to have a little talk about it, in front of the DEA brass. They won't care about your face, they'll want your ass! Then I will talk to a TV network reporter I know about the DEA's lack of cooperation with local law enforcement." Fred was all bluster, " You wouldn't dare do that! I bet you don't even know a reporter." Bill stood up and looked down at the shorter Agent, "Are you calling me a liar?" Anita notices that Bill's voice got louder without getting higher pitched. That was dangerous. She stepped up to Fred, "Look, you moron! He does know a reporter. He will probably have dinner with her tonight. I think he could make one phone call, and you'd be sent to Butte, Montana." Between Bill's large presence on one side and Anita's words of warning on the other, Fred's nerve began to crack." Bill saw it, so he offered words of encouragement, "Make up a cover story. I'll let you save face. But you need to be careful who you call a liar. Make sure he can't kick your ass!" The look on Bill's face took all the fight out of him. Fred knew this man could destroy him. It did not matter how much older Bill was. "Could I have the schedule, Sir. I'll get with Sargent Yeager about the changes." Bill kept his stern look, but gave the paper to Fred, "Special Agent, you are dismissed." A beaten Fred turned and slowly walked out of the vehicle. A smirking Anita came around the table got on her tiptoes to kiss Bill on the cheek, "Thanks Bill, I needed that." Bill spoke as she walked away, "So did Fred." He spoke to her in the bathroom, "I have to deal with the Homeland Security Brass, then we can make some plans. Ones that involve a good deal of close contact." "It had better, Bill. Or I might take you right here, on the conference table!" It was close to the time for the DEA brass to arrive. Anita gathered up her documents, tossing them into a folder. Having already checked her makeup, she headed out to the Helicopter Pad. Bill wished her luck. Bill thought about what he knew about the Assistant Secretary for Homeland Security. He was retired Navy, an intelligence professional, not a career politician like his boss. Bill knew him by reputation, Admirals moved in different circles from Reserve Commanders. The man was reportedly very sharp, some said too sharp. There were several versions of why he retired, early. He had been known to eat errant Ensigns, raw. Errant Commanders too. Bill heard the Helicopters approaching, two at least. "Well, the DEA dog and pony show is about to begin," Bill could not help thinking, "Good luck Charlie." He decided that he would walk outside to see the landings. Bill stood by the end of the mobile unit, this rolling Command Center, and saw two Black Hawks flair and land about fifty feet apart. "Showboating for the Brass, I wish Joyce wasn't on one of them." The landings were uneventful, and Bill watched the Brass embark from the closest Black Hawk. Charlie and Fred were there to greet them. They were all smiles. The Press Party emerged from the second Black Hawk. Anita was there to greet them. She does have a beautiful smile. Suddenly he saw a beautiful woman waving at him, he waved back. Joyce did look stunning in a pastel sun dress, her hair loose and flowing. Anita spoke to the group, then checked the credentials of the six assembled reporters. He saw her say something to Joyce, then they both laughed. Soon Charlie led the Brass toward the Midas Mine, describing the Raid as he went. Anita and the Press followed close behind, taking notes or talking into mini-recorders. Bill thought about getting one for his work. He had a brief description of the Raid in the car, maybe he'd borrow a mini and finish the report. Sgt Yeager approached him. Bill noticed that he was wearing a fresh uniform. "I wanted to thank you, Sheriff. Fred handed the duty schedule to me for revision. We're going to work on it together, when he's done with the PR show." "I'm glad to hear it. Guess my little talk with Fred did some good." "Someday, you'll have to tell me just what you said to old Fred." "Someday, I might." They shared a laugh over Fred's discomfort and his well deserved comeuppance. Then the two men went into the Command Center. Yeager went into the Conference Room to work on the duty schedule. The phone in the communications room rang, Bill answered, "Command Center, Sheriff Andrews speaking." "Sheriff this is Homeland Security, has the Assistant Secretary landed yet?" "No, he has not." "Is Special Agent-in-Charge Stevens there?" "No, he is out on tour with the DEA Brass." "Sheriff Andrews, I have a Priority Fax for the Assistant Secretary. Can I trust you to deliver it?" "Would it help if I told you that I am a Commander in the Naval Reserve, Vice Admiral Saunders in Special Ops can vouch for me." "Please hold, Commander." Bill waited, wishing that at least the phone should play music while you're on hold. After two minutes, the gentleman returned, "Very well Commander. Admiral Saunders sends his warmest regards. The Fax will follow shortly. Goodbye." Bill didn't know whether to laugh or cry about the man's performance. "How secure could a fax be?" He was about to find out. The Fax machine became alive, the first page emerged. It was marked: Priority Fax! Eyes Only-Assistant Secretary of Homeland Security. The second page contained the body of the message. Bill had no hesitation in reading it. It was background on the 'dirty bomb' plot. Seems that there were several people involved. They were going to take the Nuclear Waste and the Ammonium Nitrate to a hillside in Marin County, where they would meet a tanker truck of diesel oil. There would be a big blast, and the Waste would be blown all over the Bay Area, helped by the prevailing Northerly winds. "Very good plan, except for a careless drug operation, and an old Indian man looking for special pigments. One of the plotters was dead, two were in custody, and four were being sought." Bill was amused at how easily it had all come unraveled. It could have just as easily have all worked. Bill remarked at how none of this plot had reached the media. He took the fax and folded it in half. There were several questions that the fax did not answer. First, how did they buy the Ammonium Nitrate? Access to purchase explosives was restricted. Did Johnny Eagle set that up through one of his companies? Why would a man trying to build a casino here, help to irradiate the Bay Area? Did Bob Moore see what was in the Molly Bee Mine and Johnny had to kill him. Secondly, did Russ know about the terrorist plot? It looked like he parked his Jeep in the next cave to the Nuclear Waste, but did he know the trailer and men were there? He was taking drug money, but what about our Middle Eastern friends? "Just like old times, no black and white. Only shades of gray. Only more questions." Russ Baker's body was lying in a body bag, in the Morgue. Johnny Eagle rested in a Jail cell. Two men for whom people held such high hopes. Several of the dead men were missing all or part of their head. One man was in pieces, nothing larger than his foot existed. All of them dead due to greed, except one. Perhaps the teachings of Islam are correct. Perhaps one man died a martyr, a golden throne waiting for him in Heaven. Or is he sitting in it now? Bill could not understand how they could believe that it was okay to kill thousands of innocent people in the name of Islam. His Muslim friends told him that was not the Islam they knew. To them, Islamic extremism was a dark perversion of their religion. Like the Inquisition had been to Catholicism. The Protestants had their Witch Trials. "I'm getting philosophical in my old age," Bill admitted to himself. Then his ears caught a familiar sound, a helicopter was approaching. Bill went outside, the sound was getting louder. He headed for the logical landing site. Bill noticed that the DEA group was still on their tour of the Midas Mine. They would end up at the trailer full of dope. Bill stood next to the trailer to wait for his party. He made small talk with the two DEA agents on duty. Of course the DEA would be stationed here, leave all other duties for the Deputies. The helicopter appeared in the southern sky, "Probably coming from Sacramento," he observed. It was logical, that was the nearest major airport. It was nearly two hundred miles away. "Once more, I am reminded of just how isolated we are up here," he reflected. The machine got closer, Bill could see that it was a Jet Ranger, not a Black Hawk. "Rank has its privileges." Soon the Jet Ranger was flaring and landing fifty feet from where he stood. As the blades slowed, the passenger door opened and stairs folded down. A man about thirty got out, obviously an aide. Then the Man himself appeared. Rear Admiral Raymond Stark, Retired, Assistant Secretary of Homeland Security was a graying fifty-three year old of medium height and weight. His black rimmed glasses gave him an owlish look, like the intellectual that he was. Bill stepped forward, "Mr Secretary, welcome to Sierra Vista County." He did not extent his hand. "Call me Admiral Stark, Commander." He did not extent his hand either. "I was told, Admiral, that you are known for your command of facts, I see that information was correct." "Knowledge is power, is what I was told. I have found that information is also correct, Commander." Bill offered him the fax, "This just came for you, Admiral." Stark took it, unfolded it, and read it. "Are you aware of the contents of this fax, Commander?" "Yes Sir. I took the liberty of reading it." "Do you have anything to add to this?" "No Admiral. I just have questions that fax doesn't answer." "Yes, it is shy a few detail. Well Commander, shall we get on with it?" He handed the fax to his aide, who slipped it into a binder he carried. "Mr Kinney, you may stay here if you wish," Admiral Stark spoke to the burly man in his

308

forties standing behind him. "Sir, I don't think I should leave you." "The Commander here was a SEAL Officer, Desert Storm, etc. Just two days ago, he killed a Mexican Cartel assassin with a double tap to the heart. Yesterday, he defeated an El Qaida operative in a knife fight. I do think that he could protect me very well." "Admiral, Mr Kinney is Special Forces, I assume." "Right you are, Commander. They promoted him to Warrant Officer, then tried to assign Mr Kinney to a desk job, but he did not share their opinion. Did you." "Damn straight, Admiral," snarled the old warrior. "Very well, Mr Kinney, you may accompany us on our little tour. Shall we, Commander?" Bill began, "Gentlemen, the Trailer behind me contains several tons of assorted drugs. The Semi ran into several fifty caliber rounds when it tried to flee. The driver lost most of his head." They could see the shredded Semi tractor. He gestured toward the nearest mine, "This is the Molly Bee Mine. There was a hostile firing an RPG from the entrance." Mr Kinney spoke, "What happened to the hostile?" "My sniper put a four oh eight round through his chest from the ridge behind us." "Nice shooting, Commander." "On behalf of my Sniper team, I thank you, Mr Kinney." Admiral Stark had his own comment, "The man's name was Sidde El Sharif, an Egyptian dissident thought to be affiliated with Al Qaida. Wanted for questioning by the Egyptian Government about several bombings of tourist sites." They continued on into the Mine, Stark continued to talk. "The Commander shot it out with a Cartel soldier, on the ridge above us." "What happened to him, Commander?" Mr Kinney inquired. "I put three bullets in his head with an AK-47." That got a grunt of approval from Mr Kinney. "The Commander failed to mention that the man had an AK also," added the Admiral, "the night before, he did the same thing with a pistol, put three shots into the head of a renegade. His Cousin was a Captain in his own Department!" Mr Kinney was impressed, "Killed your own Cousin when he turn traitor, damn straight! Did you know before the night?" "I suspected him for a while, then I got conformation that he was taking bribes. I was ready for it when it came," Bill spoke with little emotion. Mr Kinney looked on Bill with a new interest. He considered that this man was no whoosh, Naval Officer or not. Bill took them to the trailer of Nuclear Waste, now uncovered. There were the bags of ammonium nitrate on it. "I never heard about this missing trailer. When was Law Enforcement going to be so informed?" Bill asked, staring right at the Admiral. "Commander, the FBI assured us that they could find it without causing public panic." "Without the eyes and ears of local law enforcement? How did they do, Admiral?" Admiral Stark had the resigned look of someone who had been through this before, "Commander Andrews, this is neither the time nor place for the discussion." "Begging your pardon, Admiral, but this is precisely the time. You say that Homeland Security accepted the FBI's premise that to notify local law enforcement means to invite public panic. Speaking for the Sheriffs and Police Chiefs of this country, I resent that. We are not the illiterate, potbellied old farts the Bureau seems to think we are. Most of us have a college degree, some of us have advanced degrees. There are many MBAs and PhDs in our ranks. This stolen trailer of Nuclear Waste was discovered because a tip came into my Department of night truck activity. We investigated and I suspected a drug operation. I notified DEA and we conducted a joint operation. Then we discovered the Nuclear Waste. An old man started this off, not the FBI! The Department of Justice recently awarded us with a grant for equipment and training. They helped us to improve our capabilities, then accept the Bureau's belief that we have none. Make up your minds!" The Admiral looked at Bill with interest, so did the aide and Mr Kinney. Admiral Stark seemed to be making a decision, "Commander, you speak with great passion, and not without affect. Would you consider coming to Washington and making this argument to the Secretary? This is a hot topic in Homeland Security, we need your point of view in our discussions." "Admiral Stark, I would be glad to come. This is something that needs to be said. Perhaps while I'm there, I could find out more about this plot. More about the Dubai connection." This brought an odd smile to the Admirals face, "Commander, I believe that I can arrange it so you can pursue the Dubai connection where ever it leads. We need to talk about this further. Is there somewhere secure where we can talk?" "Our Command Center is as secure as it gets around here, Admiral." Gesturing toward the mine entrance, the Admiral urged them on, "Lead on Commander. I and my associates could use something cold to drink." "Admiral, I think some ice tea could be arranged. Perhaps Mr Kinney would prefer something stronger?" "Damn straight!" Admiral Stark didn't even turn to look at Kinney, "Mr Kinney will have ice tea with the rest

310

of us, Commander." Bill turned to Kinney, as they walked, and shrugged. Kinney nodded that he understood. They exited the mine and headed for the Mobile Command Center. As they did so, Bill noticed that the DEA group was at the dope trailer. Charlie was motioning toward the Center. Bill suspected Charlie was after the same Conference Room that he was. Bill picked up the pace. The Admiral got that funny little smile on his face as he realized why Bill was rushing them past the DEA group. He nodded to the DEA Brass, neither of which he recognized. Bill nodded to Joyce and Anita. Charlie had a look of concern on his face. Once they were past the DEA group, Bill knew they were home free, Charlie would not make a move with the Admiral present. Just a little one upmanship between colleagues. He got the party settled in the Conference Room, and served them all bottles of ice tea, with a plastic glass. Add your own sugar and lemon. "Commander Andrews," the Admiral began, "it has come to my attention that you are an accomplished man. A SEAL officer with many decorations, holder of an MS in Chemistry from the University of Virginia, NCIS team leader with a very good record, and popular Sheriff of a rural county in California. You speak intelligently and with passion. You stick to facts with a minimum of name calling. You just might have the skills to make it in Washington. Come work for me." Bill was surprised, "What would I do for you?" "I would create a position for you where you could act as liaison between Homeland Security and local law enforcement. Work out the bugs. Kick butts if necessary." "What about my Reserve duties?" "We could bring you back on Active duty. As a Navy Commander, with a chest full of ribbons, you would carry weight. I would push for you to receive a fourth stripe." Bill looked at the group in the room for a bit, then spoke, "A very interesting proposition. I will need some time to think about this. Admiral Stark, I do appreciate your offer. I am sure you do not make such things lightly." "Commander, take all the time you need. I realize it is not a small thing. Please call me at this number." Stark handed Bill a card. Bill put it in his shirt pocket. "It may interest you, Bill. I didn't like your Libyan Mission either. It was one reason I retired." Bill surprised, by both his informality and his mention of a 'secret' mission. "Admiral, I appreciate your candor, but should you be discussing a mission that is still 'classified'?" "It is common knowledge how you saved the life of a young Ensign on that mission. A mission that was not well conceived. The young Ensign who just happens to be the son of the now Deputy Director of the FBI, and is a rising FBI agent in his own right." Bill looked sternly at the Admiral, "As far as I know, you are simply repeating rumors. No one knows what happened on that mission except those of us that were there." Admiral Stark had a rueful look, like he was not real happy with how that went. Mr Kinney looked smug, like he would have said much the same to the Admiral. "I consider myself properly rebuffed, Commander. Perhaps that you can do that is one reason I want you." "Duly noted, Sir." The little conference was disturbed by the noise of one, and then two Black Hawks taking off. "There goes the Dog and Pony Show," announced Mr Kinney. The rest of the party chuckled. "They're entitled to their publicity. They made a very big bust, millions in captured drugs." The Admiral tried to look sincere, but somehow failed. Even his aide laughed at that. At that moment, Anita and Joyce appeared in the Conference Room doorway. The Admiral was quickly on his feet,"Who do we have here?" Bill rose and went toward the door, "Admiral Stark, may I introduce Anita Brubaker, PR person for the local DEA, and Sheila Andrews of KNBC-TV in Los Angeles. This is Rear Admiral Raymond Stark, Retired. Assistant Secretary of Homeland Security. His Aide, Mr Humphrey. And Mr Kinney of the Special Forces, in charge of security. All three men looked appreciatively at the two beauties. The Admiral was first to speak, "Sheila Andrews, any relation to the Commander here?" "Yes, I'm his Daughter, Admiral Stark." Stark looked at Bill, "this could be very interesting. Miss Andrews, I have just offered your Father a post with me in Washington. But then, I am sure he will tell you all about it." "Admiral, you obviously do not know my Father. Nice fishing expedition." Stark smiled coyly at the young woman, then addressed Bill, "Beauty and brains, that could be dangerous in a reporter." Bill smiled coyly back at him, "Dangerous for those who lie to her." "Well said, Commander. I am sure our time together in Washington will be interesting." Mr Humphrey stepped up behind the Admiral, "Sir, we need to get back to Sacramento if we are to make our flight to Washington." Over his shoulder, "You are right about that. Gentlemen, we need to leave!" With Bill leading the way the party headed for the Helicopter, the ladies just got out of the way. After the door closed, Anita grabbed Sheila by the arm, "Your

312

Father can't take that job in Washington. It's a school of sharks in Homeland Security, everyone fighting for turf." "Anita, all of Washington is like that. My Father learned that as a SEAL Officer, why do you think he left?" "You don't think he'll take it?" "No, I don't. Anita, you can help me with something. That Jet Ranger didn't look like a Government unit, how can I find out?" "All right, Sheila. It's simple. Get the tail number for me and I'll check with the FAA." Sheila squeezed her arm and ran outside. Quickly she came back, tore a page out of her small notebook and gave it to Anita, "Please see what you can do with that!" "Wait here," Anita went into the Comm Room. Sheila tried talking to her, "Anita, how do you like working with the DEA?" "It's like being the only girl in a boy scout troop." "That bad?" "I made it worse by dating one of the agents." "How did that work out?" "He asked me to marry him." "Anita, obviously you refused." "I told him no, we broke up. Now I have to dodge him." "Won't take no for an answer?" "You got it. I'm gong to drive back to Susanville tonight, or I'll have to fight him off. Last night, he went after a female firefighter by mistake. He got a face full of pepper spray for his trouble." They both got a laugh out of that! "Anita! That's horrible. Why don't you come home with Dad and I? I know he wants to see you, and it's much closer. I think Dad will be back here tomorrow." Anita came back into the room and handed a sheet of paper to Sheila, "Here! This should answer your questions." "Thanks, Anita this is great!" "Sheila, do you think it would be all right with your Father. I mean, it won't interfere with something he's got going?" "Anita, my Father wants you with him. Please come with us." The Jet Ranger took off over them, delaying the conversation. "How can I resist. Okay Sheila, you talked me into it!" "Good! Get your stuff together. I need to take off as soon as Dad can. I need to file my story." "You could file it from here!" "Thanks, Anita, but I'd rather do it from Dad's. He has a good wine cellar, and he's a great cook. We just have to get him in the mood." About this time, Bill came back into the Center. Entering the Conference Room, he and the two women looked at each other. "Why is it that I get the feeling that something has been decided involving me, to which I was not privy." "Every once in a while, Dad likes to remind me he graduated from U.S.C., I graduated from UCLA." Anita slipped by Bill and started down the hall, "I graduated from Georgetown." Sheila got excited about that, "Anita, some of my friends graduated from Georgetown." "After I was there," she said from the bedroom. "Maybe a couple of years later." "Bless you my child. Your Father has taught you to be kind to your elders." "Anita, your what, four or five years older?" "Try ten, Sheila." Sheila looked odd. "Now you know, Joyce Elizabeth, why it is not wise to try and guess a woman's age," Bill intoned. "Did you know how old she is?" "Yes I did, she told me." "Do you think she looks it?" "No I don't, Sheila. She does look younger." Anita appeared at his side, carrying a small suitcase. She kissed him on the cheek, "Thank you for that, kind Sir." Sheila picked up her own case, "Shall we go. Anita's coming home with us." Bill jumped on that, "I knew something was afoot!" "Look Dad, she was going to drive to Susanville rather than stay here and fight off an old boyfriend." "Fred! Has he been bothering you, Anita?" "Well, he did a bit last night." "That's it! Your coming home with us. Come on!" He led the way. The two women looked at each other, then followed. Anita took them to meet Brenda, she had to stay until the Molly Bee was empty. Bill got to hear about Fred and the Pepper Spray. Bill was not amused.

The ride to Bill's was uneventful. After alerting Dispatch that he was en route home, he was told that all was well. Sheila talked about how things were going in her career. Anita envied her career, and complained about how she scrambled for a living. She had left her PR job in Washington, DC to tend her sick Mother. Mom died last year, now she lived with her Dad. Dating was limited, hence Fred. Bill talked a little about his favorite places in DC. Anita and he had some in common. Sheila found that interesting. She found she liked Anita, she knew her Dad did too. She was their kind of people. The ladies prevailed on Bill to pick up something special for dinner, so they stopped at the Reservation Store. Home made tortillas made a good lunch. Bill selected some beautiful steaks, made from cattle grown and butchered on the Reservation. Bill regretted that most residents of the Reservation could not afford this meat. They drove on to the Andrews home. Bill parked in front of the house, he took in the groceries, the ladies carried their own suitcases. When they entered the central Hall, two sleepy animals were waiting for them. Anita was again charmed by the miniature blonde cocker mix, Susie was delighted with her. Tiger got a thorough rubbing from Sheila. Bill took the food into the Kitchen. Sheila took Anita upstairs and they both

314

unpacked. Both guest rooms were ready (does Mrs Garcia ever fail?). Then Sheila went downstairs and into the Den to file her story. Anita came down and just toured the house. She had taken off her jacket and had on a short sleeve, light blue blouse. Eventually, she found herself in the Kitchen. Bill was pouring marinate from a bottle without a label onto the steaks. "What kind of marinate is that?" She asked. Bill told her about the old family receipt. She was skeptical, until he pulled out an old notebook and showed her a yellowed sheet of paper containing the recipe. "Of course, if you read this, I'll have to kill you." She moved close to him, looked up and told him, "I'll risk it." He looked down on her, leaned over and kissed her. She let him, "I was hoping you would do that." "Were you now," he said as he put down the bottle. He turned to her, put his hands on her shoulders, and kissed her again. This time, she kissed him back, putting both her arms around him Then he whispered, "Anita come with me. I have a hunch." With his arm around her, he escorted her out to the staircase. He looked at the study and whispered "The Little One is busy." "Little One," Anita hissed back, "She is taller than I am, and makes me look like a boy!" Bill lifted her onto the first step, "Not even close." She kissed him warmly. She could look into his dark eyes and he could see her blue ones. Chuckles from the Den caused them to walk over and find the cause. Sheila was chuckling over the response to her story summary from her Boss. Hearing the pair behind her, she ex- plained, "He wants to know how I knew that the Assistant Secretary of Homeland Security was flying in a Helicopter registered to Lockheed Missile and Space, a major Defense Contractor." Anita stepped forward, "Tell him you got it from the FAA. He doesn't need to know how you got FAA confirmation." Sheila smiled at her, then typed her reply. His reply was swift in coming, "He bought it! Thank you, Anita! Dad, I think it is time to break out your good white wine!" "Not my Spatlase!" "Yes Dad, your Spatlase!" "Anita, I hope your not wedded to Chardonnay. Spatlase is a German white wine that is a touch sweet. Very fruity." Anita looked up at him, "I'm game. It sounds interesting." Bill ushered the two women down into the Basement. There they found a complete gym setup. "So this is how he stays in such great shape," Anita thought as she took it all in. She had to go to a gym to use this kind of equipment. It wasn't cheap. "Why didn't he show this to me before?" Then, she recalled their wonderful time in bed! Sheila slid back the heavy wooden door on one side of the room. Inside there were racks of bottles, some red, some white, and some pink. Bill selected a bottle, and they headed back upstairs. The ladies escorted Bill into the Kitchen. There, he place the bottle into the refrigerator removing the open bottle already there. Sheila had produced three wine glasses and Bill poured each glass part way full. He handed each of them a glass. Sheila offered a toast, "Here's to life in California and staying the Hell away from Washington, DC!" They all drank. Then the wall phone in the Kitchen rang. Bill reached for it, "Hello, Sheriff Andrews." A booming voice burst out of the phone and in to his ear, "Bill, this is Roy Saunders. Can we talk, alone?" "No problem, Sir. I can put you on hold and pickup a more secure phone." "Why don't you do that." Bill pushed the Hold button, hung up the phone, and headed for the Den,"Excuse me ladies, I have to take this call." Once in the Den, Bill shut the door, sat in the computer chair, and picked up the phone. He pressed the Line One button, "Hello Sir, to what do I owe the pleasure of this call?" "Lord, you reserve officers sure are long winded. Save it. We need to talk." "Yes, Sir. What topic did you have in mind?" "Have you been talking to Admiral Ray Stark?" "Yes, Sir, I talked to him this morning." "Did he offer you a job, working for him?" "Yes Sir, he did." "Did you accept?" "I told him I would think about it, Sir." "Are you going to accept his offer?" "Sir, I thought that after a reasonable length of time, I would politely decline." "Good for you Bill! Stay away from Stark, and that whole damn Department. They couldn't find their ass with both hands! It is one big turf fight." "Yes Sir, so I discovered. They allowed the FBI to withhold important inform- ation from local law enforcement because that might create public panic. Then my little department solved their problem, from a local tip." "I heard something about a big gun fight that you were involved with." "Yes, Sir, my people and the DEA, we killed eight and captured four. We only had three wounded. Captured millions in uncut drugs. I am sorry about Jennifer." "Unfortunate about her. What was she doing there anyway?" "Coming to see me, although we had broken up, Sir. I am seeing someone else." "That sounds like her. If my Daughter did half the things she's done, I'd disown her!" "I appreciate your calling to warn me, Sir." "I heard that Stark was sniffing around asking about you. I was afraid that he might get you before I could ask." "Ask what, Sir? " "Bill, I need

316

you to work for me. The position would be Assistant Chief of Staff, with the rank of Captain. I don't think I'd have much trouble getting your reserve commission transferred back to the regulars. That would put you on the promotion track." Bill was stunned for a moment. "Excuse me Sir. This is a lot to take in. Why me?" "Your SEAL experience, your firm convictions, your combination of brains and guts. I need someone to tell me no, if that is the right answer. My Brother, and some of your old COs tell me that you are that man. Think it over. How much time do you need?" "I'll take three days, Sir." "Very well, three days it is. Bill, there is so much going on. I need your help." "I appreciate that, Admiral. I will be in touch." "Goodbye, Bill. I'm counting on you." "Goodby, Sir." The line went dead in Bill's ear, he hung up, then sat there for a few minutes, wrapping his mind around what just occurred. "It could be an important job, but a demanding one. I'd be living back in the DC area, this time working in the Pentagon." That put several images in his head. Not all of them pleasant. He heard a faint whimper from the door. Opening it, he found Susie sitting there, looking up at him. He reached down and picked up the little blonde dog. He carried her on her back and scratched her tummy. He walked this way back to the Kitchen. The two ladies were amused at the big, tough Sheriff and the little dog. "There's a macho scene," announced Sheila. "I think they look adorable," said a smiling Anita. "Who was that on the phone, Dad?" "Vice Admiral Roy Saunders. He wants me to move to DC and be his Assistant Chief of Staff. I'd be a Captain in the regular Navy with chance for promotion." "Flag rank, Dad? That is an awfully big carrot. There must be a big stick there too." "You can bet there is, Little One. It's a lot to think about. I should start by finishing my wine. Could one of you ladies assist me?" Anita was the closest one to his glass. She put hers down, and brought his glass over to him. Carefully, she put it to his lips and tipped it gently. He took a drink of the wine, this was repeated until the wine was gone. "Never enough. But thank you for the assistance Kind Lady." "You are quite welcome, Kind Sir." Anita put his glass on the Kitchen counter. Bill and his little friend went through the Dinning Room into the Living Room and sat in his favorite chair. The two ladies took seats on the sofa opposite him, with their wine glasses. "Are you really thinking about this job, Dad?" "Yes, I am giving it serious consideration." "How serious could you be with an upside down puppy in your lap?" Asked a smirking Anita. "You're right, Anita. I usually have a cat in my lap when I have an important decision to make," responded Bill, with a straight face. The ladies both chuckled over that one. "You laugh! Studies have shown that people think more calmly with a cat in their lap. It's either be calm or they'll shred your pants." This was received with a chorus of boos from the women. Anita grew serious, "What department does this Admiral control?" "He is head of Special Operations for the Navy. That puts him in charge of anything involving unconventional forces, like the SEALs, or the new Stealth Boats. But his next assignment might be bigger, and I would probably rise with him. To Rear Admiral or higher. Of course, if I piss off too many, I might find myself retiring early. This move has its risks. Some officers will resent me, I did not go to Annapolis, and my duty was all in SEALs. Most of them spent all of their duty in Surface Warfare, after graduating from Canoe U." Both women smiled at that term for the Naval Academy. Both of them had heard it before. Susie flipped herself over and got down, she stretched and sauntered toward the Kitchen. The three humans all watched her go. Bill looked at his watch, "Time to build a fire!" "Can I help?" Offered Anita, with a warm smile. Bill got up, "Follow me!" Bill led the way and Anita followed. Sheila watched this with interest, so far she had not seen them so much as touch each other. She wondered if they had. Building the fire gave them opportunity to do so again.

Dinner was great. The steaks were excellent. Anita thought that the marinade was very special. They had a good Cabernet with dinner, and the Spatlase with cheese and fruit afterwards. The evening was spent in talk of the job offer, of DC, and what to do with the house, if he were to move. Many ideas were expressed, few decisions were made. There was time to think, wasn't there? Sheila told about some of the unusual stories she had covered. Many of them never were aired. Anita told about some of the stunts lobbyists pulled in Washington. Some of those had been aired. Sheila announced that, "It has been a long day. I'm going to hit the sack" Anita started to follow her, but Bill stopped her on the first step of the stairs. They had a long kiss good night. Then Anita climbed the stairs, and Bill toured the house. Turning off lights, checking the doors, and adding water to the animal bowls, Bill made his rounds. Then he too climbed the stairs and went to his room. He took a quick shower, then changed into just the pajama bottoms. That was all that was necessary right now, it would be cooler later on. He finished in the bathroom, then climbed into bed. He had things to read, but none of them seemed very interesting. So he just laid there, staring at the ceiling, unwilling to turn out the light. This went on for a while, then Bill heard a noise on the landing. Soon, there was a form in the doorway. As the form came into the light, "I saw your light on." It was Anita. "I can't sleep,"Bill admitted, "Too much on my mind." "I have something on my mind, also." She was wearing a thin "Baby Doll" night gown. Bill could see her shape very clearly. "Bill, I was so worried! I could have lost you." With that, she pulled the night gown over her head and dropped it on the floor. She stood there looking at Bill. Bill was certainly looking at her. There was not a brick out of place. Her lovely breasts were high and firm. She climbed onto the bed and went on her hands and knees up to Bill. "Does this approach work for you?" Bill asked, sitting up. She put her face up to his, "I don't know, I've never tried it before." "I bet you'd be very surprised if I kicked you out of my room." "You bet I would! It's been three days!" "Well, I do have this strong urge to kiss you!" They kissed. Bill laid back on to the bed, Anita was on top of him. The light went out, and his pajama bottoms came off. It is such a joy to find an experienced lover in one of which you are already fond. Like and lust go well together. Much pleasure was derived from many positions. They were both quite limber. Bill never gave a thought to the sick Jennifer.

Chapter Twenty-two

Wednesday:

They lay together, his arm around her, her head on his shoulder. They slept the sleep of satisfaction, sexual and otherwise. Bill and Anita knew they liked each other, they might have even realized that they respected each other. But respect, like love, was something that required time to grow. Three men were on their way to Bill's house, intent on insuring that no one in the house had any more time for anything.

Enrique Calderone was an experienced assassin, he had long ago killed his first enemy of the Cartel. At thirty-eight, he had earned a place in middle management, as befitting the eldest son of the Cartel's number three leader. The loss of two Semi loads of dope at the Mines was a major blow to the Cartel, the fact that a member of the Calderones was in charge was a major blow to the family. The death of his little brother, Juan Carlos, made it personal. Enrique had been flown to a small airstrip nearby, where he was met by three Cartel soldiers. Two of them were to accompany him on his mission, to kill the men responsible for their loss. Enrique took that to mean the Anglo Sheriff that had led the raid, and who had killed Juan Carlos. He was taking a chance, the Cartel expected him to kill the Cousin who failed to manage the drug operation. Then he could worry about the DEA and Sheriff. Enrique had his own priorities. He wished that he knew the two men now making their way through the forest with him. They were interested in the reward offered by the Cartel. The two had been already in the area, it was expediency, time was most important. Each of them wore US issue camouflage fatigues and jungle boots. Their pistols, ammo, and gun belts were all from US Army stocks. Enrique told them to leave the M-16 rifles, the Beretta pistols would be best for inside a house The men knew what to do, try to find an unlocked door or window. Then quietly find the Sheriff. They knew he lived alone, but sometimes had the company of a tall blonde woman. If she was there, she too would die. It would send a clear message.

"Dispatch calling Unit One! Dispatch calling Unit One!" Bill's radio blared from the dresser top where it sat, recharging. Bill and Anita were quickly up and he grabbed the Mic., "Unit One to Dispatch! Over!" "Mrs. Grimes reports that three men were dropped off in front of your place and they disappeared into the woods. They were wearing fatigues and gun belts. Over." "That makes twice to be thankful for her insomnia. (Russ was the first.) Send in the Cavalry! Consider these men armed and dangerous! I have two female guests. We will hold the house. Over." "Roger cavalry. Roger civilian females. Out." A worried Bill turned to Anita, "Can you shoot a pistol?" "I learned to shoot my Dad's 1911 Colt." "Good! Anita, go wake Sheila. Both of you get dressed, then come back here." A naked Anita left the room. Bill got on some fatigue pants and shirt, plus his running shoes. Out of his closet, he got out his fanny pack and belt, plus an old canvas Navy bag. On the dresser, he laid out his Glock 23 and two magazines from the fanny pack. Out of the canvas bag, Bill took an UZI 9 mm submachine gun and three thirty round magazines. He inserted one of the magazines into the weapon and charged it, turning on the safety. He stuffed the other two magazines into the utility pockets in his pants. Anita and Sheila both joined him, they were both wearing jeans and a blouse, with running shoes. Bill saw Sheila's fanny pack, "Have you got your Sig?" "Yes, with two mags. Just like you taught me." "I hope you can shoot that thing." "Watch me!" Anita was anxious, "What about me?" He picked up his belt and fanny pack, and put the belt around her, "I think we can make this fit. There!" He grabbed the Glock and its mags, "This is a .40 caliber Glock. Each magazine has thirteen rounds. You have one in the gun and two in the pack. It has less kick than a .45." He replaced everything into the fanny pack. "That's an UZI, isn't it?" Sheila stared at it. "Yes, its an UZI. A gift from an old Israeli friend. I want both of you to stay in this room. If anyone unfriendly comes up the stairs, shoot to kill!" He started out of the room, Sheila wondered why, "Where are you going?" Bill stopped and looked at the two women, "These gentlemen will be looking for an unlocked door or window. I'm going to give them one, in the basement. Then I'm going to wait with my friend for them to enter. You stay alert, in case one gets by me!" He was gone.

"What does he mean, get by him?" Sheila anxiously asked. Very calmly Anita replied, "If they kill or capture him." Sheila just stared at Anita. Anita stared back, "If one of them hurts your Father, I'll kill the Bastard!" Sheila looked at Anita, "You'll have to get in line." Bill stuck the radio headset on his head as he went down the Stairs. He stopped at the Hall closet and got out his gun belt. He put it on and clipped the radio pack to the belt. "Here we go!" Bill thought as he walked to the basement door, opened it, and went down the stairs. He threaded his way through the familiar obstacles, to the rear door. Very quietly, he unlocked the deadbolt, then retraced his steps back to the stairs. There was a very large treadmill back there, Bill laid down behind it. The UZI rested on top, Bill flipped the safety off. He couldn't help but think, "Now if they only do what I want them to."

Enrique did not count on finding an opening unlocked, he had his own method. When the three men approached the rear of the house, the motion sensor turned on the floodlights. Enrique rushed up to the back wall of the house, the other two followed suit. Soon the lights went out. However, Bill had heard the relay for the lights click on, then click off. He knew they were there. The two Cartel soldiers worked to the left, checking windows. Enrique went to the right. Hugging the wall, he worked his way around the corner and along the side of the house. He found the large window for the Den. Meanwhile, his two friends found the unlocked rear door. What luck! One man quietly opened the door and stepped in, his companion was right behind him. The UZI exploded. Four slugs ripped into the first man's chest, he went down. The second man hit the floor. Finding that the floor was the safest place, he popped up only to fire his Beretta at Bill. They exchanged shots. Enrique heard the shots, but was not fool enough to investigate. He intended to attack from a different direction. He pulled a glass cutter from his pocket to help with his plan. Quickly, he cut the glass, and removed the piece. He was able to pull himself up on the sill and slipped into the room. He heard the gunfire from the basement."That is the Sheriff. I will find the door and kill the man," he thought as he panted by the desk. He had been eight years younger and twenty pounds lighter the last time he had done this kind of thing.

Sheila heard the gunfire continuing from the basement, "He's down there with them. I'm going to join him!" Anita grabbed her arm, "Your Dad said stay here. We don't know where they all are!" "He may need my help! I'm going down!" She pulled away and charged on, walking quickly along the landing and down the stairs. Enrique heard her on the stairs, quietly he came close to the doorway. Sheila rushed down the stairs and turned to her left at the bottom. Enrique emerged from the Den right behind her. His left arm went around her neck as the right hand grabbed her gun. Sheila was disarmed and in a choke hold before she knew anything was wrong. As he saw the redish hair, he thought, "This is not the Blonde. This man has many women. This one will be his last!" "Help me!" Sheila yelled, before he choked it off. Anita stepped out of the bedroom, but stepped back when she saw why Sheila yelled. "I don't have a shot. They're too close together," she thought. The head of the five foot nine Enrique and the five foot seven Sheila were over lapping. Enrique started to force Sheila toward the open basement door, "Come! We will go see your man!" He had Sheila's own gun at her head. "Move!" He still had to half drag her. Anita could see enough to guess their destination. This gave her an idea. She watch the pair move until they approached moving under the landing. Then she stepped up to the landing rail, she had the Glock in her hand. She looked down onto the tops of their heads, aimed, then fired just once. It had been a moving target, but so were the rats she use to shoot at. The one hundred eighty grain JHP (jacketed hollow point) slug hit Enrique in the top of his skull. The bullet expanded, shredding his Cerebrum, nasal passage, pallet and tongue. It exited under his chin. Enrique's corpse hit the floor behind a startled Sheila, who scream mightily. Anita peered down at the carnage she had caused. Bill heard the shot and yelled, "Joyce, Anita are you alright?" Sheila, who was reclaiming her gun, ran to the basement door, "We're okay, Dad! Anita killed one up here!" The last assassin heard that too. He decided that retreat was the best idea. "Even their women are armed!" He fired several shots at Bill, then broke for the door. He fired high, Bill didn't even flinch. The UZI nearly cut the man in half. But he did make it out the door, before he died. "Dad, are you okay?" "Yes, Little One. I just need to check the bodies." Cautiously, he approached the first victim. He was dead, four holes in his chest. The second man was obvious, his torso and hips pointed in totally different directions. Two here and one upstairs, that's three. Is that all? Bill hit the Talk switch,

"Dispatch! This is Unit One! Add Coroner and Crime Scene Unit to call. Three dead. Over." "Dispatch to Unit One. Roger Coroner and Crime Unit . Good shooting, Sir!" "Thanks Dispatch. I only got two. Over and out." The motion sensor switched the flood-lights on. Bill tensed and raised the UZI. "Cease fire! We're friendly!" It was Jim Bearpaw and two of the Deputies, M-16's at the ready. They came through the back yard and gathered around Bill and the body on the ground. Bill pointed to the doorway, "There is another one in there and one upstairs." "Jesus!" exclaimed one of the Deputies. Jim was quick to comment, "Randy, this is an average day for our Sheriff." "Look who's talking!" said Bill, pointing at the 'Sniper'. Bill headed inside and up the stairs to the Hall. He found a shaken Sheila and the body of Enrique. "He had me, Dad! He jumped me and took my gun! He would have forced me to the basement if Anita hadn't shot him!" Bill went to the body. He saw the head wound, then looked toward the stairs. Anita was standing on the bottom step, watching him, and holding on to the hand rail, "You're all right!" She exclaimed. Bill put the UZI on the floor and went to her. He held her by the shoulders, just looking at her. She smiled, and he kissed her, then hugged her. "What a shot!" He whispered to her, "What guts!" "It was the only thing I could do!" She said in her defense. "And you did it, Kind Lady." "It's all that I could do, Kind Sir," Bill saw that she was crying. "Everything is okay, the bad guys are all dead and we're all fine!" "I know, I'm just so happy!" She said, smiling through her tears." Bill had never known a woman who could smile and cry at the same time. But he wanted to know this one better.

Jim and the deputies swept the area, and found the driver waiting to pick up the assassins. He could not believe that all three were dead. Barbara arrived, rather upset, "Where am I going to put these three? You've already filled up the Morgue! These three will have to go in the grocery store freezer!" Sheila was incensed, "They tried to kill us! What did you want us to do, kiss them!" Bill sat on the stairs with Anita and watched the two yell at each other, "Doctor Barbara Davis went to Cornell and Cornell Medical School, she did her Residency at John Hopkins. My Daughter graduated cum laude from UCLA." Anita smiled and laughed at the whole thing. Bill had his arm around her. Soon, the Crime Unit showed up and started taking photos. Anita got Sheila to shut up and go to the Kitchen with her. They made coffee, a lot of coffee. Barbara took her measurements and noted the various holes in each corpse. Bill described the attack to Jim who used one of those mini-recorders. After he had Anita described her part, Jim insisted on thanking her. Then Jim told Barbara, and she wanted to thank her. Through it all, Bill was at her side, usually with an arm around her shoulders. Jim and Barbara noticed. So did Sheila. Anita didn't seem to mind.

Barbara and the Crime Unit people quietly went about their duties. The crime areas were photographed and measured in great detail. As the sun peaked over the Cascades, Jim and Randy helped Barbara place each of the three bodies into a County body bag. Sheila thought it was cute, the way that Jim helped Barbara with her tasks. She wondered where Barbara had been sleeping when called for this job? She envied them that kind of relationship, but she had no great desire for one herself. There was plenty of time for that. Anita was older, and of a different cut. She did want a solid, intimate relationship. She knew that they all could have been killed. She did not want to die, not for a long time. She wanted that happiness in life that we all want, and so few get. She thought about her life as she and Sheila fixed breakfast. Bill had made a survey of the damage to the house. Nothing major, except for the missing glass in the Den and the blood stains on the floors. There were numerous marks on the cinder block walls of the Basement, where bullets had hit. Some of the gym equipment had been hit, but the stainless steel of the pro quality equipment hardly had a mark. He announced his findings in the Kitchen, as the women prepared the food. As he left to tell the others that breakfast was about ready, he touched Anita's arm. Sheila caught that. Anita saw her. Sheila had to say something, "Anita, my Father feels a lot of gratitude toward you, we both do. But my Father has had a lot of disappointments in his life. I don't want him hurt again." Anita was cooking scramble eggs. She continued stirring them as she spoke, "I have no intension of hurting your Father. I have had a lot of disappointments in my life, also. Your Father is a good man. He is also a great lover. A woman would be lucky to have him. If that woman is me, I think it would make me very happy. Does that tell you what you wanted to know?" Sheila was smiling, "Too much information Anita, but thank you." Anita served the eggs, Sheila added Canadian Bacon and toast. They ate in the Dining Room,

326

Bill, Anita, Sheila, Barbara, Jim, and Randy. After breakfast, and tidying the Kitchen, Anita and Bill quietly went up stairs. They went into Bill's room. Bill started to change, Anita picked up her discarded night gown and started to leave. "Don't go," Bill said to her. The little boy look on his face, caused Anita to walk over to him. She went on tip toes to kiss him, "Since you asked, I won't." She went in to the bathroom and changed. She came out wearing the night gown and crawled into the bed, beside Bill. He put his arm around her, and they went to sleep. They were both exhausted.

About eleven, they woke up, made love, then got up and got dressed. When they opened the bedroom door, they found a note taped to the railing opposite. It told Bill that Sheila had written a story about last night. It was on the computer screen, to be reviewed. The note went on, "If you disagree with something, do not edit, let me fix it! The DEA promised Jim to identify the dead men as soon as they could." Curious, the two went downstairs, to the Den. Sheila's room had been empty. They scrolled through the story, reading as they went. A warm breeze came through the open window frame. Bill was pleased, over all. It was a factual account, even to the details of Sheila's own errors. Bill thought it gave him too much credit. "They didn't have a chance. I had them out gunned!" It certainly lauded Anita. Bill thought that only right. Bill wrote her a complementary note, and taped it to the screen. Then the pair went over to the Kitchen. Mrs Garcia was there. When she saw Bill and Anita, she cried and hugged them both. The Deputies had told her about last night. Bill thought that Anita looked like she was enveloped by Mrs Garcia. After the hugs, she insisted on making them a big lunch. While that was being prepared, Anita went upstairs and checked in with Charlie and the DEA. Charlie wanted more detail about last night. Then Charlie told her that he could use her as a field agent. Would she like to go to DEA training? Anita declined. Bill called Jim to check in. Jim went over the details of what they knew about the three would be assassins. "Bill, the one Anita killed is the big brother of the one you shot three days ago. He was high up in the Cartel middle management. Looks personal. DEA says there are two more brothers. The other dead were just soldiers. All three were here illegally. I'd like to know where they got their gear. It was all US Army issue. Most things had serial numbers on them. Barbara and I like Anita." "So do I, Jim. I'll check with Homeland

Security about a timetable for removal of the terrorist equipment. Then we can bring our people back." "Yeager told me he asked for Denise as his No 2. He said you approved." "That is correct. Is there a problem? Not with me, oh great leader, but some of the good old boys are senior to her. They're pissed." "Jim, they may be senior to her, but she makes most of them look like they're standing still. She works while the rest of them are drinking coffee and playing with themselves!" "You have such a way with words, oh Slayer of Men. Yeager, Wolfe and I will seek to placate the savage hordes." "I think that you've been hanging around a certain Doctor too much. Do I have to remind you, that you do very well with your "Thunder Stick", oh God of Lightning." "Okay, Bill. You got me there. Oh, yes! Barbara and I want to invite you and Anita over to my place for Dinner." "I'll have to check with Anita. What night?" Anita walked into the Kitchen in time to hear the last part, "Check with Anita about what?" "Barbara and Jim want us over to Dinner." "When?" "Let me find out. Jim, what night.?" "How about tomorrow night?" Bill put his hand over the phone, "Tomorrow night." Anita was concerned, "Bill, I need to get back to Susanville and take care of some things." "If I drive you over to the Mines first thing in the morning, you could pick up your van and go back to Susanville. Could you handle your business in time to be back here for Dinner?" Anita did not relish the round trip drive to Susanville and back. But the anxious look on Bill's face, and thought of two more nights in his bed, made it seem trivial. "Tell Jim okay." So the Dinner was set. Mrs Garcia made them a beautiful lunch, which they ate it in the Dinning Room. They talked about his job offer. The pros and cons of a job in Washington, in the Navy. "What about your Department here?" Anita asked, "Wouldn't you be leaving them without a leader?" "Anita, look at last night. Even short handed, they responded correctly. They got the job done. It isn't their fault that you and I took care of the bad guys." She smiled at that. Bill went on, "The leadership may be young, but they are experienced. The courses I mapped out will round them out and broaden their outlook. We already have new technology that will help hugely." "If you took the job with the Navy, you would not be the one in charge. You would be in a junior position. Would you like that?" He thought of how wise this beautiful woman was. "I would probably be the only one there with real Special Ops experience. It will be my job to insure that the missions are realistic." "Bill, look at how things were in the past Administration. They make policy decisions without any real thought about how the troops are going to accomplish them. They seem to be always running with theories that don't quite work!" "You have a point there, but Special Ops is different. Most problems in that field occur because the local commander made a bad decision. Not because the operation from the Pentagon was wrong." She was concerned, "I hope you are right." Her hand was on the table and he put his hand on it. She clasped his hand. "Anita, I do appreciate your comments. Your discussing this with me means a lot. Will you take a walk with me, after lunch?" She said yes. That afternoon, Bill and Anita walk along the lake and talked. It was a meaningful time for both of them. There was one interruption, a phone call from Marion Metcalfe. She called to tell Bill that Two Maryland State Troopers picked up A W today. She was on her way to Baltimore.

Sheila spent the afternoon with Dr Barbara Davis, observing autopsies. The first one was Bill's victim from the hillside. Killed by three gunshots to the head. "Dad sure did a job on him." that made Barbara comment about Anita. "What is it with your Father and gun toting women?" "Barbara, that was Dad's gun Anita used last night. I don't think she had shot one for a while." "Well, what a relief if I ever spent an evening with her." "That's not fair, she seems to be a very good person. Dad sure likes her, and she likes him. She told me." "Well, that answers that question." Barbara dropped an AK-47 bullet into the steel dish being held for her. "I just wonder how long she will last." "Barbara Davis! You make it sound like Dad uses then discards women by the score." "Sheila, that is not what I meant! Your Father has a demanding, high profile job. He is a complex man with a lot of baggage. But another man might not have given up on Jennifer." "To my Father, any mental problem reminds him of my Mother. She never got any better, only worse. Is Jennifer getting better?" Barbara dropped another bullet into the dish. "I don't believe so. I think they're trying hypnosis to reconcile her with what happened to her. I hope they don't run into other problems. It amazes me that she could be stripped and raped, then deny it in her own mind." "I know what you mean. Anita used a gun to kill a bad man, then the only emotion that she showed was joy that we had all survived. I mean she did cry while she was smiling, that could be seem as strange." "Joyce Elizabeth Andrews, I have sometimes smiled and cried at the same time! I do not find that at all strange!" "I stand corrected. I suppose it is one of those female things." "You sound like an outsider!" "Barbara, sometimes I feel like it. I don't think I am very emotional. While most girls in college worried about getting pinned, I was hustling stories for the school paper and radio station. I've never wanted to belong to a man." "Sheila, I don't belong to Jim. We belong to each other. It's a blending, not a domination. You are afraid of losing yourself, because your not that sure about yourself." Sheila thought about that as she watched Barbara begin removing the victim's organs.

After dinner, Sheila sent off her story, then went straight to bed. She was bushed. Bill and Anita did the dishes. Afterwards, Bill poured them both some wine, and they carried it into the Living Room. They sat side by side on the sofa. The conversation was still about the Navy job. "If you took the job, Bill, where would you live?" "I don't know. The Pentagon is in Virginia, I suppose it would be wise to live there." "My Aunt and Uncle live in Vienna, Virginia. I spent a lot of time there, with them. When I was married, we rented a townhouse in Alexandria. Then there is Arlington. All connected by the Metro to the Pentagon." "Anita, you get a far away look on your face when you talk about the area. Where did you live last?" "I was in Georgetown, a few block form the University. I had this great old apartment. My landlady was this sweet old gal. The house had been her family's, then she and her husband inherited it. They had to turn it into apartments or lose it. Then he died and left her alone. All she had was her tenants. No kids, no nieces or nephews." "I am sorry you had to give up your apartment and come back to nurse your Mom. But then, I would have never met you. And that would have been a tragedy." They kissed. "Bill, I bet my Uncle would help you. Of course, he's a retired Marine and you're Navy. But he might overlook that, if I asked him." "I would appreciate that, Kind Lady. If I take the job. I just don't know how much more I could accomplish here. Next year, I would have to stand for election. Someone might run against me. I could go back to NCIS in San Diego." He looked at Anita, "I now know one thing. Wherever I am, I want you beside me," Anita inhaled suddenly. Her mouth dropped open, "Bill! We haven't known each other long. We hardly know each other." "I know enough to realize what a special person you are. I know that

330

I want to be with you as much as possible. Now I want to know how you feel. What do you think about it?" Anita looked a bit startled, "I don't know what to say. Bill, this is a major thing." "I know you"re startled by this. Anita, I don't expect an immediate answer. Take your time. I won't pressure you about this, except to say that I need you very much." "Oh Bill, I do feel something for you. I don't know anyone that I respect more than you. You are a special person to me. We will be apart most of tomorrow, that will be a good time for me to think. I'll try not to keep you waiting too long." He touched her cheek, "I won't like it, but take what time you need." Bill leaned over and gently kissed her, she kissed him back. Afterward, Anita's mind was awhirl. Part of her wanted this more than anything. Part of her feared such a huge move. It was just so soon! Can I trust this man? Then, she could not help thinking about where she would like to live. Bill tried to be positive, but what if she says no? He had that butterfly feeling in his stomach. It had been a long time since he had this problem over a woman. It had been a long time since he had stuck his neck out for another woman. What if she said no! Anita was watching him. She saw the worry momentarily cloud his face, then it disappeared, only to reappear. "He is terrified I will say no! He really loves me! He has told me so many ways that he cares. He is such a strong man, but he needs me. He seeks my input about his decision," she saw it so clearly. She reached out and touched his cheek, "Don't worry Bill, I will go with you wherever you go. I'm not asking for a ring, yet. I will go to Susanville tomorrow and tell my Dad." Bill's face turned from clouds to sunshine. He held her hand in his. He was stunned by her quiet declaration. She leaned over and kissed him. He held her face with both hands and kissed her back. They embraced and held the embrace for a long time. The rest of the evening was one of quiet joy. A communal shower, then bed. Love making with more emotion. Two hearts filled with warmth. Two minds filled with joy.

Chapter Twenty-three

Thursday:

Wanda was the first one in, she preferred it that way. She was sleeping alone for the time being, Jason was preoccupied by Jennifer's problems. She was not doing well, which meant her Father was traveling back and forth to LA. Documents in the Fax machine was nothing new. She grabbed the sheets, depositing them on her desk. Then, it was time for coffee! She sipped the fresh perked brew, as she scanned the faxes. What was this! A bulletin from the Department Of Homeland Security! A demand to arrest and detain Linda Littlewolf, on charges of Terrorism and Treason! Captain Jim Bearpaw came in, just in time to be handed the fax. He was reading it in his office, when Lieutenant Wolfe joined him. Tom showed him the note and Arabic documents from the night Deputy. Now they knew what prompted the upset at Homeland Security. Wolfe had a patrol car meet him at the Eagle residence. Jim called ADA Metcalfe, and the Court about the Homeland demand. Judge O'Reilly was quick to request a copy, an arrest warrant was then generated. Tom had the three Deputies surround the house, while he knocked on the front door. No answer, so Tom used his shoulder. The cheap door splintered! A search of the interior showed signs of a hasty departure, and no Linda! A check showed one vehicle missing. The Deputy that had been watching the house was questioned. No, he saw nothing. He was suspended without pay for dereliction of duty. Tom Wolfe was sure that the had been sleeping in his patrol car. An APB was put out Statewide for Linda and her car. Jim notified Homeland Security of her flight, they flooded him with requests for information. It was only then, that Jim found out that she had been an Arab Language Specialist in the Army. Linda had a faculty for languages! Armed with a Search Warrant, the Forensic Team began a detailed examination of her house.

When they arose, Bill and Anita told Sheila. Anita was moving in with him! She was happy for them, especially for her long alone Father. Breakfast was a happy time, Sheila wished them every happiness. She had her doubts, but kept them to herself. Later, Bill drove Anita over to The Mines. Sheila called Barbara with the news. Anita and Bill checked in with Charlie. The first trailer full of dope was in San Francisco. The DEA was making plans to pull out, as soon as the next load was gone. No word about when the Nuclear Waste was to be removed. Charlie was apologetic, but it was not really his problem. He had other fish to fry. He and Fred were about ready to leave. Fred saw Anita and Bill holding hands. Bill saw Anita off, then got on the DEA secure line, a call to the FBI was in order. The direct line of the Deputy Director was just the ticket. He answered on the third ring, "Hello." "Hello Mike." "Hi Bill, I am hearing all kinds of things about you!" "Good things, I hope." "Bill, the stories around here say you and your boys captured fifty million in dope, cracked a terrorist plot, and wiped out a small army of Mexican Cartel Soldiers." "The local DEA did help some. It's about the terrorist plot, I need your help." I'm glad you're on a secure line, Bill. Talk to me." "Mike, we have your missing trailer of Nuclear Waste." "You what!" "The trailer and bright yellow containers are sitting in an old gold mine about fifty yards from here. Right next to several tons of ammonium nitrate." "My God! How long have you known about this?" "Two days, about. I did tell Admiral Stark when he was here yesterday. He told me that your Department didn't want local law enforcement involved." "Bill, we have been scouring the West for that truck! And that bastard didn't even bother to tell us. It was he and his Boss that insisted no local involvement. Who's guarding it?" "The DEA and my Tactical Team, but the DEA is pulling out today, and I have no budget for this. I need help." "I guess you do! I'm going to get a Security Team in there by tonight. What facilities have you there?" "Mike, the DEA has a Mobile Command Center here now, hence the secure line. They will try to pull it out. There is landing area for two helicopters. We sleep in one of the Mines." "Let them try to pull it out! I do appreciate this Heads Up, Bill. I owe you." "One more thing, Mike. Stark offered me a job working for him." "He what! I hope the hell you're not going to take it!" "Mike, I'm about to call him and politely decline. I have another offer, this one from the Navy." "You have been busy! This Navy job, you like it?" "I've got to admit, it has me interested. I'd be Assistant Chief of Staff for Admiral Saunders in Special Ops with the rank of Captain." "Nice. It would be good to see you again. You know the wife will want to see you. She will probably try to line you up." "Mike, if we do see each other, I won't be alone. Her name is Anita." "Bill, I met the young lady, remember? You can tell me about it later. I've got to make some calls." "Go for it, Mike. I'll tell you about Anita and the three gun fights later." "You big Bastard!" The line went dead. "Now, on to Admiral Stark!" Bill dialed the number from Stark's card. "Admiral Stark's office, Justin Humphrey speaking." "This is Commander Andrews. I would like to know when will the Nuclear Waste be removed? The DEA is pulling out today and my men will be leaving tomorrow." "Ah Commander, we are making arrangements for the Nuclear Waste. These things take time. The FBI is being most uncooperative." "On the contrary, I found the FBI very quick to respond. I complimented the Deputy Director when I spoke to him. I found him very informative." "Ah, Commander, we were handling this situation. You may have undone many carefully negotiated arrangements." "Carefully arranged Photo Ops, more likely. As of tonight, the FBI will be in charge here. I will not be joining you in Washington. Please pass that to the Admiral, with my regrets, I found his offer lacking in appeal. I wish I could say it's been fun." "Commander, the Admiral will be very unhappy with your decision. I am sure he will be most displeased with your actions today." "Mr Humphrey, we all have our own agendas. Please remind the Admiral that it is hard to make an omelet without breaking eggs. Goodbye." He hung up. "Is it so hard to find good help? Slimy and second rate! I feel like I need a shower." Then he thought of his Daughter. A moment later he was talking to his Little One. He explained the terrorist plot to her, the lost Nuclear Waste, Homeland Security's duplicity, and the holes in our defenses. "God! Dad, this is huge! This will make the evening news as in New York! It might even rate a special. But how do I break this story without nailing you as the source?" "You can say that while you were on the DEA dog and pony show, you saw the Jet Ranger and investigated. You recognized Admiral Stark, the Assistant Secretary of Homeland Security and followed the trail. You have a choice, you can nail one of the DEA agents, Fred for

335

instance, or Stark's Aide, Justin Humphrey as your source. He is a slimy little leach, who probably does much of the Admirals dirty work." "I could say a source close to the Assistant Secretary! Dad, they will want to know who leaked the info. Won't Stark or his aide point to you leaking the info. Stark can't be caught in this, he won't get directly involved. He will probably deny any knowledge of it. If a scapegoat is needed, his aide will serve nicely. The poor fool will have served his purpose. Stark will have to find a new aide." "It is a cold business. I thought TV news was tough!" "The stakes are much bigger in this game. The power is greater, so are the risks. The only rule is don't get caught. Plausible deniability is the name of the game, Little One." "Dad, maybe you can survive in Washington. You seem pretty savvy, are you going to take the Navy job?" "I don't think I will. Anita and I have talked about it a lot. This thing with Homeland Security has reminded me just what Washington can be. It seems to be always a matter of who should you trust." "Sounds good, Dad. Well, I have to get going on this story. When will you be home?" "I'll see you in about an hour. I can go over the details with you then. Bye." "Bye Dad" "Two down and one to go," he thought as he dialed the number for the Pentagon switchboard. When the Pentagon operator answered, he asked for Admiral Saunders. She put him through, "Admiral Saunders' office, Lieutenant Earl speaking." "Lieutenant, this is Commander Andrews. Is the Admiral available to take my call?" "Yes Sir, Commander! I mean, I'll check, Commander, Sir!" Bill was put on hold. A minute later, the Admiral came on the line, "Bill, how are you? Jason called me about what happened. Are you all right?" "Yes Sir, not a scratch. We can talk about the events here later. First, I think we should talk about your offer." "Bill, talk away." "Sir, this business with Homeland Security has opened an old wound. I transferred to the Reserves, because I found the life at higher ranks can be very political. That means you may have a problem knowing friend from enemy. I don't think I can accept your offer." The Admiral was concerned, "Bill, I can't deny things can get political, at times. That is my lookout, mine and the Chief of Naval Operations, my boss. You could be shielded from the flack." "Beg your Pardon, Admiral Saunders. If the storm is big enough, it could easily swamp my small boat." The Admiral had no answer for that one. "I am afraid that you have me there, Bill. I was hoping that you

336

would be one willing to brave the storm. I and my Chief of Staff could offer you some protection." "Sorry, Sir, but I have seen too much of the damage politics can do to plans and careers. My stock is pretty high around here, strong enough for me to get elected. I think Anita and I will make a life here, in the Valley." "You have time to reconsider, Bill. I have done without you unto now, that could go on for a while longer." "Thank you, Sir. Anita and I will talk about it." "Anita? Someone you met locally?" "Yes, Sir. She has a degree from Georgetown and a background in Public Relations. She is currently working with the DEA, in that capacity." "Well, you and Anita talk it over. I really need you here. We could find something in PR for Anita, if she was interested." "Thank you, Sir. Is Lieutenant Earl new to your staff?" "Yeah Bill, he is green, isn't he. He looked good on paper, but we'll see. You take care, Bill. No more gun fights." "Yes, Sir. I will try to remember that. Goodbye, Sir" "Goodbye, Bill." Bill sat in the Comm Room after he hung up. His mind went over what he must do. There were so many people to tell, so many details to handle. He thought of the huge labyrinth that was the Navy. "At least this time I could be higher up in the food chain." He recalled that his Daughter was waiting for him at home. He did not know when Anita would arrive. He did not like her driving alone all that way. "I just want her here with my arms around her. But I don't want to smother her, she has been on her own for awhile." Bill ended his meditation and tracked down Sgt Yeager. He passed on the FBI info, they were to take over. When the FBI team took charge, he was to pull all the Deputies out and head home. Yeager quietly slipped him the M-16 with grenade launcher, and three boxes of assorted Grenades. They went quietly into Bill's car, under cover of course. Bill talked to some of the guys, a little moral boosting. He made a point of telling Denise that there would be a Sergeants exam next month. He and Brent had a little talk about the future, then he drove over to the Sheriff's Department. The word was all over about the three dead assassins. Their curiosity was overwhelming. He promised to return the next day and tell them all about it. He stopped by Wanda's desk after locking up the special M-16. Jason had just returned from LA, Jennifer was not doing well. Hypnosis was not working, a drug regimen and hypnosis was next. Bill thought of Mary, his late wife. All of the treatment, all of the drugs had only been a band-aid. Like giving aspirin to someone with AIDS. In the end, she was never normal, she was never whole. He wished Jennifer better luck with the next round of treatment. Wanda said she and Jason would be at Jim's tonight. That made him think of Anita, what would they think of her, and him for loving her? Driving home, he thought about it. What he was experiencing was a full blown case of love. "I cannot remember experiencing anything like this since Mary. I have had some strong sexual relationships, but I never cared about them this way. I sure don't give my love easily." That brought him to a question, "If I love her, what will I do about it?" That question was still unresolved when he got home. Sheila was waiting with a multitude of questions about the Raid and the Terrorist Plot. He got them both a glass of ice tea. Then he sat there sipping his drink, petting Susie, and answering Sheila's questions. Sheila repaid him by fixing their lunch. Gwen called, to tell him that Russ would be buried tomorrow morning at ten. He would be buried in the veterans section, but there would be no military honors. His Mother requested that Bill be there. Gwen told him that his Aunt did not blame him for killing Russ. She felt that he was only doing his duty. She did not know what made Russ so bad. "None of us ever did know why he did what he did, Gwen. Now, we never will. I will be there." The call left him with thoughts of Russ in happier times. It could have been so different. Perhaps, if he had been blessed with a better Father, he might have been a better man." He watched his Daughter working on his computer. She seemed so alive, so dedicated, so bright. "How good a job did I do with her? Time will tell." As if she read his mind, Sheila turned to him at that moment, "This story is turning out great! I know it's not for the LA market. I need to pitch it to New York, to the Network. I wish I had better contacts." "What about Liz Caldwell? Didn't she jump to Network News?" "Liz and I did not part on the best terms. We had a fight, about you. But she owes me. Maybe I can work through her.... Thanks, Dad!" She ran to get her phone book. She had a call to make.

About four-thirty, Anita pulled in. Her Civic was packed with her personal items, including her computer. Bill was drafted to help carry it all in. She found that Bill only used two draws of the dresser. She took over the other four. A slight rearrangement of the walk in closet, allowed all of her clothes to fit, almost. The winter clothes went into the Guest Room. Bill decided that a shoe tree would be needed for the multitude of multicolored footwear that emerged from her small white car. As she agonized over what to wear tonight, Bill came up behind her. He put both arms around her waist, and whispered in her ear, "Anita Louise Brubaker, I love you. Welcome to your new home." He felt something like electricity flow through her body. Then he saw that she was crying. "I'm sorry I surprised you, Anita." She turned and grabbed his face with both hands kissing him, tears and all. Then she just looked at him, "You dear, sweet man. I hope you go on surprising me this way. I love you too." Then she cried some more, smiling and laughing all the time. Bill did the smart thing, under the circumstances, he hugged the crying, laughing woman. She hugged him back and cried all over his uniform shirt. Attracted by Anita's blubbering, Sheila came upstairs to investigate. She was relieved to find that it was an impromptu celebration. She tiptoed away form the happy couple, and returned to the computer. The crying was soon replaced by giggling.

On the ride to Jim's house, Anita sat right against Bill. Sheila thought that she would have sat in his lap, if it had been allowed. Sheila sat in the back, observing the phenomenon as a good reporter should. Now she did not think that Anita and her Father were crazy in love. She just didn't think that they were exactly sane. At Jim's, Barbara and Wanda noticed Anita's joy right away. Anita wore an off the shoulder, off white dress with a full skirt short enough to show off her gorgeous legs. Matching heels and her shoulder length light hair completed an outfit designed to show Anita to her best advantage. Given her current state of mind, she glowed. Bill's announcement of their cohabitation was almost an anticlimax. Barbara and Wanda were very happy about the match. Jim gave his guarded congratulation to this surprising event. Bill was concerned about Jason, especially since he had heard of Jennifer's slow progress. But Jason was his usual effervescent self, his congratulation seemed both warm and genuine. The dinner was a warm affair. The humor and good spirits hid many concerns. Jason was genuinely concerned about Jennifer. Barbara had been appalled by the damage Jim had done with his rifle. She could hardly speak to Jim. Working with the wounded Deputy and Agents made her realize how bad it could have been without Jim and his Sniper rifle. But she had nightmares about his victims. She just could not get past all of those horrible bodies. The reality was too much for her. Jim had been concerned about Bill, it was not like him to stay away from the office so much. Now he understood why, Anita had his much of his attention. He brought Bill up to date on the Linda Littlewolf matter. Bill approved of the actions taken. Bill let him know that he would push the Board of Supervisors that Jim be appointed Captain, permanently. "Jim, I am very proud and pleased with the way you and the other leaders in the Department handled yourselves. I have some ideas on training to talk about." "Thank you, Bill. I have a few ideas of my own." Bill announced his plans for 'Captain' Bearpaw, and 'Lieutenant' Wolfe. There was a flurry of applause, then a round of congratulation for the pair. Jim quietly needled him about "leaving the job to the underlings", while he was with Anita. Bill knew that he and Jim would have many talks over the next few weeks, there were plans to make. The women found Anita to be bright, friendly, and very genuine. The men found her to be cute, bright, and very appealing. Everyone, even Sheila, thought that they were a lucky couple to have found one another. Jason wondered if Bill and Jennifer would have ever been happy. Wanda was unreserved about Anita and Bill. She thought they were the greatest thing since sliced bread or the Morning After Pill!

At ten the next morning, Russ was buried. His Mother sat with Gwen, Marlene, and her two grandchildren. She was stoic, Russ had never been a good son. Her Daughter Della attended with her fiancé. Bill attended with Sheila, and Anita, who insisted on coming. Jim was with Barbara. A group from Monty's attended, they were both sober and reverent. Old Puma Lee led a delegation from the Lee family and the Washo tribe. Don Lee and his parents were among this group. Tiffany Abbot was somberly dressed, standing beside Don. She clung to Don's arm, the picture of devotion. Reverend Phelps was brief, there wasn't much to gush about this time. There was no ceremony, just the quiet regrets of those that knew him. So few really knew him well, fewer still loved him. Gwen, his estranged wife, summed it up best, "He lived doing what he wanted to do, and it killed him. We can get on with our lives, they will be simpler now." Bill and Anita spent much time at the reception, cousin Della and her fella were delightful.

Sheila thought of how Della's life story would make a great news special!

Linda Littlewolf was arrested at JFK, as she tried to board a plane for Dubai. She was surprisingly loud in protesting her innocents of any wrong doing. She was shocked to learn that Homeland Security had all of her papers! The laptop computer in her possession held a copy of every letter that she had written to her Al Qaida contact. Other letters showed her hatred of the US, and her desire to cause it great damage. She saw it as revenge for what the Government and people of the US had done to Native Americans of all tribes. Her denouncement of the US was loud and bitter, after her activities were reveled. Not even her husband seemed to be aware of her duplicity. Bill wondered just who was using who. Johnny Eagle was speechless, when some of her activities were revealed to him. Homeland Security held on to her, since her crimes seemed to be all Federal. She may have known about the Drug operation, but there was little proof of her involvement. Linda considered herself a patriot, white people were the traitors. Given the sad treatment of Indians by the US Government, she had a valid point.

Bill had a special task to handle, a few days after the party at Jim's, he received a call. Wanda told him that a Jeff Worthing was calling from the FBI. Bill had her put it through. "Hello, Jeff. How is it at Quantico?" "How tacky of you to ask, Bill. Both the temperature and the humidity are at ninety-five. But then I did not call you to discuss the weather. Mike said I was to give your case special treatment. I want you to know I don't usually call hill-billy Sheriff's with their forensic results." "Jeff, do you have something for me, or are just calling to abuse my esteemed office." "Bill, I have plenty for you. With the use of polarized light we found tiny blood drops. The newest DNA Sequencer let us identify these tiny drops. But let me read the report. "One and two mm blood spots were found on a mans right sock. Blood was identified by DNA as belonging to the Victim, Joyce E. Andrews. Sock was certified as having been removed from the Subject, Raymond Van Cleef. This was confirmed by DNA. Investigation has shown that the blood spatter could not have formed on the sock unless worn by the subject while driving the vehicle at the time of the victim's injury. Victim was moved to the Drivers seat, exacerbating her injuries.

Victim was subsequently left to bleed out." Mike told me she was your Sister. I am sorry for that. But now you can nail the bastard that killed her. I will fax you a preliminary, the Certified copy will take a couple of days. What happens next?" "Your fax and this call will be enough to get an arrest warrant. Someone from your lab will be called to testify at the trial." "Maybe I'll be the one, Bill. It will be good to see you again." "Jeff, I hope you are the one. If you come, I can introduced to Anita." "You don't mean to say that you found an old woman!" "Not old at all. She's young and beautiful, and she graduated from Georgetown!" "Well, maybe the wait was worth it! I look forward to seeing you both. Talk to you later, Bill." "Bye. Jeff." There it was. He had the evidence to bring Ray to trial. The death of his Sister was solved! Twenty years waiting to catch her killer! A call to Marion Metcalfe would start the process. He made the call. Marion came over to get the faxed report. She combined it with evidence already on file and presented to Judge O'Reilly. The Judge gave her a quick appoint-ment, went over all of the evidence, and had his Clerk draw up an arrest warrant for Ray Van Cleef. The Judge examined the Warrant, found it correct, then signed it. Marion hand carried it to Bill. When presented with the Arrest Warrant, Bill marched it down to Jim's office. "Captain Bearpaw." "Yes, Sheriff Andrews." "I have a task for you and one of the deputies." "What would this task be?" Bill presented him with the Arrest Warrant. "Bill, are you sure you don't want to do this?" "No Jim, if the Bastard opened his mouth, I'd probably kill him!" "Bill, you know he will. Tom Wolfe and I will do it." They did do it. Marion and the DA's office staff watched as they arrested the DA. Van Cleef blustered, then he pleaded, then he cried like a baby as they handcuffed him and led him to jail. Wanda was there, smiling. The jail staff kept him on suicide watch. It meant that the light in his cell stayed on all night. One of the jailors watched him twenty-four hours a day. They made a lot of noise. Bill called Sheila and told her, she made sure it made the news. Later he went home and told Anita all about it. She was very sympathetic. They had dinner, drank some wine, and made love They also made a lot of noise

Jim was saddened by Barbara's coolness, but he had seen it before. Some women just could not get their head around his sniper victims. They could not distinguish between just killing, and

342

taking a life to save others. They could not balance one with the other. Brenda Dawson had no such problem. To her, Jim took lives in the performance of his job. They were bad men, deserving what they got. As a firefighter, she had a practical outlook on life, much like Jim. When he first asked her out, she was pleased. She was happier still, to find that Barbara Davis was no longer in the picture. They quickly became an item. Bill and Anita saw a lot of them, of course Anita already knew the young Amazon. It was inevitable that Jim's bedroom should again be the focus for more nights of powerful sex. Their attraction was strong, both were fit, athletic people. When they could, the couple spent some quality time together. Brenda was introduced to both his Sister, and his Mother. Like Brenda, Jim had never known his Father. They had that in common, and so much more. Brenda practically moved in with Jim, she loved his house. Together, they finished off the interior. She had no trouble responding to fires from the house, it was only about one mile from the Station. Stan was accepting, her choice was understandable. Besides, he had caught the widowed owner of the Market giving him the eye. Martha was an attractive, full figured gal. It was only a week or two, before he made his move. He knew love would take time. For now, there was some very fine sex!

Deputy Brent Carter found himself riding with an experienced Deputy in a patrol car! He was to be backup, for when a regular patrol officer needed time off. He could not always drive Mona to and from work, so she drove his car. He added her to his insurance. It was not cheap, she fussed about the cost. She was contributing to the household expenses, and to Brent's happiness. She was a good house mate, and a great bed mate. They were very fond of their times together. Mona went on the Pill, Brent fretted about that. She tried three different prescriptions, before she and Doctor Sarah were satisfied. One evening, she confided in her female boss. She told her that she and Brent were living together. She was told that the owners already guessed that fact. Her employers were overjoyed! The little redhead was hugged and kissed. She had never been so happy. She had come so far from living with her Mother. Brent loved his little partner, but would he ever understand how the orphan thought? Small things upset her, but small things could fill her with joy!

Jason and Wanda surprised people by announcing their engagement at a small party. Bill and Anita were there, and so happy for the middle-aged love birds. Jim brought Brenda. The others saw how devoted they were to each other. Anita stole some of the attention, when it was noticed to be wearing an antique ring. It had been Bill's Grandmother's. It should have gone to his Sister. Barbara wished the engaged couples happiness, but the sight of Jim with Brenda did bother her. She knew that it was her own fault.

Chapter Twenty-four

After her capture, Linda Littlewolf, a.k.a. Mrs Eagle, was questioned in Manhattan. Homeland Security found her totally uncooperative. When she found that they had many of the letters laying out the plot, she fell silent. After she was arraigned, it was decided to transfer her. One rumor had her at Guantanamo, but it was never confirmed. Within a month of her transfer, men in Dubai and Egypt began being arrested. Often, they simply disappeared. Their families asked about them in vain. Their governments acknowledge nothing about them. Homeland Security concluded that twenty individuals were involved in the plot. The man who survived Bill's knife gave up some of them. Water boarding has it's uses. The group was vigorously suppressed by their own governments. Al Qaida was a threat to them all. Linda has not surfaced, yet. No one really thinks that she ever will. Treason and Terrorism carry severe penalties. What amazes some, is how she expected to survive the plot. If it had succeeded, Al Qaida, or her husband, would have killed her to keep her quiet. They did not trust her, she was a woman, and she was not Muslim. Did her hatred blind her to the danger? She may have a long time to consider that question, if she is lucky.

Johnny Eagle may have known about the plot, but had no hand in arranging it. He did use access to the Mines to his advantage. He and Senor Calderone were arraigned in San Francisco, on multiple drug charges. Johnny's included the Marijuana Field, and the Meth Lab, both tied to him by the testimony of his men. In addition, Johnny was charged with one count of murder, and one count of kidnaping. Charlie, Bill, and Jim testified in both trials. Both men were found guilty of all charges. In Federal Court, both men were sentenced to life without parole on the drug charges. In addition, Johnny got fifteen to life for Second Degree Murder, and twenty years for kidnaping, in State Court. An agreement allowed The State of California to have Johnny first. When they were done with him, he will spend the rest of his life in a Federal Prison. So smart, so much promise, so wasted. Despite all the security precautions by the Feds, Senor Calderone did not live for even a year. Although he was kept in solitary confinement, completely isolated from the prison population, he was found dead in his cell. The Hispanic Trustee they blamed for stabbing him, claims the Cartel threatened to kill his wife and child, if he did not do as they wished. Johnny was told about the death. He lives in complete paranoia, new faces in his cell block terrorize him. He knows not a moment of peace, in his solitary cell. Gone was the superior air, the lofty wit. He just exists, in constant fear.

Ray Van Cleef asked for a change of venue, his trial was moved south, to Fresno. Of course, he had to resign as DA. As senior ADA, Marion Metcalfe took over. Family money bought Ray a team of top defense attorneys. They immediately attacked the FBI lab report. They brought in expert witness to explain the evidence away. Wanda testified that Ray brought Joyce to the party, and that Joyce left with Ray. Attempts to trip her up failed miserably. Jeff testified for the FBI, a veteran of countless trials. He was solid, unshakable, in defending the lab standards in the FBI's Quantico Laboratory. Since he ran most of the samples himself, they could not blame nameless technicians. Whenever the Defense thought that they had Jeff on a point, his deep knowledge of the topic unraveled their attempt. Marion Metcalfe was coprosecutor, along with the local DA. Her probing questions helped to solidify the Prosecution's case. Sensing that he was losing, Ray defied the advice of his consoles, and took the stand. His self-serving version of the night Joyce died, served only to highlight the Prosecution's case. Marion adroitly lured him into contradicting the evidence at several points. Bill and Anita watched the faces of the jury. Their skepticism of Ray was obvious. His voice rose in pitch, it became a whine. In the end, he was pleading for the jury to believe him. It was an unnerving display of desperation. In the summation, Marion detailed the holes in his defense: 1) No one on record having seen him during the entire party. 2) Two witness saw him drive away with Joyce. 3) No reasonable explanation for victim"s blood on his clothing. 4) He appeared very drunk at the party, too drunk to drive. The Defense tried to cast doubt on the witnesses. The blood evidence they called "a lab error". The Jury took all of two hours to find

Ray: Guilty. After more than twenty years, Ray Van Cleef was found guilty of Second Degree Murder, in the death of Joyce Andrews. During sentencing, the Judge was harsh. Twenty-five years to Life was the sentence. He moved her to the Driver's seat, then left her to die. All to avoid a DUI involving an accident with injury. Afterwards, Marion dined with Bill and Anita. Jeff attended, as did Sheila, who was in town to cover the trial. Wanda and Jason joined the party. Justice was finally served. Ray did not fare well in prison, his patrician manner, and having been a prosecutor, did not endear him to the other prisoners. Beatings were frequent, and he was raped on occasion. He put all of his hopes on an appeal. Ray's wife divorced him, taking their children to live in LA. She changed back to her maiden name. His membership in the State Bar was revoked. Ray was stripped of his State Law License, he would never practice law again. He never once expressed a shred of remorse for the death he caused. Bill doubted that there was any in him.

Dr Barbara Davis realized that moving to the Valley was a mistake. Aunt Sarah was understanding, she had seen this coming. Her resume went out, there was much interest. In the end, she chose the Presbyterian Medical Center, in San Francisco. Barbara felt more at home there. She loved the shopping possibilities. She tried not to dwell on what happened with Jim. She was a while in dating. Barbara considered that she had made two wrong choices in men. She might have be surprised to find that Jim considered her a bad choice. She was a Staff Attending at the Hospital, and she taught one class at the UC Med School which was nearby. Her happiness returned, there was satisfaction in her work. She was a popular date, but she did not remarry. The beautiful Brunette was in no rush to tie herself to another man. She soon developed a reputation for coolness, as many female professionals do. They seemed to realize that for them, finding a mate is very difficult. They often felt no great desire for children. There are many opinion on why they feel this way. Most are very uncomplimentary, to the Ladies.

Cal Fire Station One was a smooth team again! Gene had accepted a position with Cal Fire. He did not like starting out on Probation, but he understood why. He found that he was now junior to the twenty year old Danny! Still, it was a lot better than unemployment. Gary found that he had a efficient engine crew again, it had been a while. Things were decidedly happier around the Fire House. They were a bit surprised, when Brenda started responding from Jim's house. No one was surprised that she found someone. She was a bright, beautiful young woman. Gary had his family. And Gene was building his, the wife announced she was pregnant with #2! Danny and Sally saw each other, whenever they could. She had her own room now, with it's own entrance. Sally went on the pill. They were a happy couple. Danny wanted to make Firefighter II, then he was going to propose! Brenda found her life full of contentment and joy. She loved her time with Jim. He was good lover, a great friend. They did things together, just like a family. That was so important to the child of foster care. In September, the thunderstorms hit! Lightning cause numerous forest fires, activating the entire firefighting community. All Cal Fire Units hit the forest fires, with the Volunteers caring for the residential properties. Soon, more Fire Units arrived, from out of the area. Battalion Chief Stan was a very busy man. When the out of area city and county units arrived, Stan spent much of his time on the radio. The urban firefighting units drew the property protection role, Cal Fire, and the Volunteers, fought the forest fires. Helicopter and fixed wing water bombers added to their efforts. Ground units from as far away as San Jose, and Los Angeles were on line in Shasta, Trinity, Lassen, Sierra Vista, Siskiyou, Modoc, and Butte Counties. Before it was done, Federal Forestry Fire Units from Idaho and Wyoming were also involved. The air assets were augmented by a DC-10 from Southern California, and a huge four engined flying boat from Canada. The latter had to land on one of the two large local reservoirs in order to fill up with water. It took one week, for this massive effort to control all of the fires. Mop up took another week. One of the city units from San Mateo County was taking a break near Engine One. The crew wanted to know about the Sheriff and his men that stopped the Terrorist plot. It could have irradiated their homes and families. Brenda was able to introduce them to Jim Bearpaw, the Sniper. He was heaped with praise, due in no small part to the news story put together by Anita and Sheila. The crew from San Mateo could not miss that Jim and Brenda were holding hands. All too soon, the firefighters had to go back to work. It made a big

348

impression on Brenda, how important Jim and his Department were. She knew, Jim had done a lot of good with his sniper rifle. Brenda was held in much respect by her crew, and the rest of the firefighting community. It was not lost on Jim. She was much on his mind. There was none of the uncertainty he usually experienced with a Lover. After the Fires, Brenda moved in with Jim. She was no longer just visiting the house on the lake. She felt that she was home.

Mona and Brent continued to live together. Working night shift had some disadvantages, but neither would have changed, even if they could. They loved their days together, and the nights were so good! He was learning about patrol work. Traffic stops, writing citations, pursuits, there was so much to learn. Then came the time for him to take patrol duty one weekend. Saturday and Sunday nights, Brent was one of the two patrol units on the four to Midnight. One DUI traffic stop, and a small bar fight to break up. Nothing major, just good experience for the young Officer. She was learning about preparing guest statements for next morning checkout. She knew that it could be a big help to her bosses. Sister Ellen, and his Folks came back to the Valley for the Holidays. Mona was treated as one of the family. Brent's Parents knew her, they accepted her relationship with their son. They made no comment about their sleeping arrangements. They stayed in their Motor Home, at night. Mona was so happy, she had a family! He never saw Donna again, but she sent him a Christmas Card. At the Department, he received her card, complete with a note and photo. The photo showed a cute Brunette in skirt and tight sweater. Only her smile revealed that the slim lovely was Donna. Her hair was styled, the make up well done. Gone was the bulging waist, although the prominent bust remained. She thanked him for his attention during the Summer. She had been dealing with a family problem, and her talks with him helped her to make a decision. Inclosed, was a newspaper clipping about Donna charging her Parents with Sexual Abuse. She charged that her Father had been abusing her, starting at age nine. Her Mother knew, but did nothing. There was talk of a Civil Suit seeking damages from her Parents, the amount mentioned was five million dollars. In her note, Donna told him that she was graduating in June. Next Summer, she would be back at the Indian Village dig, this time as

Crew Head. She hoped that they would be able to renew their 'friendship'. Donna wanted to give him a big 'thank you'. Brent was alarmed and intrigued by her note. Part of him really wanted to see the new Donna, but what would that mean about him and Mona? Brent had a lot to think about, between then and June. It would be for the period of June to September, then she would go on to Grad School. Temptations are always with us.

Corporal Denise Deertail had a boyfriend! One of the DEA Agents had found her at the Mines. He was a Mohawk Indian, from upstate New York. He visited her often, driving over from Susanville. At first, he slept on her sofa. The attraction was strong, he soon shared her bed. She studied for the Sargent's Exam, and entertained her lover. She soon found out that he had a law degree from Cornel. After that, he started studying for the California Bar. They had it all figured. He would pass the Bar, then become the Attorney for the Washo Tribe. They would need legal advice, what with Jason assisting them in getting a Casino. Along the way, she rather hoped they might get married. He saw the situation as very promising. A California Indian Tribe with a Casino, could mean a good income for their Attorney. Denise was a good partner, in bed or out. He saw the future as very bright. She wondered about being married, and a Sargent. Would there be children? She approached that with mixed feelings.

Jason Saunders was indeed planning a Casino. He helped the Washo Tribe to find a good Management Company, to handle the facility. The chosen one had plenty of Casino experience, with various Indian Tribes. One of Jason's Companies would supply the construction capital, for a small part of the Casino. The contract allowed for the Tribe to buy them out, if they so chose. The Casino was attempted with his usual high energy. Things happened very quickly, once Johnny Eagle's mess was cleaned up. There was a break in the action, come October. Jason and Wanda got married, in a small ceremony, just family and friends. Jennifer did not make it. Jason arranged for them to honeymoon on a private island in the Tahitian group. Not his island, but he did rent the entire place for two weeks! Wanda had been dieting, and working out more. She was all fit and toned for the island. Jason loved it, they made love frequently. After they returned to Sierra Vista, Wanda found that she was pregnant! It was not exactly an accident. Dr Sarah and the fortyish Wanda had conspired. Jason was surprised, but when Dr Sarah approved, he was delighted! Later, Ultrasound showed that Wanda was carrying a boy! All of this helped to offset the lack of progress by Jennifer. It was as if she did not want to improve, she did not seem to care. There were reports of her vocal outbursts, "Why are you keeping Bill away from me?" She was adamant, insisting that Bill would come for her. She would hear nothing to the contrary. Jennifer acted like the rape never happened, attempts to discuss the event met with a blank stare. She referred to that night as her last time with Bill. All her memories, were fantasies of what she wanted to happen with Bill. She was dogged, that dream was her reality. When Sheila visited her, she was greeted as an old friend. However, the conversation quickly went to talk of Bill, "How is your Father? When is he coming to visit?" The reporter was told that Jennifer refused to take her Meds, they were given to her as 'vitamin injections'. After the visit, Sheila decided not to call her Father. There was no good news here, Jennifer was still delusional. Anita and she talked, she knew how well the couple was doing. If they wanted to know about Jennifer, they could ask Jason, or Wanda. The young woman now saw something of how it had been for her Father, with her Mother. The idea depressed her, she now had so much sympathy for her Father. Thank God, he now had Anita.

The events in Sierra Vista, and at the Mines got Sheila a lot of visibility. Her expose` on Homeland Security's mistakes, took the young LA reporter to a prime time special. NBC tried to out do '60 Minutes' with the attractive redhead. She followed that up with a request to profile her cousin, Dr Della Baker. Her stock was high, so permission was granted. Sheila and her crew went with Della on her Hospital rounds, watched her perform surgery, then covered her personal life. Many thought that the parts about Della and her fiancé were the best parts. Sheila wanted to show how much alike the dwarf couple were to every other young couple in love. Some came to see that we are beautiful to those that love us, dwarf or not. The documentary created a demand for more, she received an offer to do a series. Reality documentaries were all the rage. The series brought her into contact with a young Producer, together, they would develop the show. Sheila directed, he produced, they collaborated on the scrips. Soon the tall dark haired Producer, and the redheaded Director collaborated on other things. Sheila discovered just how emotional she could be. The pair fell into a passionate affair. Where it led, neither of them knew. It was just what both of them needed. They found a joy in creating a show with their lover. It could have been a disaster, but turned out so nice! They had thirteen shows to tape, then they could take a break. Sheila wanted to take her love to meet her Father. She thought of that as the acid test. Would they like each other? Would he be intimidated by Dad? Her Father's opinion mattered to this Daughter of a single Dad. Her Father was a dominating man. She thought that he had an aura about him. How many others felt it?

Jim Bearpaw felt it. He was sure that it was Bill's Washo blood. The Lee Clan was know for its strength of spirit. Old Puma Lee was over ninety, but still mobile, still clear headed. He knew what was happening in the world around him. One sometimes heard his disapproval. The intimidating mound of paperwork Jim had inherited, was soon reduced. Updating emergency plans now occupied much of his time. It felt different, turning over Patrol responsibilities to Tom Wolfe. Jim was now Operations head, planning and communicating with other Counties was now his to handle. He found it very fulfilling. When Bill found something lacking, it could be something else. Yes, Bill was a hard task master, but everyone knew that his goal was a very worthy one. Bill's hard standard kept the Department sharp. Jim recalled the young Deputy Brent Carter, he used his head to capture Johnny Eagle. It was that kind of thinking that Bill wanted from all of his manpower. For Jim, this is the way it should be. Hard work for a tough boss, in a good cause. His Ranger duties were that way, now his law enforcement position was the same. Bill's Dad was sometimes slack in his standards. Not everything held importance for the Viet Nam vet. He had been too easy to dismiss things, for Jim's taste. Russ encouraged him, that man wanted no change. Things were different, now. Bill was cleaning house, the dust and cobwebs were swept away! Next Spring, Bill had him attending a thirty day Course with the FBI. A month at Quantico, Virginia! Jim wondered about that. Would he and Brenda still be together? She had just moved in, it felt strange to help her put her things in his house. Her rapid departures still took some getting used to. She could be called at any time! But then, so could he. Jim had to reflect on the lovely Brenda, she was solidly in his life. She made less waves than Barbara had. Brenda tried to fit in, not change things. She was in better shape than Barbara. He took a moment to recall her shape. Those long legs, those tits! Really something worth coming home to! Thinking about her made him smile. Most everything she did made him smile. She was a beautiful, sensuous woman. But, Jim had other thoughts, the Casino gave him concern. Jason had the support of the Tribal Council, Jim and his Uncle had talked long about it. They seemed to be handling it in the proper way. But what would it mean to his people? There would be jobs and revenue for the Tribe, but what about crime? Would it mean more crime for the Reservation? Jim could envision the type of customer that would be attracted to the Casino. Some would be cheats, or con artists. What about employee crime? Greed could cause problems, temptations were not always resisted. No, as Jim saw it, the Mill reopening was the better solution. But how would business be for the Mill, in this Recession? For Captain Jim Bearpaw, the future seemed filled with uncertainty. Not particularly new, for a Ranger and Sheriff's Captain. But then, he did have Brenda. At least until the next alarm. But she always came back. He could then have her freshly scrubbed, right out of the shower. He was smiling again!

With the business at the Mines settled, and Ray Van Cleef in prison, Bill smiled more often. Anita certainly helped in that department. At first, he had tried giving her space. He did not poke his nose into her business, allowing her to have time alone. The young woman found things not to her liking. Sheriff Bill Andrews was informed that, "She had been on her own for several years, now she preferred to share his space." She said this while seated in his lap. A point well made, by a most effective young woman. She made some changes in the house, but since Bill was only recently moved in himself, it was more like they made changes together. The animals fared very well, they received loving from two humans now. Anita quit the DEA, she now split her time between the County, and the Memorial Hospital. She had a small office in both facilities, nothing fancy. The staff of both institutions found her to a bright, happy person. The females knew that she lived with Bill. They were sure that would make them happy. There was probably a bit of jealousy, over her lover, but no one saw any sign of friction. When you are a cordial coworker, petty things are usually forgiven. She moved her charges into the 21st century, as far as their publicity was concerned. Both now had web pages, Anita designed them, a young Mother laid them out on the Web. Anita saw how she worked from home, while caring for her baby. It made her think, could she do that? Bill continued to make plans for his Department. With Jim and Tom, they bounced ideas off of each other. Some were developed, while others did not survive study. Three heads were definitely better than one. Both Jim and Tom, were made permanent by the Board. There were only five member on the Board of Supervisors now, the other two gentlemen were awaiting trial for accepting bribes. The State Attorney General indited twelve individual, in the Johnny Eagle matter. With Johnny convicted of multiple felonies, it was felt that he had received punishment enough. With his promotion, Tom Wolfe announced that he was marrying Betty, the Dispatcher. She was the Widow of his best friend, they had all gone to School together. Congratulations flowed in, everyone liked the couple. The Mines had been seized by the Federal Government, it followed from their use in Drug and Terrorist activities. Dubai protested, on behalf of the owner. The US State Department released excerpts from Linda's letters, and the responses from Dubai. They clearly detailed the developing Terrorist Plot. Dubai grew silent on the whole issue. One of Jason's Companies was able to lease the area from the Government. Most residents assumed they would be mining the gold. Oh, they had geologists go over all of the mines, all right. However, the report was disappointing, low grade ore was available only in two of the mines. Large scale mining was deemed uneconomical. That was never the intension anyway, but wholesale excavation was commenced for quite a different reason. The new business venture was Mushrooms! Electricity was brought to the mines. Many workers were hired, most of them Washo. An office build sprang up, near the Springs. With Jason, and the EPA, looking over their shoulders, everything was done in the Green way. There would be no toxic waste at this site! Anything that could not be recycled, was hauled away. Proper disposal of all materials was the order of the day, every day. Bill viewed this, and the reopening of the Mill, as major improvements to the Valley. Jobs meant an improved economy for the area. What the proposed Casino meant, remained to be seen. As Sheriff, Bill

354

was asked by the Board to provide an analysis of its impact on the Valley. He, Jim, and Tom spent many hours on it. The Board was not pleased by their report. The three Law Officers were asked to defend their rather negative report at a closed session of the Board. At the heart of the problem, was their insistence that the Casino would require many more Deputies, on top of the Security Department of the Casino. Bill had to remind them that the Reservation was outside of County jurisdiction. What security the casino would have was unknown. His Department would require more manpower, to handle the increased tourism that the Casino would bring. More traffic, more crime, and more violence, was how the lawmen saw it. They defended their views, by quoting statistics of other areas where Casinos were built. All of them were Indian land, all had gone through problems of high crimes and increased violence. The members of the Board found it sobering, no one had mentioned this before! Ray Vinders made it clear, there would be more talks with Jason and the Tribal council! The three lawmen left, knowing that the Casino would have to police itself. What about the Reservation? Would it have its own police? Jim knew that he would be talking to his Uncle about this. Anita was waiting for Bill, that evening. They talked about the problem in some depth. Then, she brought out the familiar Hawaiian brochure. She thought that it was a good idea for them to take a vacation. The first one, together. He saw the wisdom of her plan. Their schedule was set, two weeks at a remote resort on Lanai! Jason had mentioned to them. They used his name when making their reservations. Before the trip, Bill had a conversation with Jason about a security system for the House by the Lake. Bill conferred with Jason's head of Security, they were both experienced, agreement was rapid. Jason insisted that he would have his people install the system, they would also monitor it. Bill and Anita were touched by his generosity. The pair went about their duties, as an array of infrared sensor, and low light level cameras were installed on the grounds. Patrols made sure that the work was unobserved. By the time the couple took off for Lanai, the new system was being tested. Five days later, Jason's night crew noted two men sneaking through Bill's" property, then setting up near his driveway. The experienced warriors were sure, ambush! A four man patrol was organized, all ex-Special Forces. Silently, the four spread out. No sound betrayed their travel through the woods. This was old hat for the four veteran warriors. Shortly, they merged on the two hapless invaders. The attack was swift, the pair was taken. One resisted, he died, his blood flowing into the dry soil. Brent and another Deputy were sent to pickup the would-be assassin. Charlie, and the DEA, were able to identify the pair as Cartel assassins, both wanted on Federal Murder charges. They took care of both, Jim did not mind ridding his County of such scum. When Anita and Bill returned home, Mrs. Garcia was first to tell them all about their two 'visitors'. It was a grim reminder of the threat that the Cartel still presented to their futures. To himself, Bill wondered how many more attempts would be made? They had attacked the house, now they attempted a driveway ambush. Would they try something on the road next? On the other hand, would they now see this as a foolish gesture, too expensive in time and manpower? He knew that it was no longer a smart business move, it was now simply revenge. Would the Cartel stop the Calderone family? He assumed that was who continued the vendetta. In the end, he knew that only time would tell. For now, he ran with his Lover. He and Anita worked out together. He loved her shape, and visa versa. Thanksgiving saw them all gathered around Jason's table. He and Wanda hosted Bill and Anita, Jim and Brenda, Joyce, and Anita's Dad and Stepmom. Christmas time was marked by a wedding! On Christmas Eve, Bill and Anita were wed. Jim was the Best Man, Joyce (Sheila) was the Maid of Honor. Judge O 'Reilly did the honors. Wanda and Jason were prominent among the few guests. Anita's Father got to give her away, something he was unable to do the first time. Mr and Mrs Andrews had already made a life for themselves. The new year allowed them ample opportunities to enjoy it. The Spring brought the reopening of the Mill, although orders for lumber were small. Spring also brought an announcement! Anita was pregnant! Joyce visited to celebrate the news. She brought her 'friend' Richard. Rich was twenty-eight, tall, fit, and obviously taken with Joyce. The two couples had a good visit. Before they left, Bill had a brief conversation with his Daughter. The gist of it was, "I approve of Rich!" That phrase meant so much to the young newswoman! Bill and Anita watched the young couple from the doorway. As the drove away, Bill kissed his pregnant wife on the cheek, "Do you think they will ever love each other as much as we do?" She looked up, into his eyes, "Not possible!" They shared a long kiss.

Table of Contents

www.ingramcontent.com/pod-product-compliance
Lightning Source LLC
Chambersburg PA
CBHW072312020726
47501CB00002B/485